THE SWORD OF ANTON

Novels by Gene Del Vecchio:

The Pearl of Anton
The Sword of Anton

Other books by Gene Del Vecchio:

The Blockbuster Toy: How to Invent the Next BIG Thing!
Creating Ever-Cool: A Marketer's Guide to a Kid's Heart

THE SWORD OF ANTON

By Gene Del Vecchio

Pelican Publishing Company
Gretna 2006

The word "Pelican" and the depiction of a pelican
are trademarks of Pelican Publishing Company, Inc.,
and are registered in theU.S. Patent and Trademark Office.

ISBN-13: 9781589803046

Printed in the United States of America

Published by Pelican Publishing Company, Inc.
1000 Burmaster Street, Gretna, Louisiana 70053

To Linda and Megan for their encouragement, thoughts, and improvements. To Matthew for the original inspiration. To Pelican Publishing for its gracious support. And finally, to all Dels of noble blood, particularly to those few who know of their true lineage.

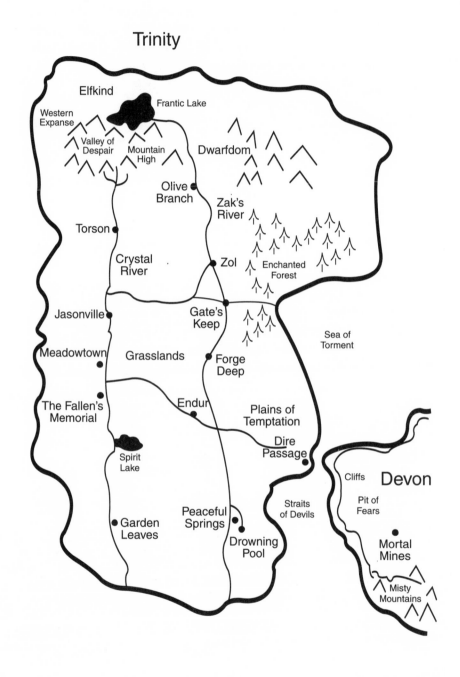

Trinity

Elfkind

Western
Expanse

Frantic Lake

Valley of
Despair

Mountain
High

Dwarfdom

Olive
Branch

Zak's
River

Torson

Crystal
River

Zol

Enchanted
Forest

Jasonville

Gate's
Keep

Meadowtown

Grasslands

Forge
Deep

Sea of
Torment

The Fallen's
Memorial

Endur

Plains of
Temptation

Spirit
Lake

Dire
Passage

Devon

Cliffs

Pit of
Fears

Garden
Leaves

Peaceful
Springs

Straits
of Devils

Mortal
Mines

Drowning
Pool

Misty
Mountains

CONTENTS

Trinity

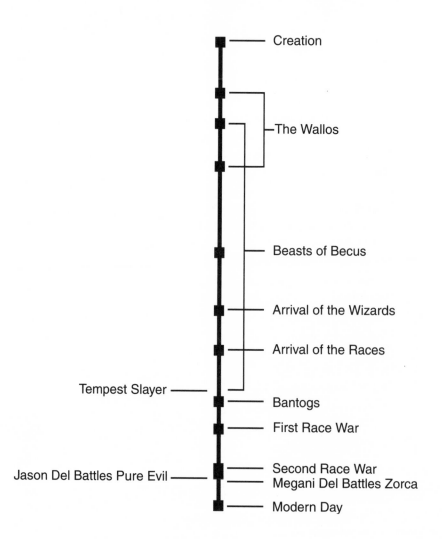

Creation

The Wallos

Beasts of Becus

Arrival of the Wizards

Arrival of the Races

Tempest Slayer

Bantogs

First Race War

Jason Del Battles Pure Evil

Second Race War
Megani Del Battles Zorca

Modern Day

INTRODUCTION

If you are reading this, then chances are you have read my first published history entitled *The Pearl of Anton*. Translated from the ancient Book of Endur, it told the saga of Jason Del and his quest to find the Pearl of Anton in order to use its mysterious powers to defeat Pure Evil in the Final Contest. He was victorious, though it cost him dearly.

Many asked that I offer another history from the Book of Endur. In particular, interest has been expressed in Jason's daughter, Megani, who was a mix of both human and Ethan blood. As it happens, Megani inherited a world of great dangers, and her greatest challenge came a mere month after her father's death. A cunning beast had been in hiding, waiting for a day when her father, Jason, would be gone so that it could reign.

The historical account of this incident is offered here. I call it *The Sword of Anton* because the ancient blade, used by the Dels for thousands of years, became central to this telling. The story begins with a prologue written many years before the history of Megani and ends with an epilogue written a few years after the account of the Sword. I pray that this satisfies those who are curious about Megani's heroic life.

Gene Del Vecchio

PROLOGUE:
THE SWORD IS FORGED

A History from the Book of Endur,
Submitted during the Watch of Lorelii

In a desperate quest to aid a desperate cause, I, Lorelii from the Race of Etha, gave witness in the very bowels of the Earth as a great Sword was forged. The blade's purpose was to meld the powers of the last remaining three Wizards so that the Sword, when given to the Royal House of Del, could be used to defeat the last of the great Beasts of Becus.

Streaming lava boiled up from a deep well that touched the center of the Earth. Red light from the bubbling brew bounced about the large, dark cavern as thick steam rose continuously from the scorching-hot well. The master Wizard Zorca stood over the brewing lava pit. Beside him were the last of its Wizard kind, Zemba and ToKi. Their thin, bony features, aging, wrinkled skin, and long white beards gave them a weakly look. Yet vibrant powers still lived beneath the skin that was forever cloaked in deep-blue robes. These were entities created by the God Anton in order to protect the land of Trinity and Anton's Elf, Dwarf, Man, and Ethan Races from the hideous Beasts of the God Becus. The powerful Wizards had won many agonizing battles, but their time on Trinity was running short and so they worked now to ensure that their powers would remain with Anton's Races. To this end, we are here this day to forge a Sword so great that the Races will be protected even after the Wizards have passed to whatever fate awaits them in the mysterious heavens above.

Zorca picked up a cauldron of scarce Tork rocks and poured the many small boulders into the lava well. Sparks splashed upward as the metals plunged beneath the surface of the lava. The brew within the well suddenly boiled up, reaching higher and higher until a thick

11

fountain of searing hot lava met the height of Zorca. Though I was still a distance from the sight, I shielded my eyes from the intense light, intermittently peeking between the fingers of my hands to catch a glimpse of the progress.

Boom!

A massive explosion suddenly blew in all directions within the large cavern. It threw me to my knees, as it had all others. When we recovered, the fountain of lava was gone, but floating in midair where the fountain had been was a massive Tork Sword revolving as a top. Its blade reflected a brilliant shine that speckled the cavern with a rotating light. Even from my distance I could see my own reflection in the spinning Tork blade. Beneath the Sword's handle was a gray gem Stone that was affixed to the bottom of the Sword's hilt. Zorca reached quickly above the lava pit, grabbed the hilt of the Sword, and brought it to his bosom. The heat of the Sword sizzled in the Wizard's hand, melting its skin, but Zorca did not flinch. The calm yet mighty Wizard paused for a moment and stroked the blade almost lovingly. Zorca then seemingly whispered to the brilliant Sword. He walked across the cavern to a cascading waterfall that originated from the Drowning Pool far above, on the surface of Trinity. The Wizard thrust the blade within the cold waters. White, billowing smoke rose from the blade as water instantly evaporated under the intense heat. Gradually, the blade cooled.

Zorca moved stridingly to his fellow Wizards and stood before them. He nodded to Zemba, and the fellow Wizard nodded back. Without a word, Zorca plunged the massive Sword through Zemba's chest. Half of the blade sliced through its back. Zemba shrieked in pain. The white magic within Zemba poured from the Wizard's body, flowed through the Sword, and settled in the Stone at the base of the Sword's handle, turning the gem a brilliant white. Suddenly sucked of its power, Zemba fell back to the cavern floor, dead.

Zorca stepped to ToKi and gave a nod. ToKi took a breath. I was surprised at the Wizard's calm under the shadow of death. Zorca plunged the Sword within ToKi's chest. Again, white magic was pulled from the Wizard; it danced and sparkled along the length of the Sword before settling in the Stone at the Sword's base, making the gem twice as brilliantly white. Tapped of all its magic, ToKi fell back dead. Two of the three Wizards had fulfilled their final purpose.

Zorca motioned to two figures that had been waiting in the shadows. Angeloti Del emerged. He was a small Man in stature but in possession of a strong, solid frame. Behind him followed his only child, a daughter, fifteen-year-old Pita Del, possessing her father's strength but with sleek features. Both had the bright-red hair and sharp green eyes of Dels past, their bodies clothed in the modest leathers of frontiersmen. Theirs is the family in whom the Lord Anton and all of the Races of Trinity would place their trust to defeat the last of the Beasts of Becus.

Zorca handed the Sword to Angeloti. The senior Del took it.

"I am sorry for what I must do," Angeloti said. They were the first words uttered in the cavern. They felt foreign and lonely.

"Nonsense!" mocked Zorca. "The Lord Anton chose you . . . for reasons I do not know nor could possibly comprehend." The Wizard's voice was accepting of his fate, yet displeased with it.

"I'm sorry nonetheless," Angeloti repeated.

Angeloti plunged the Sword through Zorca's chest. Magic was sucked from the very marrow of the Wizard until it fell back, as had the others. But this time, a fragment of the Wizard's magic was left so that it did not die. For what future purpose, only Anton would know. The Sword began to vibrate in Angeloti's strong hands, but he held firm. The gem Stone at the base was now three times as brilliantly white.

Boom!

The cavern rumbled and rocks fell from the ceiling. When I looked back, the Stone had fallen from the Sword. Pita quickly picked it up and gazed into its aura. And there they were: father holding the Sword of Legends and daughter, the Wizard's Stone. These precious, powerful implements were the final hope for the Races in their quest to defeat the last of the great Beasts of Becus, but only if the Dels could muster the strength and courage to use them. It was not long before they were put to their first test.

The ground trembled at the feet of the fallen Wizards. Dirt and gravel blasted up and a huge beast suddenly emerged. It was nearly fifty feet long and snakelike, with deep-blue scales and a white mane atop its lizard head. It must have been one of the many Beasts of Becus, though it had never before been seen. The demon snapped at Angeloti with sharp, yellow teeth. The elder Del stepped forward and thrust the Sword toward its belly again and again, but to no avail.

"Pita!" he called. "Bring up the Wizard's Stone!" The father knew that the magic that had been sucked into the Stone must be great, if only they could unleash it.

But Pita took a step back . . . then another! I could tell from afar that fear gripped her soul. She gazed into the Wizard's Stone, knowing full well it possessed great powers, but she could not find the bravery to wield it. She took a third step back.

"Pita!" called her father again. The desperate cries echoed throughout the cavern as Angeloti wielded his blade back and forth to ward off the massive strikes of the lizard beast. He was in dire need of whatever help Pita might muster, but his calls went unanswered.

The beast suddenly pivoted about and pounded its tail into Angeloti. The elder Del tumbled into the darkness of the cavern and out of sight. Pita was not as fortunate. First frozen in terror, she now turned to run instead of fight. The beast lunged at the girl, grabbing her around the neck within its massive jaws. It raised her to the very top of the cavern and began to squeeze the life from her body.

"Father!" screamed Pita with her final, frantic, choking breaths.

Angeloti recovered and threw himself toward the belly of the monster with great force. He saw an unprotected flap of skin and thrust the Sword deep within the beast.

Bang!

Light exploded within the cavern. I was thrown against jagged rocks and did not recover for many hours. When my mind cleared, smoke and ash were all about the cavern. The beast was gone. I found a grieving Angeloti cradling the lifeless form of his precious daughter. She was the first Del to die while the family was in the possession of the Wizard's Sword and Stone. Perhaps worse, she failed to prove her bravery— failed to prove her potential—and thus risked the lives of all the Races upon Trinity. She shamed the Royal House of Del. It does not bode well for future women in the Royal House . . . nor throughout the land. As painful as it is for me to decree, I hereby order that from this day forward, only sons will be groomed as the rightful heirs to the powers of the Royal House of Del. I would wish to do otherwise, but I cannot.

This was the account of the birth of the Sword and Stone. May the Dels use their powers well to eradicate the Beasts of Becus from the land and in every other toil for which these implements will be in need.

Faithfully, *Lorelii*

A History from the Book of Endur, Submitted during the Watch of Lorelii

My life is draining from me. My ancient body may have a day more
. . . perhaps two. I am not afraid to die, but I am afraid to sleep, for I
have been haunted by night terrors these last days. The dreams are
intensely vivid. They catapult me back to the day over one hundred
years ago when I witnessed the birth of the Sword and Stone. But rather
than reflect what I thought transpired on that day, the dreams are different, relating a different series of events. It's as if something beyond our
Earth is ripping a veil from my eyes so that I can see that day for what
really happened . . . what really transpired!

Was I fooled, as were all in the deep cavern that day? Was the history that I wrote incorrect? Did Pita and Angeloti not perform as I had
first recalled? Was my memory altered? And if so, who altered it and
for what purpose?

I cannot write down my entire vision, the one I now know to be true. I
fear that it will be discovered. The implications of my dream are too far
reaching and so it is best that no one, absolutely no one, has the full knowledge. But I have done this: I committed one sentence of most importance
to parchment. I cut that parchment into ten pieces, each containing one
word. Then I entrusted ten Guardians to hold their piece in trust within their
families for generations should the day arrive when they will be called.

On that day, they must seek the *Historian.* He will understand what
to do; he will know the value of the message I leave. I will see to that
as well. The free will and thus the livelihoods of all those on Trinity
will depend upon him and the rightful heir to the Royal House of Del,
whoever will be unfortunate enough to have that title when the time
arives. I know now that the Beasts of Becus are not nearly as deadly as
I first thought. They will be defeated. But a greater evil exists among
us that remains hidden, in wait for a time when it can reign supreme. It
is for that purpose that I leave this message.

And now . . . I die . . . and leave the responsibilities of my kind to
my eldest daughter, Tara.

Faithfully, *Lorelii*

P.S.: Forgive me, Pita. But your truth, the truth I now know, will have
to wait.

THE SWORD OF ANTON

CHAPTER 1

A BLOODY BRIDGE

On most days, the new township of Olive Branch was a peaceful haven in the east. It sat on the western bank of the mighty Zak's River. The inhabitants of the town were mostly farmers, tilling fertile land in a place that just seventy years before was an arid desert. That was before the Chosen One, Jason Del, fought and destroyed Pure Evil in the Final Contest, a battle between the champions of the Good Lord Anton and the Evil Lord Becus. On that day, the last of the great Beasts of Becus was destroyed and all of Trinity and the Races of Lord Anton rejoiced. Once Pure Evil was no more, Jason went about the task of rebuilding the eastern lands, which had been devastated by the former Beasts of Becus for many years. In one effort, Jason found the source of an ancient eastern river. With the vast, inner powers bestowed upon him by the magic of the Wizard's Stone and the great confidence given to him by the Pearl of Anton—both of which were a part of his flesh—he made the river flow again from north to south as it had ages ago. Called Zak's River in honor of an old king who once had tested Jason's fortitude, the water's flow blossomed the land about it. The fertile ground made ideal farmland that burst each year with abundant crops of wheat, barley, and corn.

But Olive Branch was more than a newly prosperous township of some one hundred farmers. It was the site where The Binding Treaty was signed, in which Elf, Dwarf, and Man pledged to never war against each other again. It took the arrival of Pure Evil to make the Races realize that those things that united the Lord Anton's Races were far more important than the trivial disagreements that separated them. Olive Branch stood as a monument of peace. The people themselves were a mixed breed. While the northern kingdoms of Elfkind and Dwarfdom kept true to their lineage, as did the Man Race in the south, Olive Branch was a place where the blood intermingled. It was common, for example, for an inhabitant to have the solid frame of a Man but with slender Elf ears or the stockiness of a Dwarf but with Elfin grace. Olive Branch stood for so much promise and peace.

But this was not true today.

"Send me another!" laughed the Gorgon as the massive beast tossed another dead human, its tenth, over the side of the long bridge that crossed Zak's River just outside of Olive Branch.

The women and children of the town were locked away in their cottages as the men huddled nervously behind green foliage on the western edge of the bank just outside Olive Branch. They could not believe their eyes as they gazed at the huge creature that stood at the midpoint of the bridge. The green, scaled beast was twice the height of a man, with two thick legs and a grossly misshapen head that had huge bones protruding over its thick, bushy eyebrows. The most deadly features were its two scaled, serpentlike arms, each capable of lashing out some fifteen feet to grab its victims with powerful, teeth-lined jaws where fingers would naturally be found.

Blood from the last victim still dripped from the two serpents' gaping mouths. The Man had been brave enough, or stupid enough, to confront the beast with the only implements he had—farming tools. These people were not skilled in war. They were certainly not the Races who had defended Trinity under the skilled defiance and mastery of Cyrus Del, Jason's father, during the Final Contest. The ways of battle and war were a memory among most Men in Trinity. Seventy years of peace made them weak. History repeats.

"Send me another!" mocked the Gorgon again as its two serpent arms snapped before it, yearning to sink their teeth into more human flesh. "Or I'll come to your feeble town and take them myself!"

And so the slaughter continued throughout the morning. Brave Men reluctantly went forth to face the beast and died in the feeble attempt. In one noble effort, ten farmers raced toward the beast at once to try to overpower it. But in mere moments, ten more bodies, sliced open, were tossed over the bridge and into the river. The Gorgon's long serpent arms were no match for farmers. Nor were the few arrows that the men sent toward the beast of any use, as the Gorgon was swift to knock down most. The few arrows that did manage to plunge toward the beast's scales simply glanced off its body.

It was curious that the beast made no demands of the town other than to send it more fresh human meat for its amusement. By midday, the bridge dripped with red blood until the flow reached the end of the western end of the bridge and dribbled toward the town itself. Until this day, the town had lived in idyllic peace. No one could imagine from where such a beast had come. The Beasts of Becus were long gone, as the last of its kind—Pure Evil—was defeated by Jason Del during the Final Contest some years before.

Some of the peoples of Olive Branch began to pack their belongings in hopes of fleeing the town to the west. They placed goods in old wooden carts and began to pull them along the main road. But the Gorgon could see all from the bridge that looked through the center of the town.

"Run if you like!" it shouted as green saliva dripped from the corners of the crooked mouth upon its head. "But if you do . . . I'll come for you first!"

And so the half-hearted attempt at a daring escape ended as the peoples retreated once again to their homes. If only Jason Del were still alive, the townspeople collectively thought, they would be saved. They deeply missed his wisdom. But more than that, they deeply missed his power and the safety it brought. Though few in their lifetime had ever seen Jason Del unleash his full forces, his reputation was formidable. He was the destroyer of Pure Evil! Nothing could compare to the great Jason Del. Wherever he traveled, people instantly recognized his white robe and gentle ways, which masked the intense powers that had become part of his very flesh.

But Jason Del had died a month before of old age, and now Olive Branch was defenseless. The town council had sent a messenger to the north hours ago in hopes that the runner could find Jason Del's daughter. She was seen passing quickly through town the day before in her travels to the northern country. Some said she possessed powers similar to her father's, but none had ever witnessed them. However, there had been no word from the messenger and so the peoples of Olive Branch grew hopeless.

The blood continued to flow for another hour's time. The bravest men had been the first to volunteer to face the beast, and so they were dead already. Most of them included the members of the town council. Those remaining were the not-so-brave and the last member of the council, Mayor Fin, who was a shrewd, middle-aged politician. With the brave and town council gone, Fin took greater charge and began to select the men who would face the Gorgon next. His judgments were based upon politics. His political rivals went first. Anyone who disagreed with his assessments often went next, which silenced many. The weak went before the strong because he knew they could be more easily forced. Old men went before middle-aged ones for the same reason. The crowd supported every decision he made, mostly because each among the dwindling men was glad that he had not been chosen.

"Send me another!" slurred the beast yet again.

Mayor Fin was about to choose. He never thought about how to avoid the circumstances altogether. He only knew that the beast had to be fed. His shrewd brown eyes scanned the crowd of some fifty remaining men about him. The people held a collective breath. Someone was about to be sacrificed. Each prayed silently that it would not be him. The Mayor never felt such power before. He smiled inwardly. Life or death.

"Look!" shouted a Man as he pointed toward a figure that suddenly emerged from trees to the north.

A murmur of tempered relief and excitement rose from the frightened men. The figure was cloaked in a familiar white robe. Excitement turned to jubilation.

"The Robe!" one Man shouted. It was the nickname given to Jason Del years earlier.

"But it cannot be!" said another. "Jason Del is long dead."

Mayor Fin felt a tinge of disappointment as the attention shifted to the approach of the figure. The crowd parted and the slender, robed form entered their frightened circle and stood amongst the remaining men at the western edge of the bridge.

The figure threw back the hood. Though it was beyond reason, the townspeople hoped against hope that Jason Del was back from the dead. But it was not true. The crowd went silent upon seeing long, red hair fall upon a woman's slender shoulders. It was Megani Del. She was wearing the white robe her father had worn nearly all his life.

Megani saw the disappointment in the people's faces. Only then did she realize that by wearing her father's robe, she had given them a false hope of his resurrection. She shook her head, angry at herself for donning the garment. She meant only to assure them that she carried her father's blood. Now, she had to prove to the people that she had the right to wear the garment her father left for her. After generations of women being in the shadows, perhaps she could even prove to all within Trinity that she, a woman, could wield the power that previously had been given to male Dels alone.

"Thank you for coming," said one young Man, struggling to turn a disappointed expression into a hopeful one.

"But can you help us?!" snapped Mayor Fin, skeptically. "You're a woman!"

Megani gazed at the gruff Man. Though she had been in his presence many times when accompanied by her father, this was the first time he had addressed her directly . . . the first time she could recall that he actually had looked in her eyes. Before this, he only paid attention to her father. That was the way with Mayor Fin. He divided all those he knew into two groups: those who mattered and those who did not.

Megani gazed into his eyes but remained silent. She knew that she must answer his question with deeds and not words. Many generations of Del women were labeled weak and ineffectual because of one ancestor who had shamed them all. It was a cross that many women in Trinity bore, more often subjugated to lives of follower and not leader, of nurturer alone and not defender, too.

Megani turned and gazed downward at the human blood that now touched her leather boots, the red flowing from the bridge beyond. She slowly looked upward toward the Gorgon. Megani's green, hardened eyes glittered in the sun.

The Gorgon smiled when it saw her defiance. "Good!"

Megani looked upon the beast with surprising reserve and confidence. She had good reason. After all, she was the daughter of the great Jason Del, the destroyer of Pure Evil, who captured the confidence of the Pearl of Anton within his very being. She was a descendent of Matthew Del, Tempest Slayer, who merged the magic of the Wizard's Stone into his own flesh. And so Megani inherited much. The two gems, the Wizard's Stone and the Pearl of Anton, spun forever within her mind. With just one thought, she could merge the icons so that the confidence of the Pearl would access the Wizard's magic. The beast before her was not a match for her powers, she knew. But she was patient, her reserve due to her mother, Bea, who hailed from the stern and dedicated Race of Etha. While other children played games, Megani learned the uses of power from her skilled father. While other children engaged in childish pranks, Megani was taught dedication to the Races and to Trinity from her austere mother. She had much to prove . . . to her descendents and to herself. She was the first daughter to inherit the powers since the era of Pita Del.

That burden was great. After Megani's birth, her parents tried desperately to have a son, but none of the pregnancies were successful. Each time they tried, it reminded Megani that she was not considered strong or brave enough to be worthy of the powers. The disappointment she saw in her parents' eyes each time a pregnancy failed was devastating, for the true disappointment was with her gender. They were left with a daughter as the sole heir of the responsibility for the protection of the Races. Megani knew she had to be better, faster, stronger, and braver than any male Del that came before her. It wasn't easy. Everything was a test.

With Jason Del's death one month earlier, Megani was now in charge of the protection of all of Trinity. Though in human years she was a full adult, in Ethan years she was barely a teen, owing to the long life span of her mother's Race.

How odd, Megani suddenly thought, that this beast did not make itself known to the world before her father's death. Did it believe, thought Megani, that with her father's passing it was now safe to emerge from the shadows . . . safe to battle a *woman,* a descendent of the coward Pita?

"What are you?!" Megani called as she took several confident steps toward the foot of the bridge.

"A Gorgon!" the beast replied, smiling while its serpent hands snapped at the air as though trying to consume Megani even before she was within reach.

Megani threw her mind probe forth, yet another inheritance, and brushed the essence of evil. The darkness was formidable, but the beast was flawed. The creature is stupid, she instantly knew, not possessing enough intelligence or experience to be a great foe. How odd, thought Megani as she continued to probe its mind. The creature also had little knowledge of its own creation. Its mind possessed no memories of the previous day. It knew only that it was here, on this bridge, and that it was to taunt the inhabitants to battle it. Megani was careful to keep her own mind protected from the mind probe of another, a skill her father taught her years before. She was taught to be forever on her guard.

Megani looked back into the grateful but still fearful eyes of the Men huddled behind her. Though she had helped her father resolve minor disputes among the Races these many years, Megani had never before been put to the full test. All of the great battles of this era occurred long before she was even born. But now with her father dead, she was their savior. The Races of Trinity would look to her. She had to prove she was worthy . . . that a *woman* was worthy. She could not fail her first real test as Pita had thousands of years before.

"And what's a Gorgon?" Megani asked. She took another striding step toward the beast, her feet splashing through blood puddles as she stepped upon the bridge.

The beast hesitated, then slurred, "I don't know."

Odd again, thought Megani. How can a beast not know its origin or its very essence?

A few more steps brought Megani within striking distance of the creature. She looked up towards its massive height. "Who commands you?"

It snapped, "I do!"

The Gorgon's right serpent arm suddenly shot toward Megani. She pivoted to one side and let it pass. It snapped again, but Megani easily pivoted right and left to avoid its sharp teeth. The left serpent arm plunged toward Megani. She ducked and grabbed the arm from beneath and was lifted upward as the beast's left arm jerked back and forth to break Megani's vice-like grip. The right serpent arm dove toward Megani, but just before it struck she swung from the left arm and jumped onto the Gorgon's right shoulder. Missing Megani, the serpent's right arm bit deep into its own left arm and sheared it off below the shoulder. Megani drew her sword and sliced off the remaining serpent arm. Green blood exploded from the beast and the Gorgon began to fall back. Megani jumped to the bridge as the beast crashed with a heavy thud. The armless Gorgon, now void of its serpent arms, rose to its feet and dashed toward Megani to crush her with its massive weight and force. She stood immobile for a moment as the beast hurled onward. At the last moment before impact, she ducked low and sliced her sword through the beast's legs. It fell dead upon the bridge. Green mixed with red.

"Hurrah!" the townspeople cheered. Only Mayor Fin did not rejoice. But the jubilation was short lived.

Two Gorgons raced from the eastern foliage toward the bridge. Megani spied them instantly. She held her sleek sword firmly. It was not as formidable as the Sword of Legends that her grandfather Cyrus Del carried when he came to the aid of her father in the final, cataclysmic battle with Pure Evil. But it would do. In no time, the beasts were close enough for Megani to use her mind probe. Like the Gorgon that was now dead at her feet, these creatures had great evil intent, but it was focused entirely upon seizing the bridge, with no memory of where they had been yesterday nor any thoughts of where they might be tomorrow. Her mind probe was useless to tell her more.

The two Gorgons arrived. They lashed at Megani with their four serpent arms. But each that came within reach was beheaded. With several more sure strokes, two more Gorgons lay dead.

Sixteen Gorgons dashed forward from the forest beyond. Megani wavered just a bit, but her confidence held. She stood her ground.

"Where are they coming from?" she wondered aloud. Why now? Why here?

The sixteen Gorgons stopped short and their serpent arms—thirty-two in all—detached from their bodies and slithered forward. The bodies paused as sixteen of the serpents went straight to the bridge while the others waded in the water and, reaching up, gained the side of the bridge next to Megani. Others waded farther west and gained the bridge behind her. In a moment, Megani was surrounded by the serpents.

The townspeople covered their eyes, certain of the outcome.

The thirty-two serpents lunged at once!

Megani jumped upward some thirty feet into the air as serpents gashed at her from below. She came down spinning like a top, headfirst, as her blade cut deep into the beasts that came for her. She landed atop a pile of thirty-two corpses. The Gorgon's sixteen bodies charged at once. Megani raced toward them.

"Always forward!" she said to herself as she flew, a phrase cemented into her mind by her sonless mother. "Always forward!"

Megani jumped high, landed upon the shoulder of the lead Gorgon, sliced it fatally with her sword, and without ever losing her forward momentum continued to leap from shoulder to shoulder until all were dead.

"She is lucky!" spit the frustrated Beastmaker as he watched the carnage from a ridge a mile away. A massive beast that continuously altered its shape from one creature to the next, the Beastmaker was now in dragon form. It had created the Gorgons, and they were as much his pets as they were his tools.

"Not really lucky," said an ancient creature cloaked in darkness at the Beastmaker's side. "She's skilled."

"Luck!" shouted the Beastmaker, now in the form of a raging bull.

"Well then," crackled the ancient one, "let's see how much luck she has left. Send thirty-two Gorgons, each with two serpent arms."

The Beastmaker stomped his hoof. The signal was relayed until it reached the eastern forest.

Thirty-two Gorgons sprang from the trees and dove toward Megani. Too many for the sword, she thought. Megani had never used her magic in battle, but there was no better moment than this one. After all, this is why she existed in the first place. She looked back toward Olive Branch as the townspeople continued to huddle and watch in horror. Dozens of women and children had joined the men in their watch. She saw a mixture of both hope and doom. She looked back at the raging beasts. "Where did all these things come from?" she breathed.

The Gorgons came onward. The icons of the Wizard's Stone and the Pearl spun in Megani's mind. The combining of both—the force of the Wizard's Stone and the confidence of the Pearl—were the sources of the power. The beasts swept closer. The ground trembled.

"Merge!" she commanded, and the icons overlapped by a quarter.

Boom!

White magic shot from Megani's clenched fists and pounded into the beasts. They exploded in a fierce, sizzling ball of fire and were gone.

"Ahhhhhhh!" grieved the Beastmaker. "She has magics! I didn't know she had magics!"

"No matter," said the ancient one.

The Beastmaker pounded his gorilla chest. "My creatures can't fight against magics! It's as ancient as you are . . . as powerful as nature."

"We are not here to fight against it," said the ancient one. "We are here to find the magic's limit . . . her limit." The shadowy figure thought a moment. "Send five hundred Gorgons," it said casually.

"Five hundred?!" shrieked the Beastmaker, now circling about the ancient one as a lion. "I won't . . . I won't send my pets to die . . . not by magics!"

"You're right," said the ancient one as if in agreement, until its voiced hardened. "Send one thousand!"

"But . . . ," began the Beastmaker as it slithered about on its snake-like belly. The ancient one cut him short, turning its hardened, blood-red eyes toward him. The Beastmaker grunted in frustration, knowing better than to disagree.

"Wooaaahhh!"

One thousand Gorgons exploded from the forest, howling as they came. The townspeople shrieked in horror and bolted westward to save themselves from the sure onslaught. Megani's jaw dropped as her eyes widened in disbelief. But she instantly bolted forward, toward the beasts, leaving the eastern bank behind her. She refused to run away.

She could never, ever run away. She could never be like Pita, the first Del to have shamed the Royal House. She was Megani, and that meant she must move forward, and never, ever back. Megani knew that she would need the full power of her magic, but she did not know if that would be enough to thwart the tsunami of flesh before her. She knew only that this was her moment to discover its strength. If she died, Megani thought, it would be while running forward!

"Merge!!" she screamed as she flew into the horde of one thousand beasts. The icons of Wizard and Pearl fully joined within her mind.

KABOOM!

White fire engulfed Megani as a searing, white wave of intense magic flew before her. The Gorgons entered the massive flow and were incinerated as they screamed and shriveled into nothingness. The peoples of Olive Branch fell to their knees while the ground beneath their feet buckled and heaved. Their hearts pounded with fear, not just of the beasts, but of the powers unleashed by she who sought to save them. When the ground ceased its rumbling, the men, women, and children rose sluggishly, nervously to their feet and gazed east of the bridge. They suddenly paused, transfixed. Silence reigned. They saw Megani on her knees amidst falling ash that looked like a gentle snowfall. The Gorgons were gone, though their smoldering carcasses remained, obliterated by a force that Trinity had not seen since the day that Jason Del destroyed Pure Evil. Cheers broke out. Men spoke in whispers, finding it both a blessing and a curiosity that a woman could be so powerful. Women sensed a pride they had never felt. Mayor Fin walked away.

Megani Del, the last descendent of the Royal House of Del, was exhausted and dizzy. Sweat dripped down her face and neck. All her strength was spent. And in that moment, her guard fell and her mind was unprotected.

"Ahhh," said the ancient one from far away. "There it is."

"There's what?" asked the grieving Beastmaker as the massive bat darted about his master's head. "My pets are dead!"

"There's her weakness . . . one among many."

"What weakness?! She killed nearly all of my precious ones. It will take me days—weeks—to create more."

"She has many faults," teased the ancient one. "She's vain, thinking herself invincible. Why else would she rush a thousand Gorgons without knowing if she could defeat them? Next, she is weakened by the full force of her powers. I could have finished her off with another hundred Gorgons or so . . . too bad I needed them elsewhere. She also does not protect her mind fully when pressed to exhaustion, and so it can be planted with fresh memories if ever I get close enough. Finally," the ancient one concluded, its voice crackling with delight, "the young girl is so easily fooled. She will be fun to play with!" Wrinkled lips cracked a thin smile. "And . . . she's just a girl, after all."

The ancient one nodded, pleased with the progress. "Go to the Valley of Despair," it told the Beastmaker. "Tell me what you see. I need to be sure that my other plans are on schedule."

The disheartened bat darted west. With each flap of its wings, it turned into a different soaring beast . . . first a massive crow . . . then an eagle . . . then a dragon . . . then a huge dragonfly . . . .

Megani rested for several hours in Olive Branch, where grateful townspeople regaled her with food and drink in the town square. As many of the couples danced, their affection was evident. Megani was never allowed to engage in such trivial pursuits, she thought. "It's a waste of your time," her mother would say. Besides, Megani spent her life proving she was better than Men and had little experience trying to gain their affections. Though there was one who was close to her heart . . . more than she dared to admit. But that notion was too distant, too much a luxury, particularly now with a new danger afoot.

Megani smiled as she watched the townspeople celebrate in her honor. It felt good that in her first real test since her father's death, she had succeeded. Her parents would be very proud, she thought. She protected the Races. She could feel the cowardice of a thousand years begin to erase from the history of the women who carried the name of Del—and from all the women in ages past who were cast aside so that their brothers would inherit the powers and the responsibilities.

A middle-aged woman carrying two pails of water crossed between the dancing couples, making her way to tables filled with food and drink. She suddenly tripped and fell hard to the ground. Her pails smashed upon the dirt and the water splashed upon those nearby. Mayor Fin was among them.

"Stupid Pita!" he spat as he raised his hand to strike the woman who was still upon her knees.

As his hand came down hard, it was stopped by a strong grip from behind. He looked back into the menacing eyes of Megani. Old prejudices are thick, she thought. She released Fin's arm and then helped the woman off the ground.

"What's your name?" asked Megani.

"Beth," she said.

Megani smiled. "My grandmother was named Beth! She was a warrior at the Battle of Meadowtown alongside my grandfather Cyrus. He was one of the few who knew her potential. She helped save the town just prior to my father's battle with Pure Evil."

"I know!" said the old woman. "I was named after Beth Del."

Megani gave her a hug. She held back tears. "Then wear the name proudly."

Megani sent her on her way. She turned to Mayor Fin. His face was a menacing red and a vein in his neck pulsated to the beat of his angry heart. She moved in close so only he could hear her words. "I expect you to treat her—and all women—with the same respect that you gave my father."

Megani then turned to the assembled town. "I must leave you to continue my travels north!" she began. "I suggest you travel to Meadowtown. They are still skilled in battle there. You will find protection and training should Gorgons still be a danger."

"Let's not be so hasty!" said Mayor Fin. "I think we can take care of ourselves."

Megani stared at him, knowing full well that it was his power, not the people's lives, he sought to save. "Recent events say otherwise!" Megani countered. She turned again to the townspeople. "Again, I suggest you pack all of your belongings and journey to Meadowtown." She then walked through the crowd to continue her trip. A cheer rose as she left them behind. It was a good feeling. She searched the forest east of Zak's River to ensure that no more Gorgons remained. Satisfied, she began her trek north once more.

Before she was delayed by the events in Olive Branch, Megani had been on her way to meet with Elf King Alar and Dwarf King Dal to resolve some sudden and urgent dispute between their two Races. There was even a rumor of conflict between them. The day before, news of the dire events had reached Zol, where Megani and her mother were lodging. It was so bizarre, thought both, that the Elves and Dwarves would even consider war when the Races were so much at peace and for so long.

Near sundown, Megani once again started north to lend what aid she could to the northern Races.

"Good travels north!" laughed the ancient one as it saw Megani leave the confines of Olive Branch. "I have an even bigger surprise waiting for you there!" The creature then smiled wickedly. "So much like Pita," it cackled. "So much like Pita."

It was the only creature in existence who would know that firsthand.

CHAPTER 2

A BATTLE TO THE DEATH

*B*oom . . . *Boom* . . . *Boom!*

The eager drums of war pounded. The aging Elf King Alar could barely hear himself think. But that's what Dwarf war drums are meant to do. The ground rumbled to the maddening beat. The Elf monarch, dressed in full battle mail and helmet, surveyed his ten thousand warrior Elves, who stood in rigid formation at the eastern edge of the Valley of Despair, where the slope rose upward to the snowcapped Mountain High. Though the pounding pierced their ears, it could not pierce their brave hearts. It was high noon. The sky was filled with dark clouds. A steady, cold breeze blew from the west. Alar knew it would not be long now until the evil Dwarves would attack. Snow began to fall lightly.

"How did we get here," he whispered to himself, "when just a week ago Elfkind was at peace with Dwarfkind?" For many years he had even counted Dwarf King Dal as his closest friend. As noble princes many years before, they had fought valiantly beside each other in the famed Battle of Meadowtown to aid Cyrus Del and pave the way for Cyrus's son, Jason, to battle Pure Evil in the Final Contest. Elf King Alar's mind drifted back to that day and to a moment when the Dwarf Prince Dal actually pulled Alar from the carnage to mend his wounds after the battle. If not for the Dwarf's tender care, Alar would have died decades ago.

"How did we get here?" asked Alar once again, shaking his head as he scanned his able troops. Dwarf King Dal had been his friend for so many years, he recalled again. They had shared so much together. They each took part in the other's wedding. They became godfathers to each other's children. But that was long ago, it seemed. Those times were almost as distant as the peace that existed a week earlier. The world had changed . . . in that one week. And yet he and Dwarf King Dal had been the closest of friends. If only . . .

King Alar's mind suddenly sparked with the vivid memory of his son's murder, and his heart hardened. The atrocities conducted against Elfkind by the sinister Dwarves were beyond belief, yet they were as true as the sun rises and sets. If Elf King Alar had not seen his only son, Prince Allo, butchered at the hands of Dwarf King Dal one week ago, he would not have believed it. He had vividly seen the Dwarf king ahead of his massing army upon the plains just east of the Valley of Despair while he and his son, Allo, were hunting. They were both surprised that the Dwarves beat the drums of war. While King Alar stayed to tend to their game of deer, he sent Prince Allo to greet the Dwarves and determine why they were at war and with whom. But as King Alar watched from afar, he saw the Dwarf king pull his ax and slice Allo through the heart. The Dwarf King Dal and his army then marched eastward toward Dwarfdom. Elf King Alar remembered racing forward to aid his son, but he was already dead. Alar swore a blood vengeance upon all of Dwarfdom and then returned home to the land of Elfkind to raise his army.

Elf King Alar closed his eyes as though to blot out the memory, but it stayed fresh in his mind. And eyes and minds don't lie. So a lifetime of friendship and trust was shattered by an act so vile that it demanded the greatest retribution.

Dwarfdom must perish, thought the Elf King as he scanned the mountaintop to the east, and Dwarf King Dal must die.

Boom . . . Boom . . . Boom continued the Dwarf war drums, echoing throughout the valley. But no Dwarves could yet be seen. Loose rocks rolled down the slopes to the beat of the drums. The sound prevented the Elves from using their fine hearing to detect where the Dwarf troops might mount their first wave of assault. Elf King Alar had hoped to reach the summit of the mountain before the Dwarves had arrived from the eastern lands, but it was not to be; the Elves must battle in the pit of the Valley of Despair. He smiled sadly to himself, knowing that the valley would once again earn its name. Ages ago in a world that no longer exists, the Valley of Despair was the first battleground, as the Wizards and Races, all sent by the Good Lord Anton, fought the gruesome Beasts of the Evil Lord Becus. Only about one hundred years ago, this was also the very spot of the Second Race War, when the Dwarves and Elves nearly annihilated each other in a desperate struggle over territory.

"We won't be so lucky this day," Elf King Alar mused, recalling how the able Men of Trinity, led by the great Major T, came to prevent the northern Races from carrying out their own destruction. "Not today," the wise king thought again.

"Bukaaa!" came a shout as a cold wind blew, chilling the bone. The voice emanated one-fourth of the way up the slope. Before the first echo resounded, a roar rose above the drums.

"Bukaaa Taaa!"

One thousand mail-clad Dwarves simultaneously appeared upon the slopes and flew down the mountainside. Each whirled a leather sling around its head and then let the rock within it fly. One thousand boulders flew toward the Elf lines. Then another thousand. Then another. The sky darkened as a shower of rocks raced overhead. The boulders began to crash into the army at the base of the slopes. But the Elf warriors were quick to raise their metal shields and the stones glanced off.

"Hold those shields!" shouted Elf King Alar. Ten thousand Elf troops stayed safely behind their barriers. But the king saw that the Dwarves were advancing rapidly and he needed to return fire. The only way to do that was to sacrifice a line of troops.

"Second line, ready your arm!" commanded Elf King Alar. While nine thousand Elf troops stayed behind their shields, one thousand Elves in the second line put their shields down and raised their bows. With many shields down, thousands of Dwarf missiles began to crash into the exposed second line of Elves, immediately killing dozens of the Elf warriors. Those who remained steadied their aim.

"Second line . . . find your Dwarf marks to the east!" shouted Elf King Alar. "Release!"

The second line of one thousand Elves shot mostly true, sending their arrows into the horde of one thousand Dwarves that descended upon them from the mountain slope. Dwarves fell as pointed shafts of death avoided the chest plates and iron helmets and pierced exposed necks and faces. Hundreds of Dwarves fell in the first assault. And so too did hundreds of Elves in the second line as the boulders continued to crash among them.

"Second line!" shouted Elf King Alar. "Continue to release. First line, hold those shields. Lines three through ten . . . reverse and ready your aim!"

Eight thousand warrior Elves turned to face west . . . away from the slopes! They put down their shields and raised their bows. The Elves began to get pounded by the rocks coming from the slopes behind them. Elf King Alar was in the middle of his troops. His aides shielded the king as best they could. In seconds, hundreds of Elves lay dead, their red blood mixing with dirt and a light covering of snowfall.

King Alar shouted above the battle. "Lines three through ten, elevate to hit in a semicircle between two hundred and five hundred yards west!" The Elves obeyed. "Release!"

While the first line kept their shields high for protection and the second line continued to shoot with deadly accuracy into the Dwarves who descended from the slope to the east, the remaining Elf lines shot some eight thousand arrows as Elf King Alar had commanded, directly west and seemingly into the dirt. But King Alar knew otherwise. Though he could not hear or see the warrior Dwarves advancing from the west, he could smell their approach. He knew that for hours they had been gradually oozing their way along the surface of the ground, wearing camouflage and blending in as dirt, rocks, and brush. So the skilled Elf king decided to spring their trap before the Dwarves did. He knew that the Dwarf assault from the slope was a diversion to draw their attention eastward while the main body of Dwarf warriors had already arrived at the Elf's rear position.

As soon as the westward bound arrows hit, screams arose from the ground.

"Bukaaa!" shouted a command to the west. The Dwarves who remained alive, some four thousand, rose and rushed the Elf lines, throwing axes with deadly accuracy. Hundreds of Elves fell instantly dead—among them were three of King Alar's aides and the standard-bearer.

"Perimeter shields up!" shouted the Elf king amidst the furry.

The Elves about the perimeter of the lines raised their shields to provide more protection for those in the center of their force. Between slits in the shields, Elves flew a continuous stream of arrows into the advancing Dwarves, killing hundreds at a time. With the closing of distance, the Dwarf slings grew more deadly. Within minutes, one-third of King's Alar's warriors were dead, as were thousands of Dwarves.

As they raced nearer their enemies, Dwarves launched spears into huddling Elf defenses. More Elves lifted their shields to gain desperately needed protection, but hundreds of spears pierced the shields, killing many. The spearmen fared no better, for each Dwarf that exposed himself to launch his spear was dead soon thereafter, pierced with many Elf points.

Suddenly, the pounding drums grew more intense. As they did, the advancing Dwarves suddenly disappeared. That was not a good sign, Elf King Alar knew, for it meant they were about to launch another phase in their attack. The Elf king looked up toward the mountain's snow-covered summit to the east. He saw a large bat dart far above in the gently falling snow. The king blinked his eyes, and the bat appeared to have changed into a large, ominous crow. Bad omen, he thought.

Elf King Alar gazed beyond the bird to the very top of the mountain and saw for the first time the large, flowing flag of Dwarf King Dal. Beside the standard-bearer was a mail-clad warrior whose armor sparkled in the light . . . the Dwarf King himself.

From far above, the battle-clad Dwarf King Dal was pleased with what he saw. The Elves had poor position. Days ago the Dwarf king knew that if he pushed his army hard enough, they could reach the summit of the mountain while the Elves were still crossing the floor of the valley. And now the Dwarf army reaped the fruits of their hard struggle. Despite King Alar's good intuition to attack west, this day would still go to the Dwarves, he knew.

"But how did we come to this?" wondered the Dwarf King quietly to himself. A week ago they were at peace. And it was a good peace. He wondered how he could he have trusted Elf King Alar for all those years. He had always treated the Elf like his own brother. The Dwarf king suddenly recalled that, as a prince, he gladly nursed Alar back to health after the Battle of Meadowtown. He danced at his wedding. And now, the supposedly righteous king of Elves had started a war against Dwarfkind by butchering the Dwarf king's own son, Prince Drak, right before his father's eyes. And eyes don't lie, thought the Dwarf King.

Had Dwarf King Dal not seen his only son, Prince Drak, butchered at the hands of Elf King Alar one week ago, he would not have believed it. He had vividly seen the Elf king ahead of his massing army upon the plains just west of the Valley of Despair while the Dwarf King and his son, Drak, were hunting. They saw the Elf war banners from afar and were alarmed. While Dwarf King Dal stayed to tend to their game of elk, he sent Prince Drak to greet the Elves and determine why they were at war and with whom. As Dwarf King Dal watched from afar, he saw the Elf king pull his sword and slice Drak through the heart. Elf King Alar and his army then marched northward toward Elfkind. The Dwarf King remembered racing forward to aid his son, but he was already dead. And so Dal swore a blood vengeance upon all Elves and then returned home to the land of Dwarfdom to raise his army.

And so a lifetime of friendship and trust was shattered by an act so vile that it demanded the greatest retribution. Elfkind must be erased from the face of Trinity, thought the King of Dwarves, and Elf King Alar must die!

"How did we come to this?" the Dwarf King questioned again as a dark haze began to lift from his brain and reasoning began to seep in again. But quickly it was gone. It is what it is, thought King Dal as his mind sparked again with the memory of his only son's murder. The Dwarf King glanced up and saw a large black crow. He blinked his eyes and in the crow's place was a red hawk. Not a good omen, he thought. But he looked down into the valley and smiled at the Elves' poor position. His heart was gladdened.

"They are squeezed together like the vile rats that they are," he seethed from his high vantage point. He turned to his aide. "The time is right. Bring on the mammoths!"

King Alar was alarmed by the sudden disappearance of Dwarves, particularly since the Dwarves already had strong positions. It could only mean that King Dal wanted them out of harm's way while he unleashed something even more deadly. The pounding of Dwarf drums became furious. The ground trembled violently. Loose stones from the mountain above them continued to fall, creating a steady rockslide. But the pounding now came from more than the drums alone, noted King Alar.

"King Alar!" shouted an Elf at the northern edge of the battle, "Mammoth Riders!"

The King whipped his gaze toward the north and spied nearly one thousand huge woolly mammoths with long, sharp tusks racing toward the Elf encampment.

"Form islands amidst the storm!" shouted the Elf king.

Seven thousand remaining Elves formed dozens of piles of flesh and mail, each measuring some twenty feet high. Their aim was to trick the mammoths into venturing around the piles instead of through them. But the mammoths skillfully took the orders from the Dwarf riders atop them.

The beasts pounded into the Elf islands, throwing many Elves far into the air while trampling others. Again and again they plowed through flesh, using their sharp tusks to gouge many Elves at a time while crisscrossing back and forth along the Elf position. Brave Elves caught the legs and tails of the beasts and began to pull themselves upward to attack the Dwarves that guided them. In no time at all, battle raged atop the mammoths, and the Dwarf Riders, so intent upon controlling the beasts, were no match for the Elves that gained position from behind. Within minutes, Dwarves were replaced by Elves. But the beasts had fulfilled their purpose, killing thousands of Elf soldiers.

At the sound of a sharp bugle, the trained mammoths dropped to the ground and rolled over, crushing the Elves that remained atop them. The giant, woolly beasts then turned and trotted west to the renewed Dwarf lines there.

King Alar was alive. But he knew that it would not be for long. He could not wait for a renewed onslaught of Mammoth Riders. He had to attack.

"Elfkind!" he shouted as he raised the torn Elf flag. "To the Dwarf king!" The battered King Alar raced up the slope of the mountain toward King Dal. Thousands of Elf warriors flew up behind him. Many passed their king in order to carve a way through the grim Dwarf battle lines.

"So be it!" spit King Dal. "To the Elf king!" he shouted in return as he grabbed the Dwarf flag from the standard-bearer and rushed down the mountain toward his mortal enemy. The Dwarf king's pace was swift, as gravity pulled him toward his destiny.

Within minutes, thousand of Elves in their ascent clashed in hand-to-hand combat with the thousands of Dwarf troops from above. The Dwarves that were west of the Elves' position were pinned down by Elf archers that formed a line to protect King Alar's back. But arrows were soon depleted, and the Dwarves gained valuable ground. Elves drew swords and Dwarves readied long knives and axes.

Thousands more were killed within minutes. New Dwarf Riders on mammoths returned from the west and began to chase the Elves farther up the mountainside, but the battle was so close that Dwarves died under the beasts as easily as did Elves.

Through the carnage of the battle, two flags skidded and dashed about the clash of warriors as they dove toward each other, one from below and one from above. Though warrior Dwarves had opportunities to cut down the Elf King, they did not. Though Elf warriors had opportunities to cut down the Dwarf King, they resisted. The troops instinctively knew that these two kings must meet—must collide—to administer the ultimate justice . . . and to right a grave wrong.

Thirty minutes later, surrounded by the clash of battle, screams of death, and the smell of blood, the flags met!

"Devil!" shouted Elf King Alar as the towering Elf jabbed his sleek sword downward at the advancing Dwarf King Dal. But the old Dwarf, clad in full battle dress, was still surprisingly agile. He ducked and rolled beneath the blade and came up just before the Elf's waist. Dal jabbed a ten-inch, jeweled blade hard, piercing Alar's breast mail and sending the knife into his lung.

"Demon!" Dal seethed as he twisted the blade. Alar fell back and rolled many yards down the mountainside even as the battle raged about him. He came to a sliding stop and pulled the blade from his body, tossing it aside.

The old Dwarf flew down the slope and jumped toward the Elf. Alar painfully jerked his feet forward and hurled the Dwarf over his head. Dal rolled many more yards down the mountain, cracking his head upon an outcropping of boulders. Blood flowed. The Dwarf stumbled to his feet, pulled his ax from his side, and spinning about, he hurled it at Alar just as the bleeding Elf king had gained his footing and launched his own sword at the Dwarf king.

As the Dwarf ax plunged into King Alar's chest, the Elf sword sliced into the Dwarf king's shoulder and knocked the Dwarf off his feet. He spun head over heals and landed hard on his chest. The fall pushed the blade deeper. Blood flowed, and the Dwarf king felt his life slipping away. He looked up at the mountain and saw the evil Elf king pull the ax from his own chest. Blood spurted from the gaping hole. Their eyes met.

Broken, bloodied, and dying, the former friends dragged themselves toward each other, gaining precious inches along the rugged mountainside until they met face to face again. Each managed to grip the other's throat. Each squeezed with every ounce of life he had left, hoping to kill the other before he himself died.

In a moment, they were both dead, their battered flags beneath them. Elf King Alar carried a mortal wound of the Dwarf king's ax, just as Dwarf King Dal carried the mortal wound of the Elf king's sword.

Neither king had ever thought to question each other's version of the past week. Neither had thought to question what their eyes told them: that their sons were killed by the other king. Neither thought to understand, beyond their grief, what forces beyond each might have been affecting them both. While each had sent a message to the only one in Trinity who might aid their individual causes—Megani Del—neither thought to stress the true urgency of the situation.

But why not? Odder still was that these two kings lived as friends and died as enemies, a change that occurred in only a week's time.

They trusted their eyes, which affected their hearts, which clouded their reasoning. Had they only known the truth . . .

What had been thousands of proud Dwarf and Elf warriors was now but a trickle, but they fought until the last among them was dead or dying. They fought for their kings. They fought to right a grievous wrong that many also claimed to have seen with their own eyes. Many hundreds saw each king slay the other king's son. They saw it clearly.

And yet it should have been a happy time, for Prince Drak of the Dwarves and Prince Allo of the Elves were both about to celebrate the passage into adulthood—their fifteenth year. They were to live in the forest together, far to the west, for two weeks with only a couple of hunting weapons and a pair of leathers each. They were to hunt their own game and make their own lodge, as wild bears do. Once they returned, they would have been greeted as full warriors. But that was not to be, as hundred of Dwarf eyes saw Elf King Alar of the Elves kill Dwarf Prince Drak right before the Dwarf prince was to leave on his quest. And hundreds of Elf eyes saw Dwarf King Dal kill Elf Prince Allo right before the Elf prince was to leave on his quest.

After the clang of battle had subsided for some time, dirt began to roil upwards all along the blood-stained mountainside. Beasts slithered from their shallow burrows and tunnels where they had hidden weeks before. Hundreds of massive, green slithering serpents spied the remains of the battle. They smiled, revealing glistening, sharp teeth. They knew only what they were supposed to know: They were to wait until the earth above them grew turbulent and then still again. And when the quiet came, they would rise to the surface to kill those that still lived. Their task was soon complete. They then followed their next directive, which was to slither away to the Elf and Dwarf kingdoms to devour the remains of the unprotected Races that had been left behind. Their deeds were handily, mercilessly done.

In one swift, maddening, and incomprehensible moment, Elfkind and Dwarfkind were gone.

From a distant mountain along the western edge of the cold and gloomy valley, a young woodsman of nineteen years sat among the brush. He looked in wonder and disgust at the bloodshed in the depths of the valley to the east. He had been there for many hours, drawn by the sounds of war and the ominous signs he had been taught to recognize— the madness among the Races. These were not good . . . not good at all.

He shook his head in disgust. How could two Races, friends for so long, perish so quickly and so violently? What madness could do this so neatly? The questions were not easily answered. It wasn't natural, he thought.

And then it got worse. The young man's sharp eyes caught sight of strange serpents slithering about the carnage. They tracked down the dying and put a quick end to them. His heart froze. He had spent most of his life in the deep forest and had seen many beasts that few men had ever witnessed. But never had he seen beasts such as these. They were not of the world that the Good Lord Anton had created. They were something much different. He then caught sight of an even stranger beast that flew far above the battleground. It had been circling for hours. It was a crow . . . that became a hawk . . . that became a dragon . . . .

"Supernatural," he thought as the beast momentarily disappeared into the clouds.

His right hand slightly trembled as the young Man gently rolled up the sleeve to his left arm. It revealed a tattoo that he had had since birth. He suddenly rubbed it as though trying to remove it, but it could not be erased so easily. "G," the tattoo read. It stood for "Guardian," for that's what he was, though he did not know what, exactly, he was guarding. But he did know that he somehow carried a message, one that he was obligated to deliver or die trying. That's what he was raised to do—was trained to do—what he swore to do so long ago.

The young Man lowered his sleeve and threw his thick brown hair back from his sparkling blue eyes. He again caught site of the strange, flying beast. This time it changed from a dragon to a bat as it departed the Valley of Despair and headed south. Strange.

The Man had no idea why he was thrust into the middle of this day's events or where his involvement might lead. But he had a duty to perform, one that he promised he would fulfill.

"Supernatural," he said again as he slowly rose to his feet. He dusted off his leathers and gazed again at the slaughter in the valley below. He had seen death many times before and in many hideous ways, and he knew that if he did not fulfill his mission, his quest, there would be more. Much more. He knew that the battle below was simply the beginning of a tortured end to Trinity. But his thoughts also went to the only woman for whom he had ever cared. He instinctively knew that she, too, would be hurled into this devastation. It was only a matter of time. But he pushed her image from his mind. His quest had to be of primary importance.

"Well," he said with a sad smile as he began to stroll down into the valley, "I gotta find me the Historian."

CHAPTER 3

DEVASTATION

Through the early evening and late into the chilly night, Megani raced northwest toward Mountain High, where she had heard that Dwarves were moving west and into the Valley of Despair to meet the Elves. She skirted easily about the brush and trees, drove through meadows, and crossed small streams whose chilly waters came from freshly melted snow from Mountain High.

She was deeply troubled. Where did the Gorgons come from, she wondered? There were so many. How could they have come to Trinity without notice? Why now? Was it truly because her father had died the month before, and so the beasts felt the land was unprotected? Perhaps the Gorgons thought she would be no match without her father, Jason Del, the Destroyer of Pure Evil. However, she had proved otherwise. Perhaps that would prevent the beasts from trying to attack Trinity again.

Now and again, her thoughts would bounce to Devon, a mysterious land southeast of Trinity. Could that be the origin of the Gorgons? she wondered. The land was first discovered decades before by seafaring, adventurous Men of Trinity who sought to expand their knowledge of the unknown world. Few of the brave souls ever returned. Most were either lost to the treacherous sea in the Straits of Devils or to the fore-boding land beyond it. Those who did find their way home told tales of strange, fierce beasts and sudden, unexplained disasters. Some came back completely mad. On one occasion, a Man returned with his arms where his legs should have been and his legs where his arms should have been. He was otherwise alive and well, though he had no recollection as to how his crippling transformation came to be. Jason Del regarded it as a warning from those beyond not to venture into the land of Devon.

Megani often asked her father if she could go to Devon in order to better understand what threats might exist. But Jason Del always refused, claiming that Trinity was given by Anton to the Races, and it would show a lack of appreciation to venture beyond it. And, too, her father had seen enough war to last ten lifetimes; he was not about to involve the peoples of Trinity in another. So while father and daughter made sure that Trinity was protected, tragedies continued to haunt those who ventured beyond its borders. Now, she wondered, could it be that Devon arrived at their doorsteps?

Megani was anxious to reach the northern Races in order to warn them of the Gorgons and to gain their counsel. The Elves and Dwarves were wise and steadfast. King Alar and King Dal were not only good friends to each other, but they had been good friends to Jason Del and to her as well. She was sure that they would certainly know what to do. It would be a comfort to seek their guidance, particularly since her father was no longer there to help her.

In the early morning, Megani began to see a scattering of frantic men and women burdened with supplies moving quickly south across the plains. From afar, Megani sensed that they were fleeing from some unknown disaster. Perhaps the Gorgons had struck in the north already, she thought. She spied the nearest frontiersman with his family and made her way toward them. Their pace was hurried as they pulled an old wooden cart that overflowed with what appeared to be all their possessions. The family bowed when they saw her approach. "The Robe," the husband said out of respect, though he clearly knew it was Megani who donned it.

"Rise," Megani said. "Why do you travel south in such haste?"

"Have you not heard?" asked the man. "Dwarves and Elves ready for battle!"

"With the Gorgons?"

"Don't know what a Gorgon is," began the Man. "The Races have gone crazy. . . . They intend to battle with each other!"

"What?!" shot Megani. "I heard there was a disagreement . . . but battle?"

"Battle," he confirmed.

"Why?!"

"Don't know . . . and I was not about to find out. It's too dangerous in the north, so we're heading south until they make peace or kill each other trying."

Megani raced toward Mountain High. It was insanity, she thought, that Elves and Dwarves would be at war. She had visited the region one month ago to tell the kings of her father's passing, and all seemed well within the kingdoms. What madness is this, she wondered again and again, that would first bring the Gorgons and now pit the northern Races in conflict? She admonished herself for staying so long in Olive Branch. She should have left soon after the battle with the Gorgons and not wasted time partaking in the celebration afterward. Was it exhaustion that delayed her . . . or vanity?

By midafternoon Megani reached the eastern face of Mountain High and found the Sky Tree, a huge oak of immense height and girth. Its strong, massive limbs climbed straight up through the low-hanging clouds. Some said that the tree was as old as Trinity itself. She paused at the base of the oak and looked about to be sure she was not detected. Megani then quickly climbed far up into the tree and disappeared into its many branches and abundant green leaves. She climbed higher and higher, pulling herself from one limb to the next until she passed above the clouds, about one-third of the way up the tree. Megani found a large hole in the arm of an upward-reaching branch. She glanced about herself once more to be sure she was undetected. Seeing that she was completely hidden in the lush-green foliage, Megani jumped headfirst into the hole.

Megani hurled downward, sliding within the core of the ancient tree's trunk. Her stomach tickled at the feeling of plunging weightlessness. Far at the bottom of the trunk, the plummet began to level off and turned northwest as Megani's path took her gliding within one of the tree's massive roots. She continued to hurl at great speed, owing to the slick oils of the inner root and the slight declination of the root as it approached Mountain High from below. The path would take her beneath the mountain and to the Valley of Despair, saving her a time-consuming climb over the top. Megani knew this path well, having found it while with her father some years before. Trinity was riddled with wondrous passages beneath the surface, testimony to the craft of the first beings to grace the land, the Wallos. But she and her father had kept such passages a secret so that the riches of the Wallos would not be plundered or destroyed.

As Megani slid underneath Mountain High, her mind filled with histories of the land's origin. The Wallos were Anton's first children, sent to create the mountains, rivers, and even the smaller life forms. They were great architects and builders. They lived as such for thousands of years until the Evil Lord Becus sent his Beasts to destroy them, which they did. In retaliation, the Lord Anton sent the Wizards, cold, exacting beings whose responsibility it was to destroy the Beasts. To aid their cause, Anton then sent the Races of Elf, Dwarf, Man, and Etha to help the Wizards achieve their task. The Wizards tired, however; but before they perished they placed their remaining magic in the Stone and Sword. It was then up to the Royal House of Del to wield them to protect Trinity and the remains of what the Wallos built. Eventually, the magic of the Wizards merged with the Dels' own flesh, making them the eternal protectors of Trinity. While many Races played an important role in Trinity's past, she thought, the Wallos held a special place in her heart. They must have been immensely talented and creative beings to create such a fantastic world as this.

The root came to an abrupt end, but Megani continued to slide onward along a tube of slick, pure-white marble. A widening opened in the tube. It was lined with sleds with razor-thin metal runners. Without slowing, Megani grabbed a sled and pulled it beneath her. Her speed instantaneously doubled as she zoomed along the narrow tunnel. This path would catapult her to the Valley of Despair faster than any other.

Chambers opened up along her path as she dove deeper and deeper beneath Mountain High. Some of the chambers bore huge, glowing crystals of red, blue, and yellow light that guided her way. Other chambers were filled with large, deep-green gemstones that sparkled brightly. Some caverns contained groves of fruit trees, some of which, like the apple and orange trees, Megani and her father had introduced to the peoples of Trinity some years before. Other harvests were not as suited to the surface, so they remained here. How sad, thought Megani, that thousands of skilled Wallos were all destroyed so long ago, leaving their rich bounties unappreciated. What wise, old creatures they must have been. If only she could have met one of them, she had often thought. What a grand experience that would be.

But beneath the wonders of the Wallos, Megani could not stop thinking of the northern Races and the horrific folly in which they might be engaged. Her heart pounded with each passing moment, hoping that the report she had heard was wrong and that the noble Elves and wise Dwarves were still brothers.

After an hour, Megan's sled began a long incline as the tunnel began to reach upward toward the valley. The force of her long descent and the slickness of her route kept her moving rapidly. Finally, she entered a huge cavern and slowed to a stop. She placed the sled in a row of ten others. Her mind could feel the kind and astute essence of the Wallos even after all these years.

The chamber was filled with dozens of tunnels coming and going in various directions. Megani found the one she needed, an upward-reaching tunnel with a marble stairway that rose to the surface far above her. As she stepped into the opening, she suddenly paused at an unexpected, distant sound. She looked back to the many tunnels behind her, but the sound had vanished. She shook her head, thinking she was in error. It had sounded like a human voice . . . a child's voice. But that could not be. Just as she turned back again to step upon the stairway leading upward, the sound boomed.

"La de da . . . la de da . . . hoop a da . . . la de da!"

Megani turned abruptly to follow the noise. Her sharp eyes scrutinized the many openings within the chamber. She could not discern which tunnel it came from, nor could she ascertain what distance it had traveled. The echo could have been traveling for many miles before it even reached her.

It boomed again. "La da da da . . . de da la la . . . da hoop da . . . la de da!"

Megani was sure of it this time. It was the childlike sound of laughter and song. She sent her mind probe down the various tunnels and let her thoughts meander around a multitude of bends in the rock, but she could not find the origin of the voice.

"Who are you?" Megani yelled into the void. "Where are you?" But her words were not answered, and the voice ceased. Megani waited several minutes, but the voice did not come again. It was very odd indeed to hear anything humanlike within these passageways, especially the sound of a child's merriment. It was also a foreign sound to Megani, even upon the surface. She never really had a childhood, for Trinity had needed attention for as long as she could remember. Laughter and song were for the childish ones, her mother often said, and not for those with responsibilities.

But this puzzle would have to wait. Her time fleeting, Megani dashed up the marble stairway. After an hour's climb, the stairway connected to a huge opening in a massive tree root. Megani pulled herself through the opening and climbed the many natural notches that lined the interior of the dark, hollow root. Within the hour, the root connected into its large tree trunk. Up she climbed, toward a slice of light that emanated from far above. When she reached the opening, Megani pulled herself through. She found herself upon a thick branch atop a tall tree about one hundred feet above the western edge of the Valley of Despair. She could see nothing, as the leaves were thick about her. Megani jumped downward from one branch to the other, moving closer and closer to the floor of the valley while still within the thick of the foliage.

Halfway down she came to an abrupt stop upon a branch as the sickening smell of death reached her nostrils. Massive death. Her heart pounded, not just at the smell, but at the chilling silence. She raced downward from branch to branch. The foliage became less dense. Through the leaves Megani caught sight of gently falling snow, and now and again, a fallen warrior. But her view was still too obstructed by the leaves. Impatient, Megani leaped and fell fifty feet to the lowest branch. Her view was suddenly unobstructed. Her shoulders sank. Her mouth fell open. Her eyes widened in stunned disbelief.

Devastation.

Megani froze. She saw thousands of Elf and Dwarf warriors . . . motionless . . . meshed together in death as they had been in the throes of battle. Dwarves and Elves were still in each other's death grip as a light snow fell upon them. She turned about in all directions, and it was the same everywhere for nearly as far as her eyes could see. Birds of prey were feasting upon the remains. Some carcasses were almost entirely eaten, leading Megani to believe that larger predators had come and gone. The smell of blood and sweat continued to mix within her nostrils. Megani slumped in her perch above the carnage. Her head spun. The safety of the Races was her responsibility. And she had failed. In the one month since her father's death, his legacy was gone. All he had lived for was gone.

Megani was too late to prevent the insanity. If only she had left Olive Branch earlier, she thought. If only she had not gone to Olive Branch at all! Maybe she could have prevented this. She looked about again, trying to comprehend the vastness of the disaster, hoping to find an ounce of life beneath the madness. But none came. Rage suddenly consumed her.

"What did you do?!" she cried at the dead souls. "How could you kill each other? And for what purpose?!" Her voice did not echo within the valley.

Megani suddenly spied the dirtied banner of the two kings draped upon the mountain's slope. She jumped from the tree and dashed to the site, kneeling beside the battered remains of King Alar and King Dal. Her eyes filled with tears. These monarchs had been like uncles to her. She spent years at a time in the kingdoms of each, as her father felt that she should come to know his friends as he did. Now they were dead at her feet, each in a death struggle with the other.

"Why?" she asked, her fingers gently stroking each king's brow.

Through the grief, she sent her mind probe into Elf King Alar.

Though his brain was dead, she reasoned, it still might contain fragments of memories that she could dissect. She found them, but they were fading rapidly. One memory was the most prominent because of its appearance . . . a large, dark, oozing morsel. She plunged within it. Her eyes shot open.

"Can't be!" she proclaimed. "King Dal would never kill Allo! Never!"

Megani pulled her mind from that of the Elf king and plunged it deep into the mind of Dwarf King Dal.

"Can't be!" she said again, seeing a memory of Elf King Alar slaying Dwarf Prince Drak. "King Alar would never do such a thing!"

Bewildered and exhausted, Megani sat on the bloodied ground. She placed a hand upon each friend's face.

"I'm sorry," she sobbed, devastated. This was the first time she had ever fully cried. Her mother, Bea, would never allow it, for tears were a sign of weakness. Her mother's Ethan blood was as thick as it was stern. And Megani could never show such weakness in front of her father, the great Jason Del. But that didn't matter now. She was nothing more than a lone, white robe amidst the hideous, silent blackness. She had failed, and she was utterly alone.

Megani stayed there for hours, motionless. Her mind could not comprehend the past day. First the Gorgons, she thought over and over, and now this. It could not be a coincidence, she reasoned. But she could not fathom how the pieces fit together.

"I have failed!" she whispered repeatedly. It was a devastating thought, for Megani was taught never, ever to fail. But this nightmare was beyond her control. If she had left Olive Branch earlier, she thought again, maybe this would not have happened.

Another hour passed. The snowfall ceased. Through her grief, Megani heard lone footsteps approach from the west. Still numb, Megani looked up from her vigil over the kings.

"Saw ya here," said a young Man with thick brown hair and weary blues eyes.

"Gil," Megani managed to whisper, smiling sadly to her friend. She rose and embraced him. It felt good to share this tragedy with another human being. They held each other tightly.

"I know," Gil said sadly as he felt her warmth. "I feel the same way, and I suspected that you'd be pulled into this mess sooner or later."

Though she was much older than Gil, their ages were comparable, given Ethans' long life spans. She was fond of this young man, more than she could admit. His family was from a long line of frontiersmen, as was Megani's maternal grandfather, Major T. Perhaps that's why she felt a special connection to him. He was also one of the few who was never intimidated by her bloodline. Her father saw something grand within Gil as well. "There are great things in store for Gil," Jason Del once said. Megani took that seriously. But she never thought he would see her like this.

They continued to hold each other close, comforting each other longer than mere friends would have. Then they each instinctively unlocked their embrace and gazed into each other's eyes.

"I saw most of it from up thar," Gil said as he pointed toward the western mountain range.

"What happened?" Megani asked dejectedly. "What did you see?"

"Elves came from the west," he began. "Some Dwarves from over the mountain, and others came up slowly behind the Elves." Gil shrugged his shoulders as he scanned the death around them. "Then they fought . . . not much more to it than that," he said plainly. His voice became grave. "I waited for a time before I started this way," he began as he glanced shrewdly about, "because thar was snake things that came, killin' off the Elves and Dwarves that were left."

Megani whirled, scanning the horizon, ready to unleash her powers at the slightest provocation. "Snake things?!"

"Yep . . . and them was huge . . . thick all around . . . nasty lookin' cusses."

"Gorgons!" Megani said, her green eyes darting about the terrain.

"What's a Gorgon?" Gil asked

"They are beasts with huge bodies and serpents as their arms."

"Didn't see the beasts . . . just the serpent parts, I guess. But they are gone now, headed out hours ago."

Megani relaxed her stance, and looked back at the carnage. It seemed the Gorgons somehow did have a hand in all this. Her demeanor turned to deep melancholy. "Help me," she said, taking a deep breath. "They need a proper funeral."

Megani and Gil spent the rest of the evening putting bodies atop funeral pyres and setting them ablaze. They silently watched as ashes rose steadily into the night sky. Low-flying clouds reflected the orange glow of the crackling flames as red, glowing embers rose upward, creating an aura of grief. The silence made it all the worse.

After a time, Gil was the first to break the quiet. "I am sorry that your pappy died."

Megani's heart fell. Gil was the only one who ever called her father "pappy." She suddenly realized that she had not seen Gil since her father passed to Anton.

The young Man continued, nodding, "He was a good sort."

"He felt the same way about you, too."

"Was it painful?" he asked cautiously. "Did he suffer at the end?"

"My mother told me he didn't."

"You weren't there?"

"I was there . . . just not allowed to see the moment when Anton called him home."

"What did Bea see?"

"She told me that Anton granted him his wish to be fifteen years old again." Megani then looked far off into the sky, filled with smoke and ash. "I can't even imagine what it is like to be fifteen like other fifteen year olds."

"Ain't all that great," said Gil. "Everybody tells ya what to do and nobody takes ya serious." He put his arm around her and looked into her eyes. "You're best off the way ya are."

"I'm not sure I know who I am anymore," Megani said in an unguarded moment. "A day ago I was a hero, and now I'm a failure," she said dejectedly. She looked about. "I don't even know what to do first . . . in which direction to go to stop all this. . . . And I'm the one who is supposed to know."

Deep within Megani's soul, she had the confidence to endure nearly anything. But she oddly welcomed the confusion brought on by the grief because she felt responsible for the devastation that brought it. She deserved the numb. It was a partial punishment for not arriving earlier.

"Well . . . if you're looking for the first thing to do," said Gil, "I reckon we should find out who they are."

Gil motioned to two silhouettes rapidly approaching from the west. As they came closer at a full run, Megani suddenly recognized the duo. She could not believe her eyes. This could not possibly be, she thought. They are supposed to be dead! The madness was spinning out of control, and now even she was somehow caught within its embrace.

She bolted toward the pair—her friends—yelling as she went. "You're alive! I can't believe you're still alive!"

CHAPTER 4

THE HUNTED

One day earlier . . .

A young Dwarf crawled from the thick forest and into the tall, green grass of a meadow, slowly and silently making his way toward its center, where a slender but deadly Elf stood guard over a huge elm tree. The Dwarf was careful to keep below the height of the grass while advancing so slowly that the Elf could not detect the blades of grass that he disturbed. The black-haired Dwarf was completely naked, using nothing but his wits and bravery to guide and defend himself. He was only fifteen and of a small build, even for a Dwarf, with a straggly, black young beard and patches of hair nearly everywhere upon his body. What he lacked in size he made up for in patience, strength, and persistence. He already had spent hours in this meadow, moving at a painfully slow pace that served to keep him alive. "So far," he thought, "so good."

"I can smell you!" cried the Elf suddenly, nastily, as his sharp eyes scanned the meadow, trying to discern where his enemy would strike. He too was fifteen, but the brown-haired, handsome Elf knew that being young would not save him from certain death at the hands of his enemy. He wore the green leathers of his Race, which allowed him to blend with the forest. They were perfectly tailored to fit his slender frame.

It was high noon when a short breeze gently stroked the Elf's cheek. His brown eyes flashed. The Elf turned and with deadly accuracy shot an arrow where his nose pointed him. The shaft sliced through the air, pierced the tall grass, and struck the Dwarf's shoes one hundred yards out . . . but the Dwarf was not in them! The Elf turned about and continued to pace slowly around the tree, his sharp eyes scanning everything. Again and again he went. An hour later, he heard a subtle disturbance at the other end of the meadow. With lightening speed he aimed and shot another arrow. It pierced the grass and killed a rat that was tied to the Dwarf's backpack. But no Dwarf was present.

51

This was the way of the world, each enemy knew. Kill or be killed. Make supper of beasts, or have them make supper of you. Neither the young Dwarf nor the young Elf ever felt more alert . . . ever felt more alive.

The Elf slowly paced around the tree again, defending it with his life against an unwanted attack. He had only one remaining arrow and a slender, jeweled knife at his side. He knew he would need them both. He had faced this opponent before, and he knew that if he was not careful and completely attentive to his surroundings, it would be his doom. He could not let the tree fall into enemy hands, or it would also spell disaster for all those who depended upon him to survive. A world was at risk, he told himself, and he could not let it down.

Hours passed. The sun began to fall in the west. To the east were the tall mountains that formed the western edge of the Valley of Despair. Trees west of the meadow began to cast large shadows across the grass. A chill settled over the area. The Elf remained cautious as he paced slowly about the tree, knowing that his enemy was close now . . . very close. His nostrils flared with his opponent's stench.

The Dwarf jumped from the tree!

The Elf heard him just in time and turned to face the onslaught. The Dwarf came down hard upon the Elf, smacked him across the face, and rolled away into the tall grass. Gone. The Elf fell hard onto the base of the tree, but he bolted up quickly, holding his bloody nose with one hand and his bow with the other. The Dwarf rolled to a long-handled ax in the grass some thirty yards out, where he had placed it hours before. He jumped up and launched it at the Elf with such force that the young Dwarf stumbled and fell. The blade tumbled over itself as it sliced the air in search of the Elf's heart. But the Elf jumped up just before it struck. The ax smashed deep into the tree, its handle parallel to the ground. The Elf gently landed upon the handle of the ax and spied the Dwarf. He drew his last arrow and let it fly just as the Dwarf found his footing, but the Dwarf jerked his head aside before the arrow found its mark.

The Elf dashed off the ax handle, dropped to the grass, and charged across the meadow, drawing his jeweled blade. The Dwarf knew he could no longer hide, so he bolted toward the Elf. Just before they clashed, the Elf jabbed his knife toward the Dwarf's heart. The agile Dwarf ducked and rolled beneath it, just as his father had once taught him. He rolled up at the Elf's legs and tackled him to the ground. The Elf hit the meadow hard, losing his blade in the fall. The naked Dwarf held tight to the Elf, squeezing his waist with massive arms, trying to deplete the Elf's supply of oxygen.

"Ahhhh!" the Elf growled as he fought to extricate himself from the death hold. But with the closing of distance, the Elf's own strength could now be used. He grabbed the Dwarf's thick neck and threw it into a hammer lock, squeezing it tight in order to deprive the Dwarf's brain of precious blood.

Feeling himself suddenly dizzy and knowing that he would certainly pass out before the Elf's lungs would be depleted, the Dwarf let go of his hold and socked the Elf in the crotch.

"Ooooooooohhh," groaned the Elf as he doubled over upon his stomach in pain.

The Dwarf landed upon the Elf's back and yanked his enemy's legs backward toward the Elf's head. The Elf screamed in pain as he tried to reach the Dwarf upon his back, but to no avail. The Elf knew he was trapped.

"Say it!" growled the Dwarf.

"No!" returned the Elf as he struggled to gain his freedom.

The Dwarf twisted the Elf's limb.

"Aaaaahhhhhhh!" The pain was unbearable. The Elf tried to cut off his mind to the ache, an ancient Elf skill, but he could not turn away from it.

"Say it!" growled the Dwarf again as he picked up the Elf's own dagger with his free hand to thrust it at the Elf's throat, drawing a trickle of blood.

The Elf drew a breath. "I'm dead!"

"And what else?" returned the Dwarf, twisting the Elf's legs painfully with one hand while pinching the knife deeper into the Elf's throat with the other.

"You are my king!" shouted the contorted Elf.

The Dwarf let go and tumbled onto the grass beside the Elf. The Elf rolled over and wiped the blood off his neck.

"You cut me!" complained the Elf as he shoved his blood-tainted fingers toward the Dwarf's nose.

"Then surrender sooner!" spit the Dwarf as he pushed the hand away. "We're tied—two and two," he said with boastful satisfaction in his voice.

"You got lucky," returned the Elf. "I could have killed you with my last arrow, but I held my string until you were ready. You need to bounce up faster . . . much faster."

"Agreed," said the Dwarf, reluctantly. "I saw you hold your shot . . . but you need to watch what you are protecting every bit as much as what lays beyond it. I was in that tree for an hour . . . stupid!"

"An hour?!" asked the Elf. "But how did you get up there undetected?"

The Dwarf grunted with satisfaction. "Your pace around the tree was always the same. I counted it out for hours. Ten paces. Always ten paces. And it was always at the same speed . . . slow . . . which took you five minutes to get around the whole tree. I crawled toward you in circles, always keeping the tree between us. I left items for you to find . . . like my shoes. That would give you something to shoot at."

"Clever," admitted the Elf.

"When I finally got to the tree," continued the Dwarf, "you were still on the other side. I climbed up at the same pace, circling the trunk as I went up so that you stayed on the other side of the tree as me."

"I was stupid," said the Elf dejectedly.

"Finally we agree on something," said the Dwarf. "So we're tied," he said again, looking for confirmation.

"We're tied," agreed the Elf, before adding, "And how did you get beneath my blade so quickly?"

The Dwarf smiled. "My father taught me that. Elves always lunge for the heart . . . and so I anticipated your move and plunged below it."

"The stinking shoes you left in the field were a good trick, too" said the Elf. "I'll have to remember that one. Just because it smells like a rotting Dwarf, doesn't mean it is a rotting Dwarf."

The friends laughed as they both looked into the darkening sky.

"And another thing," said the Elf. "Put your clothes back on. You looked like a giant fur ball as you fell from that tree. A naked Dwarf is far uglier than a poorly clothed one!"

This was the Western Expanse at the western edge of Trinity. It was a truly wild and rarely traveled land. Filled with dense forests and wild game, it presented a virgin landscape, nearly untouched by the Races or the Beasts of Becus before them. It was considered sacred, in a way, because of its lack of Race-made development and was used only ritually by the Races, often to test the young to determine if they were ready to attain adulthood. Dwarves and Elves and Men—especially frontiersmen, the most rugged and adventuresome of Mankind—had sent their young men to this area for ages, to live with nature, to test their fortitude, to test their skills. Always sent in pairs, the friends would test each other for weaknesses here so that such weaknesses would not appear for real, in battle. The pairing was historically among one's own Race: Dwarves with Dwarves, Elves with Elves, Men with Men. This was the first pairing of Elf and Dwarf. Their families had sent them here with great promise and hope that more of the Races would follow their lead and join in partnership when young.

The young lads were Dwarf Prince Drak and Elf Prince Allo, sons of kings. They grew up together, as friends, just as their fathers had hoped. But as King Dal and King Alar became friends on the battlefield of Meadowtown, they wanted their sons to become friends outside of the specter of war. So two weeks earlier, the fathers sent their sons into the Western Expanse not only to mark their sons' ceremonial entry into adulthood, but also to cement their lifelong friendship. The experience achieved both objectives.

Now their time in the Western Expanse was drawing to a close. They had lived by their wits and strength for two weeks, and both were stronger for the experience. Though darkness had fallen, both boys packed their few belongings and began the long trek back through the thick, green forests on their way toward the western rim of mountains surrounding the Valley of Despair. They were to meet their families in celebration there. It would be the ideal homecoming for such a momentous time in their lives.

As they trekked through the forest, the sound of playful crickets echoed, punctuated now and again with the sound of hooting owls. The moon was high above when the Elf stopped and sniffed the air. His senses became alert.

"What is it?" questioned Drak excitedly, fully aware of the Elf's ability.

Allo sniffed the air again. The scent of the beast was new to his senses. It smelled as though it were a commingling of snake and eel. But Allo could not only detect the beast's scent, he could also smell the fine oils that are excreted when beasts wait in anticipation of an attack. He knew this was a hunt. Allo also knew that whatever the beast, they would be ready for it. They had already faced bears and lions in the Western Expanse, so they were ready for anything.

"Something hunts us!" the Elf whispered.

"What is it?" Drak asked, his eyes bouncing about with delight.

"It's new to us," Allo said quietly.

Drak smiled. "Good," he breathed as he slowly scanned the forest, turning his big Dwarf ears toward the seemingly cheerful nightly sounds of the forest. "But the forest sounds okay," he ended, disappointed.

"It's not," whispered the Elf. He scanned the ground beneath their feet and pointed downward. Drak grinned as he pulled his ax. The Elf silently pulled his bow. They began to pace slowly backward to extricate themselves from this dangerous situation.

The ground beneath the boys' feet suddenly heaved violently upward! A ton of dirt and rocks flew in all directions. The boys were thrown aside and hit the ground hard.

A huge serpent rose from a shallow hole. It was a twenty-foot-long, scaly, green beast with razor-sharp teeth. Seeing the two boys apart, it lunged at the nearest, Drak. The Dwarf ducked and rolled beneath it. The beast smashed into a tree, sinking its teeth deep into the thick bark. The beast pulled its fangs from the wood and quickly turned for another attack.

Allo was already on his feet, his bow in hand as he took deadly aim.

"Don't kill it!" yelled Drak, waving him off. "It's mine!"

"Crud," said Allo as he paused and sat upon a nearby rock. He could do nothing but watch the event unfold as a bystander because Drak was the first to call possession. Both hated the rule, but it helped keep the peace between them.

The serpent lunged again at Drak. This time the beast dove low to prevent the Dwarf from rolling beneath it again. Drak jumped upward and landed upon the serpent's back, facing its tail, straddling it just behind its head. The serpent reared up as it tried to unseat the Dwarf, but its efforts did not work. It rolled over upon the ground again and again, but the Dwarf, spitting dirt, held firm.

"Stupid beast!" yelled Allo. "Use your tail!"

As if in answer to Allo's suggestion, the serpent whipped its tail around and struck Drak hard, tossing him headfirst into a tree. The Dwarf turned about quickly, holding his aching head while sitting against the tree trunk.

"Whose side are you on?!" yelled Drak.

"Well," thought Allo. "Your side, I guess, but the beast has to give you more of a challenge. . . . How are you ever going to learn?"

With its gaping mouth spread wide, green saliva dripping from its fangs, the beast struck again. Still sitting, Drak had nowhere to move. He had to face the onslaught head-on. He grabbed his long-handled ax and launched it. The beast recoiled quickly leftward, away from the blow, and then continued its plunge forward. Drak was fully exposed and unable to move out of its path!

But the beast gained no ground. An arrow pierced its brain from behind. The creature squealed loudly; its body heaved upward and convulsed, then fell dead. Its massive head landed in Drak's lap.

"Get this stinking thing off of me!" he yelled, annoyed.

Allo was there in a heartbeat and pulled the large beast back by the tail.

"I was going to kill him!" growled Drak. "You broke the rule. You interfered too soon!"

"What were you going to kill him with . . . ," Allo began sarcastically, "the smell of your feet?" Then he added. "You just lost a point because I had to save your big butt. The score is two to one again. I'm up by one!"

"But I didn't ask for your help!" shot Drak.

Allo shook his head. "Then you'd be dead now. You lose a point. Don't cheat like the time you found the dead tiger and then told me you had slain it!"

"I did slay it!" Drak growled.

Allo shook his head again. "Here we go again. The tiger had been dead for weeks; it was decaying. You don't get a point for killing a dead tiger!"

Drak turned red, and the veins in his thick neck popped as he roared, "But I didn't know it was dead when I killed it! I thought it was *playing* dead when I threw my ax!"

Allo smiled. "Right . . . a vicious tiger *plays* dead. I can't wait to tell your family that story."

Drak went silent for a moment, thinking of the embarrassment he might face at home. "You won't tell them . . . right?"

Allo leaned in close, knowing he twisted his friend into submission. "Then you lose a point for having to be saved from this thing . . . right?"

"Agreed!" Drak reluctantly grunted.

"Agreed," said Allo. "I'm up by one!"

The Elf turned and examined the serpent's carcass. "I have never seen the likes of this before. . . . Have you?"

"No," Drak grunted as he kicked the serpent hard, punishing the beast for making him lose a point.

Allo became suddenly alert, his eyes shooting into the forest beyond.

Recognizing the sign, Drak smiled. "Are there more?"

Allo nodded, returning the Dwarf's smile. "Several more . . . on their way. They must have heard this one squeal."

"Where from?"

"Above ground . . . just east . . . we have only a few moments to prepare!"

The natural sounds of the forest went silent as four serpents suddenly emerged a moment later and sped to their dead companion. They sniffed the beast thoroughly, as they did the plot of ground where the Dwarf had lain. Then they jerked about, their noses searching for prey. Two converged on a nearby, large tree while the other two dove across a short clearing toward a large bush, following a scent. Sensing something they could not see, they lunged within the foliage. They emerged with a pair of Dwarf underwear. The two beasts ripped them to shreds.

"Nasty," said Allo as he rose from behind the bush and shot an arrow into the head of one of the beasts. The serpent screeched and fell, its body jerking in the throes of death.

The serpent beside it lurched at Allo, but the Elf jumped into the tree above and disappeared from sight, hidden in the branches. The serpent recoiled and shot into the tree, searching for its prey.

The two beasts that had converged upon the large tree on the other side of the clearing slowly rose into its branches. They slithered around the trunk as they ascended. Some thirty feet up, they followed a scent toward the very end of a large limb, coiling around the thick branch as they went. They paused at the end as they came to a pair of the Dwarf's shoes, dangling by their laces. They sniffed them and then looked about, surprised that no Dwarf was in them.

"Hey, stupid!" cried the Dwarf from where the branch met its trunk. The serpents turned. With two massive chops of his ax, the Dwarf sliced through the branch. The Serpents crashed upon the forest floor far below. One was crushed under the limb and died, while the other landed safely upon the ground. It immediately slithered to find its only remaining companion, who returned from the other tree, absent the Elf it hoped to find.

Across the clearing, Drak and Allo emerged, standing rigid in the moonlight. The beasts turned. But this time they paused, more cautious of the Races this time.

"Thanks for the use of the underwear," said Allo to Drak, "but I'm afraid the beasts ate it."

Drak glanced over and saw his shredded undergarments. "Another reason to kill the beasts," he seethed.

Allo smiled. "It's probably best anyway since you never washed them."

The two serpents slithered slowly toward the Races. Allo and Drak came slowly forward. The beasts circled separately until Allo and Drak were back to back, with one serpent facing each.

The beasts lunged.

Drak threw his ax slightly off target, to the right. It spun with a strange rotation. The beast pivoted to the left to narrowly avoid the blade, but the ax suddenly curved left and struck the beast dead center in its forehead. The serpent convulsed upon the ground and then went still . . . dead.

"Can't fool me twice," growled Drak. The Dwarf turned to see how Allo fared. He found the Elf with his hand outstretched, holding his bow, which was now wedged longwise into the serpent's mouth, holding it open. The beast was struggling to get free, but three arrows pinned its tail to the ground.

"What do you make of this?" asked Allo calmly as the beast continued to struggle, its saliva dripping down its fangs and upon Allo's bow and hand.

"It's pretty dumb," said Drak, "and clumsy."

Allo nodded. "Agreed."

Having retrieved his ax, Drak walked around the serpent. "It's not from this forest," he said as he prodded the beast with his blade to test the resiliency of its skin and frame. "Solid, strong."

"Agreed," said Allo again as he rotated his bow back and forth to get a better look at the beast's head. It continued to struggle to get free, but it could not. Its slender eyes bulged in frustration and fear. "Could it have come from the north . . . perhaps the ancient Dwarf lands?"

"No," said Drak as he prodded the beast again with his ax. "Maybe it came from the lands to the far south? Our Races know little of that region."

"Maybe," answered Allo. "But I doubt it," he added as he pulled the bow toward himself until he gazed directly into the serpent's struggling eyes, its body still trying to break free. "I don't think this is from Trinity at all."

Drak paused. "You mean . . . ?"

Allo nodded. "Yes, I think this might be from Devon. I don't think it even has a name here in Trinity."

Drak shot to attention. "I claim it!"

Allo shook his head. "Will you please stop claiming everything?! Besides, this could be serious."

"I double claim it! I hereby call this Drak's Beast!" The Dwarf puffed his chest out proudly as he placed a hand on the serpent.

Allo glared at Drak, saying sarcastically, "And so for the rest of eternity, your name will be used whenever anybody thinks of this smelly creature." Allo smiled. "Maybe that is a good idea!"

The Elf drew close to the beast's mouth and sniffed it strongly to punctuate his humorous words. With the Elf's nose that close to it, the beast's inner reaches were gradually becoming known to Allo's senses. The Elf's smile suddenly vanished as a light, foul scent reached him from the beast's stomach. He sniffed again. The smell intensified. Allo's expression turned to dread.

"Something's not right here," the Elf said as he used his free hand to draw his blade. He instantly sliced the beast down the stomach, killing it and spilling its guts. The remains of Elf and Dwarf bodies fell onto the ground. Allo and Drak looked in horror upon remnants of hands and feet, some still wearing Dwarf and Elf sandal leathers, wrist guards, and the like.

Drak and Allo fell to their knees and gently touched remains. Their minds were filled with disbelief.

"Can't be!" cried Drak. "Our peoples could never lose to these stupid things!"

Allo slowly stood up. "Unless these Elves and Dwarves were already dead or dying."

Drak's eyes were suddenly on fire as his hand gripped his ax strongly. He spied a Dwarf ceremonial wrist band that was reserved for battle. He seethed, "The Dwarves prepared for war."

"And so too did the Elves," added Allo as he spied similar Elf trappings. Allo recognized the other contents of the beast's belly as well. It contained half-digested shrubs and berries that grew in only one place.

"This happened in the Valley of Despair," the Elf said grimly as he, too, rose to his feet.

The two friends looked at each other in horror. Dwarf and Elf nations were in trouble. How this could come to pass so quickly was incomprehensible. They gathered what little they had and bolted east, across the meadow, through the dark forest, and toward a hideous rendezvous with destiny. They had no idea of the horrors that truly awaited them, that their lives were about to change forever. The fragile world that they knew was mostly gone, and what little remained was in jeopardy. Allo and Drak were about to be called to a duty so dire, so grand, that the fate of all living things would depend upon them. But at this moment all they knew was that they had to come to the aid of those in need in the Valley of Despair. Sadly, they did not realize that they were far too late. Nor could they even fathom that the destruction that awaited them was, in fact, because of them, or rather, because of what their Races thought had happened to them.

As they ran, their hearts still filled with dread, they sparred with words as they had all their lives. It kept them sane.

"So . . . do you really want the creature to be named Drak's Beast?"

asked Allo with a forced smile as the Elf jumped over low tree branches in his path.

Drak grunted as he ran beneath the same branches. "No, I hereby unclaim it."

"Good idea," added Allo as he raced across a shallow stream, Drak beside him all the way. "We should name undergarments after you instead. Seems more fitting."

"Drak's Fine Ware!" suggested the Dwarf as he crossed the stream and raced onward.

"How about . . . Drak's Ugly Pair!" suggested the Elf, maintaining the fast pace.

They shared a sad smile as they entered the forest on the other side of the bank. Cheer above the ruins.

CHAPTER 5

THE PLAN

Without sleep or nourishment, Allo and Drak raced up the rugged, western end of the snow-capped mountain and then began a long descent into the Valley of Despair. They knew instantly that this had been an immense battleground. Allo could smell flesh, blood, and the angst-ridden sweat of the newly dead. By the patterns of chaos etched into the land, Drak could discern where each battle formation had fought, skirmished, maneuvered, and died. Both were unnerved by the sight of huge funeral fires that sent ashes into the dark sky. The light of the flames bounced off the clouds, basking the entire valley in an ominous red glow. It had taken a full day and a half to get as far as they had, but neither would succumb to the grueling pace as they finally reached the valley floor and began to make their way across its wide expanse.

After hours of running, interrupted now and again by brief periods of walking, Allo and Drak reached the eastern edge of the valley. They spied two figures standing alone, tending the fires. Allo and Drak hurried toward them. They needed desperately to hear the ill news of what had transpired, but they equally dreaded it.

"You're alive!" called a woman upon seeing their approach. "I can't believe you're still alive!"

Allo and Drak knew this voice instantly. And they recognized the robe she now wore, the one that was once her father's.

"Megani!" they cried in unison and desperation. They met and hugged.

"What happened here?!" shot Allo, panting as he tried to suck in air, sweat glistening on his thin brow. The last of many bonfires surrounded them, sending pillars of smoke into the thick air already clogged with sorrow.

Megani put a hand on each friend's shoulder. Her mind was reeling and deeply confused at the tragic, unexpected events of the past day. It pained her to speak, the guilt of responsibility weighing her down. "Your Races . . . ," she paused, struggling to find the right words, yet realizing that no *right* words existed to deliver such painful news, "they battled each other . . . and died to the last."

"Each other!" roared Drak. "You mean Elves and Dwarves battled each other?!"

Megani nodded, "Their full armies . . . thousands . . . ," then added, "and your fathers died with them."

Allo dropped to his knees, head in his hands, his mind spinning in grief, lost in his worst nightmares. His father was gone. Memories of his father shot before his mind. How could this be? This ground, this moment, should have been one of celebration of his adulthood. But now it was a funeral ground. Rather than rejoice life, he sorrowed death. How could this be?

"Why did this happen?!" barked Drak in disbelief as he broke his ax over his knee, converting his sorrow into anger as Dwarves do. "Why did my father die?! By whose hand did he fall?!" The Dwarf was already looking for vengeance.

Megani could not bring herself to tell them that their fathers had killed each other. She instinctively knew that the sons might treat the other as an enemy. She could not risk that. But Megani knew that each needed to understand why the Races battled.

"The Races believed that each king killed the other king's son."

Allo and Drak glanced at each other in disbelief.

"What?" Allo questioned as he rose wearily to his feet. "We are here . . . alive . . . our fathers sent us off together nearly two weeks ago. . . . They knew that!"

"But they did not know!" said Megani. "I touched their minds before they faded, and each king had a vivid recollection of your deaths. I could not believe it myself, but it was there."

Megani paused a moment. Given the strange events of the last couple of days, she had to be sure of even the most vividly real things. "I know this is an immense loss," she began, "and I don't mean to offend you . . . but I need to be sure that you are . . . you!"

"Test me!" said Allo, knowing Megani's ability to probe minds. Megani placed her hand upon Allo's forehead and sent her mind within his. She stoked thousands of memories, including those of Allo and herself years before. In just a few moments she emerged and was satisfied that the Elf before her was indeed Allo. She did the same with the Dwarf and saw a vast assortment of memories of family and friends. She realized that the most precious memories were those of Allo and Drak together. These were true friends, she knew. Megani hoped they could remain as such.

"Okay," she said, hugging Allo and Drak. "That leaves us with a sad puzzle: Why did your fathers think you were dead?"

Allo shook his head. Answers would not come. "They killed each other to avenge our deaths . . . and yet we are alive and well. I talked with my father about my eventual return from the Western Expanse. He should have known that I was well. Why he thought differently is far beyond my understanding."

"Madness!" barked Drak. "It must have been some sort of madness that infected them all. Both fathers saw us off . . . together. They even planned to meet us on this very day—on this very spot—to celebrate our return. I have heard of strange diseases in the past, those that can infect. It must have been a contagious fever!"

"Odd," Megani returned. "What infection could possibly have given each the same vision . . . the same memory . . . the same madness?"

"Where . . . ?" asked Allo, his mind elsewhere, "Where are my father's remains?"

Sadly, Megani pointed to a nearby bonfire that was still ablaze. Nothing within it was discernable. "I laid both kings there."

Allo slowly approached the fire and knelt beside it. He looked up, following the ashes as they floated wistfully up to join the red, glowing clouds.

"I'm here, Father," the Elf choked, fighting the tears. "Still here . . . alive and well . . . may you find your peace in Anton!"

"Who killed my father!" demanded Drak angrily as he intently scanned the same funeral pyre. "Which Elf did this?!"

Megani could not tell the truth. Dwarves, like Elves, are bound by blood to wreak mortal vengeance upon those who kill their kind. She was sure that if her friends knew the whole truth, their friendship would become something far more sinister . . . and potentially deadly.

"I don't know," Megani lied convincingly, "but they are all dead. Those who were killed have passed on with those who killed them." Then she drew closer to Drak and placed a hand on his shoulder. "But this was no fault of theirs," she said as she gestured to the funeral pyre. "This battlefield is absent of guilt. Something else made them act this way."

Unsatisfied, Drak stalked off and joined Allo at the fire. His father is dead, thought the Dwarf, and so someone living must be at fault . . . or at least those who shared the murderer's blood. The Dwarf looked uneasily at Allo, but he shook his head to rid his mind momentarily of thoughts of revenge. He told himself that it was not Allo's fault. Drak repeated it again and again. The Dwarf then examined the funeral pyre. Its glow tinted his face red, as it did Allo's. He was close to his father's ashes as they mingled with the Elf king's on their way to the heavens. Drak looked up into the red-hued clouds and jabbed his fist skyward to punctuate his words.

"On my blood," began the Dwarf, "I will find and kill *all* those responsible for this, Father. Their blood will flow!"

Allo glanced at a nearby pile of weapons taken from the fallen. His eyes landed upon a jeweled sword, his father's own. He shot toward it and grabbed it. Its metal was still bloodied, but little did Allo know that it was the blood of the Dwarf king. Drak was at his side, looking through the armaments. He found what he sought, his father's own ax. It, too, was still bloodied, but like his friend, he did not know it was the blood of his father's killer. Drak quickly sliced the palm of his hand with his father's ax and let droplets of his blood drip upon the fire. The droplets sizzled as they hit the flames. Allo impulsively did the same with his father's sword.

"Upon my life!" shouted Drak into the sky. "I will avenge your death upon those who did this and all those who descend from them!"

"I will send them to hell!" shouted Allo.

Megani shivered, for she knew the demands of a blood oath, but for the presence of a lie, her lie, Allo and Drak could remain as friends. If they knew the truth, they would assuredly fight each other to the death. She was sure of that now.

Allo and Drak were silent for an hour's time, sitting by the remains of the fire. Allo's mind was filled with grief, Drak's with anger. After a time, Megani broke the silence.

"The question remains," Megani said as she approached, "Why did your fathers believe that you were each killed by the other's father?"

Gil, having hung back for a time for fear he would intrude upon a deeply personal moment, now joined them. Allo and Drak knew this frontiersman, one of the few among this era's Men to test his skill in the Western Expanse. And more. If stories were true, Gil had ventured into the Expanse and not returned for two full years! He was given up for dead. No one among Dwarfkind or Elfkind had ever done as much. They could only imagine what terrors he must have faced, both from within and without. They nodded in recognition of his accomplishment.

Allo suddenly sniffed the air, his nostrils on fire. "They were here!"

"Who?" shot Megani.

Allo sniffed again. "Serpents!"

"I saw them, too," added Gil. "They scavenged after the battle."

"They are gone now," Megani said. "I have checked many times."

Allo sniffed the air again. "But not before they murdered the last of the dying. We killed five of the beasts in the Western Expanse. . . . They had come to hunt and kill us."

Megani's mind spun. These were undoubtedly the same beasts she had faced. "The beasts had a hand in this . . . somehow," she began. Megani scanned the horizon as she recalled the events of the past two days. "They attacked Olive Branch, where I first met them. There, they were as arms in a larger beast that called itself a Gorgon. Then they watched as the Races killed each other here. Then they came to kill you." Her mind grasped at a conclusion. "That means they knew you were still alive. But how did they know that when all others thought you were dead?!"

"This is not madness," began Gil. "This is beyond us. It's beyond Trinity . . . beyond natural. They must have been a part of a bigger plan," he finished, his eyes gleaming.

"Yes," agreed Megani. "Yet the beasts I found were without any knowledge beyond their immediate task."

Gil joined in Megani's analysis. "Somethin' else guides them, sends them, creates them."

Megani nodded in agreement. "Of course . . . that must be right."

"What became of those you encountered?" spat Drak.

Megani turned. "Many Gorgons attacked. I killed them."

Drak grunted. "How many? How many did you kill and how many are left for me to butcher?"

Megani shuttered at the Dwarf's cold, distant question. The Dwarf had one motive now, and it was to kill any thing involved with his father's death.

Megani pulled the red hair from her eyes and hooked it behind her ears. She took a deep breath. "I killed a thousand or so a day ago, outside of Olive Branch. I don't know how many remain."

The three young men looked at her in amazement.

"You killed a *thousand* of them?!" Allo asked in disbelief.

Megani nodded, realizing that her friends had little knowledge of the full extent of her powers. She took pride in their discovery and that she was, after all, her father's daughter. Yet, she was still devastated by the destruction of the Races. If only she had come immediately north, she thought, reliving her tumultuous thoughts of earlier, she might have prevented the battle and the Races might still be alive. If only she had not been diverted to Olive Branch. She saved a hundred Men, but lost thousands of Elves and Dwarves.

"What did all of this? Where did this come from?" asked Megani as all eyes turned to the bonfires.

"This is supernatural," Gil answered. "This is Devon!" he proclaimed.

"Devon," agreed Allo. "I thought as much."

"Devon," chimed Drak.

"Devon," Megani said, her own suspicions confirmed.

Megani turned to face her friends. As though a dam had burst, she was no longer held in a state of confusion; Gil had given her direction. She would find her answers in Devon. It was the only place where these beasts could have been in hiding for so long, and the only place where she might gain the answers she needed. Though she did not yet have a name for the faceless threat that sought to destroy her world, she knew that it was her responsibility to discover it. The funeral flames were partially her responsibility. She had to redeem herself. But she also needed to maximize her strength. The past few days proved that the creature that created and commanded these Gorgons and serpents, whatever that creature might be, was all powerful and intensely shrewd. It made the Races believe falsehoods and then created armies to devour the remains. Megani knew that she needed much more power than she possessed, and possibly far more than she would be able to muster.

"I need powers from beyond us," Megani began. She shivered slightly. "I need the Sword of Anton, the one used by Matthew Del ages past to slay the last Tempest, the same one used by my grandfather Cyrus when he came to the aid of my father during his battle with Pure Evil. We will need its powers, whatever those might be, to help us destroy what lies ahead."

"But the ancient Sword is lost . . . destroyed!" said Allo. "My father told me so. Many tried to recover it but could not."

"Yes . . . lost during the battle with Pure Evil fought by my father," stated Megani, thinking. "But was it really destroyed? If any fragments are left, they would be beneath the Fallen's Memorial where the Circle of Wisdom had collapsed during the battle with Pure Evil. That's where they would be found, if any fragments exist at all."

"My father searched for the Sword for days after the battle with Pure

Evil!" exclaimed Drak. "He did so with your grandfather Cyrus. They found nothing!"

Megani looked south and wondered about the Sword, something she had not done in years. She let her mind casually consider its recovery. But her mind was suddenly yanked upward. It traveled over the mountains, across the plains and forests, and toward the Fallen's Memorial that lay south of Meadowtown. She had never used her mind probe over a distance of more than a few hundred yards, but it was suddenly pulled onward at a devastating speed. She tried to cut the probe off, but she could not. Something was drawing her mind out, stretching it beyond her limits. Her mind ached as it drew nearer and nearer to the memorial. It also grew weaker with each added foot it traveled. Her mind then plunged deep into the soil at the foot of the memorial, where the Final Contest with Pure Evil took place. Her thoughts tingled as though something of value lay far beneath the surface. Something was definitely there, she knew. An intense light blasted through her mind, and Megani saw fragments of the brilliant Sword, lying in wait. Megani wondered why she had never felt this before, nor had her father or grandfather. It was the feeling of smothered power . . . a power she recognized. The fragments began to pulsate wildly as though trying to draw her attention. It knew that she was thinking of it, and it responded in kind. Her heart leaped with optimism and understanding. Without warning, her mind probe snapped, and Megani found herself upon her knees, her worried friends about her.

"Are you okay?" asked Gil as he knelt with an arm around her shoulders. "You were in a trance for minutes!"

"Fine," said Megani, sluggishly rising to her feet and gazing into the eyes of her friends. "Maybe the Sword didn't want to be found years ago," she said quietly as she rubbed her temples. "But it wants to be found now!"

Her voice was committed and sure when she continued. "I need the three of you to venture to the memorial to find what remains of the Sword."

"But . . . ," began Drak.

Megani placed a hand over the Dwarf's mouth. "No 'buts'," she began. "I can feel it . . . somehow. It is far below the surface. And it is expecting us."

Allo's and Drak's eyes sparked with duty even as remorse was thick upon them. This was the Sword of Anton, and to be on the hunt for its recovery was the greatest of tasks. If it truly existed, and if they recovered it, the task would bring pride to their fathers' memories. Drak and Allo glanced at each other and then gazed back at Megani.

"Honored," said Allo as he pounded his chest once.

"Honored," returned Drak as he did the same.

Gil, however, looked concerned. "My quest is elsewhere . . . ," he said quietly to himself, his words trailing off. But it was not quiet enough.

"*Quest?*" said Megani suspiciously. "Did you say *quest?*" That was a word used sparingly in Trinity and with great reverence. To be on a "quest" is to be sent by a God. She was about to probe Gil's mind, but she held back. She would not intrude in such a way upon her closest friend.

Gil stumbled over his words quickly. "Not exactly a *quest,*" he faltered, "an errand really." He pulled Megani aside to speak to her alone.

"I'm supposed to do somethin'," he said. "I have to find somebody named . . ." He paused, afraid of uttering the identity of a person kept secret among his family for centuries. But he could not hold it back from Megani. "I have to find someone named the Historian."

Gil felt an immense burden lift from his shoulders. He looked eagerly into Megani's green eyes, hoping that she could help him on his own personal journey. "Do you know where he might be?"

"The Historian . . . no." answered Megani. "I have never heard the name before." It was strange indeed, thought Megani, that anyone would be bold enough as to call himself the Historian. After all, her own mother, Bea, was considered the most knowledgeable of all histories, as those from the Ethan Race had been for centuries. If there were someone named the Historian, Megani knew that her mother would have told her.

"Why do you have to find the Historian?"

"Well . . . I'm not really sure," Gil said truthfully. "All I can say is that I have somethin' that belongs to him."

Megani could see the truth in his eyes. Her friend had a mission that was part of a larger scheme. Very curious, she thought. Things were spinning all at once.

Gil could not divulge what little else he knew, not even to his friend. Yet he could not refuse her aid, either. If he had to find the Historian, Gil suddenly thought, then what better place to find him than near the Sword of Legends . . . the Sword of Anton.

"Well," said Gil, "I guess my journey can wait a spell. I'll help ya find the Sword, and then ya can help me find the Historian."

"Of course," said Megani, pleased that Gil would provide the stability and guidance that Allo and Drak would need. They returned to the younger lads.

"Here's my plan," she explained. "It's simple for now because we know so little. I entrust the three of you to venture to the Fallen's Memorial to find the Sword. It will be buried, perhaps hundreds of yards beneath the surface. It was shattered into three pieces during the battle, so all the pieces must be recovered."

"But in the final Battle of Meadowtown," interrupted Allo, "many died in a clash of swords. We are apt to find many beneath the surface. How will we know which sword is the Sword?"

Megani smiled. "You will know it when you find it . . . even in fragments. Its luster is ten times anything you have witnessed before. The strength of its metal is unparalleled. Its size is substantial."

Allo and Drak glanced at each other, in awe, a spark of intrigue helping to ease, for a brief moment, their immense loss. They had a mission that in some small way would make things right.

"Once you have it," continued Megani, "travel to the town of Dire Passage at the mouth of the Straits of Devils. It is there that we will unite again . . . before we travel to Devon."

"Where will ya be in the meantime?" asked Gil.

"I'm traveling back to Zol, where my mother and I were investigating histories at Libra, the ancient library. That's where we received news of ill happenings in the north. I need to seek her counsel before I continue further. Her knowledge may aid us in this. Any questions?"

"No," said Allo and Drak.

"None," said Gil. He then looked hard into the eyes of Allo and Drak. He knew that while skilled, they were still young, wounded tiger cubs. He hoped that they truly understood the responsibilities they carried. Gil, beyond almost anyone else in Trinity, with the exception of Megani, knew what it meant to have fate own your life. The tattoo on Gil's left arm, a flesh-and-blood reminder of his responsibility, suddenly tingled. Gil jabbed his fist toward Allo and Drak.

"We find the Sword of Anton," he began, his voice grave, "or we die tryin', and may a painful death strike those that get in our way."

A chill passed through all those who heard his words.

"To the Sword of Anton!" shouted Allo as he grabbed Gil's fist.

"To the Sword of Anton!" growled Drak as he did the same.

Megani closed her two gentle hands around theirs and looked into the heavens. "Dear fathers far above, protect us and give us speed!"

CHAPTER 6

JUST LIKE PITA!

After Megani bid her friends well and watched as they began their long climb up the slippery slopes of Mountain High on their way south, she hurriedly sped toward a portal to take her once again beneath the earth and to the tunnels built by the long-lost Wallos. She wished she could spare her friends the long walk over the southern mountain, but she was sworn not to divulge the whereabouts of the Wallos' previous kingdom to anyone. Finding the Tree Portal that brought her to the valley, she climbed into its branches once more. She found a different entry used for going in the opposite direction, jumped into the trunk, and slid through the base and along hollow roots. As before, she was hurled along passages and tunnels with the aid of sleds on her journey far beneath Mountain High on her way toward the southeast.

Her heart was low as she sledded through caverns and passages. She was concerned not just for the loss of the northern Races, but also for her last remaining friends. Foremost, her thoughts often went to Gil. She feared for his life in these dangerous times. Her feelings went beyond mere friendship, but she suppressed them. Where there was responsibility to Trinity, she reminded herself, there could be no time for frivolous emotional ties. With her father's death, the world depended upon her, and so far, she more often met with failure than success.

After an hour's ride, the tunnel shot Megani up to the surface of Trinity just east of Mountain High. She sped south toward Olive Branch on her way to Zol. She was anxious to see if the peoples of this town were still safe.

They were not. On her approach, Megani spied the town, engulfed in flames. Black smoke billowed high into the blue sky. As she rushed nearer, she saw clumps of people standing nearby, watching intently as their livelihoods were being destroyed. Angry stares from grief-ridden people greeted her as she approached. Mayor Fin was among them.

71

"How nice of you to join us," the Mayor said sarcastically, his eyes stabbing hers.

"What happened?" Megani asked.

"Well . . . let's see," began the Mayor. "You left us defenseless and so we were attacked by Gorgons again. They killed about half of the townspeople, some of the rest fled west to Anton knows where, and the rest of us hid until it was safe to come out again."

"But I told you to evacuate to Meadowtown!" argued Megani.

"Because you refused to stay here and help us yourself!" spat Mayor Fin.

"I lost my husband!" shouted one woman.

"And my children!" cried another.

"I was needed up north," pleaded Megani.

The Mayor mocked her. "There is no *north* anymore! Woodsmen have been streaming past here for the last two days. Not only are there rumors that the Dwarves and Elves have killed each other, but that their homelands were devoured by the Gorgons as well."

Megani wavered. Until that moment, she had not considered that the homelands of the Elves and Dwarves would have been in danger. All the Dwarf and Elf women and children . . . gone! She took a breath and spoke to the remaining people about her, some two dozen.

"You must prepare what you can, as this darkness is apt to become graver still. There are more evils than just Gorgons, I fear. As I said before, go to Meadowtown. Its fortress is mighty and the people there are still trained in battle. I must leave now to go to Zol to seek my mother's counsel."

"Stay with us!" pleaded a mother. Her two young, fearful children were huddled at her feet. "We can't survive the trip without you!"

"We need you!" called a farmer, his voice desperate. A roar exploded as more desperate voices were added, begging Megani to stay and protect them.

"You see," said the Mayor, a shrewd gleam in his eyes. "You must help us now . . . or our doom will be your responsibility."

Megani noted a thin smile come to Mayor Fin's lips as the people continued to beg for help. He was an evil man, she knew. He gained power by masterfully concentrating the people's anger at others.

"I cannot go with you to Meadowtown!" Megani yelled, the words breaking her heart. "Nor can I stay here any longer. If you are able, follow me to Zol. But I won't be there long, as I intend to travel to a place where you cannot follow . . . to Devon."

The people gasped.

"Devon?!" asked the Mayor. "Why run to Devon when we need you here?!"

Every choice Megani made had an evil consequence. By helping Olive Branch before, it meant she was too late to stop the Elves and Dwarves from destroying each other. By seeking her mother's guidance in Zol, it meant she could not help these people reach the safety of Meadowtown. By thinking so narrowly of a single task before her, she had not considered that the homelands of Elves and Dwarves were also at risk. And now by going to Devon, she left Trinity even more unprotected.

"Gather your things as fast as you can," she began. "Head toward Meadowtown. . . . You will find greater protection there. Or come with me now, and I'll protect you as much as I can before I leave Trinity."

"No!" screamed the people. "We'd never make it without you."

Megani drew a breath. "I must leave now. That's all I can offer." Megani then pushed through the crowd on her way south.

"Your father would have protected us!" shouted Mayor Fin, pleased with himself.

"Your father would have stayed!" complained a man, echoing the Mayor's words.

"At least he could have waited!" added an angry farmer. "Coward!"

"Now we see your true colors!" yelled Mayor Fin. He turned to the town. "Do not worry," he said loud enough for Megani to hear as she departed. "You'll be safe. I'll guide us to Meadowtown. We don't need a *woman* to show us the way."

Megani paused, her head spinning. Thoughts of Pita struck her like a hammer. Perhaps her father would have stayed to protect them . . . would have waited until they were ready to follow. Perhaps her grandfather Cyrus Del would have done the same. After all, it was her grandparents Cyrus and Beth Del who trained the peoples of Meadowtown to fend off beasts prior to the Final Contest. They lost much, but they saved the town. Perhaps she could do the same now. But all decisions have risks, she knew. All decisions are not equally popular. Megani could not stay in Olive Branch when the real threat was probably in Devon. She could not wait another moment if it meant missing an opportunity to discuss the dire news with her mother. Megani spun and faced the crowd.

"To Meadowtown!" she shouted. "That's all the comfort I can give you this day. Leave your possessions. Your family is all that matters!"

Megani turned and left. She felt the weight of dozens of worried, angry eyes as they watched her leave. A couple of days ago, she was their hero, she suddenly thought, and now she was a failure—even here. The difference between success and failure seemed suddenly so slight, and yet so vast.

"Go! Coward. Go, Pita! Your father would never have left us!" shouted Mayor Fin as Megani entered the forest just west of Zak's River.

Megani headed south, but her troubled thoughts were still north. How could the people of Olive Branch have been so ungrateful? She was suddenly angry at the Race of Man. Elves and Dwarves never treated her as such. It must be an imperfection in Mankind alone, she thought. She was suddenly thankful to be only part human. Her stoic Ethan blood, owing to her mother, saved her from Man's inconsiderate nature, she reasoned. But then her thoughts drifted to her father and his descendents, all from the Race of Man, and to their great accomplishments and sacrifices. Jason Del lost a hand and his sight—and nearly his life—in the Final Contest with Pure Evil. The children of Meadowtown lost half their parents during the battle. Megani's own maternal grandfather, IAM, lost his life that day as well, alongside his Ethan wife, the great Sarawath. Megani's thoughts shot to Gil, and she admonished herself for thinking that Mankind was less than it is. Perhaps she was seeing Mankind at its worse. Hopefully, it would not be repeated.

After a half-day's trek, Megani entered Zol. Years before Zak's River had resumed its historical course through the area, Zol was a barren town of sand-dome dwellings in the desert. Now it was a thriving township with merchants lining the streets and farms surrounding the town. It was three times the physical size of Olive Branch, with as many more inhabitants. Her robe billowing behind her, Megani was greeted with smiles once again. Dire news from the north had not yet spread here, she knew. But before she would inform the town of the ill news, Megani needed counsel from her mother, Bea, so she flew to her mother's retreat, a small, austere cottage near a cliff overlooking Zak's river, fifty yards below. The sun was shining bright, much in contrast to the dark news she carried.

From the outside, Bea's cottage was stark looking, much in keeping with the homes of all those of the Ethan Race. It was built from gray slabs of granite carried from Endur. A simple door made of oak and a small window graced the front of the cottage. A similarly small window graced the rear, beside which was a simple stone fireplace. Within, Megani knew, she would find it as it had always been: a small bed and a hearth for the fire.

Her father did not like this retreat, Megani remembered, because it was too sterile. He preferred their home in Meadowtown, built by his father, Cyrus Del. But this retreat in Zol was satisfactory for times when Jason Del lodged in the east. It made Bea happy, Jason would tell Megani, because the cold granite suited her disposition. Bea was the last of her kind, descendents of Ethan Teachers whose sole function in life was to guide the descendents of the Royal House of Del and attend to their histories. Bea's mother, the great Sarawath, had guided Megani's father, Jason, through his trials and tribulations before the Final Contest in which she gave her own life. So it seemed fitting that Jason and Bea should marry, thus merging the ancient families that depended so much upon each other. Megani Del grew up in a family in which Bea administered the discipline and Jason the powers.

Megani approached the cottage quickly, yet with reserve. As much as she would have dreaded telling her father about the destruction of the northern Races, she dreaded telling her mother more. Megani was always a child to Bea despite the fact that Megani was an adult in human years and nearly an adult in Ethan years. With the passing of her husband a month before, Bea had been more dour and demanding than ever, and . . . Megani was not the son her mother had always wanted. With the sound of the river rushing over a cliff behind the cottage, Megani drew a breath and entered.

Bea was sitting at the fireplace, stirring soup in an old cauldron. She looked over her shoulder at her daughter. The matriarch's snow-white hair and large, sparkling blue eyes were still strikingly youthful, even though she was over one hundred years old, barely middle age for an Etha. Bea rose and stood by the fire as Megani shut the door. Their eyes fully met. Silence rang out, but only for a moment.

"You failed!" accused Bea.

The words stung Megani. Ethas could read much in the eyes of those they meet, though they did not have the power of the mind probe that Megani inherited from her father. If Bea knew she failed, it was because Megani projected it.

"How many died?" Bea interrogated.

"Nearly all the Races . . . all Elves and Dwarves . . . save two. The Races killed each other."

"All of them!" exploded Bea, the anger boiling within her. "All the northern Races?!" She drew closer. "Why?!"

"They each believed that the other killed their prince, but it was not true. Allo and Drak live."

"When did this happen?"

Megani hesitated. "Two days ago."

Bea's eyes flashed. She took another step toward Megani until she gazed directly into her eyes, searching them for clues to the disaster. Megani could feel her breath upon her cheeks.

"Two days ago?!" Bea repeated. "But I sent you three and a half days ago. Why were you late in resolving their dispute? Why didn't you arrive in time?! Did you run . . . like Pita?!" The words cut deep.

"No!" shot Megani. "Olive Branch came under attack by beasts that called themselves Gorgons. I had to save the town first. I faced the beasts with honor!"

"Gorgons!" said Bea, considering her daughter's words carefully. "But while you faced them with honor, you saved a hundred of Mankind and let thousands from Elf- and Dwarfkind perish. That was not the best of choices!"

Bea looked deeper into Megani's eyes. "But you did not leave Olive Branch in haste after your victory . . . did you? I see guilt in your eyes."

Megani again paused. She knew these words would come, for she had thought earlier of the same.

"Your father is dead but a month, and you have lost nearly everything he worked for . . . that our descendents worked for . . . that I worked for . . . that all the previous *sons* of the Royal House lived and died for!"

Megani suddenly realized that her mother's successes and failures were tied to her daughter's successes and failures. She tried to shake it off. At least she still had her mother, and she needed her counsel more than ever.

"I think Devon may be involved," she spouted. "I've sent Drak, Allo, and Gil to find the Sword."

"What?!" snapped Bea. "The Sword could not be entrusted to anyone but you!"

"They are responsible," returned Megani.

"And you have proven not to be!"

The criticism stabbed Megani. All her life, she had prided herself upon being responsible, and now her own mother, the one who taught her responsibility, stripped her of it. And worse, it was for good reason!

"You must find the Sword yourself!" Bea demanded. "No one else in Trinity can wield it but you. No one else can touch it but you."

Megani shook her head. "They will bring it to me at Dire Passage."

"Dire, indeed!" Bea shouted.

Megani tried to shake off the rebuke by changing the subject to another quest. "Gil searches for a Man named the Historian. Do you know of him? He might be involved in all this."

Bea stepped back a pace, then another. Her eyes grew wide with concern. "This cannot be!"

"What?" Megani asked as she pressed forward. "What cannot be?"

Without another word, her mother grabbed a shawl and sped toward the door. "I need to warn the elders of Zol to prepare for war. I'll be back in minutes, and I'll explain then." She was gone.

Megani looked about the cottage. It felt suddenly cavernous. She stepped slowly to the fire and sat upon a stool, placing her head in her hands. It was too much for a young girl to accept, too much for her to suffer, she thought. She was not ready for such vast responsibility. Her father died a month too early.

"I need help, Father," she said and glanced up. But it was not help that came.

The door blew open, and a chilly gust of wind entered and swirled about the room. The fire flickered wildly. A huge bat entered and darted above Megani's head. She frantically waved it away, but it continued to dive and soar. A dark-blue-robed figure hobbled into the cottage, and an even deeper chill came with it. Megani rose to meet the ominous visitor. The robed figure's face was not visible; she could see only a long, white beard flowing beneath the hood. The intruder was hunched over, a mark of age. An old man? she wondered. The bat landed on the figure's shoulder, but the devilish, winged creature instantly turned into a snake and wrapped itself around the figure's neck.

Startled at the ominous sight, Megani shot her mind probe forth. Instead of piercing the intruder's thoughts, Megani's probe suddenly bounced back with such force that it knocked her to her knees.

"Delighted to meet you," said a chilling voice as Megani rose to her feet. Her blood ran cold.

"Who are you?!" shouted Megani as she drew her sword.

A flash of light exploded from the intruder's hands, and the sword vaporized. Megani shrieked as the intense heat burned her skin. The snake slithered to the floor and became a jackal. It paced anxiously back and forth behind its master, howling with each stride. Its master took a step forward.

Megani knew instantly that this was the demon, the mind that controlled the Gorgons, the entity that sought to destroy all that her father had worked so hard to build. In one move, she could make things right, she thought. She could gain redemption for her failings. With renewed vigor, Megani turned deep within her consciousness and sought the icons of the Pearl and Wizard's Stone. They hurled upward from the depths of her soul.

"Merge!" Megani screamed as she pushed the two powerful gems fully together within her mind.

Boom!

The intense power threw Megani's head back as it forced her fists toward the intruder. Light exploded in the small cottage, and the walls shook with the devastating force. The figure raised its bony, wrinkled hands and caught the beam of power as it poured out of Megani. Megani's eyes widened. The blast did not destroy the figure—it didn't even harm it!

"Good," said the figure as the power continued to flow from Megani, "very good!"

Megani felt herself weakening; yet the figure seemed to grow larger and stronger. The intruder's hunched back began to straighten. Its wrinkled hands began to turn supple.

Megani concentrated, trying to unleash every ounce of power within her in order to damage the creature before her. She concentrated so fully on the task that she inadvertently left her mind unprotected.

"Aaahhh!" An ancient force tried to gain access to her thoughts, but she immediately held it at bay. She could feel the beast try to enter her mind from all directions. Megani fought off the onslaught, but it was massive.

"Silly *girl,*" said the figure, its voice more vibrant with each passing moment. "What can you do that I cannot undo?"

Megani suddenly realized that her powers were of no use, and worse, the powers she shot at the beast appeared to make it stronger. She tried to end her force, but she could not. They continued to be pulled into the robed figure.

The creature bore down harder upon Megani to pound its way into her mind, but it could still not gain access. Megani fell to her knees under the assault. She could sense the creature mentally weakening, even becoming desperate. But she grew weaker as well, and it was becoming increasingly difficult to shield her mind. She was about to be exposed. She feared what might happen if the creature had her thoughts . . . if it could gain access . . .

Bea suddenly entered the cottage, breaking Megani's concentration. Her mother's eyes widened in terror, a sight Megani had never seen before. However, more than terror, there was recognition. Bea knew of this beast, this creature. Megani was about to send her mind into that of her mother's to understand what stood before her, but she could not; she was drained.

Bea pulled a knife and lunged at the robed figure.

"So nice to see you," said the beast as it blasted Bea with a fireball and sent her tumbling to the ground. Bea began to rise, but the jackal turned into a large scorpion and raced toward the Etha. With one jab, it stuck Bea in the heart and killed her instantly. Megani's mother fell to the floor, dead.

"Noooooooooooooooo!" Megani screamed. She could feel herself weaken further, her fists still bathed in the massive white power that blasted toward the figure that fed from it. She did not know what to do, how to fight, in which direction to mount another attack. Megani suddenly broke and ran. She jumped through the back window, crashing through the glass. When she hit the ground, she rolled many yards toward the edge of the cliff. Zak's River rushed far below on its way south. She turned, wavering. All her life she had been taught to run toward battle, not from it. But she could not destroy this creature. Megani did not know what to do, where to turn.

Boom!

Her mother's cottage exploded. Rocks spewed in all directions. Megani was hit with shards that ripped her robe and cut into her body. She landed hard on her back, blood pouring from her. She looked back and saw the intruder standing where the cottage had been, a snake wrapped around its neck, its face still shrouded beneath its hood. It moved toward her.

Instinctively, Megani pulled herself painfully toward the cliff. It was her only hope of survival. She grabbed the edge of the rocks and with one last yank she hurled herself over the edge.

"Just like Pita!" Megani heard herself scream as she fell away from bravery and toward her shame.

Through clouded eyes, Megani caught a brief glimpse of the water below, its surface rippled with white foam as it cascaded over rocks. She felt a cold, shivering plunge and then a dull thud when her head struck a boulder beneath the surface.

Unconscious.

CHAPTER 7

ROCK BOTTOM

Zak's River was twice a gift. Trinity's first builders, the ancient Wallos, created several waterways, including one in the East that served to bring both life and transportation to that region of Trinity. They crafted it so that water poured from the hot, boiling surface of Frantic Lake. It flowed into the Eastern lands along a mighty river that circumvented the mountains toward the east before heading south to an end that was beyond Trinity itself. The life-giving liquid sustained the lesser life forms that the Wallos created, such as insects, birds, and deer. When the Races, created by the Lord Anton, arrived in Trinity, they found their Eden waiting for them. It was a land rich in fertile soil, game, and abundant vegetation. But they also found ferocious Beasts who had been sent by Anton's evil brother, Becus, to destroy all that Anton had worked to achieve.

The Eastern River was one of the first targets of the Beasts of Becus ages ago. The evil creatures knew that if they disrupted the river's beginning in the north, it would devastate the Races that depended upon it in the south. And they were right. The Beasts had merely to damn the river at its source, Frantic Lake, for the sinister task to be completed. Once done, the southeastern realm of Trinity stayed arid for thousands of years.

When Jason Del defeated Pure Evil in the Final Contest, it was decreed that the Beasts of Becus would never be allowed to touch the land of Trinity again, so Jason set upon returning Trinity to its pristine condition. The Eastern River was one of his first great tasks. Using the powers of the Wizard's Stone and the Pearl, he reforged the riverbed at its source, thus allowing the life-giving waters to flow once more. It was the second time the river was given as a gift to Trinity. Jason called it Zak's River in honor of Dwarf King Zak, who tested Jason for courage before the Final Contest.

But that was a pleasant moment long ago. The present day was an ominous one, and the river knew it. How a river could have the consciousness to *know* anything was a mystery, but it knew nonetheless. It knew that a descendent of the great Jason Del was in need. So as Megani plummeted into its waters to escape certain death, the river rose up to meet her, thus softening her fall. Despite its best efforts, however, the water could not prevent the girl from smashing her head against the deep rocks in the riverbed. The river could feel her life slipping away through a thousand cuts that poured warm blood into the water's cool embrace. It shoved the girl upward to help her gain air. Megani broke the surface of the river. Though she was unconscious, her lungs sucked in the precious air they needed, and she took several deep breaths.

A figure appeared atop the cliff from which Megani had fallen. The river knew this creature, too. It was not as old as the Beasts of Becus, but close. The water shivered and grew cold at the thought of this ancient one. The water feared it. From atop the cliff, the creature threw a lightning bolt toward Megani.

Boom!

The water pulled her back down to the riverbed and yanked her farther south. The blast of light exploded upon the water, and a pillar of white steam erupted as the water screeched in pain. But Megani survived. The river had pushed her just far enough downriver to escape the fiery bolt. The water shoved her to the surface again to help her gain another breath. She took it. And then another.

Boom!

Another blast came from above as the beast walked along the ridge, keeping pace with Megani's movements in the current. A wave of water instantly flowed over her and plunged her as far from the assault as it could while forcing her farther south. But the lightning bolt was mighty. It struck the surface of the river and drove deep, scorching Megani's legs. However, the cold waters and fast current kept her from greater harm. The water thrust her to the surface again on its way south. Again Megani took huge breaths, her mind still not alert to the danger.

The river's flow was very fast now, and it outpaced the figure that stood on the ridge. But a hawk suddenly flew from the cliff and plummeted toward Megani. Just before it struck, its shape changed into that of a huge, sleek devil fish with sharp, glistening teeth.

The river knew that this beast was equally evil. The water pulled Megani beneath the surface once again and continued moving her away from her attackers. The menacing devil fish plunged beneath the surface and raced toward Megani. It opened its massive jaws to strike. Long, sharp teeth sparkled in the clear waters. Closer and closer it came. The water tried to divert it by creating powerful, whirling currents, but the beast easily mastered the changing flow of the waters. It flapped its massive fins to propel itself mightily. Its jaws still open wide, it prepared to clamp them shut upon its prey. It closed in upon Megani's legs, about to strike.

But it never got a chance.

The devil fish was attacked from beneath by hundreds of river fish that inexplicably had banded together for this very cause. The demon rocketed into the air, flipping in circles from the force of the attack. It turned into a bird once again, but a damaged fin became a damaged wing, causing it to fall quickly, fluttering clumsily to the ground. Just before it hit, the creature turned into a butterfly and spiraled softly to the earth, where it began to tend its wound.

"Come back to me, Beastmaker!" yelled the ancient one from far behind and atop the ridge. "I'm weak . . . very weak . . . and must return to Devon!" The powers the ancient one had used had taken their toll.

A wave of water pushed Megani farther downriver, far from the creatures that sought to harm her. The fish that had come to Megani's aid were now grouped beneath her. They forced her head above the surface to keep her nostrils free of liquid. Still unconscious, Megani was at the crest of a huge wave. The wave then surged even faster, chilling the girl with a cold breeze that passed over her. Megani's wounds began to close as the cold constricted her skin. The wave flooded the bank of the great river for many miles as she remained on its crest. After a time, the river had done all that it could. Its momentum, and its awareness, was coming to an end, owing to natural forces that took over its current.

The fish deposited Megani upon a gentle bank of sand on the eastern shore of Zak's River just north of Gate's Keep. Like the river itself, the collective minds of the fish began to dissipate, and they swam away. An ancient, gentle force had made them act as such. It was built into the very fabric of their being; they were Wallo-made.

Megani was still unconscious. Her head was upon the bank even as her body gently bobbed to the flow of the current. Her robe was dirtied and ripped and still spotted with blood. Her red hair was a tangled mess. Her eyelids were swollen shut. Blood began to seep out of the wounds once more, dotting her robe with fresh red. Brush was scattered about the bank, as were some trees, filled with birds whose chirping pierced through the sound of the rushing water. Farther to the east was thicker brush that signaled the beginnings of the Enchanted Forest, its massive trees dotting the horizon beyond.

"What's this?" said a haggard-looking Man as he bent beside Megani. A shrewd gleam in his eyes, he grabbed a dagger off her belt.

"We will split that evenly!" said the other, beginning to search Megani's robe. He found another knife and stashed it in his own belt. "And this too."

Both Men were unshaven vagrants, the kind that move from region to region looking to make a living from the sweat and toil of others. They wore dirtied leathers that were as unwashed as they. Their black beards were as tangled as their motives, and their yellow teeth were as crooked as their souls.

"She's got nothing else!" complained the first Man as he finished his search. He kicked Megani to punish her for the lack of belongings.

The second Man rubbed his chin. "Maybe we can sell her in Devon. I heard one guy got fifty gold Daca coins for a girl."

"We *might* get a good price," began the other and kicked Megani again, this time to inspect the weight of the goods, "except the demons in Devon might take us just as well."

Megani suddenly stirred. The Men rose to their feet and backed up a step. She bent to her side and coughed violently. Water poured from her lungs. She heaved again and again for several minutes as water continued to spray. With the last of the heaves, Megani rolled upon her back and tried to open her swollen eyes. Sunlight seeped in. She looked at her bruised, cut hands and saw blood begin to squeeze from the wounds. Megani then noticed the Men near her. She tried to stand, but she fell with a heavy splash near the water's edge.

"Damaged goods," said one Man, disappointedly.

"I'm Megani Del!" she gasped as she found her footing and rose. She ached and her balance was unsteady as her drenched body swayed back and forth upon weak legs.

The Men glanced at each other and then back at their find.

"She thinks she's Megani Del!" laughed the first Man.

"So she's crazy!" said the second. "That could hurt the price we get for her, particularly if we sell her in the south. I doubt that anyone in Devon would care though."

Megani's head spun. The last day's events were a blur. She glanced wearily through her tangled hair. Where was she? How did she get here? Who were these Men? The last thing she remembered was the Valley of

Despair and entrusting Gil, Allo, and Drak with finding the Sword. That seemed ages ago. Megani sent her mind probe forth to touch the thoughts of the ill-mannered Men before her. Perhaps their recollections could fill in the blanks of her own memory, she thought. It didn't work! She tried again. It still didn't work. Her mind could not fly beyond her own.

The Men suddenly grabbed her by the arms. Megani was startled by their filthy, insolent touch. She had never been handled as such by a fellow human—or anyone. She pulled abruptly away, repulsed by the behavior. Megani tried to hit one of the Men, but she was too weak. She missed and fell forward and into the mud of the bank.

Splat! She rolled upon her back. The Men shot toward her.

"Merge!" she choked, attempting to unite the icons of the Pearl and Wizard's Stone in her mind in order to unleash just enough energy to knock these vagrants senseless. Nothing happened. Megani panicked. She searched her mind but could not find the gems within it. They were gone—both gone! She hoped reason would work.

"I'm Megani Del," she screeched. "I have to find the Sword of Anton. Dwarves and Elves have destroyed each other. There's danger everywhere!"

"Danger!" mocked the first Man. "Oh . . . you didn't tell us there was danger. That makes it all different, my queen."

The Men laughed once again as they grabbed Megani and threw her hard upon her stomach. She whipped around and smacked one of the Men hard. He fell upon his back. She tried to rise, but the power she had just exerted depleted her. Megani fell forward into the mud once more. The second Man jumped upon her back to hold her steady while the first Man recovered, grabbed a rope from within his backpack, and began to tie Megani's hands behind her.

"That hurt!" he said as he tied a tight knot. He struck Megani hard across the back of her head.

"Hey!" cautioned the other Man. "Be careful not to damage the merchandise. It's pretty cracked already, and any more bumps or bruises will reduce the price we get for her."

"Merge!" Megani wailed again as she tried to muster her powers, but to no use. Her mind spun in a blur.

The second Man mocked her, chanting, "Merge! Merge! Merge!" He then spat at her. "Look at me, I'm Megani Del come to save you!"

The other grinned. "She's crazy all right. If we play our cards right, maybe we can get more money for her madness. It's kinda like an attraction. People might pay to see this. Throw in a three-legged bear and a two-headed chicken, and we might have a traveling show we could take from village to village."

"Great idea," added the second. "I bet we could get a Daca coin or two for a peek at our strange beasts." He turned to the other. "Then we keep her until we can get the other parts of the show . . . right?"

"Yep. That's the plan."

Once Megani's hands were tied tightly, one of the Men took the other end of the rope and pulled it toward his captive's feet, tying them tight as well. He cinched the rope until her hands were pulled back toward her ankles, arching her back. Megani's head and legs were raised aloft, leaving only her stomach to touch the ground. She was devastated: Two *Men* had so easily disabled her. Perhaps she was Pita, undeserving of all the trust placed in her. This must be a nightmare, she thought again and again, except that nightmares were never this real or this wet or this helpless.

One of the Men wobbled her back and forth like a seesaw. "All we need now is a good pole to hoist her up," he began, "and we are good to go."

"Here we are," said the other as he pulled a fallen tree limb from the bushes. He quickly cut off a couple of branches and fashioned it into a pole. Just as he began to slip it through Megani's tied ankles and hands, leaves hustled at the edge of the forest across the clearing. The Men looked up and saw three figures slowly emerging from the trees. The first appeared to be a little girl with curly blond hair, the second appeared to be a hunter with a bow draped over his strong, yet slender shoulder, the forth was an old Man, limping as he came.

"Dang!" said one of the vagrants upon seeing the threesome approach.

"What should we do now?" asked the other.

"We can't outrun them with her in tow. And she would be too hard to explain. I guess we have to leave her behind."

"But our plans . . . our fortune . . . our traveling show . . . "

"We'll just have to find another crazy woman who thinks she's someone important." He thought a second. "Hey . . . I have a cousin who thinks she's a duck."

"That would do," said the other, smiling. "I think people would pay to see that!"

Without another word, the two robbers gathered up what little they had and sprung south along the bank, leaving Megani tied and helpless.

"Oh, joy!" shouted the little blond-haired girl with deep-blue eyes when she spied Megani from across the clearing. Dressed in a simple, green robe, the little girl bounced with delight across the grass.

"Wait!" called the hunter.

Without responding, the little girl continued skipping across the clearing. Upon her quick arrival, she jumped upon Megani's back. The little girl weighed the rope downward, which pulled Megani's head and feet even closer together behind her back. Megani shrieked in pain.

"Mammoth Rider!" squealed the playful little girl as she rocked Megani back and forth, pretending to ride a much larger animal. "Mammoth Rider, Mammoth Rider!" she continued to shout with delight.

Megani could not believe her senses. Still dazed and confused, she wondered if she were caught in a devilish dream in which she was the plaything for this wretched little girl. How could all this have come to be? But such thoughts were subservient to the pain that seemed to be everywhere at once. In her whole life, she had never felt such ache, made greater by the shame of being made into a child's plaything.

"Mammoth Rider, Mammoth Rider!" the girl continued.

The hunter dashed forward and lifted the little girl off Megani. He drew his blade and cut her ropes, and Megani's face and feet landed on the damp soil of the bank.

"I'm sorry," said the hunter, his black, youthful eyes matching his black hair. He pulled Megani over to her back and knelt beside her. "Are you okay?" he asked as he inspected her wounds.

Megani didn't answer, her mind still shrouded in confusion.

"My name is Kendro," continued the hunter. "And this is Lyndi," he said as he tapped the little girl on the head. "She didn't mean any harm. She's actually very sweet when you get to know her."

Lyndi looked sad. "But I was just playing Mammoth Rider." Then the little girl stomped her feet. "If she didn't want to be the mammoth, then why was she pretending to be one?"

Megani rolled into a ball. A couple of days earlier, she was the most powerful being in a peaceful land. Now all that had changed. The Gorgons attacked; the Races killed each other; she had failed to keep the land the way her dear father had left it a month before. Megani suddenly needed to tell her mother of all that had happened. She started to stir from her coiled position, but a memory dropped upon her hard, crushing her lungs and stealing her breath. Her mother was dead, destroyed by a huge, hideous scorpion that was in league with an ancient, robed menace. And Megani had run . . . just like Pita. She shook violently. Then she did something that confirmed her newfound weakness.

Megani sobbed and sobbed. Unbelievable, undeniable grief held her tight. It was a foreign feeling. She had lost everything. Everything! She continued to cry, her brain sapped of any reason, her body numb and limp.

"I'm sorry I thought you were pretending to be a big, hairy, stinky mammoth," comforted Lyndi. "I am really, really, really sorry. I didn't mean to make you cry."

"Shhhh, little one," said Kendro.

Megani did not hear the apology. The little girl within herself cried out for parents that were not coming, could not come. She was alone in this world, and nothing on Trinity could possibly ease the pain and loss she felt. She had failed. And without her powers, she could not recoup her strength or the Trinity that she loved so dearly. Not even the Sword, she thought, could save the earth because she lacked the strength to carry it. Megani looked at her blood-soaked hands. She wiped them on her robe, but the stains remained.

"Blood is not so easily wiped off," coughed an old voice.

Megani looked up and into the weary brown eyes of an old Man who had now joined them. His immensely wrinkled brow, deeply etched leathery face, bent back, bald scalp, and yellowing beard said much about this Man's great age. But it was his lack of a left arm that most caught her notice as he removed a crutch so that he could lower himself to her side. The old Man touched her cheek with his right hand and then gazed deep into her tearful green eyes.

His eyes grew worried, and they widened in recognition of her. "I can see that greatness has fallen," he said sadly.

Megani was startled by his immediate awareness of her identity. Suddenly, she would have preferred that he did not know who she was. Embarrassed for the immense distance she had plummeted in such a short time, Megani rolled back into a ball. She felt it would have been best if the old Man had as little knowledge of her as did the vagrants who had just departed.

The old Man raised her chin. "Can't hide from the world . . . ," said the crusty voice, "or from your blood."

Curious at the mystery in the old Man's words, Lyndi dabbed her finger into one of the many droplets of Megani's blood that squeezed onto the robe. The little girl examined it carefully, her sharp, blue eyes squinting hard. After a moment, she smiled exuberantly.

"It's you!" Lyndi proclaimed, looking cheerfully at Megani. "It's really, really you!" The little girl suddenly gave Megani a huge hug. Megani winced with pain. Madness was overtaking her, she thought.

Kendro pulled Lyndi off of Megani once again. "Leave her be," he said.

"Leave me alone!" shouted Megani to all three. She suddenly needed to be by herself in order to sort out what had happened and why. She rose to a sitting position. "I don't need any of you!"

The old Man's voice turned grave. "Perhaps not," he said. "Then again, perhaps you need us more than you are willing to admit."

Megani wavered. Her body was too weak to sustain her mind. She suddenly fell back and lost consciousness.

"Who is she?" asked Kendro, motioning toward Megani.

"A little girl with great responsibilities," said the old Man. "She's Megani Del."

Kendro's eyes flashed. "How could this be? She's the daughter of the great Jason Del. It's told she has great powers, great strengths. But those beggars tied her up as though she were a pig prepared for slaughter."

"Mammoth Rider, Mammoth Rider!" squealed Lyndi with delight.

The old Man patted Lyndi on the head and smiled. "We'll have to get you a mammoth another way," he said. "For now, please stop riding the rest of us."

"Is she part of our *quest?*" asked Kendro as he gazed at Megani.

The old Man nodded. "In many ways, she *is* our quest."

"But how can she help us in her condition?!" asked Kendro in disbelief.

"I've seen worse," said the old, one-armed Man. "Much worse!"

Megani stirred briefly. The old Man bent toward Megani just as she reached consciousness for a fleeting moment. Their eyes met.

"Who are you?" asked Megani, breathlessly, her face a mix of blood, dirt, and sweat.

The old Man spoke, his voice filled with great responsibility. "They call me the Historian."

As Megani drifted off to sleep, the familiar name continued to ring in her mind, though her thoughts were far too jumbled to know where she had heard it before. Then, at the edge of awareness, just before she plummeted into a deeper sleep, she heard a playful little voice that sounded very familiar, too. It was the sound of a child singing.

"La de da . . . la de da . . . hoop a da . . . la de da!"

CHAPTER 8

A LEADER EMERGES

Just over the rim of Mountain High, Gil scanned the southern horizon, which was blanketed in dark night. Snow-capped peaks were just behind him. The sky was clear of clouds, and bright stars shone high above as he stood knee-deep in frigid water that, just feet away, plummeted over Crystal Falls. The flow emptied a mile below into a huge pool that formed the genesis of the Crystal River. A cold wind tousled his brown hair as he gazed at campfires dotting the land below. He could see the lights of Torson and, beyond that, even the lights of Jasonville, a town once known as Charity, until it was renamed to honor the great Jason Del.

Gil had not set foot in the south since he was five years old. It was then that his family moved to the northern wilderness in order to begin his introduction to the ways of the wild. Their sole goal was to train him to survive under the most treacherous of situations, so that should a great dread come to fruition, Gil could complete a task that had been handed down within his family for generations. The destruction of the Races and the emergence of the strange beasts were telltale signs. He had to find the Historian to deliver his message . . . or die trying. He would begin by searching the south. Simultaneously, Gil had to uncover the long-lost Sword of Anton and return it to Megani in hopes that she could use it to thwart the rising menace. Though his own quest was great, he could not help but aid Megani first. He was hoping that both tasks would somehow merge in the near future, but meanwhile he would have to rely on time, skill, and a certain degree of luck.

Allo and Drak sluggishly approached Gil, but they stayed on the water's bank. Though the trek to the top had been strenuous, none would dare complain. Nor had any words been spoken among them during the entire ascent. Gil knew that both of his new companions continued to grieve deeply for the loss of their families and their Races. He let the silence remain unbroken.

Drak peeked over the falls and along the jagged rocks beside it. It

89

was surprisingly quiet given the amount of water that rushed over the edge, for the sound created by the water's impact was too far below for those above to hear the ultimate crash. The trio heard only a low rumble at the fall's edge.

"We can't climb down from here," the Dwarf rightly observed. "There are no grips to hold. The cliff is too shear, and the stone is far too wet and slippery this close to the falls." The words were deafening after so long a journey in silence.

"I agree," said Allo as he joined his friend and looked over the falls as well. The Elf scrutinized the mountain cliff in both directions in an effort to discover a more suitable path. He could not immediately find one.

Still knee-deep in the frigid waters of the falls, Gil stretched his arms far above his head and twisted his back. *Crack!* He lowered his hands and began to wiggle his arms and legs.

"Then I guess we have no choice," said Gil as he continued to limber up his body.

"What do you mean . . . *no choice?*" asked Allo. "What are you planning to do?" he added suspiciously.

"Preparin' to go over," said Gil in a surprisingly calm tone.

"Over the falls?!" Drak questioned.

"Over," confirmed Gil.

"It's a mile down . . . if not more," said Allo, an eyebrow raised high. "You can't be serious. We would be crushed when we hit the bottom. That's if we don't drown before we even reach the bottom!"

"Then I suggest ya begin to loosen them muscles," Gil said with a twang as he wiggled his head back and forth. "Ya need to be limber; ya need to make your whole body nice and loose. When ya jump, just imagine that you're a part of the water, a part of the liquid. Jump into the falls farthest from the cliff. Flow with it and don't fight it. The water knows what to do. And don't forget to take breaths now and again as pockets of air open up around ya. At the bottom, the force of the water crashin' down in front of ya will help blunt your fall and pull ya under. Just stay underwater and swim downstream as quick as ya can before ya swim to the surface. Ya just need to get out from under the waterfall real fast. That's all there is to it."

Crack went another of Gil's bones as he loosened them.

"All there is to it!?" Drak shouted. The Dwarf stared at Gil in disbelief, assured that the young Man was truly insane. The Dwarf suddenly tingled at the madness of Gil's plan.

Allo whispered to his friend, "And yet he looks so normal."

Without a word, the Dwarf dashed several yards west of the falls, looking for footing to help them climb down. "I'll find a path!" he shouted, completely ignoring Gil's plan.

Allo was quickly behind his friend, scanning the edge with sharp Elf eyes. "There . . . a mile west . . . I can see surer footing there!" he shouted to Gil. "We could be there in just hours, and then down by midday tomorrow."

"Thank the Gods!" said Drak, relieved. They ran back to Gil.

"We wasted nearly a day walkin' up this rock," said Gil. "I'm not goin' to waste another to go down it." He took a couple of steps then leaped over the edge!

"Wait!" gasped Drak as Gil disappeared over the falls. The two friends dashed to the edge and gazed into the falling water. Gil seemed to have become one with the liquid as he plunged downward, spiraling gently as he descended. Then they lost sight of him and the water swallowed him up.

"He is crazy!" spit Drak.

"And probably dead already," added Allo.

They glanced at each other and then peeked over the edge again.

Drak raised his fist. "He's insane. Megani left us with a madman!"

"Maybe," said Allo, reconsidering. "But if Gil lives, he will know that we did not even try. Then he'll go on without us and recover the Sword alone. How would that look, particularly after we swore to recover the Sword? We would be known as the cowardly Elf and Dwarf."

"But if all three of us die in these falls, there will be no hope," Drak countered.

Allo took a deep breath. "Then that's the choice: Either we die now, or we suffer embarrassment for the rest of our lives." He turned to Drak, gesturing to the falls. "You next!"

Drak grunted. "You go next. I thought Elves were brave."

Allo smiled. "Yes . . . but not stupid!"

Allo shook his head and exhaled a deep breath. He took his bow and arrows from around his shoulder and his sword from his waist. He held them tight and waded into the shallow water that fell over the falls.

Drak shook his head. "Elves are stupid!"

"Maybe," Allo said. He began to loosen his muscles, recalling what he had seen Gil do a couple of minutes prior. "But should I die, it will be on a quest to recover the Sword." He then smiled as fears turned to sarcasm. "Besides, if I take the falls and you walk down, I'll be up another point." Allo dashed toward the falls and jumped.

Drak ran to the edge and peered over it. "They are all crazy . . . all crazy!" Despite his words, he knew he was trapped by pride. He had to match madness with madness. The Dwarf removed his ax and held it high. He waded into the breathtakingly cold water and began to wiggle his stout body as much as he could in an attempt to loosen rock-hard muscles. It did not happen easily.

"For Father!" Drak yelled as he dashed to the edge and dove into the waters. His stomach immediately tightened at the feeling of weightlessness. His lungs emptied. The Dwarf was encased in solid water as he helplessly plummeted. He waved his arms to push water from his face, opening up a small tunnel to the air beyond the falls. He took a deep breath just before the wall of water closed in again. He anticipated the hard entry on the surface below, but it was still far off. And so he waited . . . and waited . . . and waited. His lungs began to ache once more. Drak desperately tried to push the water from his face in order to find a pocket of air again, but he could not. In a futile attempt to breathe, he sucked in water instead. He immediately coughed it up as his lungs tried to expel the liquid, but he took in more.

Smack!

Drak hit the surface of the pool and was pulled far under. He suddenly remembered what Gil told him: stay beneath the water and swim downriver to get out from under the falls. He kicked his arms and legs wildly, but in an effort to refill his lungs, he broke the surface of the pool too soon. Drak was immediately knocked under the surface by cascading waters from above. His lungs still depleted of air, he lost consciousness.

The next thing he remembered was the searing pain in his lungs. Drak turned over and coughed wretchedly, hurling up water. Again and again he heaved. It took several minutes before he realized that he was on dry land.

"Not a bad choice," said Gil from above him, dripping from head to toe. "It took us a minute to come down and five for me to fish ya both out of the water." Gil strolled off to wring water from his leathers.

Drak looked over and saw Allo. The Elf looked as bad as the Dwarf. Between both of them were Drak's ax alongside Allo's sword, bow, and arrows. The two of them looked wearily into each other's eyes.

"A point a piece," hacked Drak, "so you're still up by only one."

"Agreed," coughed Allo.

Drak glanced at Gil and then whispered to Allo. "He's still crazy, you know."

Allo whispered back, "We followed him. What does that say about us?"

In the thirty minutes it took for Allo and Drak to gather their senses, Gil had found a hollowed-out log and fashioned it for use as a canoe. With suitable tree branches as paddles, the trio began their passage down the Crystal River. The banks were filled with Farlo trees whose bright-green leaves glowed and glistened in the night, providing ample light to guide their way.

After several hours, they approached the town of Torson, or rather, what used to be Torson. Smoke billowed from where the town had once stood, and floating ash was testimony to the destruction carried out by the Gorgons and serpents. The trio paddled silently by the ruins. They soon found that Jasonville was similarly destroyed. Both were very recent events, the trio knew, as both towns were alive and well just hours before, when seen from atop Mountain High. Gil saw a thin smile reach his companions' lips. They liked the thought that the beasts were close—very close.

Just before daybreak, Gil saw the fortress of Meadowtown through the trees. It had been spared from the fires and destruction that took Torson and Jasonville. Meadowtown was once a small township with craftsmen and farmers living in peace, but that was before the town was viciously attacked over seventy years ago by beasts who sought to find and kill Jason Del before his Final Contest with Pure Evil. At the time, Jason was on his quest to recover the Pearl of Anton, so his father, Cyrus Del, organized the men and women of Meadowtown. Along with Cyrus's wife, Beth, they taught the peoples of the town to fight back against overwhelming hordes. Hundreds of people died over several days, both in the town and at the Circle of Wisdom, where Cyrus decided they would make their final stand. Once the darkness passed over them, those who lived rebuilt the town into a fortress, one that would never again need to be evacuated. Thousands now farmed or crafted either within the walls or beyond it. And all citizens of Meadowtown—both men and women—were required to serve at least three years in military service. After the tragedy that had befallen so many, the township decided never, ever to be caught off guard again.

Though Gil wanted to keep his quick pace toward the Fallen's Memorial, where the Sword was lost, he decided to take a detour. Working a branch as a tiller, Gil guided the boat toward the western bank.

"I need to see someone in Meadowtown," he said.

"But we'll waste time, and . . ." began Allo.

Gil cut him short. "It will take but an hour, maybe less," he said as he jumped from the boat and pulled it ashore with Allo and Drak still within it. Gil then marched west through a thick of Farlo trees with Allo and Drak close behind him.

"So he expects us to jump over the falls to save time," whispered Drak to Allo, "but then we waste an hour in Meadowtown."

"Shhhh," responded Allo. "The falls saved us a day. This is only an hour. Besides, we are likely to find our enemy nearby."

Drak grunted.

After traveling a hundred yards through the forest on their approach to the town, Gil stopped suddenly as something tickled his senses. Allo and Drak halted just behind him. Gil began to move slowly to his left to circumvent the area that caused him concern. He waved at Allo and Drak to follow his cautious lead.

"They are here," whispered Allo to Drak as his shrewd eyes darted to the trees.

"What's here?!" asked Drak.

"Serpents . . . ," Allo sniffed, "and something bigger . . . perhaps the Gorgons that Megani described."

Drak smiled, "Good, very good."

Allo and Drak glanced at each other, their eyes gleaming. They suddenly bolted past Gil, accidentally knocking him to the ground as they charged toward devils they could not yet see.

Fifty yards ahead and within a grove of Farlo trees, six Gorgons fell from the branches in front of the Elf and the Dwarf. Each of the massive beasts had two serpent arms lashing from its body. A quick arrow and a steady ax fell two Gorgons, but the arms shot from the wasted bodies and continued the advance. Drak and Allo worked masterfully, ducking and jumping and twisting as the beasts came toward them. They sliced and hacked at the beasts.

"For my father!" growled Drak as he cut a Gorgon in half with his father's ax.

"For justice!" said Allo as he did the same with his father's sword.

Having picked himself up from where his supposed comrades had tossed him, Gil retreated to a nearby rock, sat, and watched. He did not like what he saw: Allo and Drak were gleeful as they hacked at the beasts, not killing because they had to kill to defend themselves, but because they wanted vengeance. And they were skillfully deadly. Gil had lived among many animals in the wild, living as they did, and knew that animals only killed for food or protection, but never for sport or madness or revenge. But that's what he witnessed as the two youths continued their killing spree.

Three of the Gorgons were already slaughtered. Some of their serpent arms were as well. Three Gorgons remained. Within another minute, all the beasts lay dead. But Allo and Drak continued to hack at the remains, green blood splashing them. They looked around in hopes of finding more of the beasts, but none came.

"Four for me!" growled Drak, dizzy with a vengeance that could not be quenched.

"Three for you . . . three for me!" corrected Allo.

Drak looked about and counted the dead. "You're wrong!"

Allo counted again and realized his error. He had counted a couple of serpents separately from the Gorgons that carried them. "Four Gorgons for you . . . two for me," he moaned.

Drak smiled as he sliced at the dead Gorgon at his feet. "I'm up by one!"

"Yes," said Allo as he took a whack at his last kill.

Gil shook his head, whispering sadly, "Six beasts are dead, but two remain." He rose and marched past Allo and Drak. "Then we are done here," he said as he pushed through the edge of the trees and entered the clearing surrounding Meadowtown. He paused at an equally hideous sight. Allo and Drak did the same, though their expressions turned to smiles.

A line of stakes surrounded the high fortress walls. On each stake was the head of a serpent, as though posted to ward off any others that might try to storm the walls of this fabled city.

"Who goes there?" challenged a lookout from atop a twenty-foot stone wall.

Gil took a step forward. "Gil of the Wilderness."

Allo did the same, shouting, "Allo of the Elves!"

Drak followed. "Drak of the Dwarves!"

"You may enter!"

The trio followed a path through the clearing, past the heads of the serpents on spits, and through a large iron gate that cracked open just long enough for them to enter.

"Follow me!" demanded a warrior who was dressed in full armor.

Gil, Allo, and Drak followed the Man as he marched down a central road lined with two- and three-story buildings. Torchlight guided them though the sky was just beginning to brighten with the rise of the sun. Past the buildings, large areas opened up, filled with grasslands where crops grew abundantly, allowing the city to have its own food source. Underground springs continually bubbled to the surface to form pools of water held within rock fountains. Everywhere, soldiers, both male and female, walked about with a steady purpose—one of battle.

Drak and Allo were intrigued to see the women dressed as warriors. They knew the history of this town, though they had never set foot here. They could only imagine years past, when thousands of beasts hammered the township. They wondered at the skill and defiance required of Cyrus Del, aided by Drak and Allo's own fathers, to save both the city and its people. This was where Beth Del taught the women how to fight, which helped save everyone from utter destruction. But it was an anachronism: In all of Trinity, only here were women treated as equals.

"Do the women *really* fight?" Drak asked of their guide as he spied several women marching in formation, swords at their belts and bows draped over their shoulders.

"As well as I," said the guide. "Half of the dead serpents you saw upon entering the gates were killed by a woman warrior."

"Impressive," said Allo. "Very impressive."

They passed women in a plaza who were practicing swordplay. Others were shooting arrows at targets. Drak watched the women intently as they passed.

"You know," Drak began, "there's something attractive about a female holding pointy swords and arrows." Women nearby overheard his words and glared menacingly at the Dwarf.

"Don't say any more," Allo interrupted as he slapped his hands over Drak's mouth. "Does everything you think need to end up on your lips? Please . . . I beg you. . . . Don't say any more."

Drak went silent.

Another plaza opened before them. It was filled with dozens of large tents about which sat hundreds of careworn-looking men, women, and children.

"Who are they?" asked Allo.

"Refugees," explained the warrior. "They began arriving several days ago from all across Trinity. Their towns and villages were destroyed by the beasts. It seems that Meadowtown has become a haven once more."

The trio was brought to a gated barracks in the middle of the town. Sentries threw open a large gate, and the group made their way to a great hall lined with large wooden benches. At the front of the hall was a raised platform with nine huge chairs. Men were sitting within each, their voices echoing slightly in the brightly lit chamber. They stopped their discussion and looked up as the visitors approached. The guard who guided them raced to the platform and spoke quietly in the ear of an old Man who sat in the centermost chair.

"I see," said the old Man upon hearing the warrior's words. His skin was wrinkled with age, and his hair was a mix of yellow and silver. He rose from his chair and slowly made his way toward the trio. He wore a simple gray robe and a battle-worn sword that was affixed to a thick leather belt.

"We are surrounded by beasts," the Man said, "but you seemed to have cut a path to get here. You must be skilled indeed. We typically send a regiment of fifty or so warriors outside the walls when we see refugees approach. But when the guards saw you rush and kill the six Gorgons, we decided to hold back."

"I see from your postings," said Gil, "that you have already encountered many of the creatures."

"Yes," said the old Man as he hobbled closer. "They have attacked us many times, but they are no match for our warriors." He reached the trio. "You must be Gil of the Wilderness," he said as he motioned to Gil. He nodded. "And Drak . . . and Allo," he continued, nodding to each. They nodded in return.

The old Man stepped closer, looking at Allo and Drak. "We have heard much sadness of the northern Races. First the warriors die in battle, and then their homelands are destroyed."

"What?!" asked Drak. "The homelands as well?!"

Allo sank into a bench. Drak joined him. Neither had considered that their homelands would be devastated. They were truly, utterly, alone.

"I'm sorry," said the old Man. "I didn't realize you had not heard. News reached us from frontiersmen far to the north, as well as from refugees from Olive Branch."

Gil motioned to Allo and Drak. "Then Drak and Allo are truly the only Elf and Dwarf remaining in Trinity."

The Man shook his head sadly and sat slowly, uncomfortably on the bench between Allo and Drak.

"Unbelievable," he said, scratching his head. "The Elves and Dwarves were such good friends." He then gazed directly at Gil. "And I could have used their might in battle, as we did so many years before." He looked off into the distance.

Gil suddenly knew the identity of the Man who was in front of them. He knelt. "Sir Joh," he whispered, "I apologize . . . as I did not know it was you."

As a boy, Squeaky Joh had been a childhood friend of Jason Del, long before the Final Contest. Later, Squeaky Joh fought in the famed Battle of Meadowtown alongside the greats of history.

Though dazed, Allo and Drak still had their wits about them. They slid from the bench and similarly knelt beside the old Man and kissed his hands.

"You fought with our fathers in defense of Jason Del and Meadowtown," said Allo. "I pledge my life to you."

"Say it," said Drak to Sir Joh, "and it is yours."

"That was a long time ago," Sir Joh said, "and any debt your Races owed to me was repaid by your fathers long ago." His mood turned remorseful. "I am sorry for your loss," he said to Allo and Drak.

Gil rose, knowing that time was fleeting, particularly since Gorgons were becoming bolder with each day. "Megani Del has sent us on a quest to recover the Sword of her fathers."

Sir Joh shot a glance at Gil and smiled. "The last time I saw it, the blade sparkled with power in the hands of Cyrus Del, many years ago. . . . But it is lost."

Gil nodded. "Yes, but we intend to recover it where it was last wielded, beneath the Fallen's Memorial."

"And if you find it, what then?" asked Sir Joh.

"We will bring it to Megani, who will carry it to Devon to destroy whatever power controls these beasts."

Sir Joh nodded. "What can I offer you? Troops . . . armaments . . . ? Name it and it is yours. I owe Cyrus and Jason Del my life. I would gladly give my own for Megani."

"Thank you. The offer is most gracious," said Gil, "but your forces are most needed here, to protect those who cannot protect themselves."

Gil took Sir Joh aside to speak privately. "I've also come because I have heard that you know just about everyone in Trinity."

"Some say so," said Sir Joh.

"I seek the Historian," Gil whispered. "Do ya know of him?"

Joh's eyes gleamed. "If you seek such a Man, then you are on more than a *quest* to find the Sword. Show me the mark!"

Gil took a step back, surprised at the request.

Sir Joh moved closer. "Show me the mark!"

Gil rolled up his left sleeve to reveal the mark of the Guardian. Sir Joh quickly grabbed Gil's sleeve and rolled it back down before others could see it.

"The Man you seek," began Sir Joh, "this *Historian,* he will find you."

Gil looked on in disbelief. "But how?"

"He is connected in ways we can't begin to imagine."

"Do ya know him?"

"I'm one of the very few who know *of* him, though I don't think I actually *know* him. So find your Sword, find Megani, and may Anton bless and protect you, Gil of the Wilderness."

Gil had hoped that Sir Joh could provide more answers regarding the whereabouts of the Historian, but he was comforted by the thought that the Historian would find him. That knowledge would have to be enough for now.

The trio exited Meadowtown by the southern route and passed through a large gate. They raced through a clearing before entering the dark forest once more. Though Sir Joh had offered troops to help cut their path, Gil refused; he did not want to put others in harm's way. In no time at all, Gil paused, his senses once again alert. He began to change his course to circumvent whatever trap was ahead of them.

"Follow me," Gil whispered to Allo and Drak.

Allo and Drak knew instantly that there were new beasts to slaughter. The death of these creatures would momentarily satisfy the bloodlust that was heightened by the fresh knowledge of their devastated homelands. The two young warriors began to pounce past Gil and toward their vengeance. As they moved past him, Gil whirled about with a powerfully extended leg and knocked both of them through the air some fifty feet.

Allo and Drak bounced back up, angry. They paced slowly, cunningly toward Gil.

"You dishonor me!" seethed Drak.

"You had no right," added Allo. "You stand in the way of us and our sworn revenge."

Gil faced them. "Then make me pay for my faults," he calmly said.

Allo leaped through the air toward Gil. The woodsman jumped high and kicked Allo hard, sending the Elf tumbling head over heals and into the trunk of a tree. Drak came low. Gil rolled easily out of his way, but not before smacking Drak hard across the face, breaking his nose and causing it to spurt blood. The Dwarf exploded with anger. Running forward with his ax in hand, Drak hurled it at the woodsman. Gil caught it by the handle just an inch from his forehead and tossed it aside. As Gil rid himself of the ax, Allo grabbed the young Man from behind; however, Gil jumped backward over Allo, knocking him forward into Drak. Allo quickly rose with bow and arrow in hand and shot it point-blank at Gil's heart, but Gil caught it and broke it over his knee.

Drak and Allo raced toward Gil. Allo pulled his sword while Drak drew his knife. They lunged. With just a few jabs, the woodsman disarmed them both, sending their weapons into the bushes. Allo and Drak began throwing punches, but wherever they extended their jabs, Gil dodged them as he ducked and moved with both speed and calm. With another exploding, rotating kick, Gil knocked both of them down to their knees once more, forcing all the air out of their lungs. Until that moment, Drak and Allo had not fully realized that Gil carried no weapons. Now they knew why: He didn't need them.

While the two combatants were momentarily stunned, a serpent exploded from the forest. It was three times as big as any they had faced before. It roared as it jumped toward the helpless figures of Allo and Drak. They did not have time to move, and neither had weapons. The beast opened its gaping mouth, exposing huge fangs that were assured of the kill.

Gil leaped over Allo and Drak and landed headfirst right into the beast's mouth, sliding down into its belly! The creature stopped short, dazed at what had just occurred.

"Errrrrrrrrr!" it suddenly wailed in pain.

Allo and Drak looked up in time to see the long, snakelike tail of the beast begin to gradually disappear inside its body as though being pulled from the inside. In seconds, the tail began to exit the beast's mouth. The creature was being pulled inside out! More and more of it emerged as the creature's organs began to spill from of its frame.

"Errrrrrrrrrr!" it shrieked again.

Suddenly, Gil emerged, covered with green slim and the remains of the serpent's innards. With one mighty, last pull, even the beast's face was turned inside out.

Having killed the serpent, Gil slapped his hands together to rid them of the filth. He then leaped into the air, spinning rapidly like a top. The slime from the beast that had clung to his body sprayed in all directions. Allo and Drak shielded their faces. When Gil landed, he was completely dry. He moved toward Allo and Drak and knelt beside them. His voice was deadly.

"We must avoid these beasts in order to keep our presence a secret for as long as possible. We kill what me must, but leave what we can. Above all, our quest is to find the Sword, not to satisfy your vengeance. Disobey me again . . . and I'll *kill* the both of you."

Gil then marched south to find the Sword. Allo and Drak gathered their senses and their weapons and followed. They were torn between their blood oath to wreak vengeance and their sudden, enormous respect for the Man that bested both of them and a beast with his bare hands. But at least for this moment, they knew one thing for sure: They had found a leader. It was something that these two suddenly tragic orphans needed most of all.

Soon after the trio had left the gates of Meadowtown, Sir Joh slowly climbed the lengthy stone steps into the bell tower, a mammoth structure that allowed watchmen to see for many miles in all directions. He moved to a corner near a window where stood a large cage filled with his precious, winged friends.

"I have an important task for you, Penelope," he said to his favorite pigeon as he took her out of the cage and petted her gently. Sir Joh then affixed a piece of rolled-up paper to the bird's collar. "Take this to the Historian . . . whoever that might be," he said as he gently tossed Penelope out of the window and into the night air. "The world may depend upon you, Penelope . . ."

Sir Joh looked out into the night and watched as Penelope disappeared from view. He looked up to the stars. "Jason . . . my old friend," he began. "I wish you were still alive to give me advice, because the decision I'm about to make is enormous." The old Man shook his head, perplexed. "If I choose wrongly, it will assuredly cost the lives of everyone in Trinity."

CHAPTER 9

THE FALLEN

After a hard southern trek through forests filled with oak and sparsely planted Farlo, Gil continued to lead his companions as they approached the Fallen's Memorial. They often changed course, silently moving around serpents and Gorgons in order to remain hidden from the beasts. Allo and Drak fought the intense urge to charge into battle to exact greater destruction upon the creatures that in some way they held responsible for their fathers' deaths. But they did not, for their desire for blood was held in check by the young Man not much older than themselves. The stories that they had heard of Gil turned out to be more than fable—they were true. The years he had spent in the wilderness and the skills he developed in order to survive were formidable and not to be ignored. While Allo and Drak exchanged comments along the way, Gil said little. He was different than them in many ways, more than the difference in Race alone.

A slight mist emanated from a clearing in the distance, shrouding what lay in front of them. The muffled but distinct noise of digging—lots of digging—reached their ears. Gil found a tall pine tree in the forest, jumped ten feet to reach its lowest branch, and pulled himself up from limb to limb, hand over hand, without ever using his feet. He quickly went higher and higher. Though Allo and Drak's own climbing skills were great, they looked in amazement as Gil silently disappeared above, completely at home in the tree as though born within one. They followed, but it took Allo and Drak several minutes to quietly reach the top of the massive pine. They gazed south and downward toward a large clearing.

For thousands of years, this plot of land had been home to the Circle of Wisdom, a massive granite slab of stone measuring ten feet high and one hundred paces in diameter. Over the years it had served as many things: a place where the Races ruled, judged, traded, and fought. It was to this place just seventy years ago that Meadowtown was forced to flee and engage in a battle with the beasts that sought Jason Del. But instead the creatures first met Jason's father, Cyrus, along with hundreds of brave Men, both male and female, and a handful of Elves and Dwarves who fought to save their families from destruction. And finally, it was at the Circle of Wisdom where Jason Del soon thereafter faced and destroyed Pure Evil in the Final Contest, thus saving Trinity from any further harm from the evil of Lord Becus. But the clash of powers was cataclysmic, and the Circle of Wisdom imploded, falling into itself as ancient tunnels beneath the structure ruptured and collapsed. Jason and Cyrus fell hundreds of yards into the abyss and would have assuredly died had it not been for the grace of the Good Lord Anton and the powers he had bestowed upon them that day.

But the Sword wielded by Cyrus Del did not survive the battle. It was shattered by Pure Evil just before the Circle of Wisdom imploded and was never recovered. The charred, gaping hole in the earth where once stood the Circle of Wisdom was eventually filled in with soil, and a large granite slab of stone was raised. It contained hundreds of names from the Races of Man, Elf, and Dwarf who died on that day, and it had become a revered, sacred patch of ground over the past seventy years. Peoples from far away would come and extend their blessings and run their fingers along the etched names of loved ones who gave their lives for a noble cause. Hundreds among these were orphans whose parents had died in the desperate struggle. There was no place in Trinity that was held in such deep reverence as the Circle of Wisdom.

But this was not the case today. As the trio scanned the clearing, the mist parted just enough to reveal sacrilege.

"How dare they?!" Drak was enraged at what he saw from atop the forest canopy.

The granite slab containing the names of the fallen had been pushed facedown upon the dirt. Huge holes appeared everywhere as giant earth-moving worms bore tunnels far beneath the surface. The dirt-digging creatures were massive, thirty feet long and ten feet wide. They were a pure white, but soiled due to their hole-digging efforts. The trio watched as the giant worms brought soil up from the depths below to create huge piles of dirt, which were awaiting inspection. Nearly eighty Gorgons watched over the huge effort. Some of them picked through the soil looking for whatever they could uncover. It wasn't much. A small mound of recently discovered swords, spears, and breastplates was evident, but it was a meager find. Once the mounds of soil were inspected, other giant worms carried off the dirt and brought it back into the tunnels. But they were stopped just before entering by other Gorgons that searched their dirt-filled mouths one last time to be sure that nothing of value was brought back into the earth.

Allo looked at Gil. "The beasts are searching for the Sword. They must be trying to keep it out of Megani's hands."

"Yes," agreed Gil, "and by the looks of things, they have yet to find it."

Drak grunted. "Why do the worms bring the soil back into the ground?"

"Because," Gil explained, "if they don't carefully place the dirt back in the holes they have already inspected, this entire clearing could cave in."

Allo's sharp eyes noticed something else. To the west of the clearing was a small graveyard. It was lined with stones that marked the names of those veterans who fought in the battle but died long afterward. He knew this well, as Elves were buried here, wanting to lie with their comrades in arms when they eventually succumbed to old age. He noticed, however, one grave that was being dug up by a huge bird of prey.

"Beasts!" he said as he pointed toward the inhumanity.

Drak and Gil followed his gaze and found the same. They both knew this marker, as had all in Trinity.

"Cyrus Del's restin' spot," Gil whispered. "Why would the bird disturb his grave?" As they watched, the bird used its talons to pull an urn from beneath the ground. It smashed it open, and the ashen remains of Cyrus Del fell upon the dirt. The beast inspected it closely with sharp eyes. It then grabbed two talons' full of the ash, lurched into the air, and flew east.

"Why?" asked Allo. "Unless it thought the Sword was there!"

"Not likely," said Gil. "No one had seen the Sword for decades before Cyrus's death. It must have been up to somethin' else . . . lookin' for somethin' else . . ."

"I can kill ten of the Gorgons myself," interrupted Drak as he turned his attention to the beasts below. "But the other fifty or so I'll have to leave to you two. I assume that the giant worms will just stay out of our way." The Dwarf began to climb down the tree, but Allo grabbed his arm and held him back. He motioned toward Gil, who was already looking at Drak with a deadly gaze.

"Oh . . . ," said Drak apologetically as he returned Gil's stare. "I suppose you have a better plan?"

"A plan," began Gil, "doesn't begin and end with slaughter. It begins and ends with findin' the Sword." Gil looked back toward the memorial. He began to gently wiggle his body back and forth.

"What's he doing?" asked Drak.

Allo spied the creatures beyond. "He's mimicking the movements of the giant worms . . . I think."

Gil was in a trance, moving as the worms moved, feeling as they felt. He could ascertain the nature of the beasts by their actions, one of many skills that had kept him alive for so long in the wilderness.

"More madness," grunted Drak as he shook his head.

Allo smacked the Dwarf. "Give him a chance."

After several more moments, Gil paused. "We need to get the Sword before the Gorgons do. That means we're goin' under."

Allo and Drak glanced at each other.

"You mean underground?" asked Drak, excitedly. "I was born underground, and I'll probably die there. You can count me in!"

"That's good to know," said Gil.

Allo scanned the Gorgons. "But how can we get there unnoticed with all of the Gorgons looking on?"

Gil pointed to a large worm gathering dirt from a pile of inspected earth near the edge of the forest. It then disappeared into a nearby hole in order to bring it back into the ground.

"We're hidin' in one of them things."

Allo and Drak looked at the giant worm in disgust.

"That's just not right," declared Allo.

"I'm not getting in one of those beasts," said Drak, "unless I'm steering."

Gil looked at his companions and shook his head. "Follow me."

Within minutes, the trio was on the forest floor, secretly making their way from bush to bush and toward a huge mound of inspected dirt. Gorgons were everywhere, but they were immersed in their task of either herding the giant worms into the ground or once the worms resurfaced, guiding them toward the filtering station where other Gorgons, with the use of the serpent arms, searched for pieces of the famed Sword. The trio hid behind a large pine tree. A giant worm was feet away, around the opposite side of the trunk, as it began to pick up dirt for its return visit to fill the holes deep beneath the earth.

"I'll slit its throat," whispered Drak. "Then we jump inside. From there I'll get in the head and peer out its eye sockets. Allo, you can get in the rear; Gil can get in between us. Then we punch our legs though its belly and just stroll down into the tunnels." The Dwarf smiled at his intelligence.

Gil turned to face the smiling Dwarf. "Not everything's throat has to be slit," he admonished. "I know of these worms. They are from the deep northern wilderness. Sorta a happy lot normally. But look at 'em now."

Allo and Drak looked, but they could not discern anything about the giant worm other than that it was . . . a giant worm.

"They're sluggish," continued Gil, "and sad. They aren't doing this because they want to. They're bein' forced to. It ain't right." Gil turned back and began to make a gentle, low, and soothing gurgling sound with his throat. The giant worm looked about and then responded just as gently with a low-hummed gurgle of its own.

Drak turned to Allo, whispering, "You mean we don't get to kill it?"

"Shhhhh," Allo quietly responded. "He's talking to it."

Other worms came and went with fresh dirt in their mouths as the gurgling between Gil and his worm continued. Abruptly, the noise stopped.

Gil turned to face Drak and Allo. "She's agreed to swallow us and bring us far beneath the surface."

"Swallow us?!" said Drak, his words too loud. He was about to speak again, but Gil struck Drak gently with an open hand to the throat. Stunned, Drak opened his mouth to speak again, but he could not. He was in no pain, but his voice would not come. Drak tried again, but still he had no voice.

Gorgons turned toward them, looking for the creature that had uttered the sound. The trio froze behind the tree for several anxious seconds as watchful eyes turned their way. The Gorgons drifted toward the worm, just on the other side of the tree from them. They sniffed the air, trying to detect enemies. Gil made a low gurgle, and the giant worm immediately expelled a huge volume of gas from its rear. The companions held their breaths at the scent of the foul odor. The Gorgons backed away, waving their arms to eliminate the stench from their nostrils. They turned and continued their work, apparently content that the only danger they faced was the worm's flatulence.

"Drak has a similar ability," whispered Allo, smiling.

Gil looked at Drak and said quietly, "Do ya promise to whisper from now on?"

The Dwarf nodded anxiously. Gil gently tapped the Dwarf's throat again, and Drak opened his mouth slowly, blowing a gentle breath out of his lungs to test his voice. "Haaaaaa."

Relief washed over the Dwarf. "By the Gods," he whispered. "I thought I had lost my voice forever."

Allo turned to Gil, impressed. "How did you do that? I could have used that on him years ago."

"No time to explain," whispered Gil. "The worm, she has agreed to swallow us along with enough air to keep us alive until she can bring us to the bottom of the dig. But in return, we have to help the worms escape once we find the pieces of the Sword."

"How are we going to help them escape when they are so slow?" asked Allo as he gazed upon the dozens of lumbering giant worms that came to and from the holes.

"One plan at a time," said Gil. "One plan at a time."

The giant worm appeared from around the tree. It was as pure white as all the others, with small green eyes and a snout from which snot ran continuously. It opened its gaping mouth. It was a perfectly round hole about five feet across. Gil climbed in. The worm's lips and throat were very soft and moist. The worm immediately threw its head back and swallowed. When it brought its head down once more and opened it again, it was empty.

"You have a tradition of going first," whispered Drak to Allo. "I'd hate to ruin your record."

Allo smiled. He quickly climbed into the worm's mouth and was swallowed. As he slid down, Drak heard Allo whisper, "We are tied again."

Drak stomped his feet. The worm brought her head back down and opened her mouth, waiting for the Dwarf to enter. Drak studied the creature and then stomped his feet again. "I think I'll stay here," he said.

A gurgle rose from the worm's belly as Gil gave it instructions. The giant worm suddenly plunged downward upon the startled Dwarf and picked him up in its mouth. The Dwarf's stout legs dangled wildly from the creature's gaping mouth. She threw her head back for the third time and swallowed. The Dwarf was gone.

"I'm kidnapped!" exclaimed Drak in total, wet darkness that began to move to and fro. He slid a short distance and then slammed into a hard body.

"Stop crowding, Drak!" whispered Allo, who was pressed tight between Gil and the Dwarf, "and get your ax from between my legs!"

"Sorry," said Drak, repositioning his weapon.

"The stench is strong," said Allo while running his hands along the inside lining of the worm's stomach.

"I agree," said Drak as he sniffed the air. "I have never smelled such a foul creature."

"I was talking about you!" corrected Allo in a whisper. "When was the last time you bathed?"

"Quiet," said Gil. "Say nothin'; do nothin'—not even a whisper. Conserve your air."

The worm packed its mouth with filtered dirt and made its way toward a procession of other worms that were lined up before entering a hole that led to the deep pit below. Two Gorgons at the entrance halted each worm and inspected the filtered dirt again just to be sure it contained no fragments of the Sword. The worm opened its mouth, and the two serpent arms of the Gorgon tossed the dirt about. Satisfied, they let it pass. The worm coiled its way to a large, dark chamber where the worms worked to place filtered dirt back into old holes. The worm gurgled low.

"We're there," said Gil in the darkness of the worm's belly.

"We climb out then?" asked Drak.

"Not exactly," answered Gil. "Hold onto your possessions."

With a massive muscle contraction, the worm excreted the trio out its back end. Gil, Allo, and then Drak splat against the chamber wall, covered in slime. They were in total darkness and the heat was stifling.

"One humiliation after another," Drak said as he began to scrape the worm's stomach juices from his face.

"Drak?" asked Gil. "My eyes are good in the dark, but yours are best. What do ya see?"

Drak grunted. "Fine! Now you need me."

"Just answer his question," begged Allo as he, too, wiped ooze from his body.

The Dwarf relented. "It's a huge dig. I'd say a hundred yards in every direction. Dozens of worms are digging in various holes . . . but no serpents. I guess they don't like being this deep beneath the surface."

Gil gurgled to the worm, who in turn gurgled to others, who in turn gurgled to others. In no time, the worms began to mobilize, searching for the Sword with renewed vigor. Some continued to rise to the surface to bring fresh dirt and return with filtered dirt so that the Gorgons would not suspect what was happening below. After an hour's time, excitement broke out in one of the holes. A worm emerged as others crowded around him. On the tip of its snout was a fragment of metal that shone brightly even in the darkness. The worms passed it from snout to snout until the last placed it gently at Gil's feet. For the first time in the chamber, the trio could see each other's faces clearly, brightened by a fragment of the Sword of Legends.

Drak reached gently toward the metal to touch the piece. He glanced back at Gil and Allo for approval. Gil made no comment, but Allo smiled evilly.

"Give it a try," he urged.

Drak gently touched it. Blue sparks ignited. "Ahhhhhhhh!" gasped Drak as he jerked his burning fingers back from the blade.

Allo's smile spread. "Oh, don't you know that part of the legend? Among all the Races, only a Del can touch the Sword without harm."

Drak socked Allo in the stomach. "Now you tell me?!" he barked. Allo fell to the ground, winded. Drak dropped beside the Elf in order to care for his aching, singed fingers.

Gil ignored his companions' antics and pulled a cloth from inside his leather jersey. He used it to pick up the fragment of the blade—the central piece. It was marvelous and looked to be a third of the blade's full length. The flat of the blade was detailed with fine lettering in an ancient language, and the edge was beyond razor sharp. It glowed with a constant white light. Gil wrapped it in the cloth and placed it back upon the ground.

More worms began to bore new tunnels near where the first fragment had been found. Within minutes, the two remaining fragments were discovered and deposited upon the cloth. They fit perfectly, as a puzzle would, but the three separate pieces were just that, separate, which made the blade useless. Even in its broken state, though, it was a thing of beauty. It was massive and yet delicately crafted: The point was as fine as a needle, and the hilt was solid and perfectly molded. Gil rolled up the cloth and the three fragments with it.

Dozens of worms now surrounded the trio while fewer continued to rise to the surface to continue the deception. Those underground began to gurgle in unison. Gil looked up.

"Now we make good on our promise."

He began to converse with the giant worms. The gurgles emanating from the creatures were pleasant at times and threatening at other times, depending upon whether the worms agreed or disagreed with Gil's ideas. After several minutes, the gurgling ceased. Gil turned to Allo and Drak.

"Come with me," said Gil. "We need to race to the surface."

Allo and Drak followed Gil to a shaft that led above ground, and they began their ascent. "The plan is simple," Gil began along the way. "The worms will begin to dig at points just beneath the Gorgons' feet so that upon my signal, they will make a couple final cuts, which will collapse the tunnels beneath the Gorgons. The worms will survive beneath. They already started escape tunnels before we even arrived. But the Gorgons will be buried. Those that live will have a tough time makin' it back to the surface at such depths. The serpents and Gorgons that are left on the surface will forget about the worms."

"Why would they leave the worms alone when they prove treacherous?" asked Allo.

"Because," answered Gil, "the Gorgons will be chasin' us!"

Drak grunted. "So that's the best plan you can come up with?"

Gil did not respond. As they reached the end of the tunnel, they found that it opened up at the eastern part of the clearing. It was midday, and they needed to shield their eyes from the bright light. Only fifty yards to the west, the trio could see dozens of Gorgons as they continued to inspect dirt taken from the underground tunnels.

Gil glanced at the Gorgons and then at his companions. "Ya ready?"

"Yes," said Allo.

"Sure," Drak added, shrugging his shoulders. "No one seems to care what I think anyway," he pouted.

"Finally," shot Allo. "He's beginning to understand!"

Gil made a deep gurgle that sounded like a trumpet. It was met with the same sound far below the surface. At the commotion, the Gorgons turned and spied the trio. The beasts paused momentarily, not sure what to make of them. Gil raised his hands, which contained the cloth-shrouded fragments of the Sword. He pulled the cloth slightly downward, and the Sword caught the light of day and shone brightly. Stunned, the beasts lunged forward all at once, but the earth began to shake beneath the Gorgons' feet. The ground suddenly fell in, and dozens of the Gorgons plummeted far below to be covered by a massive avalanche of dirt and rock. It would be a while before they recovered, if they recovered at all. But dozens narrowly escaped the collapse. They charged toward the Sword with vigor. Gil wrapped the blade and bolted into the eastern forest followed by Allo and Drak.

The beasts gained ground as the companions approached the Crystal River. Gil reached the bank first. He knew they would not be able to cross the water before the beasts descended upon them. He also knew that he could not prevent the battle that was moments away. Gil tossed the cloth-covered Sword to the bank of the river and turned to face the onslaught.

"You mean . . . ?" asked Drak, hopeful.

"Yes!" said Gil as he shot forward and plummeted feetfirst toward the lead Gorgon.

"Hurrah!" shouted Drak and dashed toward the second beast, but before he reached it, the Gorgon fell dead, punctured by an arrow in its skull. A heartbeat later, its two serpents were similarly killed.

"I'm up by three!" shouted Allo. "Two for the serpent arms; one for the Gorgon itself. I've decided to count them all." Allo readied another arrow just as a dozen more Gorgons shot from the forest.

"You can't suddenly change the counting scheme!" yelled Drak as they ran toward the beasts.

"Why not?" called Allo. "As long as we count the same, the count is fair!"

"Then more points for all of us!" the Dwarf screamed as he dove into the horde that descended upon them all.

CHAPTER 10

ENCHANTED FOREST

Megani felt at peace in her dreams. They took her to the precious places she loved most: on top of the massive Mountain High, where she could see all of Trinity; along the Crystal River at night, when the fluorescent leaves of the Farlo trees would create a green aura on the water below; and within the hallowed tunnels of the ancient Wallos, far beneath the land, which boasted of such great craftsmanship. She loved all of this, as much in her dreams as in real life. But after a time, Megani felt an urgency to leave this place of dreams and rise to the surface of the real world. She could not remember the world as she left it, but she did know that it was in need. She felt herself leaving her slumber as her body began to stir, forcing her mind up from the deepness of sleep and toward the awareness of the current world.

Megani's chest felt heavy and constrained. She could not take a deep breath with the weight upon her. She heard low, steady breathing very close to her, so close, in fact, that Megani felt someone's warm breath upon her cheek. She cracked her eyes open gently.

"Oh, good!" said Lyndi, who was lying upon Megani's chest, her head in her hands as she looked eyeball to eyeball at her. "I thought you would sleep for ever and ever," the little one said rapidly. "And we have so much to talk about. Have you ever seen the ocean? I don't mean the little water in the straits; I mean the real ocean. It's bigger than big—it's the most humongous thing ever! Did you ever wonder why the sky is blue? How about tree bark? What's that all about? And why do some stars shoot across the sky and others don't? Did you ever notice that some frogs are green and others are brown and stuff? Do you like your red hair? I like my blond hair, but I think I like yours better. I heard you snore. Do you do that all the time? The Historian does. Sometimes he can snore for hours. One time I put a cloth over his mouth and watched it float up and down with each snore. One night, it went up and down five hundred and twenty-seven times. When you go poop in the forest, which type of leaf do you like to use?

Lilies are nice because they are soft. But you have to be careful with oak, and never, ever try ivy leaves because some of them can be poisonous, and you don't want to make the same mistake that I made!"

"That's enough!" snapped the Historian as he approached. "Kendro!" he called. The strong, black-haired archer arrived a moment later. "Take Lyndi in the forest and forage for dinner. It will give me time to chat with Megani."

Without a word, Kendro hoisted little Lyndi up into his strong arms and onto his shoulders. The two of them made their way toward the eastern forest while Lyndi continued to blab. "I like berries. There's the black and the blue and the red and lots more. Do you want to know why the red ones are red and not blue? It's a secret, but I'll tell you . . ." Kendro and Lyndi drifted out of range.

The Historian looked back upon Megani. "Lyndi's a sweet girl, but she lost her family some years back, and ever since she tells a lot of tales and asks a lot of questions. She really doesn't mean any harm. Though at times she can be annoying . . . like when she wants to play Mammoth Rider. But please excuse her. She's been through a lot."

"Of course," said Megani while rising sluggishly to a sitting position. "She seems like a sweet little girl." The knowledge of the last several days suddenly came to her, shattering the pleasant remnants of the dreams she had moments earlier. Megani became distraught. "I've lost everything," she said as she sadly gazed into the old Man's eyes.

The Historian smiled softly. "Not everything. You are still here."

"Barely." She took a deep breath to help her senses reach clarity. "So you are the Historian," she said.

"Yes . . . that's one of many titles I have had in my life. We can discuss that in time. But first, tell me what happened. We have little knowledge of what you've been through, though we know you have lost some of your powers." The Historian opened his pack and reached within it. "But first . . . ," he began as he handed her some bread with his only remaining arm, "you must eat something."

Hungry, Megani took several bites of the bread and washed it down with the flavored water the Historian provided. She was still weary in body, mind, and spirit, and while she had little hope that this old Man could help her in any way, she did wish to tell what happened, if only to share her burden with someone else. The Historian seemed particularly caring, making it all the more easy. If he were truly the Man whom Gil sought, he must be special indeed. After a few moments, Megani began to painfully relate her experiences over the past several days.

"My mother, Bea, and I were in Zol when we heard that Dwarves and Elves were having a dispute. She sent me to help, but I was delayed in Olive Branch when creatures named Gorgons attacked."

The Historian's eyes flashed. "How many were there?"

"First there was only one, standing on a bridge as it taunted towns-people to fight. When I killed it, two came from the forest. When I killed those, more came."

"How many exactly?" he asked again. "When and in what numbers?"

"What does that matter?" she questioned.

"Everything matters," explained the Historian, "because it can pro-vide us with clues concerning the dangers we face."

Megani thought for a moment. "First there was one . . . then two . . . then sixteen . . . then thirty-two . . . and finally about one thousand. I was left very weak."

The Historian stroked his yellowing beard. "I hope you realized you were being watched and tested for your strength."

"What?" Megani was startled by the revelation.

"Of course," said the Historian. "Why would one Gorgon taunt the town from the bridge unless it was waiting for something to happen or in this case, for someone to arrive, namely you? When you killed it, two were sent. The attack doubled in strength. It doubled again when the number of attackers went from sixteen to thirty-two. It's an old warrior's trick. Their master was watching to determine the limits of your powers and how your defenses changed depending upon the strength of the attack against you. Near the end of the test, the Gorgons' master must have grown impatient, which is why he threw so many at you at once. He wanted to discover the limit of your powers, or kill you if he could."

Megani stared at the old Man. Until that moment, she had never con-sidered that Olive Branch was a test. She shook her head. "I have failed so many times in so few days."

"I've seen worse," said the old Man with a subtle wink. His kindness pierced Megani's gloom. Though she did not feel any less responsible for the recent events, it eased a deep ache in her heart.

"Did you use your powers . . . all your powers . . . your *full* powers?"

Megani nodded. "Yes." She was suddenly cautious about divulging too much, even to a Man that seemed so understanding. Suspicion grew. "Who are you?"

"As I said, I'm the Historian."

"But I have no knowledge of any *Historian.*" She did not want to mention Gil's quest to find this Man for fear that she might put her friend in danger.

"I have kept my appearances few and my actions even fewer so as not to arouse attention. But my aim is as yours: to fight what is before us. Can you still use your mind probe that I've heard so much about?"

Megani tried to use her abilities, but her mind could not enter his, just as it would not work with the two robbers the day before. But her Ethan qualities, inherited from her mother, served her well. This Man's face spoke the truth in many ways. He was not deceiving her.

"I can see you speak fairly," she said, "but my mind probe is useless, too."

"Well, please continue with the recent events and leave nothing out, whether or not you think it is important."

"I used my full powers and destroyed all of the Gorgons, but I was spent in doing so. After some rest, I continued my journey to the Valley of Despair to help resolve the dispute between the Dwarves and Elves, but they were already dead. . . . Their homelands were destroyed soon thereafter." Megani expected to see shock in the old Man's eyes, but she did not.

Megani gazed at him intently. "You already knew. I can see it in your eyes. You already knew that the Races were no more."

"Yes, I was there as well. I saw the devastation."

Megani suddenly recalled the girl's voice she had heard echoing in the chambers of the Wallos.

"Lyndi! I heard Lyndi's voice deep beneath the surface. You were there!"

"Yes."

"But how did you find the tunnels? In order to keep the final work of the Wallos intact, no one on Trinity is supposed to know of those passageways!"

The Historian leaned close, a sad smile reached his lips. "I have special authority, as you will learn in time." He leaned back again. "We saw the armies destroyed. I'm afraid we also witnessed the devastation of their homelands."

Megani put her head in her hands. "Can it get any worse?"

The Historian shrugged his shoulders. "These are trying times. But why in heaven would the Races battle each other? Not since the Second Race War have they done so."

Megani shook her head. "When my powers still worked, I was able to probe the minds of each king before he faded. Each believed that the other king had killed his son, but their sons in fact were alive, engaged in their rites of adulthood in the Western Expanse."

"Amazing!" muttered the Historian. "The Races all believed that Kings Alar and Dal did such a thing. Yet they were friends . . . blood brothers. The beast's power is great to have done this!"

"Not only did they believe it," continued Megani, "but each believed he *saw it* with his own eyes."

"Tell me more."

"Soon afterward, Princes Drak and Allo returned from the forest. I sent them on a quest, along with a friend named Gil, to recover an item that I might use to defeat whatever is challenging us."

"Good!" said the Historian, his eyes sparkling. "The Sword will be exactly what we need."

"I never mentioned the Sword!" snapped Megani. She wondered if this Historian knew too much.

"You didn't have to mention it. You are of the blood of your grandfather. Cyrus was the last to wield that Sword to help your father destroy Pure Evil. The blade was nearly a part of him. With the dark shadow growing upon the land, Cyrus would die trying to find that Sword. I would expect the same from you. And I know of the trio you sent; there are none better."

"How do you know so much?"

He smiled. "I thought I told you—I'm the Historian!"

Megani glanced about. "But where are your scrolls, your books, your histories?"

The Historian smiled. "I am called the Historian not because I've written about histories, but because I've lived many of them. I was with your grandfather Cyrus during the Second Race War when he helped save the Races from destroying each other. I was with him again during the final Battle of Meadowntown, just before Jason launched his own battle with Pure Evil. And I was there for many other histories, both before and after."

Tears welled in Megani's eyes as she lowered her head. "I never knew my grandparents."

The Historian raised her chin. "You have much reason to be proud. Cyrus and Beth were magnificent. Their blood flows through you."

"But with less than a month since my father's death, all is lost," lamented Megani. "After I returned to my mother to tell her of the events in the Valley of Despair and seek her advice, a demon arrived, stole my powers, and used them against me. My mother died in the battle. I'm sure he was the master of the Gorgons." Megani began to cry. "And I ran . . . like Pita!"

"Bea . . . dead?!" asked the Historian, startled. "Sadly, that I did not know."

Megani nodded. "Yes. She was killed by a servant of the evil one, a beast that changed forms."

"The Beastmaker!"

Megani looked at the Historian through watery eyes. "What do you know of all this?"

"It was a concern for many ages—since near the Beginning—and it has now come to pass."

"What it is? What am I facing?"

"You mean you don't know?!" asked the Historian, truly surprised. "You haven't figured it out as yet?"

"No!"

The Historian put his right arm around Megani and held her gently. "You face a being that was created by Anton to fight the Beasts of Becus long ago. But the beast chose to use its powers to someday claim this land for itself. The evil is a memory planter; it can place false memories in people's minds in order to make them act in hideous ways. It cannot be defeated with magic because it is magic. That is why your powers were of no use against it and why it was able to steal them to make itself stronger."

"You mean . . ."

"Yes . . . you face a Wizard!" The Historian took a breath. "And not just any Wizard . . . you face Zorca, the most powerful of the creatures."

"But my father told me that Zorca died once it taught him how to use its powers," said Megani.

"That's what your father thought. Zorca was asleep for many centuries, waiting for the day when it would rise to teach your father the ways of magic. That was to be its last task and the reason it was the only Wizard that did not die ages ago when the Sword was first forged. But after it woke and taught your father to use the magic, it placed a false memory in his mind of its own death. It needed Jason and all others to believe it was gone so that they would not pursue it afterward. Then it needed Jason to destroy Pure Evil so that once Pure Evil was destroyed, the Wizard could reign instead. Only the Sword can pull the power from the beast."

"Why did it emerge now?"

The Historian took a breath, releasing his arm from around Megani. "I suppose it waited for your father to die, knowing that it did not have the power to face you both. With him out of the way, it struck and took your powers. But at least you can still shield your mind, right?"

Megani shrunk. "I'm not sure I can. Zorca tried to enter my mind, and I think I faltered."

"Not good!" said the Historian as he scratched his beard. "We can't be positive that all your memories are intact. Some may not be yours. I have learned over the years to block mind probes, but I cannot teach you in the time we have left. If that power is lost . . . then it cannot be recovered in time."

Megani sank further. "How can I know what is true and what is not?"

"You may not be able to know. But we'll try to figure it out together."

Megani felt comforted by his words. In fact, she felt confident enough about the Historian to share one more piece of information.

"I know someone who is looking for you."

The Historian's eyes flashed. "Who?"

"Gil. He said he has a message for you."

The Historian smiled. "From what I have heard of that lad, it does not surprise me. Once he recovers the Sword, where is he to meet you?"

"We will meet at Dire Passage before we cross the Straits of Devils. I believe that we will find the Wizard in Devon."

"Perfect," said the Historian. "I suspect you are right. I hope you don't mind if we tag along with you."

"Not at all," Megani said, pleased to have the company. Her quest and the Historian's appeared to be one and the same. But she knew their efforts would be gravely dangerous, for she had no powers left and Kendro appeared to be the only one of her new companions who might be useful in battle. Megani suddenly gazed at her hands, noting that they were entirely healed of the cuts she had suffered during her encounter with the Wizard. She peeked inside her robe and noted that the cuts there had also been healed.

Megani looked perplexed. "How did I heal so fast?"

The Historian smiled. "We have our ways."

Across a meadow, Kendro and Lyndi were returning with their hands filled with berries and roots of many sorts.

"But why are people's ears so small?" Lyndi ask Kendro. "People's ears could be as big as a mammoth's ears. That's what I would have done. I would have made everyone's ears as big as mammoth ears. Why not give people wings? That would have been great . . ."

Lyndi then saw Megani and bolted toward her.

"Will you be my sister?" asked the girl eagerly as she grabbed Megani's hands and swung them side to side. "Oh, please . . . please." Then the little one turned sad as she sat in Megani's lap. "All of my sisters are dead."

Megani's heart burst as she glanced at the Historian and then back to Lyndi.

"Yes," said Megani. "I would be honored." The little girl hugged Megani's neck.

"What were your sisters' names . . . and your brothers' names, too?" asked Megani innocently.

"Nooooo!" shouted the Historian and Kendro in unison, but it was too late.

Lyndi smiled wide. "There was Aacon, Aadon, Aaeen, Aaok, Aapri, Aazac, Bbren, . . ."

As the little girl continued, the Historian shook his head. "Here we go again."

An hour later, while the Historian, Kendro, and Megani were finishing preparations to leave camp, Lyndi neared the end of her list, ". . . Ztoc, Zzmat, and Zzz!"

The Historian smiled at Megani, whispering, "Overactive imagination."

But Megani wasn't so sure. She could tell that Lyndi believed what she said. There was something about her that remained a secret.

"Kendro!" called the Historian. "I think we need to skirt the western edge of the Enchanted Forest as we move south. That way we'll stay out of the forest itself, but we'll be near enough should danger arise."

"I agree," said Kendro.

The Historian turned to Megani, "Do you agree?"

Megani appreciated being asked. She had lost vast powers, yet the Historian still treated her with respect.

"Good idea," she said.

After an hour's silent walk with Kendro in the lead, they paused. The Enchanted Forest to their left was dark and ominous, with tall, dense trees and ground foliage as high as a Man. It was alive with the hooting of owls and the caw of crows. Every now and again a strange, foreboding shrill would rise from its depths. Megani had been in this region many times, but she never ventured into the forest. Her father had ruled it off limits for fear that the dangers within would harm the peoples he had pledged to protect. And so the dangers, if there were truly any, were unknown to her. But it wasn't the forest that was her immediate concern. Something else was not quite right.

"Do you know why they call it the Enchanted Forest?" asked Lyndi suddenly. "I do!"

"Shhhh!" said the Historian. "Quiet now, little one!"

"Something's amiss," whispered Kendro to the Historian. He voiced what the others instinctively knew as well. It was not the forest that troubled any of them; it was the sudden silence farther to the west. All animal sounds had suddenly vanished. The ground began to tremble, the intensity growing rapidly. Ridges of dirt along the surface of the earth appeared as creatures buried just beneath came closer to the companions.

"To the forest!" the Historian shouted, and they bolted toward the safety of the trees. Just before they entered, mounds of dirt behind them shot up and serpents emerged. Kendro turned and slew the first two with his long knife. Megani turned as well, drew the sword that Kendro had given her, and killed the third. She felt good that her battle skills were intact. Five more pushed upward and they met the same fate.

"Hurrah!" squealed Lyndi as she tried to escape the arm of the Historian so that she could get a closer look. But the old Man kept her safe and dashed deeper into the forest. More dirt kicked up in front of Megani and Kendro, and dozens of the beasts began to emerge. There were far too many. Kendro and Megani fell back and bolted to follow the Historian and Lyndi. They dashed between brush and trees in a futile attempt to gain ground. But the serpents grew closer. Some of the beasts circled farther to the north and south in an attempt to eventually head them off. Megani could see their efforts but could do nothing but charge forward while looking for a vantage point.

The serpents that had passed them came full about and now faced them. The companions came to a sudden stop within a clearing, seeing that they were surrounded. Kendro and Megani circled around the Historian and Lyndi, protecting them first and foremost. The beasts paused and then moved slowly toward their prey.

As the serpents drew closer, a strong mist blew in from the deeper forest. It smothered the clearing, leaving all nearly invisible. Megani tried to push the mist aside, but she was unable to stop its advance. Her sword suddenly felt larger, heavier, until its point touched the ground. Though she strained mightily, she could not lift it. Her robe, too, felt large and far out of proportion to her body. The sleeves fell over her hands. The mist cleared partially, enough to make out shadows.

Megani looked about and saw Kendro still standing before her. He, however, looked more animal like, with vague features of a lion, and large talons extended from his fingers. The Historian was there, but now his shape through the mist was bigger, threatening, with a warrior's stance of old . . . and with two good arms! She gazed at Lyndi's form and saw a giant of a girl, her figure towering over all.

Megani looked upon herself. Her body was shrunken to that of a child's. She tried again, but she could not lift her sword.

"Yeah!" shouted Lyndi. "I love the Enchanted Forest. I'm always biggest here!"

"It might be best if I handle this," the Historian said as he took the blade from Megani's hand.

The serpents were but shadows farther in the mist, though their forms looked to be the same. They suddenly attacked!

Kendro leaped forward and struck three beasts at once, slicing them down with his huge talons. The Historian wielded the blade and struck the first five that leaped before them. But that's all they were able to strike.

Megani watched as Lyndi plunged her fingers into the forest floor. The ground rumbled and from the soil came a thousand vines that wrapped about the remaining serpents, squeezing them tightly. With a sudden yank, the vines pulled the wailing beasts back below the soil. They were gone. A strong mist blew once more, and when it passed, all was as it had been.

Megani gazed at her newfound friends. They all looked as they had before they entered the forest. She turned to Lyndi first. "Who are you?!"

Lyndi beamed. "I'm Lyndi!"

Megani tried again. *"What* are you?!"

"The Enchanted Forest reveals us," interrupted the Historian as he handed Megani her sword. "I am surprised you never ventured in it before. Kendro was raised to be one with nature in the wilds of the Western Expanse. He is one of ten—as is Gil—who was raised to help me. I'm who you see, and who you saw, now an old Man but once a warrior. You, Megani, are still a youth whose responsibilities came far too soon. As for Lyndi, well . . . ," began the old Man with a wide, proud smile.

Lyndi bounced into Megani's arms. The little girl looked back toward the Historian with exuberance. "Can I tell her now? Can I tell her? Please, oh please can I tell her?"

The Historian nodded. With a smile reaching nearly from ear to ear, Lyndi turned back to Megani.

"I'm a Wallo!"

CHAPTER 11

FLIGHT

"And then I created ants, but they kept getting eaten by the lizards my brother Kato made," Lyndi told Megani. The companions were making their way along the eastern edge of Trinity toward the Plains of Temptation. Lyndi had been talking nonstop for a full day, but Megani was in awe. No longer did she perceive the little girl as, well, a little girl. She now knew her to be a surviving member of the Wallos, the ancient beings that Anton first created and sent to Trinity. They were the first craftsmen who forged the mountains, rivers, and created much of the lesser life forms.

"I made more and more ants," Lyndi continued, "but they got eaten too. So I created more and more and gave them really good jaws for biting. One ant could not hurt a lizard, but I trained the ants to work together to defend themselves against the lizards. I once thought about making the ants bigger, so I tried it, but they were too powerful and they killed just about everything else." Lyndi smiled. "My brothers and sisters were really mad at me that day!"

"How do you do it?" Megani asked.

"Do what?" giggled Lyndi, thrilled at any question posed to her.

"Make things . . . make life . . . change life."

"Oh, that's the fun part. Lord Anton made everything from millions of tiny, small pieces. The small pieces are in every one of us. You just have to be able to see them on the inside and then change them. It's like a big puzzle. When you change a small piece of the puzzle, then the whole life can change. We had to experiment a lot. It was fun. Change one piece there and you get a red butterfly instead of a black one. Change a couple pieces and you end up with a bird instead of a bat. I found out how to change a tiger into a cute little brown bunny." Lyndi suddenly became sad. "But that wasn't too smart because the tiger's sister decided to eat her brother."

Megani pressed on. "Did you make a lot of mistakes?"

122

Lyndi smiled. "I made tons and tons of mistakes," she said.

Megani noted that Lyndi seemed almost as proud of her failures as she did her successes.

"Every time you change one creature," Lyndi continued, "it can either help or hurt hundreds of others. That's how you learn what to do and what not to do. We tried to make as few mistakes as possible. But I made more than anyone!"

"What did you do to the serpents in the forest?"

"Nothing," giggled Lyndi. "I wasn't close enough to touch them. I have to touch them to change them, so I stuck my hands into the ground and touched vine and tree roots. They grow all over the forest. I made them grow faster than fast so that they would come to the surface and tie the serpents all up. Then I shrunk the roots real fast so they would pull the serpents beneath the ground."

"Very clever," said Megani.

Lyndi smiled. "Thanks! It's like a game I used to play with my sister Ganti when we got bored. One of us would hide, and the other would try to find her using whatever we could touch. I once found Ganti because before she went to hide, I secretly touched her to make her smell like a beehive. Then all I did was follow the lines of bees. There were millions of them all swarming poor Ganti. She didn't want to play with me after that, but she sure smelled good—like honeycombs!"

Megani smiled at Lyndi's ingenuity. "Can you do anything, change anything?"

"No," said Lyndi. "I don't know all the puzzle pieces, so I try to stay with what I know. And I can't alter the Races much because . . . ," she began with a whisper as she looked hesitantly into the sky, "I'm not allowed. That's more complicated, and it is supposed to be for the Lord Anton only."

As Lyndi began to discuss why flowers bloom, Megani's mind wandered. She gazed at the little Wallo's cheerful face and was enchanted by the playfulness of this powerful Race of beings. Megani had expected that such power would have come from a far more serious creature. But in his vast wisdom, the Lord Anton created just the opposite. The only being that could create such magnificent wonder in the world would be one that had an eternally childlike creativity and imagination. In fact, Anton gave many of the tools of life to children in order for them to unleash childlike awe.

" . . . and that's why flowers bloom," Lyndi continued. "It started as a mistake because my brother Seta was really trying to make a plant grow eyelashes, but it ended up as something that was pretty and would give my bees something to do. My brothers and sisters were all smart that way. They always knew how to turn problems into fun." Lyndi turned suddenly sad as she gazed off into the distance. "I miss my brothers and sisters."

"I'm sorry for your loss," Megani interjected. Her thoughts turned to the Beasts of Becus, which had been sent by Anton's evil brother, Becus, to destroy all that Anton had created—including the Wallos.

"Me too," said Lyndi. "It's been very, very lonely, especially since I can't talk to Togi anymore."

"Who's Togi?"

"He's my brother, the only other Wallo still alive."

"Where is he?" asked Megani, surprised that yet another Wallo lived.

"I'm not sure," Lyndi said hesitantly as she glanced at the Historian, "but Togi is not very nice."

Overhearing her words, the Historian entered the conversation. "Togi is in league with the Wizard and has been for many, many years."

Lyndi waved her index finger back and forth as though scolding her brother. "I told Togi many times to behave, but he wouldn't listen. At first he would just play pranks, like the time he put elephant noses on deer so they would tip over, or when he made eggs grow on the backsides of gorillas so they couldn't sit down without cracking them. He even made roses sneeze mucus in your face anytime you wanted to smell them!"

Megani smiled at the thought.

"But then," said Lyndi in an admonishing tone, "he began to break the rules by experimenting too much with himself!"

Megani leaned closer, intrigued. "How so?"

"First he made himself taller, then smaller. He made himself look exactly like me once and ran around naked! That was embarrassing. For two hundred years all my brothers and sisters called me 'Naked Lyndi.' But he got worse after all of our brothers and sisters were destroyed by the Beasts of Becus. The Wizards came to defend what was left, and Togi and Zorca became . . . close."

For the first time, Megani noted, Lyndi became angry as she continued to speak. "He's a bad, bad Wizard. He started to disobey Anton. I told Togi that, but he didn't listen. Togi began to change himself a lot in order to help Zorca destroy the Beasts of Becus. I saw him as a bat . . . as a mongoose . . . even as a dragon. But it changed Togi inside, in the way he thinks. He forgot about our good efforts, our reason for being in Trinity, and began only to care about helping Zorca. And so when Zorca became bad, so did Togi."

Megani's eyes flashed. "Beastmaker! He killed my mother!"

"I'm sorry," said Lyndi sadly. "I'm really, truly, very sorry that Togi killed your mother. When the Historian found me years ago and told me that he needed to defeat Zorca, I wanted to help so that I could stop Togi from being such a bad Wallo. I'm sorry I didn't find him in time to help." With tears in her eyes, Lyndi climbed into Megani's arms. "Do you forgive me?"

Megani nodded sadly, her heart breaking. "Yes . . . I do."

"Great!" smiled Lyndi. "Now, let me tell you why I had to make grass green!"

After a time, the companions made camp just southeast of Forge Deep. Lunch was gathered from the surroundings, made more delightful from the added fruits and vegetables that Lyndi knew just where to find. They sat and began to eat.

"I saw you," said Megani to the Historian. "I saw you as the warrior when we were in the Enchanted Forest."

"Yes, as I said before, I fought in many places for many causes."

"What's your name—the one before they called you the Historian?"

He shrewdly looked about. "It's best no one knows, nor that I even whisper it, for even the air has ears. But perhaps someday that will be known." His demeanor told Megani that he spoke the truth once again.

"How did you lose your arm?"

The old man stroked the stump with his right hand then squeezed it tightly.

"I didn't lose it," he said. "I gave it away."

Megani was shocked. "But why would you give it away?!"

"Some things are worth the sacrifice!" He leaned closer. "That's all you need to know for now, for as I said, the air might have ears."

She turned to Kendro. "And you?"

The archer shrugged. "I was one of many who became one of ten— as is Gil. I know him well. He is the finest among us."

"Really?" said Megani with pride. She found herself blushing, and it was noted by those around her.

"You like Gil!" squealed Lyndi.

"No . . . it's not like that," Megani said, trying to shrug it off.

"Yes you do!" continued Lyndi. "What's he like? Is he tall? Does he have nice teeth? Is he happy a lot? What color hair does he have? Do his toes collect fuzzy stuff between them like mine do?"

Megani smiled, still blushing. "He's very nice . . . tall . . . nice teeth

. . . serious more than happy . . . thick brown hair . . . no fuzz that I know of." ·

"Gil is special," added Kendro. "He was the only one of the ten to best me. Then our training sent us in different ways."

"What do you train for?" asked Megani. Then she remembered Gil's quest. "Did you have a message for the Historian, too?"

Kendro nodded. "Yes," he said, and he rolled up his left sleeve to reveal a scar where a tattoo once had been. He rubbed it. "It's inside all of us."

"Inside?" asked Megani. "What is inside?"

Kendro glanced at the Historian and back at Megani. "The air might have ears."

"Ahhhhhhhhrrrrrrrrrrreeeeeeeeeekkkkkkkkkk!"

Without warning, a deafening, high-pitched shriek emanating just north of them pierced the forest. The companions clapped their hands over their ears to shield themselves from the sound. Above their heads, dozens of birds scattered to the south. The birds were followed by dozens of deer, elk, beavers, squirrels, raccoons, and other creatures racing from the forest to escape whatever caused the sound. The shriek came again.

"Ahhhhhhhhrrrrrrrrrrreeeeeeeeeekkkkkkkkkk!"

The ground began to rumble to the north as hundreds of animals stampeded out of the forest to save themselves from whatever was rapidly approaching. The companions banded together to avoid being trampled.

"Ahhhhhhhhrrrrrrrrrrreeeeeeeeeekkkkkkkkkk!"

Just as the stampede passed, a huge black bear emerged from the forest and charged toward the huddled travelers. It stopped short. A Man who had been clinging to the bear's back was hurled forward and landed at the Historian's feet. The bear then followed the rest of the forest animals on their frantic race south. The shriek from the northern forest came again, closer this time.

"Ahhhhhhhhrrrrrrrrrrreeeeeeeeeekkkkkkkkkk!"

The Historian bent down and gazed at the unexpected young Man at his feet. Deep wounds pierced his body and blood flowed freely. He was dying, but he opened his bloodshot eyes and gazed into those of the Historian.

"It's you," the young Man said breathlessly as great relief washed over him. He glanced over at Kendro, who was now at his side. "And you . . . ," he said, forcing a smile through the pain, "my brother Kendro . . . I have been following your trail for days."

"Benkal," said Kendro as he laid the Man's head in his lap.

"Do you have the word?" asked the Historian. He rolled up Benkal's sleeve and found what he searched for, an undamaged tattoo in the form of a G.

Kendro drew a knife and cut a slit around the entire tattoo. Benkal was so delirious with pain from his original wounds that he did not feel any more. Kendro removed the skin and handed it quickly to the Historian, who turned the tattoo over to reveal what lay beneath. He then shoved the bloody patch of skin into his pocket. Benkal took one shallow breath, then another, and died in Kendro's arms.

"Ahhhhhhhhhrrrrrrrrrrreeeeeeeeeekkkkkkkkkk!"

"Devil Rays!" shouted Lyndi as she spied winged beasts approaching quickly from the north. "Darn that Togi. He's been a bad Wallo again!"

Megani caught sight of a dozen fierce-looking winged creatures in the distance. They were sleek, black beasts that glided just above the ground with a wingspan of about four feet from tip to tip. Their form and face were batlike, but she could detect long, sharp talons upon their toes, and each quick flap of their dark wings propelled them ten feet closer.

Kendro looked for cover. "Run!" he shouted as he pulled Lyndi into his arms and dashed toward a large stand of closely packed trees to the south in the hope that they might provide some protection from the large, low-flying beasts. Megani helped the Historian hobble forward, but his pace was too slow. The Devil Rays were within one hundred yards and hurtling toward them fast. A half-minute later, the beasts descended upon Benkal's body and began to wheel about it in tight circles, forming a black cyclone. Around and around they sped as they attacked the body held within their vortex.

"Ahhhhhhhhhrrrrrrrrrrreeeeeeeeeekkkkkkkkkk!"

Megani and the Historian were still twenty yards from the large stand of trees. She looked back just as the Devil Rays ended their feeding frenzy. The beasts shot forward, leaving only Benkal's bones behind them.

Kendro reached the trees, dropped Lyndi within their midst, and returned to the Historian's aid. He picked up the old Man, threw him across his back, and raced toward the trees with Megani in pursuit. But Megani knew that they would never make it to the protection of the trees unless she delayed the beasts.

"Ahhhhhhhhhrrrrrrrrrrreeeeeeeeeekkkkkkkkkk!"

Megani turned and drew her sword. The first of the winged beasts struck. She cut it down, but its forward momentum knocked her to the ground as its carcass tumbled. The other Devil Rays plunged toward her. Her actions gave Kendro and the Historian just enough time to make it safely into the trees.

From a sitting position, Megani struck at the beasts, but they avoided her blade as they whipped in tight circles about her, forming another black vortex of death. One struck her head from behind and knocked her forward. She rolled but immediately came up, blade in hand, hacking the Rays that came closer. With two jabs, she slit three more beasts in half as they rushed by her. The survivors kept a cautious distance but continued to whirl as they sought a vantage point.

Kendro raced toward the spectacle. He could not immediately see Megani within the frenzied cyclone, but then he saw a flash of the sword he had given her. He knew that Megani was still alive. Kendro had only his long knife, a poor weapon against Devil Rays; however, he was sworn to protect his *quest,* and Megani was an integral part of it now. Drawing his blade, he struck. One beast was killed instantly, but the swarm battered him. He tumbled head over heals and rolled to a stop. The beasts remained focused upon Megani; they wanted her most of all, he now knew. Why else would they ignore a Guardian for her? They must have known that Megani was of far more value. He needed to draw their attention to him. But how?

"Ahhhhhhhhrrrrrrrrrrreeeeeeeeeekkkkkkkkkkk!"

The Historian turned to Lyndi, "What can you do from here?!"

The Wallo looked for inspiration. "We're too far away!" she screamed. "Let me look around!" Lyndi dashed deeper into the stand of trees as the old Historian turned back to witness the battle. He wished he could run to his friends' aid, wished he could recover the strength that he felt in the Enchanted Forest, wished he were the Man he had been once, but he could not help. He was barely alive as it was, hanging by a thread for so many, many years. If it were not for Lyndi, he would be dead already.

Looking upon the winged beasts in their fury to kill Megani, Kendro formed an idea. He pulled his sleeve up to reveal the scar where he once carried the tattoo of the Guardian. His only hope was to draw the beasts' attention away from Megani. Long knife in hand, Kendro dashed toward the swarm and launched through it. He flew over Megani's head. With an outstretched hand, he yanked a lock of her red hair from her head and held it high when he flew through the other side of the cyclone. He was battered by the beasts as he exited the vortex. All of the Devil Rays immediately descended upon him, following the scent of Megani's hair and the remnants of the Guardian's tattoo. Kendro had no defense—he had lost his long knife in the cyclone. The Rays fell upon him in a maddening frenzy, leaving Megani battered but alive.

"Ahhhhhhhhrrrrrrrrrreeeeeeeeekkkkkkkkkk!"

Megani looked up and saw the beasts whirling about Kendro. Before she could gain her footing, the winged creatures scattered. She saw Kendro's skeleton on the ground, picked clean.

"Run!" The Historian shouted as the Devil Rays regrouped and barreled toward Megani. She bolted. When she entered the stand of trees, the Historian reached out and pulled her behind a large trunk just as a Devil Ray turned sideways and shot into the forest. The forest was suddenly alive with the beasts as they flung themselves through it in a similar fashion, crisscrossing the stand of trees in a sideways formation in search of their prey. The Historian and Megani slid around the trees again and again to avoid the beasts as they came from different directions. The winged devils shrieked as they came.

"Ahhhhhhhhrrrrrrrrrreeeeeeeeekkkkkkkkkk!"

"I couldn't save him!" Megani shouted above the wailing.

"You did what you could!" returned the Historian as he ducked to avoid a winged beast that sliced through the forest within inches of the old Man. "Their aim was to kill Kendro and all the Guardians, and me, and especially you!"

Megani spied two Devil Rays swiftly winging their way toward her from opposite directions. She ducked quickly. The beasts crashed into each other and spun uncontrollably through the forest, hitting tree trunks.

Megani suddenly, frantically looked about even as she dodged other Devil Rays. "Where's Lyndi?!"

"Don't know!" shouted the Historian as he ducked to avoid another Devil Ray, but the beast struck him hard with the tip of its wing, and the old Man rolled head over heels into a clearing.

"Ahhhhhhhhrrrrrrrrrreeeeeeeeekkkkkkkkkk!"

Devil Rays instantly darted toward him. Knowing she could never reach him in time, Megani saw him struggling to reach his feet. She could do nothing but watch him die, for she had no powers that could come to his aid.

A stream of winged creatures suddenly blew past her in a blur. Their speed was incredible despite the dense foliage that had proven an obstacle to the Devil Rays. Through the haze, she could see that these were not Devil Rays. They were faster, bigger, and darted about with intense accuracy and purpose. They did not shriek—they buzzed!

A Devil Ray shot toward the Historian, but it was knocked into the trees by this new, larger beast: a giant bee. Another Devil Ray attacked, but it, too, was killed when dozens of the giant bees descended upon it. Megani dashed toward the Historian and pulled him to the safety of the trees. Battles erupted all throughout the forest as the Devil Rays were chased and attacked.

A giant bee darted toward Megani. She drew her sword and prepared to strike, but Megani held her blow upon noticing that the bee was not alone.

"Hurrah!" shouted Lyndi, who was upon the bee's back. "My brother HoTo made bees lots of years ago. He wouldn't like it if he knew I made them bigger, so I'll have to make them small again as soon as we're done!" Two giant bees landed beside her. "Get on!" said Lyndi. "We have to fly!"

Megani helped the Historian mount one of the bees. She mounted the other even as the Devil Rays continued to battle with the giant bees around them.

"Beezzz ah ra!" shouted Lyndi, and the three giant bees darted straight upward, above the trees, and then south. The trio held tight as the wind blew past them.

The remaining five Devil Rays followed in close pursuit. Bees followed them, but without the forest trees to restrict their wings, the Devil Rays easily outpaced the pursuing giant bees and rapidly gained on the three bees in front of them.

"They are gaining!" shouted Megani as she looked behind.

Three Devil Rays attacked the Historian's giant bee at once and sliced through one of its wings. The bee tumbled and fell, throwing the Historian into the air. A moment later, Megani's bee was attacked, and it, too, fell.

"HoTo would really hate this!" Lyndi said, and she touched her bee with her index finger.

Megani saw the ground approach and knew she would certainly die. But she landed with a *thump* upon the back of another flying beast.

"Got you!" said Lyndi, who was just behind her.

Startled, Megani looked about. The beast that had caught her had the general shape of a giant bee, but it had scales and an extended head that looked like . . .

"What is this?!" yelled Megani.

"It's two parts bee, one part dragon!" yelled Lyndi. "Let's call it a Dragon Bee."

The Dragon Bee abruptly swooped downward, but Megani held on tight. Wind rushed past her. A moment later, the Historian fell into her lap.

"I'm too old for all this," coughed the old Man.

"Better hold on!" squealed Lyndi with delight.

The Dragon Bee shot up and toward the remaining Devil Rays, which were already on a dive toward it. The Rays opened their jaws and their large talons, but they never got the chance to use them.

The Dragon Bee spewed fire! Caught in the path of the deadly flames, the Devil Rays exploded into ash and smoke. The Dragon Bee then punched right through their remains and zoomed toward a clear blue sky. Moments later, the creature landed at the northern edge of the Plains of Temptation. The rest of the beehive arrived soon thereafter, and Lyndi changed them one at a time back to their former selves. They buzzed away.

When Megani, the Historian, and Lyndi were finally alone, the little Wallo grew sad. "I'll miss Kendro. He made a good mammoth."

Megani shook her head, angry. "Why did Kendro have to die?" She was crushed by Kendro's sacrifice, but her mind also strayed to concerns for Gil. She knew that if the beasts found him, he would meet the same fate as the two Guardians they just left behind.

The Historian leaned close. "Some histories that we think we know are not in fact true. Kendro and Benkal died in order to shed light upon the real past—the *true* past—in hopes that it could be used to defeat the foe before us."

"What *true* past?" questioned Megani.

"I'm not sure myself," said the Historian. "But when all the messages from all the Guardians are assembled, we might have the clue we seek to help us destroy Zorca. That's why Kendro and Benkal died—to save the millions that still live."

Exhausted from the ordeal, the trio fell fast asleep that evening. But the Historian tossed and turned restlessly. In the middle of the night, he rose quietly and moved to the firepit that still burned. He removed nine patches of skin from a pouch within his robe and laid them upon a log. The fire shone dimly upon them. Each patch of skin contained a tattoo on its surface but a word upon the other side—the side that was beneath each man's flesh. The Historian arranged the skin in a line before him, leaving one place always blank because he had only nine of the ten words.

The Blood of ___ Defeats the Blood of the Wizard.

The Historian gazed upon it for a time. He mentally placed potential words in the blank space in an attempt to discern the entire message. Eventually, he rearranged the words.

The Blood of the Wizard Defeats the Blood of ___.

Again he analyzed the sentence, trying to decipher what word might be missing to make this sentence complete. The Historian rearranged the words again.

The ___ of the Wizard Defeats the Blood of Blood.

A pigeon quietly landed upon the old Man's shoulder. "Coo," it called gently.

"Hello, Penelope, my old friend," returned the Historian.

The old Man quickly placed the skin flaps back into his pouch and unrolled the note that was affixed to the pigeon's leg. His eyes opened wide.

"Joh has been busy," he said. The Historian then lifted his right hand and the bird hopped upon it. He brought the pigeon close and whispered into its ear. After a moment, the bird nodded and flew away. The old Man followed it with his eyes as it disappeared into the night.

"I need you, Gil," he said to himself. "You are the last of your kind, and you have to stay alive long enough to get to me. The world depends upon it!"

CHAPTER 12

BATTLE RUN

The trio was weary from the hard-fought battle the day before. Allo's right arm was in a sling, having taken a brutal gorging by a serpent. Drak had a blood-stained bandage around his head. Only Gil was unscathed as he led the way through the sparse wilderness just east of Spirit Lake. His plan was to guide them across the southern plains of Trinity to reach the Straits of Devils in order to deliver the fragments of the Sword to Megani. The pieces of the blade were still wrapped in cloth and now strapped to Gil's back. The responsibility was far heavier than the actual weight. It was midday, the sun was shining bright, and a gentle breeze came from the east. They had not spoken for hours.

Gil stopped and scanned a meadow that was nestled within a stand of tall pines. "We can rest here a while."

Allo and Drak sat upon a fallen tree.

Drak fumed, "I shouldn't have to lose a point because I hit myself with my own ax!"

"It's a self-inflicted wound," said Allo. "All self-inflicted wounds take points away, and in your case, caused your skull to crack open." Allo smiled. "So I'm ahead by one."

"Who makes up all these rules?" grunted Drak.

"We have—for years. Three summers ago you would not let me take a point when I mistakenly shot myself in the toe with my own arrow. So I won't let you take a point now for pounding your skull with your own ax. Fair is fair."

"Then you shouldn't get a point because the serpent chewed on your arm," Drak argued. "I could have had the serpent take a bit out of me, too!"

"It's an honorable battle wound," returned the Elf. "I didn't mean for it to happen, but it did. We each get points for honorable wounds inflicted by the enemy. That rule is at least ten years old."

Gil smiled. Though he had originally found his companions' banter annoying, Gil now appreciated the sound. He knew that their friendly competition took their minds away from their grief. He suspected that they knew it, too. With the Dwarf and Elf still discussing the rules, Gil wandered away to gather wood for a fire.

When Gil was out of earshot, Drak pointed toward the woodsman and whispered to Allo, "How many?"

Allo shook his head and said in amazement, "Gil killed as many as ours combined. And he paralyzed others without hurting them at all."

"But he didn't have any weapons!"

Allo patted Drak on the shoulder. "And he didn't need any when he bested us, either."

While they were talking, a deer appeared from behind a tree across the meadow. Drak slowly rose to his feet and drew his ax, the taste of deer meat already in his mouth. He took deadly aim as the creature bent to nibble slender blades of grass at its feet. The Dwarf threw his ax. It tumbled end over end on its deadly approach, but before it struck, it was pulled from the sky by Gil, who caught the blade in midair, tumbled to the forest floor, and rolled several times before bouncing back to his feet. He tossed the ax back toward Drak. The blade struck the fallen tree just inches from the Dwarf.

Annoyed, Drak pulled his ax from the tree and slid it back into his belt. "Will somebody please tell me what I can and can't kill, and when? I think I need it written down so I can refer to it often. Maybe it should be a nice chart with pictures. Kill the serpent, but not the deer— but only if Gil says so!"

Gil approached the deer quietly, and they sniffed each other. The young Man began to make clicking sounds, and the deer did the same. Gil patted the deer for a while and then followed it into the deeper forest. He returned minutes later with his firewood, along with assorted berries.

"Here's lunch," Gil said as he placed the food in front of them. "The deer showed me where to find it."

"Great," said Drak sarcastically. "More berries. We've been eating these for days. I was hoping for a real meal. You know, meat, and perhaps some more meat—and then maybe more meat. I think my skin is beginning to turn blue with all these berries. And worse, eating just berries makes me . . ."

"Constipated," finished Allo. "We know. We all know." Allo turned to Gil. "This will do nicely, thank you." Allo truly was thankful for the meal, and he had come to greatly admire Gil's respect for life.

Drak threw Allo an evil look, whispering, "And I suppose you get a point for kissing Man butt!"

Allo ignored the gruff Dwarf and turned to Gil while they ate. "What was it like to be in the deep wilderness for so long?"

Gil looked north as his mind wandered. "It was hard at first, strange later, comprehensible at last. Everythin' has a rhythm to it—the seasons of course, but also the plants and the animals—and even the rain and the rivers. More things can *think* than we give credit. There is a vast awareness out there. Most people can never see or appreciate it."

"We were in the deep wilderness," Drak added proudly. "We just completed our two weeks of warrior training before tragedy befell us."

Gil shook his head. "I'm sure you proved much and have a lot to be proud of, but you were not in the *deep* wilderness."

"Of course we were," contradicted Allo. "We marched a week due west into the Western Expanse and then a week's march out. We confronted a bear, a lion, a tiger, and even the giant serpents."

Gil smiled. "Walk west in the Expanse for a hundred days, and that begins the true deep."

"It doesn't go that far!" exclaimed Drak.

"How would you know if you've never been there?" asked Gil. "But that's where the deep truly begins, and then it continues for ten times that far. There are beasts in the deep that are too gruesome for words. The lions and bears you speak of stay near the edge of the forest because they fear the deep. The serpents would not survive it either."

"Then how did you?" asked Allo.

Gil looked at each of his companions and drew a breath. He had never told a soul about his experience in the true wilds. In part, his secrecy was because of his responsibility, his quest, which needed to be guarded. But it was also a painful memory. However, with the world in turmoil, he now felt a bit comforted to share at least some of what he could.

"Thirty of us started. All were skilled, but only twenty of us lived long enough to make it to the wilds. Ten of us survived the rest."

"If they were so skilled, why did so many die?" asked Drak.

Gil closed his eyes, but he could not close out the memories and the screams of those who had met a hideous fate. "Some were killed by armies of killer ants that were as big as bears. Hundreds swarmed about us for days. Some were killed by packs of Terra Lizards that could spit poison a hundred yards. Still others died in swamps, pulled under by giant squids. And then there were giant flowers that ate meat—human meat. Others among us were never found, so we have no idea what became of 'em."

Allo leaned close. "But why? What's the purpose for so many to die? Why did the thirty venture that far into the Western Expanse to begin with?"

Gil rubbed the tattoo on his left arm, still hidden by his brown leather jersey. "They want the strongest—always the strongest—in body, in mind. They look for those who can learn and adapt, for those who can become a part of the wilds itself. So in each generation, the youth are selected from the descendents of those who have gone before. Those who are judged good enough are sent as a group into the forest . . . to find the wilds. The ten who emerge are the very best. And so their descendents are sent again and again. It has been that way for more than a thousand years."

"Why?" asked Drak.

Gil knew he could not provide the whole truth, but he would tell them what he could. "So that we are ready to confront dangers," he said. "In one way or another, the world always seems to get itself in a fix. We were trained to look for signs of trouble, and should they come, to be prepared to defeat 'em."

Drak grunted. "Like now."

"Like now," confirmed Gil.

"How long were you there?" asked Allo.

"Couple years. Ten of us survived, as ten always do. That's when the Shaman came."

Drak gasped. "I have heard that name—an ancient people. I thought they were a myth to scare children from venturing into the forests."

Gil smiled. "They scare more than children. They are ancient, datin' back to the first arrival of the Races. If you can make it as deep into the wilderness as where the Shaman live, they figure your worth trainin' further. Each Shaman took a different youth. From then on, it was me and a Shaman. He taught me a lot about the world: about how we are all connected, about the wilds in the forest . . . and the wilds within each of us. In many ways, the Shaman were the first Races. They stayed pure to Anton's creations. They didn't take part in the so-called civilization that began to pull us from bein' in touch with the natural world."

Allo nodded. "I see."

Drak grew restless. "I don't know what that nature stuff is all about, but tell me how you kill a giant ant."

Gil smiled. "You kill it with patience, lots and lots of patience." Then he winked, "And a bit of poisoned sugar."

Allo smiled wide. "If it's patience that's needed, then Drak would be dead."

Gil became silent. Even though he felt connected to nature, and to his new companions, he also felt very alone. That was the way of the Shaman. They lived alone and died alone. It was a life of self-reliance. It was a life of *one* against the forces of nature. And that's what they taught the Guardians—to survive no matter what, to use God-given natural instincts to stay alive—no matter what. Gil was an orphan, every bit as much as Allo and Drak, and though he did not feel entirely comfortable being the caretaker of his new companions, he felt a deep kinship in the hardships they had each faced together. Gil was a loner by training, but he appreciated the company of Allo and Drak more than they could ever know.

A deer appeared at the edge of the meadow and began to gently nibble at the slender blades of grass. Drak spied it first.

"I can be every bit as patient as any Elf," the Dwarf said as he rose and gently strolled over to greet the deer.

Allo grinned. "A point if you can even touch it!"

Drak nodded, smiling. "That's very generous of you. Agreed."

Gil looked past the Dwarf and saw the deer. He knew instantly that it was not the one he had befriended earlier. Drak crept closer. The deer moved slowly toward the Dwarf, sniffing the air cautiously as it came. Gil rose to his feet and inspected the creature from afar. It looked exactly as a deer should, but Gil's senses told him that something was not right. The deer did not move altogether like a deer, and only Gil could sense the difference. Its footsteps were more like that of a small horse, and the slight bobbing of its head was more like that of a jackal. The creature was trying very hard to be a deer, but it was not. Gil suddenly saw its small tail. It was a deer's tail in form, but it was arched slightly upward and curved forward like a . . .

"Stop!" shouted Gil to Drak. "Back up!"

"I want this point," said the Dwarf while moving closer to the advancing deer.

But it was too late. The deer transformed into a giant scorpion. It shot its tail forward and punctured Drak's left shoulder. The Dwarf fell to his knees, shuttered, and then dropped hard upon his back.

Two arrows sped toward the beast, shot by Allo, who had whipped his arm out of its sling in order to deliver the points. Easily, the scorpion brushed the arrows aside with its tail. Blood oozing from his wounds, the Elf loaded his bow a third time. Gil was suddenly upon the scorpion, tackling the beast by the tail and holding firmly so that the deadly point could not be used against him. The creature tried to turn itself upon Gil but could not remove itself from his grip. Unsuccessful at ridding itself of Gil, the scorpion turned into a giant snake, but the young Man immediately reached out and grabbed it by the back of the neck. The snake recoiled about him, but the frontiersman braced his vicelike knees against the coil and refused to let it tighten further. The end of the snake's tail began to wrap about the cloth containing the Sword, which was still strapped to Gil's back. At that moment, an arrow struck the snake in its mouth.

"RRRRRRRRRRR!" it shrieked in pain as it turned into a raging bull, the arrow stuck within its massive jaw. Gil grabbed the beast by its horns and threw himself upon its back. He locked his arms about its neck in an attempt to strangle the creature. Another arrow struck its chest, then another, as the beast struggled to dislodge its unwanted rider. The bull suddenly reared up and Gil was thrown wide. The bull leaped into the air, instantly transforming itself into a huge eagle as two more arrows sped toward it, narrowly missing their target. Gil recognized the eagle immediately as the same beast that had robbed Cyrus Del's grave of its ashes. It must have been the same bad omen he had seen in the Valley of Despair. The bird escaped, but it still had three arrows embedded within it.

Allo and Gil raced to Drak. The Dwarf's eyes were nearly shut, and his body was shivering with cold.

"We're tied," Drak said to Allo just as his eyes rolled back into his head.

"What attacked him?!" shrieked Allo.

"The Beastmaker. Yet another sign of the *Coming.*" He wondered again why the creature had stolen Cyrus Del's ashen remains. But that would have to wait.

"The coming of what?"

"Of another age, a deadly one . . . unless we can prevent it."

Allo swallowed hard, motioning to Drak, who was now in his arms. "Is he dead?"

"No, not yet . . . ," began Gil. "But we need to get some toga roots to prevent the poison from spreading." Gil dashed into the forest. He returned in moments, bearing a handful of freshly cut roots. He chewed some of them in his mouth until they had the consistency of juicy syrup. Opening the Dwarf's mouth, he spit the contents into it. He moved the Dwarf's jaws back and forth in order to send the syrup into Drak's stomach.

Allo followed Gil's lead and did the same. "Just nasty," he said the first time he spit the juice into Drak's mouth, but then he repeated the process again and again.

Gil spat some of the syrup into the Dwarf's wounds as well and then bandaged them. "That's all we can do for now. We'll know in an hour or so if the roots will do any good."

The ground suddenly rumbled. Gil and Allo looked west to see nearly a hundred serpents absent their Gorgon bodies slithering toward them. Even if Drak and Allo were well, Gil knew, they would be no match for the vast numbers of demons that rapidly approached.

Allo threw Drak across his back. "Lash him to me!"

In a moment, Gil had tied the Dwarf tightly to his friend.

"Follow me!" Gil shouted as he began to sprint east—on all four limbs! Allo was shocked at Gil's ability to run like a leopard, bouncing over fallen trees and rocks as though born a beast himself. Allo followed behind him as fast as he could.

Despite Gil and Allo's quick retreat, serpents appeared in front of them. Gil leaped high into the air and bounced only feet above their straining jaws. Allo stayed low and managed to duck beneath the beasts, which were more focused upon Gil, or more accurately, they were focused upon the Sword fragments that were still strapped to Gil's back.

After several miles at a full run, with one hundred serpents behind them, Gil dashed toward a narrow ravine that plunged between two sharply rising hills. He sped to the opening of the crevice and ran to the end of the pass. Allo barely followed his lead, as Drak's weight was formidable. After several minutes, the serpents charged into the ravine in full pursuit. The crevice proved narrow for their numbers, so they began to slither atop each other as they pushed forward. Reaching a jagged wall of rock at the end of the ravine, Gil scampered upward, leaping from rock outcropping to rock outcropping as a mountain goat might. Allo struggled but did his best to mimic Gil's animal-like movements. It brought him to the top of the cliff just as the serpents reached the end of the ravine and began to slither upward along the same path.

Gil looked about and found several huge rocks. He used Drak's ax as leverage to pry the boulders from their resting spots. One fell with a heavy thud upon the serpents that were rising to the top. Crushed, they fell back into the hordes below. Allo and Gil began to drop more rocks into the ravine, creating an avalanche. Hundreds of rocks and tons of dirt began to fall upon the beasts, which began to wail in pain.

Gil bolted over the hill and down into the eastern plains with Allo beside him all the way. For the moment, they were free of the serpents, but they kept a brisk pace nonetheless.

"Let me carry Drak!" Gil shouted as he reached for the Dwarf on Allo's back.

"No!" came the Elf's response. "He is mine!"

After an hour's run, Gil repeated his request. The answer was the same; the Elf harshly refused to relinquish the weight of his friend. It was testimony, Gil knew, to the depth of their friendship.

After several hours of running with little rest, they spied columns of smoke rising from the land beyond. As they approached, they saw farms on fire, and just northeast of their position, the township of Peaceful Springs was consumed by a fiery blaze. They knew there was little help they could offer. They waded across Zak's River, drinking precious water as they hurried, and then continued their trek east.

Dashing over a rise, they came to a skidding stop. A thousand Gorgons stood just one hundred yards before them, milling about. The beasts suddenly turned and gazed at them. A moment of silence reigned.

Allo gasped for air. "Any ideas?"

Gil breathed hard. "None whatsoever."

The twosome dashed south, Drak still strapped to Allo's back, the Sword still tied to Gil's. One thousand Gorgons gave chase. Allo and Gil were spent, and they knew they could not outpace the Gorgons in their current condition. The beasts were now only ninety yards behind them. Then seventy. Then only fifty.

A pigeon soared past Gil's head. "Coo roo-c'too-coo."

Gil, though still at a dead run, looked up excitedly. He answered the bird's call: "Coo roo roo rah."

The pigeon circled and appeared again near Gil's shoulder, flying to keep the slower pace of the humans. "Roo-c'too-coo-roo."

Gil responded again. "Coo roo coo."

The pigeon then flew due south. Gil followed, trying to keep pace with the bird. A pool of water became visible in the distance. Steam rose from its surface. As the group drew closer, they could see that the water was fed by a large stream running off Zak's River. The water coalesced and whirled toward the center before being pulled downward to an unknown destiny. This was the Drowning Pool, a liquid death that all in Trinity avoided.

The mass of Gorgons was thirty yards behind. They began to scoop up huge boulders as they ran, hurling them at the companions. The rocks pounded the ground just behind Gil and Allo's feet.

"You're going to have to trust me on this!" shouted Gil.

"With my life!" answered the Elf.

The pigeon flew to the pool and hovered momentarily right above the surface of the water, which swirled and plunged downward beneath its wings. It then shot across the pool toward the forest beyond and was gone.

"Haaaa!" screeched Allo as a rock hit the back of his leg. The Elf went down hard and Drak with him. Gil immediately turned, pulled Allo to his feet, and yanked Drak into his own arms.

"He's mine for the moment!" Gil shouted as the beasts drew nearer.

They lost what little ground they had gained. The serpent arms of dozens of Gorgons in the lead shot outward toward Gil and Allo. Gil turned and bolted once—then again—and landed with a heavy splash in the Drowning Pool. Allo plunged in beside him. The serpents and Gorgons stopped at the shore and watched anxiously as their prey were pulled under by the strong current. It whipped the trio in circles, around and around, and closer and closer to the center, where the water plummeted downward. In a heartbeat they were gone, sucked beneath the surface.

The beasts hesitated. One Gorgon stepped into the shallows of the pool.

"Not good," cautioned another. The first Gorgon stepped out again.

The beasts knew very little, but one thing had been made clear to them by their master: They were never, ever to enter the Drowning Pool. It was forbidden. So a thousand Gorgons—with their two thousand serpent arms—surrounded the pool's banks for many hours in the hope that their enemies would suddenly reappear. But they did not. And to the world, they were certainly dead.

CHAPTER 13

PLAINS OF TEMPTATION

"Kendro saved my life," lamented Megani again as she and her companions marched south.

"And in so doing," said the Historian, "he probably has saved Trinity."

"He played a good mammoth, too," said Lyndi sadly.

Megani pleaded with the Historian to share more. "Where did he come from? He died so that I would live; I deserve to know more about him."

The Historian looked toward the retreating sun and paused, scanning the beginnings of the Plains of Temptation before them. He knew it was best that they rest before they entered the foreboding lands on their journey toward the narrow waterway that separated Trinity from Devon. "Let's stop for a while."

The trio found a clearing, foraged for food, and began to eat. The Historian glanced about the clearing and then turned to Megani. "Well, if the air has ears," he began, "it probably already knows what I can tell you."

"Oh, goodie!" said Lyndi as she drew closer. "You know, I never tried to give the air ears, but I could try if you want me to." The little Wallo began to examine a miniscule spec of air in front of her nose. She brought her finger up to it.

The Historian closed his hand around hers. "That won't be necessary," he told Lyndi.

Megani smiled at her young, yet ancient friend. She turned to the Historian, "Please continue."

"As you probably know, the Sword and Stone were forged ages ago by Zorca in order to transfer the magic from the remaining Wizards. The magic of the Stone was eventually transferred to your bloodline so that you would possess it at birth. While the Sword is a magnificent weapon in its own right, the true purpose of the blade was to pull the magic out of the Wizard."

"That account is in the Book of Endur," said Megani. "I'm aware of it. The birth of the Sword was also when my ancestor Pita faltered and ran—ran from a beast and nearly got her father killed." Megani's heart sank. She, too, must have looked so much like Pita when she bolted from the Wizard after her mother's murder.

The Historian's eyes met hers. "You are not Pita," he said, knowing full well the burden of her thoughts. "More importantly, we cannot be sure of the history that transpired on that day. Some histories are not as accurate as we might hope."

"But it was recorded in the Book of Endur," said Megani, "by the great Etha Lorelii. . . . It must be true! I read it myself."

"Truth can be manipulated, created, changed. Just as Zorca manipulated the Elves and Dwarves into believing that the other was guilty of murder, so too is it believed that Lorelii and all those present that day were deceived by Zorca."

Megani's eyes grew narrow. "So the Wizard was planning his betrayal from the beginning."

"Yes."

"But how do we know what truly happened on the day the Sword was created?"

"Near her death," began the Historian, "Lorelii came to believe that there was an alternate history—a true history—that transpired that day. She could not commit it to the Book of Endur for she was afraid that it would be too easily captured or misused. Instead, she convinced a society of ancient ones known as Shaman to be responsible for training ten Guardians of each generation to secure a part of a message that she devised. Should the time arise when a Wizard threatened the world, the Guardians would seek me, the Historian, to deliver their messages. Each message alone means nothing. Together, they mean everything. I only discovered my role a couple of decades ago by another message handed down within my family for generations. Lorelii was very cautious and shrewd."

Megani leaned close. "And what is the message supposed to reveal?"

"Yes!" said Lyndi. "Tell us. I love secrets!"

The Historian patted Lyndi on the head. "I don't know. Hopefully it will tell us how to kill the Wizard, but I don't have all of the messages yet; I'm missing just one more."

Megani raised an eyebrow. "You are missing Gil's message."

"Yes. He's the last Guardian. He holds the final message, which will help me decipher the rest."

"What pieces do you have so far?" asked Lyndi. "I'm good with puzzles. I once turned a river into jelly with just fifty tries. It took me a long time to figure out how, but I did it. Then one time my sister Jenta asked me to help her make bananas with arms so that they could peel themselves. We did it! But it didn't turn out too good. They kept slapping people away who wanted to eat them."

"Not this time," said the Historian with a gentle smile. "This is a puzzle for me alone to solve. Your lives would be in even greater peril if I shared it with you. It's my burden."

"Why were you chosen?" asked Megani. The Historian always spoke the truth, she could tell, but there was still a mystery surrounding this Man. Why him? She thought of his bigger-than-life appearance in the mist of the Enchanted Forest. He was connected to this in more ways than he would tell.

The Historian's shrewd eyebrows arched upward. "It has fallen to me because my work on Trinity is not yet done." He nodded toward Lyndi. "It's like her work. I believe that Lyndi's escape from the Beasts of Becus ages ago was a result of a higher power who knew she was needed here . . . now . . . with us."

"If Anton is watching," said Megani as she grew rigid, "why can't he just take Zorca out of Trinity? Why put us through all of this torment?"

"Because," began Lyndi in such a mature tone that it stole Megani's breath away, "our Lord created each of us to do as we would in this world. The Wizard is as much his creation as are you. He puts his faith in us, but we are the ones who must demonstrate that his faith is warranted. These events will either sharpen our ability to survive or destroy us completely. If we are destroyed, then Anton's faith in us was unfounded to begin with."

Megani put an arm around Lyndi. "Is that what you discovered when nearly all your brothers and sisters were destroyed by the Beasts of Becus?"

Lyndi nodded. "Had we been stronger, we would not have been killed so easily. But we were too trusting—too innocent—to destroy the Beasts, and so they destroyed us. We could not see their evil. We thought they would eventually be good, but they wouldn't. We were too good to see the evil in others and so my brothers and sisters were destroyed. It proved we were not strong enough to be given this land as our own; we trusted too easily. Anton then sent the Wizards to destroy the Beasts of Becus, but they were too cold, too prone to evil themselves, and so Anton sent the Races, which are mostly good but with just enough specks of distrust and evil that they can better recognize and battle greater evils. But it can be their undoing as well."

"The Elves and Dwarves . . . ," began Megani. "They were made so rigid by honor and duty that they could not pause long enough to understand what was being done to them."

"Just like the First and Second Race Wars," interjected the Historian. "The Elves and Dwarves fought mostly for so-called honor. It got in the way of reason and compassion. Only Man could see the difference, and it was our Race that sought to end both wars because of it."

Megani could see the logic of it. While Zorca had provided the spark, it was truly the Elves and Dwarves that created the bloodshed. The Wizard knew that their imperfections could be used against them. She wondered what the Wizard would use against her. What was the imperfection it could exploit? Megani shook her head. She seemed to have more imperfections than she could count.

Lyndi suddenly grew a big smile. "Do you want to know why we made it rain from the sky down instead of from the ground up? There's a reason, you know. Or maybe you want to know why we gave birds wings to fly? Because we could have made them fly around by expelling gas out their behinds. We tried that once, but the birds had trouble stopping; they kept slamming into trees. It made a big mess—feathers everywhere. Not to mention the smell. So we took the gas power away and gave them wings again. There were fewer crashes after that, and the air smelled better too."

After dinner, the trio approached the northern origins of the Plains of Temptation.

"I have never entered this land," said Megani. "My father kept it off limits, as he did the Enchanted Forest, and for that matter, Devon."

"He was wrong to do so!" snapped the Historian. "What a stupid decision!"

"How dare you!" cried Megani, more forceful than she had planned. No one had ever admonished her father before. "Have you forgotten that he destroyed Pure Evil?!"

"And yet," said the Historian, "he was still wrong!"

"Why?!"

The old Man shook his head. "You can't understand the world around you by avoiding it. You have to seek it out, face it, understand it . . . and defeat it if need be."

"But my father protected the peoples of Trinity from anything that would do them harm."

"That was the problem," explained the Historian. "After Pure Evil was destroyed, his responsibility to protect the Races ended. By trying to protect them further, he made them rely too much on him and not on themselves."

"That's not true!" blurted Megani.

"Then how do you explain Olive Branch?" asked the old Man as he continued to hobble along. "They were so defenseless it was shameless. They so expected to be taken care of—for you to fight their battles— that they surrendered themselves to fate. All those people, and not one among them could face a Gorgon on a bridge. Ridiculous!"

Megani glared at the old Man, but his words rang true. Following her father's lead, she too rushed to help others. In Olive Branch, instead of training the people how to kill a Gorgon, she had done it for them. Did she contribute to Man's weakness? Those in Olive Branch proved they were so accustomed to being taken care of that they began to expect it. Gratitude turned to entitlement. Could her father have been wrong to protect the peoples of Trinity so thoroughly? Among the Race of Man, only those in Meadowtown were altogether different. After the famed battle, the inhabitants rebuilt their town into a fortress. History made them cautious, and the events of the past week demonstrated that it was for good reason.

"Jason Del was too stubborn," continued the Historian in a disapproving voice. "He thought his reasoning was as strong as his powers. That's always a mistake. For many years there were hideous stories coming from Devon, but he paid little attention to them. He saw his task limited to Trinity. He protected the people from minor things here, while allowing a great threat to grow elsewhere."

Megani fumed. "But Devon was not our task. It has only become a threat now, at this time."

"Wrong again!" the old Man barked, his face flustered. "You cannot wait until a growing danger strikes; you must act while it is small enough to handle. But your father would not listen to reason. At the same time that Jason made the Races in Trinity too dependent upon him for their safety, he also allowed the danger that would undo them to expand. So it's no wonder that terror struck at the moment Jas died. He should have listened to . . . to . . . ," he stumbled as though trying to find the right words, " . . . his father, Cyrus! *He* understood the threat!"

The old Man began to shake and suddenly fell to the ground. His breath was shallow and uneven, his face drained of color. Megani was at his side, but Lyndi nudged her out of the way. The Wallo placed her hands across the old Man's chest, and Megani noted a slight glow emanate from them.

"You can't get angry like you used to," Lyndi warned. "I can't repair it all." Lyndi began to gently move her hands down his chest to his stomach and then up again in slow circles. She sang softly, "La de da . . . la de da . . . hoop a da . . . la de da!"

Megani looked in awe. "You're keeping him alive!"

"Yes," said Lyndi, "but it's hard. Too many puzzle pieces no longer fit. That's what happens when someone from the Man Race gets to be around the age of . . ."

"Quiet," coughed the Historian. "Just repair me long enough . . . just long enough . . ." He drifted off to sleep.

Megani turned to Lyndi. "Will he be alright?"

"Yes . . . for now," said the Wallo.

"Then it was you who healed me of my cuts and bruises soon after we met."

"Yes," said Lyndi as she continued to rub her hands upon the old Man. "That was easy compared to this." She shook her head as she gazed back at the Historian, who was still fast asleep. "There are just too many parts that no longer fit."

The old Man stirred something within Megani. She felt connected to him in ways she could not explain. And he had called her father "Jas," short for "Jason." No one in her memory, with the one exception of Squeaky Joh, his childhood friend, was ever that familiar with Jason Del. And he admitted being at the battle with Pure Evil alongside her father and her grandfather Cyrus.

"Who is he?" she asked aloud.

Lyndi smiled. "He is someone who cares a lot about Trinity . . . and about you."

"Am I related to him?" Megani questioned as she raised his eyelids and gazed into his brown eyes.

"What are you looking for?" Lyndi asked.

"All Dels have green eyes and red hair," Megani said. "His eyes are brown and what little hair I can see upon his bald scalp is either dark blond or gray."

"Then I guess he's not a Del," Lyndi concluded.

Megani sat back, unsatisfied. The nagging feeling of familiarity remained.

Within an hour, darkness set in, and the plains turned cold. The

Historian woke with renewed strength thanks to a short sleep and the healing powers of the Wallo. With the Historian once again upon his feet, the trio turned south to enter the Plains of Temptation.

"What can we expect there?" asked Megani while keeping a watchful eye on both the plains before them and the Historian.

"The Plains of Temptation are what they are," he said with a slight cough. "It offers us what we most desire. It can be quite enticing, and always comforting. But some comforts are not what they seem."

"It's a trap then."

"No, it doesn't have to be," answered the Historian. "It can also be a way of helping each of us better understand our true selves. It becomes a trap only if you want it to become one, and then you will be lost to Trinity forever. Those who pass through are stronger for the experience. Those who don't . . ."

"You mean we might be lost!"

"We might. As I said, the plains offers you what you want most, and it is prepared to give it to you for eternity."

Megani thought of their need to reach Devon. "How do we resist?"

"I don't know; each time is different."

"Then you have done this before?"

"I have, and as you can see, I made it out safely." He winked.

"Did my father enter the Plains of Temptation?"

"Oh heavens, no," said the Historian. "I tried to convince him to enter, but he refused."

"Why?"

"He wasn't in pursuit of comforts or temptations. He wanted only to restore Trinity to what it had been before the Beasts of Becus tore it apart, and so he avoided this part of the land and cautioned others to avoid it as well."

"Did my grandfather Cyrus Del venture here?"

The Historian shot a stern glance toward Megani, but then it softened into a subtle smile. "Yes, and he was lost here."

"Lost? But I thought he died while traveling north with my father. He was cremated there and his ashes brought back to the Fallen's Memorial long before I was even born."

"He was, but only after being lost upon these plains for several years as he searched for a truth among the falsehoods."

The Historian signaled his companions to pause. He took another ten paces to a tree that heralded the beginnings of the Plains of Temptation. The land before them was sparsely dotted with vegetation. The old Man reached his hand forward, and the air seemed to ripple like water at his touch. He extended his hand another few inches, and it disappeared before their eyes. He pulled his hand out and it appeared again.

"We are here," he declared.

"Perhaps we should go around it," suggested Megani.

"But that would add to our time, and we might need every hour."

"We're here!" chimed in Lyndi. "Goodie, goodie! I always wanted to come." The little girl darted toward the barrier. Megani leaped to catch her, but the Wallo plunged through and vanished.

"I tried to stop her!" Megani cried as she rose from her belly, where she had landed after her failed attempt to catch Lyndi.

The Historian smiled softly. "Why?"

"To save her!"

"She knows of the plains and of its dangers."

Megani paused. She had done what she always did: tried to save people from whatever dangers might exist. It was habit. She tried to squeeze all the dangers out of the world in an effort to protect the peoples of the land. Yet if she did, she would be depriving them of the dangers and the thrills and the learning that living can provide. She took a breath. Megani truly liked Lyndi, and she would have to have faith that the little Wallo would be able to take care of herself.

"I guess it's my turn," Megani said.

"No . . . it's mine," said the Historian. "I'll see you on the other side, at the straits." He took a couple of steps forward and was gobbled up by the air.

Megani took another deep breath and entered.

"I found you!" said Jason Del as he pulled a seven-year-old Megani from beneath their family table and swung her to his shoulders. Megani held on tight to her loving father with both hands by gripping his forehead in a hug. She smelled his hair, still thick and red, but with gray sprinkled about the edges. His left hand held her firmly on his shoulders; his right arm steadied her from falling backward, but it was absent of a hand, a casualty of her father's heroic battle with Pure Evil. Their small, cozy cottage was warm and inviting, with a steady, crackling fire in the hearth. A window allowed the glowing light of the Farlo branches that were wrapped around the window frame to enter the cottage with a lively, dancing glow.

"It's time for bed," said Bea. Megani looked across the room and watched as her beautiful mother pulled back the sheets of her warm bed. Bea smiled wide, her large blue Ethan eyes sparkling, her face perfectly framed by her snow-white hair. Jason carried Megani to the bed and placed her among the warm sheets.

"I love you, Mommy and Daddy!" sighed Megani as she settled down for a long rest. She nestled her head deep into her large feather pillow.

"We love you, too!" replied Bea as she placed a light, tender kiss on Megani's forehead. Jason Del did the same.

"Do I *have* to learn more about my powers tomorrow?" asked Megani sadly. She had asked this question every night for as long as she could remember, but the answer was always yes. She always hoped for a no.

But on this night, Jason Del shook his head and smiled. "No, my little one, you no longer have to learn about your powers, and you don't have to use them again. Never, ever again."

Megani's heart leaped with joy. The little girl did not like the powers; they scared her. It was too much responsibility. She wanted only to be normal like all the other children in Meadowtown, surrounded by loving parents who would accept her as herself. Megani pulled the sheets up around her neck and felt the warmth envelop her. She would never, ever again have to learn about her powers or use them.

"I want to stay here forever," Megani said sweetly. "Forever."

Her father smiled. "And so you can . . . stay with us . . . forever."

"I'm so glad Anton gave us a daughter," said her mother. "It was truly a blessing."

Megani melted. All her life, she had known that her mother wanted a son, but now, Bea finally appreciated the daughter born to her. Megani faded to sleep and slept more soundly and contently than she had ever done before.

Three days went by and seven-year-old Megani remained completely, heavenly happy. She never knew such bliss. Within the four walls of the cozy cottage, there existed only fun, love, and acceptance. As she drifted off to sleep toward the end of the third day, she woke with a fright. Lightning blasted through the small window of their cottage. Thunder rumbled.

"Daddy! Daddy!" Megani screamed.

Jason and Bea Del jumped to their daughter's cot. "You are safe with us," Jason comforted. Lightning struck again.

Bang!

The door to the cottage blew open and a large, threatening figure entered. He was drenched from the rain and wearing the leathers of a warrior. A glistening ax hung from his belt, and a sword was sheathed upon his back.

Jason Del blocked the path to Megani. "You're not welcome here!" he said. Megani craned her head past her father to get a better look at the intruder.

"She's coming with me!" the stranger said, his voice deep and sure.

The warrior's face was familiar, thought Megani. Very familiar. It looked like an older version of Jason Del himself. Though they had never met, Megani strangely knew his name.

"Grandpa Cyrus!" she screamed with delight. Megani tried to rush forward, but her father held her back.

"She's content here!" said Jason Del.

"Which is why she must come with me," asserted Cyrus. "No one should be as content as this."

Boom!

A blast of raw energy exploded from Jason Del's fist and flew toward Cyrus. Intense light flashed about the cottage. Air was sucked out of Megani's lungs by the force, and the siren sound was deafening. She clasped her hands over her ears to prevent them from shattering.

As fast as Jason Del had loosed the power at him, Cyrus had drawn his blade. Its brilliance shone a stabbing bright light of its own, but Megani could not take her eyes from it. It was the *Sword of Legends,* the one Grandpa Cyrus used to help his son, Jason, thwart Pure Evil, the very Sword that was created by Wizards and entrusted to the Royal House of Del. Her father's power rocked the small cottage, but it could not touch Cyrus. As Jason directed the power so that it would avoid the Sword and smash into his father, Cyrus brandished the blade quickly and efficiently to counter the force. The fiery blasts were absorbed by the Sword itself.

Frightened little Megani could not understand why her father and grandfather were fighting . . . and over her! The small cottage rumbled, and Megani and Bea were thrown to their knees. Her mother crawled to Megani and hugged her daughter close.

"There, there," Bea soothed. "It will be alright. *We live for you alone!*"

Megani shuttered at the words. They were oddly foreign to her. Her mother would never have said that. Never. Jason and Bea lived first and foremost for Trinity, and Megani knew, deep down in her heart, that she was a second thought. She looked about. She suddenly realized that in the last several days, she had never gone outside, had never seen the Trinity that her parents loved so. The world—her world—had become this cottage . . . this place.

Cyrus continued to pivot and plunge his Sword to prevent the deadly blasts from striking him. "I can't hold him off much longer!" Cyrus yelled.

Megani was drawn to his voice. She pulled away from her mother and scrambled across the floor and under the family's large oak table. She held tightly to the table's leg.

"You have a choice!" shouted Grandpa Cyrus as he continued to swing his blade to and fro. "You can stay here or come with me!"

"How do I decide?!" screamed Megani in tears.

"I'll decide for you!" cried Jason. "You'll stay here and be content forever!" Jason Del unleashed a renewed assault, sending an unending stream of fireballs that pounded into Cyrus.

Cyrus leaped and tumbled toward Megani, stopping just short of her in order to pivot his blade and shield himself from the stronger attack. Warding off blows, he spoke to his granddaughter.

"I cannot decide for you, but I'll say this: Stay here and you will be content forever. Come with me and face a world of fears—and destroy them!"

Cyrus held out his hand. Megani did not know why, but she reached her trembling fingers toward that of her grandfather's.

"You are safe here!" Jason screamed to Megani as he unleashed a brutal new assault against his father. The roof of the cottage blew off. The back wall blew outward.

"But you could be there!" Cyrus nodded toward the front door, still ajar from the warrior's entrance.

Megani glanced back and forth into the eyes of these two Men. Her father was content in the smallness of his world, but her grandfather had the look of excitement brought forth by the larger world's dangers. She suddenly felt the yearning to explore, to try, to fail, to succeed. She wanted the bigger world and the risks that might come from them.

Megani grabbed Cyrus's hand. Still warding off blows with the Sword, he pulled Megani upon his shoulder and in one fluid jump, flew out the front door of the cottage just as it exploded behind them.

"We'll face this together!" shouted Cyrus Del to his granddaughter as they hurled through the air. Then everything went black.

CHAPTER 14

STRAITS OF DEVILS

Megani tumbled upon the ground and came to a sudden stop. Her mind spun in confusion. She was not sure where she had been, nor where she was now. Sights and sounds from her childhood mingled with her adult world. She had just seen her father and mother vividly, as well as her cottage as it had existed so long ago. Megani could still feel the warmth of the fireplace, which matched the warmth of her parents' embrace. Among the whirling images, she glimpsed a stranger entering their cottage, then confusion and a battle followed by a bright-white light, an explosion, and a hard tumble.

Megani's senses began to return to the present. She gasped for air, realizing that her fall had knocked the wind out of her aching lungs. Her body hurt. Her ears pounded with the sound of waves crashing upon surf, and she tasted gritty sand in her mouth. Megani wearily opened her eyes, lifted her head, and looked ahead. The sea was before her, its waves churning and foaming just yards from where she lay upon a sandy white beach. Gulls circled above. In the distance and across a watery strait, she could see the jagged Cliffs of Devon. She knew instantly that she was on the east coast of Trinity. How she came to be a day's walk ahead of where she last remembered being, she did not know.

Megani suddenly remembered more of her dream: the content little girl with her mother and father always there, always attentive. It was so unlike her real childhood, which was often devoid of a father who was many times on a quest to rebuild Trinity and a mother who was forever present yet distant at the same time. The warmth that she felt within that cottage suddenly vanished, pulled out as fast as the tide before her.

Megani then recalled that the stranger was no stranger at all, but her grandfather Cyrus. His bright-red hair and sparkling green eyes were striking even by Del standards. She remembered him barging into the cozy cottage to disrupt her blissful dream. Or did he save her from it? She remembered the decision she faced: to stay in the comfort of her cottage forever as her father demanded or taste the more dangerous but exciting world beyond, which her grandfather suggested. She suddenly realized that her father had given her a command, but her grandfather had let the decision be hers. Was this truly a dream or was it real?

"The Plains of Temptation!" Megani whispered to herself. She recalled entering the foreboding land. It must have instantly pulled her from the real adult world and into a make-believe child world, one she had always wished to have. It was far more enticing than she would have guessed. It knew enough about her, about her angst as a child and an adult, to craft a world that could lure her to stay.

Megani heard a groan from behind her. "Grandfather?!" she called as she looked eagerly about, the remnants of the dream still with her. But she saw only the Historian, his body a tangled mesh of legs and arms. Megani shook her head to clear her senses. Silly, she thought, that her grandfather would even be alive. She crawled to the old Man and untangled his body, placing his head in her lap.

"Are you okay?" she asked as she stroked his bald scalp tenderly, intently gazing into his moist brown eyes. The old Man's yellowing beard was filled with sand, and his face was cracked and dry.

"I'll be . . . in time . . . ," choked the Historian.

Megani felt compelled to share her dream. "I was tempted . . . ," she began, "to be young again." Intense visions swam through her mind. She closed her eyes and clearly saw her father and mother once more, as well as the stranger who was her grandfather Cyrus. He looked so much like she had pictured him.

"I never knew my grandfather," she suddenly spurted. "I never knew what, exactly, he looked like. But he was there. . . . He saved me!" She looked deep into the Historian's eyes. "Was it really him?"

"Just an image from your deepest dreams," he said. "It was made real enough for you to be lost in them."

"But how would I know what my grandfather looked like when he died long before I was born?"

The old Man sat up, breathing heavily. "Your mind filled in gaps, I suppose. You knew he would have red hair and green eyes, as do all Dels. Your mind invented the rest."

"You knew my grandfather," said Megani pushing for more. "What did he look like?"

"Like your father but older—the red hair, the green eyes—not unlike you, but with a larger build."

"And that's what I saw in my dream!"

The Historian nodded. "Of course you did. As I said, all Dels look surprisingly alike, so your dream merely filled in the gaps. There's nothing more to it than that."

Megani wasn't satisfied. The apparition was too alive, too real, but she let it pass. She helped the Historian rise and was surprised at the muscular build she could feel beneath his gray robe. He was like her vision of him in the Enchanted Forest—a warrior of old who is past his prime. She brushed the sand off his beard and clothes.

"What was your dream . . . your temptation?" she asked.

The Historian gave her a quick, serious glance and then smiled softly. "To save a world!" he said.

"Did you do it?" asked Megani.

"Yes," he said, smiling proudly. "And I could have done it again and again and again. But at some point, the world has to save itself."

The beach suddenly echoed with the sound of laughter. "Bee . . . do . . . la . . . ha . . . do rah . . . itz . . . ta . . . bee . . . soo . . . rah!" Lyndi came running toward them, her feet playfully splashing through the surf, her curly blond hair tossing back and forth in the sea breeze. The Historian and Megani walked toward her.

"I've been waiting for you for a whole day. . . . Hurrah!" she cheered. "I loved the Plains of Temptation. First I built a tower all the way to Anton. Then I took his job and made a new world. It was really fun because I could never do that before. I made the stars so they could talk to each other and play Mammoth Rider. I filled the rivers on Trinity with chocolate. I made a Race of people that was born old and died young. Then I put an ocean in the sky. Then I made huge turtles that ate stars. Then I brought back all my Wallo brothers and sisters, and we played and made all kinds of new stuff. I was happier than I have ever been. Then I made . . ."

"Why did you come back?" interrupted Megani, startled at the intense cheer she saw in Lyndi's eyes.

Lyndi saddened. "It gets boring when you can have *everything*. Gee . . . I never failed. Everything I made worked exactly liked I wanted it too; it was too easy. So then I made everything not work, but because I knew I was making it not work, it wasn't fun." She smiled and grabbed Megani's hand. "What did you dream? Tell me! Tell me! Tell me!"

Megani smiled and bent down to gaze into Lyndi's blue eyes. "I was about seven years old, I suppose, and with my parents."

Lyndi beamed. "That must have been fun! Then what did you do?"

Megani shrugged. "Not much more than that. We were in our cottage. We danced. We ate. They told me stories."

Lyndi frowned. "I can see why you came back. You didn't even create a universe. I should have given you one of my temptations!"

"But I felt loved," Megani offered. "And I didn't have to worry about saving anything."

Lyndi made snoring sounds and pretended to look sleepy.

"That's enough," Megani said, annoyed that Lyndi would find her temptation so boring.

"I'm sorry," said Lyndi. "I didn't mean that your dream was *that* boring. But how much fun can you have when you are just in one cottage for the rest of forever. You can pick the fuzz from between your toes only so many times!"

Megani smiled. She suddenly realized that her dream, in which she was so isolated in that cottage, would be boring if it lingered too long. Megani did not have the childhood she had wished, but even so, her parents had loved her and taught her many things. Maybe that seven-year-old girl is still inside me, she thought. After all, Lyndi is thousands of years old and has amazing powers, but she is guided by the child within, still in awe of everything. Perhaps that's the way to live, Megani reasoned, to have childlike wonder even when faced with massive responsibilities.

Megani smiled. "I guess you're right," she admitted to Lyndi. "Next time I'll borrow one of your temptations. I think I'd like to make a river of chocolate or an ocean in the sky. It sounds much more fun."

Their conversation was halted when the Historian began to sway and fell backward toward the sand. Megani caught him before he hit and gently lowered him to his back. Lyndi inspected the Historian closely and placed her hand up upon his chest as she had before, moving it back and forth as her healing began.

"You were fighting again!" the Wallo chided. "You know you're too old for that."

"You're older than me!" the Historian protested as he grimaced in pain.

"Yes . . . ," began Lyndi, "but I can live forever unless I'm killed by accident or intention. You're not built that way and even Anton can't fix it."

"What did you fight in the plains?" asked Megani.

"Phantoms," he said.

"What kind?" Megani questioned.

"All kinds," he responded. "Some were evil through and through. But the worst were those that looked good on the outside but within were evil. They are the most dangerous of all." The old Man's cheeks began to blossom with more color, a sign that his health was already improving. "I hoped our trek through the plains would save us time, but it cost us a day," he said. "We need to be moving on."

After a brief rest, the trio made their way south along the coast and toward the small fishing village of Dire Passage. It was here where, hopefully, they would find Gil, Allo, and Drak, who had been sent to recover the Sword. They also hoped to find boats in the village so that they could make the passage to Devon. But upon their approach, they found the town deserted and the boats along the long dock gone.

Lyndi grabbed a handful of sand at the entrance to the dock and let the grains pass slowly through her fingers. She inspected the falling granules intensely. "People . . . human blood . . . Gorgons . . . serpents . . . Devil Rays . . . and lesser beasts . . . lots of them . . . coming from the sea."

The Historian nodded. "So, they did come from Devon as we suspected."

Megani bent and grabbed a handful of sand and let it pass through her fingers. "How can you tell from the sand?" she asked Lyndi.

The little girl beamed. "'Cause everything leaves a part of itself behind wherever it goes. It can't help it. The pieces it leaves are very small, but they are there." Lyndi cupped her hands and let the sand slipping through Megani's fingers fall into hers before it reached the ground. "In your handful," she described as she inspected it intensely, "there are parts of about two thousand different Gorgons. They passed over the dock and into this sand before spreading across Trinity." Lyndi smiled as she continued to gaze at the sand. "There's also gull poop. A cow peed here about a year ago, and . . . oh . . . there's some Man spit . . ."

"That's enough!" Megani dropped the rest of the sand and quickly brushed off the remains. She gazed across the Straits of Devils and to the Cliffs of Devon. Winds blew hard from north to south, kicking up large whitecaps atop huge waves. She then looked west. "Gil should have been here by now."

The Historian nodded. "Perhaps. Or maybe he already came, and not finding us, he decided to make the passage to Devon."

Megani shook her head. Her sharp green eyes grew worried. "He would have left a message."

"Maybe," said the Historian. He turned to Lyndi. "Can you detect a specific Man in the sand?"

"If I knew him . . . met him . . . touched him . . . then I would know what he was made of and could look for it. But since I have not, I cannot tell if he was among the hundreds of humans I see here."

"Did you see the remains of his companions, an Elf or a Dwarf?"

Lyndi grabbed more sand and let it filter through her hands again. "It's too mixed up. There are some Elf remains . . . and Dwarf. But it is not fresh, and I don't know which Elf or Dwarf it is."

"Then we move forward," said the Historian.

Megani crossed her arms. "Without the Sword?!"

"I'm afraid so."

"But I have no powers," argued Megani. "I can't face a Wizard with nothing! Even a fragment of the Sword would be better than nothing at all."

The Historian nodded. "True. But for all we know, the Sword has already made the passage and we are behind it. We must get across to be sure."

Megani understood the logic, but she did not like it. Even with her full powers, she had been badly beaten by the Wizard. How could she face the same demon without the Sword? And how could she protect her new friends?

"Stop thinking so much!" the Historian exclaimed.

Megani threw him a sharp look.

"Your mind is moving so fast I can hear it from here," he continued. "We are going to make the crossing. I have faith that Gil will find us."

Megani saw trees in the distance. "We can make a raft."

The Historian shook his head. "That would take another day—too long."

"We could have Lyndi transform bees again so that we can fly over."

Lyndi looked up, gladdened that Megani would want her to use her powers. However, the Wallo looked across the straits and was saddened. "They can't fly across because the winds are too strong." Lyndi then tossed her curly blond hair back, and her blue eyes sparkled with a delightful thought. "I can't change people much, but I do know how to make small changes here and there that might help."

"What can you do?" asked Megani intently.

"Well . . . I can make it so your toenails won't keep growing. I can give you Elf ears. I could make the color of you pee green and taste like apple juice. I could . . ."

"I mean," interrupted Megani. "What can you do to help us get across the straits?"

"Oh," said Lyndi. "I can make us swim like fish!"

"Fish?" asked the Historian.

"Yes!" Lyndi began again as her friends looked at her in wonder. "I can give us gills so we can breathe underwater and fins instead of legs. That should get us across and it would be fun, too! I bet Anton won't be mad because, well, it's to help us defeat that bad, bad Wizard. So I'm sure he would be okay with it."

The Historian glanced at Megani. "Maybe we have enough time to build that boat after all," he said.

Lyndi stamped a determined foot on the ground. "I can do this! I just need to experiment a bit."

"It's too dangerous to experiment!" said the old Man.

Megani stepped forward, intrigued at the thought of a new experience, one that was clearly more exciting than the cottage of her temptation. "I'll try it."

The Historian shook his finger. "We can't be sure of the success."

"Cyrus Del would do it," Megani suddenly blurted. "If my dream was even half true, I know that he was the kind of Man who would take that risk."

The Historian softened. "I can't escape the logic of that, but let me go first. If Lyndi is going to turn someone into a squid that eats mountains, let it be me."

"Goodie!" said Lyndi. "Let's sit in the water."

The Historian waded into the water beside the dock and sat. Megani joined him as Lyndi stood between them.

"Okay . . . let me see," said Lyndi, intently inspecting the Historian's hand. "This is the one . . . I think."

"Please don't just *think,*" said the Historian. "Can't you just *know?*"

Lyndi continued to inspect a microscopic piece of the Historian's hand that was invisible to all else. "It's been a long time. Besides, we weren't allowed to experiment on humans."

"Then how can you be sure of anything?" asked Megani.

Lyndi shrugged her shoulders. "I figure that you're pretty much the same as an ape. I do have some experience with apes."

Poof!

The Historian instantly grew elephant ears.

"Lyndi!" the old Man yelled as he tried to prevent his heavy head from falling into the water. He could see the massive ears flapping before him. Megani held the old Man up.

"On no, that's not right," said Lyndi. "It's been a while since I did that."

Poof!

The Historian's own ears returned.

"Lyndi!" he said. "Please, please be careful!"

"It might be best if you close your eyes," the Wallo said. "That way you won't get so upset by my small mistakes. . . . I mean *experiments.*"

Frustrated, the Historian did as asked while Megani watched in awe.

Lyndi gazed back into the Historian's hand, astutely detecting the building blocks of life. Her experiments began once again.

Poof. Gorilla hair.

Poof. Back to normal.

Poof. Tiger tail.

Poof. Back to normal.

Poof. Ostrich neck.

Poof. Back to normal.

Poof. Frog legs.

Poof. Back to normal.

"Lyndi!" screamed the Historian. "My eyes may be closed, but I can feel my body parts. We've just covered a third of the animal kingdom!"

"Shhhhh!" said Lyndi. "I finally have it narrowed down to your legs."

Poof. Zebra legs.

Poof. Back to normal.

Poof. Spider legs.

Poof. Back to normal.

Poof. Women's legs.

Poof. Back to normal.

"Here it is!" declared Lyndi as she continued to intently scan the Historian's hand.

Poof!

The Historian's legs melded together and became one large fin that popped beneath his robe. He opened his eyes and tested it. "Not altogether bad," he reluctantly said.

"And the gills," said Lyndi as she touched his hand again.

Poof!

The Historian grew gills upon his neck.

"Not bad for the first try!" beamed the Wallo.

The old Man began to choke in the air, but Megani quickly dragged him to deeper water. He splashed beneath the surface to capture a breath. Keeping his gills underwater, the Historian popped his head above the surface. "Not altogether bad," he said again.

"My turn," said Megani, excited to change form.

Lyndi grabbed Megani's hand and gazed at it intently. "Now that I know where to look, it will be quicker for you."

Almost instantaneously Megani's legs became one large fin and her neck sprouted gills. She slipped beneath the surface. Megani was amazed at the feeling of freedom in the water. She was joined by the Historian. A moment later, Lyndi was similarly transformed, but her fin was a bright rainbow of sparkling colors. Her friends took notice.

"Nice fin," said Megani.

"A bit much," added the Historian.

"You're right," said Lyndi. She touched her fin and it became a tad smaller, but the bright colors remained. "There," she said as she admired her tail. "Let's go!"

Lyndi headed into the depths of the straits, followed by the Historian and Megani in the rear. The Wallo kept well below the surface, Megani noted, to avoid the strong currents, but there was still enough light from above to allow them to follow each other easily. With each stroke of their massive fins, they were able to propel themselves forward many yards. The trio rarely needed their arms at all, which was good for the Historian.

Megani was in awe of the wonders below. Huge turtles swam along-side them for a while, and schools filled with thousands of glowing blue fish came and went. Dolphins appeared from behind and blasted past the trio. They then rocketed toward the surface and jetted into the air. A moment later, the creatures dove back into the water ahead of Lyndi as though taunting her to play; however, the little Wallo kept moving forward with her trusting friends behind her.

Megani began to spin in circles as she moved forward, her long red hair flowing gracefully. Schools of multicolored fish continued to dash to and fro. Green and red strings of seaweed reached up from the depths, and eels slithered among the tall vegetation. After two hours of such sights, Lyndi swam to the surface in order for the trio to get their bearings. They buoyed up and down with the large waves. The Cliffs of Devon were close.

"About four hundred yards!" yelled Lyndi above the roaring of the sea. The trio plunged back beneath the waves and continued their passage. Their pace had slowed considerably since they began. They were exhausted, and the Historian, in particular, was spent, but the trio was heartened that their destination was near.

A moment later, the waters grew still. Megani twirled about and saw that all the fish had vanished. Something massive suddenly bumped her from behind! Having turned just in time to see a huge shadow disappear below, Megani raced forward alongside the Historian.

"Swim!" she gurgled. "A beast is behind us!"

Megani turned again. A large tentacle stretched from out of the darkness below and slammed into her chest. The tentacle's suckers grabbed her and pulled her downward. She saw seven more tentacles, each about thirty feet long, leading to a whalelike beast with five huge eyes above a long, pointed jaw that contained rows of sharp fangs. Massive fins propelled it from behind, and for the moment, they were driving it backward toward deeper waters. The tentacle pulled Megani toward its gaping mouth while another tentacle struck her from behind, attaching itself to her back and pulling her closer to her doom. Megani pulled her sword and struck the tentacle attached to her chest. The blade cut a quarter of the way through the beast's rubbery skin. Stung but not greatly injured, the creature let her go and disappeared into the depths. With a burst of speed, Megani swam quickly eastward to find her friends. After several minutes, she saw the Historian stopped in the water, watching intently as the monster circled him. Lyndi was nowhere in sight!

Megani swam deeper, reaching the bottom of the sea directly underneath the Historian and hid among the towering seaweed. Looking up through the sunlit ocean, she could detect the beast's circles becoming smaller and smaller as it closed in for the kill. The Historian drew a blade, but Megani knew he was too weak to wield it effectively. The monster pulled farther away for a moment, and Megani knew it was simply using the distance to pick up more speed. It was a matter of moments before it would turn to strike her friend.

Megani sheathed her own sword and forced herself upward from her hiding spot, propelled by her massive fin. The monster turned and hurled itself toward the Historian, its eight tentacles before it. Megani saw the distance closing rapidly as she surged upward. The beast opened its massive jaw, intending to gobble the old Man as soon as its tentacles captured him. Sunlight glistened off rows of sharp, white teeth. Just as the tentacles were about to strike the Historian, Megani appeared from below, grabbed her friend, and sped toward the surface. The beast pivoted upward and was close behind. With a huge thrust, Megani and the Historian breached the surface of the sea and flew fifty feet into the air. Looking back, they saw the killer beast was right behind them, rising up out of the water with its tentacle stretched before it. Megani and the Historian had reached the peak of their ascent and began to fall back toward the sea, but the beast came onward, its momentum massive. It pulled its tentacles to the side and opened its massive jaws, intending to swallow them whole.

In midflight, Megani drew her sword and rolled to face the beast head-on. The Historian painfully followed her move, somersaulting through the air. The two friends fell toward the sea, blades in hand to meet the rising beast. Time seemed to stand still as they plummeted. They readied their weapons against the onslaught. The distance closed.

It struck!

Poof!

The massive beast became a guppy. Beneath it and rising upward out of the waves was Lyndi, her outstretched finger upon the fin of the small fish.

"Wasn't that fun?!" she cheered as she rose past her falling friends.

"Nooooooooooooooo!" yelled Megani and the Historian just before they hit the surface of the turbulent sea.

CHAPTER 15

PIT OF FEARS

Megani looked west, back across the Straits of Devils, and spied the eastern shores of Trinity. Cold, salty winds brushed her pink cheeks. Whitecaps dotted the turbulent sea. Sea gulls circled above but stayed close to shore and away from the turbulent winds within the straits. It was the first time she had stepped upon another land. It was a sinking feeling. For as long as she could remember, her father and mother had praised the land of her birth and made her swear to protect and nurture it. She was now elsewhere, driven to a foreign shore to fight a demon that threatened her own land.

Megani felt small. Devon was an unexplored region, its length and width unknown. Her skin slightly tingled with anticipation and excitement. Was it wrong to feel the thrill of discovery? she wondered. Was it wrong to leave one's own land to fight in another? Her father never would have made the journey to this unknown and hostile land. She wondered what he would say now, with all that had transpired in the month since his death. Would Jason Del praise his daughter for taking the battle to Devon in order to stop a demon seeking to encroach upon Trinity, or would he demand that she fight the battle upon their own shore?

A bigger question loomed: Did the Lord Anton truly expect his peoples to inhabit Trinity alone, as they had done for millennia, or did he expect more, so much more from those brave enough to venture beyond the boundaries of their homeland?

Megani turned east to face the shear white Cliffs of Devon. They rose hundred of yards straight into the sky to pierce dark, billowing clouds. It was an imposing sight, and the cliffs seemed impenetrable.

"We can't climb them," the Historian said as he rested flat upon his back near Megani's feet. The swim and the dangers they had faced across the straits were a great strain on the old Man's fragile bones, and his back was in great pain. It had taken hours of constant healing for Lyndi to provide some comfort to him.

164

"Then we go around the cliffs," Megani suggested. She worried whether he would be able to last long enough to face the Wizard.

The Historian shook his head. "No, that might take too long. I'm afraid we need to pass underneath them."

Megani scanned the base of the cliffs. "There are entryways?"

"Yes . . . of sorts," said the Historian. "But let's rest a bit before we begin anew." The old Man reached to his right and patted a sleeping Lyndi on her head. The little girl fell asleep soon after she had mended him.

"She's very peaceful when she is sleeping," Megani whispered as she sat beside them. She stroked the little Wallo's hair.

The Historian smiled. "Yes, but only when she's sleeping." He winked. "Let's have her rest another hour or so. She has used a great deal of power these past several days, and it exhausts her."

Megani nodded. "I have never seen such innocence."

The Historian saddened. "Nor will the world ever again when the last Wallo leaves it."

Megani shook her head. "I've put her at risk."

"No," said the Historian. "The Beasts of Becus put her at risk, and now the Wizard as well. You are not responsible for the God's battles. The best you can do is be responsible for what little we can now control ourselves."

"But I could have tried harder to defeat the Wizard," said Megani. "I should have found a way. Instead it stole my powers. My mother moved forward to strike it, and I stepped back to run from it." Megani lowered her head. She let her long red hair fall in front of her face as though hiding from the world.

"Cyrus Del ran too," he said.

"Never!" denied Megani as she jerked her head upward and met the Historian's eyes.

The Historian smiled. "Of course he ran. Why do you think the Battle of Meadowtown began there but ended at the Circle of Wisdom? The town was about to be overrun by demons, and so we evaluated our position and marched south. He avoided utter destruction."

Megani shrugged. "Well, yes, I suppose . . . but that wasn't really running."

The Historian laughed softly. "Cyrus thought it was. He knew that they were surely dead if they stayed in Meadowtown, so he gathered up the people and ran . . . and ran fast. It kept them all alive long enough for Jason to arrive at the Circle and aid their cause before his own battle with Pure Evil." The Historian sat up achingly. "I don't think you ran from the Wizard because of fear. You ran because you knew you could not defeat it with the powers you had. That's not cowardice. That's strategy. You still have other powers—human powers—and soon you'll have the Sword as well."

Megani shook her head. "Human powers will not be enough, and we have no idea if the Sword will arrive in time . . . or at all. I'm not even sure how it might aid us," she continued sarcastically, "unless I find a way to sneak up on the most powerful beast in the world in order to stab him. Not to mention that he could read my mind from yards away."

The Historian nodded. "Well, when you put it like that, I guess we must all look pretty foolish out here: an old Man, a childish Wallo, and a powerless Del." The Historian grabbed some sea plants that Megani had foraged from the shore. They made a suitable lunch. "With us in charge, I suppose that the world as we know it will cease, and a new one will replace it. Until then, eat up." He smiled and handed Megani some food.

Megani took a bite and swallowed. It was surprisingly good. "Well, at least the food is better here." She forced a smile.

"You see," said the Historian. "Things are starting to look better already. There's a little good that can be found in all things."

Lyndi began to snore loudly.

"Except that," he whispered as he tenderly patted Lyndi's head.

"Did you have children?" Megani asked abruptly.

The Historian nodded, his brown eyes becoming moist. "I had two boys . . . but they died."

"Oh," said Megani apologetically. "I'm sorry. I didn't mean to bring up painful memories."

"That's alright."

"Were you close?"

"Very close," the Historian said with soaring pride in his voice. "The eldest died when he was very young. That was a devastating loss. The youngest died when he was very old, but I lost contact with him before the end. Our paths sent us down different roads later in life." The old Man stared far off into the distance. "I wish I could have been with him at the end. The world becomes very clear when you are older, and you are better able to recognize the things that truly matter."

Megani nodded, her own gaze lost in a recent memory. "I was there at the end of my father's life, at Spirit Lake, but it wasn't what I expected."

The Historian turned a keen eye toward her. "Tell me," he urged.

"I guess I expected trumpets . . . or ceremony . . . but there was only quiet. My mother told me that the Lord Anton visited my father within a moment of time, detectable to her but not to me. He gave my father all that he wanted, all that he lost during the Final Contest with Pure Evil when he was only fifteen years old."

"Jas got everything?" asked the Historian, intrigued.

"Yes . . . the Lord Anton restored the hand my father lost in battle and returned the sight that was blinded by the clash of powers. Most of all, though my father was old when he died, Anton allowed him to be fifteen years old in the afterlife. He was shed of the years and responsibilities he had endured in order to repair Trinity to its former glory. My mother told me she even heard the spirit of his brother, Theda, and his mother, Beth, call him home. Then he was gone." Megani shrugged. "But all I saw was that one moment my father was old and standing near me, and the next he was ash upon the shores of Spirit Lake. I don't know what to believe anymore."

Megani's green eyes swelled with tears. She looked into the Historian's eyes and saw the same.

"Why are *you* crying?" she asked as she wiped her tears away from her eyes.

The Historian smiled sadly. "It's a very touching story. And I knew your father well."

There it was again! Megani noted with excitement. She could sense that he was not telling her the whole truth. The Historian knew more than he was saying; he was involved more than he would dare to admit.

"What is it?" she pursued. "What don't I know? What are you keeping from me? Is this about the real history of what happened when the Sword was created, or is this about you . . . what your role is . . . about who you are?!"

The Historian's face turned stoic, and the portal to his soul was slammed shut. "Shhhhh," he said as he patted Lyndi's head. "Don't wake her. The answers to your questions are not at all important. I'm keeping nothing of consequence from you," he declared. "It was a wonderful story you told, and I'm very sorry for the recent loss of your father and mother."

Though Megani was not convinced he was being completely honest, she still felt a deep trust toward this old Man. If he was keeping something from her, it was probably for the good of Trinity. She let it pass, but she had the undeniable feeling that this would come full circle, and they would visit this discussion again.

A couple of hours later, Lyndi awoke, fully rested, and began to talk endlessly once more. The Historian tested his fragile frame and rose to his feet. He wobbled. Lyndi applied some added healing power to make him well enough to walk . . . and live. The trio packed what little they had and walked a mile to the foot of the Cliffs of Devon. As they neared the cliffs, Megani could see the slick surface, which offered little to hold onto should one decide to scale the heights. Lyndi's chatter continued.

". . . and then I thought I could help this itsy-bitsy guppy better protect itself. It just seemed so small, and all of the other fish seemed so big. Besides, I was bored from all that swimming across the straits, so when the guppy swam in front of me, I started to experiment. I gave it some tentacles, and it worked. Then I thought it might need more eyes and lots of teeth in its itsy-bitsy mouth. That worked, too. But what good are the teeth if they are too small? So I went to make the teeth just a bit bigger . . . and poof . . . the whole guppy thingy got bigger by mistake. It swam beneath me before I could stop it. I figured it just went away. I really, really did. I thought it just went away and we would never see it again."

"We know. We know!" said the Historian. "You told us already. We forgive you for turning the itsy-bitsy guppy into a cold-blooded killing beast."

Lyndi smiled hesitantly. "But it was . . . you know . . . fun. . . . Right?"

"Just promise you won't turn any more guppies into monsters," added Megani, "unless you ask us beforehand."

Lyndi smiled wide. "Okay, but did I ever tell you why rocks are hard? We could have made them soft. We even did it once, but then the mountains became so spongy that every time we climbed on them and tripped by mistake, we would bounce all the way to the bottom. You could bounce for miles on just one stumble. We could have made trees with the bark on the inside, but we found out that . . ."

"Not now," said the Historian. "We are close to the pit."

"Oh goodie," squealed Lyndi before looking confused. "What is the pit? We didn't make that. I would have remembered!"

Having reached the Cliffs of Devon, the Historian began to walk south, his friends following. "There are tunnels beneath the cliffs that can take us to the other side, where we will find the Mortal Mines, the dwelling of the Wizard."

"Goodie!" exclaimed Lyndi. "I don't remember any of my brothers or sisters making that either. But then, we stayed put in Trinity. Maybe my brother Togi made them. He was good with stuff like that."

"You've been here before?" asked Megani of the old Man.

"A long time ago . . . to see what threats might exist here. I detected a dark seed that was weak but growing. But I hadn't the power to stop it."

Megani threw him a knowing look. "You asked my father to help, didn't you?"

The old Man nodded.

"And he refused."

"Yes. He didn't want to leave Trinity. As I said before, he believed the evil that grew here was not his concern. He did not believe it would ever grow large enough to threaten us. And so it grew unimpeded."

Megani did not fully believe that her father, the great Jason Del, could have been so wrong. But he had been, and now she stood on a foreign shore to fight a battle that he could have prevented years ago. She felt an urge to defend his memory. "He was a good father . . . and protector."

"I know," said the old Man comfortingly. "But he could not recognize his flaws, so it passes to you to right a wrong."

Megani took a deep breath. She was still without the Sword and absent of powers. But there was nowhere to go but forward. "What do we do?"

The Historian turned as a small bend in the cliffs appeared. A gaping tunnel was evident around the bend. The three companions stood and looked deep into the dark, ominous hole that measured some fifty feet across.

"We enter the Pit of Fears," answered the Historian. "Though we go in together, the pit will separate us, as each will follow his or her own path. We will be confronted by our greatest fears. If we are lucky, we will meet again where all the tunnels come together at the other side of the Cliffs of Devon."

"Wow . . . ," said Lyndi, gazing into the tunnel with eager anticipation. "I don't think my brother Togi was smart enough to do this. It must have been created by someone else who's a really, really, really good inventor. Not like me when I put green streaks in my hair. That's not all that special." Lyndi touched her hair and green streaks instantly appeared. She looped the streaks around her tiny index finger and admired it as she began to hum.

"Lyndi," said the Historian as he slowly bent beside her, redirecting her attention. "When you enter the pit, don't worry about anything you see or hear. None of it is real. Just keep walking forward, and we'll meet you on the other side. If you can't find us, make your way to the Mortal Mines, which is about five miles southeast of the Pit of Fears. A huge tower is at the entrance. That's where the Wizard lives. Be careful." He turned to Megani. "Any questions?"

"No," she said. "That was plain enough."

The old Man gave Lyndi a huge hug, though it pained him to do so. Megani knelt and did the same. They then stood hand in hand—the Historian, Lyndi in the middle, and then Megani. They shared a glance. Lyndi was the only one with a broad smile on her lips. Innocence, Megani now knew, had a way of turning fears into fun challenges.

"Remember!" said the Historian. "Whatever you do, you must step forward, always forward! That's how you break the fear. You have to get it behind you. Once the fear is a step behind, it ceases having any powers over you."

"Okay . . . let's go," said Megani.

The trio took a common breath and then stepped into the tunnel that led to the Pit of Fears.

Megani was instantly alone in the complete darkness. The hand that had held Lyndi's was empty.

"Lyndi!" screamed Megani. "Can you hear me? Historian?!" No answer. Megani turned, but the opening to the cave was gone. She held her hands out in the darkness and touched solid rock. She turned again and walked forward into the black for quite some time, her hands guiding her way. A crack of light suddenly appeared. She approached it. The light came from a keyhole in a huge wooden door. Finding a doorknob, she opened the door and passed through it.

It was midday. The sun was shining and a warm breeze caressed Megani's face. She was in the town square of Meadowtown, and a large crowd of townspeople were gathered near her. She looked to each side of her and discovered that she was in the middle of a line of children that were spread along the width of the road. They all faced north toward a finish line. This was going to be a race! From behind, she felt the squeeze of a comforting hand on her shoulder.

She looked back and into the comforting eyes of her father, who bent toward her.

"Don't worry," said Jason Del. "Just try your best. You're only ten years old, after all."

"Okay, Daddy," said Megani with a sweet but determined face. The children beside her were mostly strangers, as Megani rarely socialized with any of them. She was homeschooled, which often kept her apart from the other children. Her parents always said that was because she was different and needed special care. A banner across the road read, "Town Fair." This was one of the few times she was allowed to play with others, and it was often during the fair's contests. Her mother made sure that Megani was registered in each and every one. Megani knew that her mother always wanted to see how well her daughter fared. It was important to her.

Megani looked at the line of children on either side of her. She suddenly had the strangest feeling that she had been here before—in this race—years ago. How could that be? she wondered. She was only ten years old.

The children along the line were the best runners of Meadowtown. All were boys. All were at least fifteen years old. Girls were not expected, nor invited, to enter the race, and Megani's younger age made her participation all the more uncommon. But Megani's mother demanded that she participate, and the town council was not about to ignore the request of Jason Del's wife. Megani knew that these boys didn't want her there, and as they prepared for the race by wiggling their leg and arm muscles, towering above the only girl in the race, they often snuck an angry gaze toward her. She should not be there, their eyes yelled, and they would see to it that she failed.

Megani looked at the finish line at the far end of town. She wanted to win this race for herself and for her father. She had a lot to live up to. After all, her father was Jason Del! That put a lot of pressure upon her, as always. His comforting words, however, made the prospect of losing acceptable. Though she might not come in first place, she knew she would still be a winner in his heart.

Megani made her plans. After a fast sprint for a quarter of the length of the race, she would have to wade through the twenty-foot-long pool of water. Megani thought that if she jumped far enough, she might only need to take two steps in the water before she bounced out of it. That would save time. She would then bounce over the next obstacle, a wood pile, using just one leap. She would take only five more long steps to reach the wagon that obstructed their path. She intended to climb to the top as quickly as she could before jumping the rest of the way down. From there it was a clear run to the finish line. If she made a good show of it, by beating just a few of the older boys, that would be special, she thought. That would make Daddy proud.

"Ready!" yelled the starter. The line of children focused upon the finish line.

"Set!" he yelled again. Tension began to mount.

Megani's stern mother suddenly whispered in her ear. "Don't make me ashamed that I had a daughter instead of a son!"

"Go!" shouted the starter.

Fear exploded in Megani's mind. Her father might forgive a loss, but her mother would not. Ten-year-old Megani Del dashed forward, but the line of fifteen-year-old boys was already ahead of her. Megani's heart pounded. Her mind screamed, "I'm losing!"

Some of the boys reached the pool. They splashed within it to reach the other end.

"No!" screamed Megani as she saw her failure unfold. Her mother's words pounded in her brain. Megani knew that her plans needed to change; she needed to meet her mother's expectations!

"One foot . . . one foot . . . one foot!" Megani seethed as she reached the twenty-foot-long pool. She blasted off the edge of the dirt, hurled across the water, past the boys that still waded across, and landed upon the dirt without ever touching the water itself!

"One foot . . . one foot . . . one foot!" she screamed again as three boys were still beyond her. She reached the wood pile and hurled herself over it, through the air, across the clearing, and atop the wagon! One more leap propelled her closer to victory.

Seconds later, Megani flew across the finish line—alone—putting the fear of disappointing her mother behind her.

Darkness.

Megani's heart pounded. She had just won a race, she knew, but she did not know where she was now. She used her hands to guide her along a dark, cold tunnel. A crack of light appeared ahead. She rounded a bend and entered the light.

Megani instantly recognized the clear-blue water of Spirit Lake. She looked to her side and saw her father, Jason Del, bent with age, his red hair streaked with gray, his green eyes weary of life. She knew he was about to die. This was the moment.

"Don't leave me, Daddy," she blurted while holding back the tears.

The old Man placed his wrinkled left hand, the only one remaining, upon her shoulder. He drew close and kissed her cheek. "It's up to you now, Megani. Protect Trinity. . . . Protect the Races. I have faith in you."

"It's time," said a stern voice. Megani looked past her father and saw her mother, the snow-white hair and large blue eyes of an Etha. "Your father needs his eternal rest."

Jason Del smiled at Megani. "It will be alright. Hopefully, we will all meet again."

The father pulled away from his daughter. Megani reached and touched him one last time as he walked forward and paused. He turned and smiled. Megani whispered a plea into the air: "Please, please, Anton . . . give him more time. Give my father more time."

Jason Del suddenly burst into ashes that floated unceremoniously to the ground. Megani fell to her knees, her body shaking. She did not know which was greater, the fear of the death of her beloved father or the fear of knowing that the responsibility—the trust—of all of Trinity now rested with her. It gripped her. She looked up and gazed into her mother's disapproving eyes. They said much. Bea was not pleased with her daughter's outpouring of grief, a human trait. Megani pulled herself together and slowly stood, trying to match her mother's Ethan fortitude. She struggled with the fears and finally put them behind her. Something within told her that she had to move . . . had to place one foot ahead of the next. Megani took a deep breath and calmed her nerves. She stepped forward to collect her father's ashes.

Darkness.

Megani walked slowly through a dimly lit tunnel. Her mind was still in a whirl of grief over her father's death, but the confusion gradually began to leave her. "That's right," she said, panting. "I'm in the Pit of Fears." She was amazed at how real and accurate the vision of her father's passing had been. She was equally stunned that she had not realized it was a vision. It had seemed so real, so like the exact moment that he died. She rounded a bend in the tunnel, light emerging through the opening. She ran toward it and exited the tunnel. "Always forward!" she reminded herself.

Megani was in a great valley. Dark, billowing clouds filled the sky. Thousands of Elf and Dwarf warriors lay mangled upon a battlefield as far as she could see. They were dead. She gazed at her feet. Her boots were drenched from the puddles of blood. The Valley of Despair.

The Races were destroyed, and it was because of her: She had not moved fast enough; she had wasted time in Olive Branch. Megani shook with fear. She screamed at the sky to turn back the time in order to give her a chance to make it all right. But the carnage remained, and Megani had failed. She was not worthy of the trust her father and mother had placed in her. She did not know which made her more fearful, the unknown that might lie ahead or the sinking feeling that she must tell her mother that she was responsible for the destruction of the

Races. She pulled herself together, inch by inch. She had to keep moving forward, she told herself, to Anton knows what. But she could not begin until she placed one foot ahead of the other. She decided to search for signs of life among the dead. Perhaps that might provide some small hope. She broke her fear and stepped forward.

Darkness.

Megani shook the confusion. The sights and sounds of the previous visions began to shoot through her mind. Small fears. Big fears. She felt suddenly burdened. Megani swallowed hard and walked forward, pushing cobwebs aside with her hands as she approached a huge wooden chamber door. She was suddenly cold, very cold. She grabbed the large metal knob and gave it a twist.

Clank went the tumblers as the lock opened. She entered the room. "Keep stepping forward," she reminded herself. "Get the fear behind you."

Megani found herself hanging against a wall, irons locking her feet and wrists to the stone behind her. The room was cavernous and mostly dark. Torches hung on the walls and flickered from a cold breeze that entered a window at the far end of the room. Muffled sounds of a huge battle wafted through the window. It sounded far below, suggesting that she was far above, possibly in a tower. Megani looked at the floor beneath her feet and gasped. There lay Allo and Drak, dead, blades· piercing each of their bodies. Her heart raced. Megani heard faint breathing to her right. Lyndi was next to her, chained to the same wall. The little one was bloodied and dying.

Megani struggled violently against her chains, but they would not break. She heard a whimper across the chamber. Through the shadows, her eyes detected the figure of a woman who lay on the bottom of an iron cage that hung above the ground. Megani could not detect who it was, as the person was in a heap.

Megani then saw a figure standing near the cage, its back to her. It turned to face her, and its red eyes glistened in the darkness. White, ancient hair fell from its crown to its shoulders.

Zorca!

Megani struggled against her chains again. Blood spurt from her wrists and ankles as she pulled against the irons, but they held.

"Some visions are more real than others!" Zorca laughed. "Some are real enough to kill you. Then there are those visions that *are* real!"

The Wizard took one step closer and into the torchlight. He lifted his clenched fist high, and a brilliant light flashed. It was the Sword!

"Thank you for the gift," it cackled. "It's precisely what I needed you to do: deliver the Sword." The beast looked lovingly upon the blade. "Imagine that in the entire world, this is the only thing that could have stopped me . . . and you did not even know how to use it." It laughed and the chamber echoed with its shrill voice.

"All your friends are dead or dying," it heckled, "because of you. You are so much like Pita. You have no idea!"

Without warning, Zorca threw the blade. It was aimed at Megani's heart. Fear exploded within her, and she struggled to get free. The blade looked like an icicle against the dark cavern. She tried to step forward—to take just one step—but she could not!

The blade struck. It hammered into her chest, pierced her heart, and smashed two feet into the rock wall behind her. Pain exploded. Megani looked down and saw her blood pouring upon the blade and then upon the floor below. Megani shivered with cold and fear: She had failed. Her eyes became heavy as the life flowed from her. The pain lessened, replaced by a deadening numb. Megani took a shallow breath. Then another. She tried to step forward once again, but again she could not. Her head dropped to her chest, and her entire body went limp. Darkness came.

Megani Del was dead.

CHAPTER 16

EARTH FORGE

Several days earlier . . .

Drak heaved, sending a vial mixture of poison-laced vomit onto the boulder where he lay exhausted. His limbs were weak, and his face pale. He inhaled deeply, trying to catch his breath. His stomach churned and he heaved again. The Dwarf had been through much, he knew, though many of the details were lost to him, for he had been unconscious for the past day. The last thing he remembered was a deer that transformed into a huge scorpion and then sharp pain when the beast stuck him with its deadly point. Drak was so focused on his own illness that he did not fully realize that his companions had been through much more: They had carried him across southern Trinity in order to avoid demons that sought to kill them all. The Dwarf heaved once again, spewing more poisoned vomit.

"How long will this go on?" asked Allo, who sat nearby.

Gil shrugged. "Another hour or so. He needs to get all the poison out of his body. The medicine roots we gave him are pullin' it out the hard way."

"It's not the poison that churns me," groaned the Dwarf. "It's the Elf spit!"

Allo shook his head. "If I hadn't chewed up the medicine root and spit it into your mouth, you would be dead now!"

"Like this is any better!" cried Drak. He heaved once again and came up coughing. "The human spit is bad enough, but of all the spits in the world, there is nothing more disgusting than Elf spit!"

Allo smiled. "How would you know what 'all the spits in the world' taste like," teased the Elf, "unless you went out of your way to sample them. I've heard of many strange Dwarf hobbies, but that one is new to me."

Drak heaved again and then came up yelling. "I was just exaggerating!"

"Oh," said Allo, taking delight in Drak's illness. "That Dwarf hobby is very familiar to me!"

They were in the bowels of the Earth, thousands of feet below the surface, in a cavern that had not been disturbed for centuries. Gil looked about. The water from the Drowning Pool far above poured downward in a cascading, swirling funnel. After hundreds of yards, it plunged into a receiving pool and then bent east to form a fast-moving underground river that disappeared through a dark tunnel. Faint light was provided by glowing green fungus attached to the cavern walls.

Allo turned to Gil. "How did you know this existed?" he asked. "My people thought that only death waited at the bottom of the Drowning Pool."

"I did too," began Gil, "until the pigeon told me otherwise."

"Pigeon?" asked Allo.

Drak heaved once again, the sound echoing throughout the cavern and the tunnel beyond.

"On our run from the Gorgons," continued Gil, "a pigeon flew above us and directed me here."

Allo raised an eyebrow. "You can talk to pigeons?"

"More interestin'," said Gil, "would be to figure out who sent the pigeon in the first place and why that person sent us here." Gil looked eastward, watching the flow of the water. The tunnel through which it coursed was dimly lit with the same green, glowing fungus that grew throughout the cavern. The place was very cold, and the wind created by the cascading water was constant as it whistled east along the river. The fall from the Drowning Pool had been hard. Though nearly spent of strength, Gil had had to fish Allo out of the water while he still had an unconscious Drak in his arms.

"You don't suppose the demon sent the pigeon . . . as a trap to get us down here?" asked Allo.

"Nope, don't think so," said Gil. "The Gorgons could have killed us above. I don't think their master would have saved us by sendin' us down here. No, somethin's down here . . . and somebody wants us to find it. I just wish the pigeon would have told me who sent it, but it was in a hurry to get out of trouble as well."

Gil wondered if Megani could have sent the pigeon, but then he realized she hadn't the skill to communicate with the bird. It could only have been sent by another of his brothers, one of the

Guardians. Or it could have been sent by the very person they all sought: the Historian. Either would be a good omen, he knew, for it would mean that he was not alone in his quest to deliver his message to the Man who could save the world from evil. When Allo walked over to Drak to see how he was faring, Gil momentarily rolled up his leather sleeve and rubbed the tattoo of the Guardian that was given to him by the Shaman years earlier. It was now one of two responsibilities, Gil thought. He rolled the sleeve back down and picked up the cloth bundle at his feet. He unfolded the cloth and instantly reached to shield his eyes from the stabbing light of the Sword's three fragments. The young Man suspected that both of his quests—to get his message to the Historian and to deliver the Sword to Megani—were in fact the same. Everything was connected, he knew.

"By the Gods!" wrenched Drak. "Take my sorry life now!" The Dwarf bent over the rock and heaved once more.

Allo was in an unusually good mood at his friend's expense. But in truth, his merriment was relief that his friend was still alive. "Take it like a real Dwarf!" Allo bellowed as he stood over Drak. "And by the way, I'm up one point for saving your life with my Elf spit!"

Drak gave his companion an evil stare. "Then we are even since I had to spit your kindness out of me!" He heaved yet again.

"Fine . . . be that way!" snapped Allo as he returned to Gil. The Elf then grew worried as he looked back at his sick friend.

"He'll be fine," whispered Gil.

"I hope so. I normally would have demanded another point for carrying the ton of lard across nearly all of Trinity," Allo said quietly, "but I don't want Drak to know I did that. He might think that I actually like him . . . or worse, that I care for him."

Gil shook his head. "The most complicated friendship I've ever seen," he said. "I'll keep your secret."

After several hours, Drak stopped heaving and regained most of his strength, so the trio continued their travels. They could not go up through the Drowning Pool the way they came, so they needed to find another way out. Gil led them east along the southern bank of the underground river, which was the only direction they could go, and followed the water that gushed through the tunnel. In an hour's time, they came to a parting where the water diverted into two tunnels. Gil waded through the river until he was between each opening. The water flowing into the tunnel on the left was gentle, and Gil could smell vegetation from a land beyond. That was their escape. The water moving into the tunnel on the right was faster, and he could hear waves crashing upon rocks farther below. It clearly went deeper beneath Trinity. There was something else he detected, too. It was heat, rising from among the turbulence. The decision seemed easy enough. One route was their escape to the surface; the other went deeper and into the unknown.

"I'd say go left," offered Allo. The Elf's senses could detect the differences even from the shore.

"Yep," began Gil. "That's what any reasonable person would do. Which is why we're goin' right."

Allo was taken aback. "But that leads deeper!"

Drak shook his head but then held it tight as pain exploded within it. "I agree with the heartless Elf," he said. "Deeper is not good right now. I could use some fresh air."

Gil waded back to the bank and picked up his pack. "And yet we are goin' deeper. Someone . . . or somethin' . . . sent us here for a reason, and I don't think it was simply to come down into this tunnel to immediately go to the surface again. Somethin' must be down here, and I aim to find it." He moved into the tunnel on the right and began to descend along its narrow bank. Drak and Allo held back as Gil moved out of sight.

"Tell him he's wrong," whispered Drak.

"You tell him he's wrong," whispered Allo.

Drak stomped his foot. "But you have a gift for getting people to do things they don't want to do. You tell him . . . and I'll give you a point."

"Thank you," said Allo, "but I'm not telling Gil what to do."

"Coward. Tell him he's wrong!" barked Drak.

"Ya can both tell me!" yelled Gil, his words echoing in the tunnel as he continued forward.

Drak and Allo followed slowly. They were not about to challenge Gil, not when he bested them both on every occasion.

"He heard you, stupid!" said Drak.

"Me?!" answered Allo. "You can't whisper without waking the dead!"

After another hour's climb downward along jagged, slippery rocks, they came to the head of a waterfall that rushed to a pool one hundred yards below. With the dim light of the green fungus continuing to illuminate their way, the trio carefully climbed down the slippery rocks along the side of the falls and came upon a huge chamber off the southern bank. The river continued eastward to yet another unknown destination. This cavern had an ancient, musty smell. Thick, sticky cobwebs rose up from the floor and then mingled and meshed together near the shadowy roof of the cavern, obstructing the path. Gil pushed them aside as he guided his friends toward a reddish glow emanating from the rear of the massive cave.

As the companions approached the rear of the cavern, they came upon a huge, bubbling pool of lava, its steam rising through cracks in the stone. It bathed the cavern in a red glow. The heat intensified as they moved closer, causing the trio to sweat more profusely with each step. Just as they came within five feet of the lava pool, a fountain of the molten rock suddenly surged up six feet high before them. Shocked, the trio quickly stumbled away. The fountain fell back into the lava pool. Curious, they took a uniform step forward and again the fountain of lava rose. This time they stayed put, and so too did the fountain. Its churning splashed bubbles of liquid rock along the surface of the pool.

"It's tryin' to tell us somethin'," said Gil. "Stay here." As Allo and Drak stood still, Gil took a step back. The fountain again fell into its pool.

Allo and Drak stepped back with Gil.

"I guess it wants you," said Drak, shrugging.

"Not likely," answered Gil, and he took the cloth containing the fragments of the Sword off his back. He slid the bundle to the lip of the lava pool. The fountain shot up again.

"What does this mean?" asked Allo.

Gil slowly scrutinized the cavern, taking it all in at once. This was truly an ancient, noble place that was now unknown by the world. "This is where the Sword was forged ages ago . . . in this place . . . in that fire."

Allo and Drak looked about in reverence. The Sword had meant so much to the Races for so long, and this was its birthplace.

Allo looked at the lava and glanced at the cloth. "It wants the Sword."

"Yep," said Gil.

Drak shook his head. "You mean we are going to throw it into the lava? That's not wise. We could never recover it from there. We would have to return to Megani and tell her we lost it. Then the evil beasts win and everyone dies and the world ends. We would all look pretty stupid in front of everybody."

Allo just stared at the Dwarf for a moment. "It's hard to look stupid *after* the world ends and everyone is dead," the Elf said. He turned to Gil. "I hate to admit it, but Drak may have a good point. How do we know the lava will give it back?"

"Can't be sure," answered Gil. "But somebody sent us here for a reason. Three separate parts of the Sword ain't goin' to help Megani much. But a whole Sword, well, that's somethin' else. And you saw it. The lava knows this metal somehow. What else could it possibly mean?"

"I suppose you are right," said Allo. "Besides, if the Sword fragments sink, we can always throw Drak in the lava to get them. He'd drop right to the bottom."

"Better that," spat Drak, "than waiting for a sissy Elf with pointy ears to do something useful!"

Gil moved slowly to the edge of the pool while Drak and Allo stayed safely back. He grabbed the cloth and unfolded it, exposing the three fragments of the Sword. Their shine illuminated the cavern. In response, the top of the lava fountain formed three fingers and arched halfway toward the fragments as though waiting to grab the bundle. Gil glanced at his companions. "See what I mean? Somethin' is going on here."

Allo nodded. "It can't be any clearer than that!"

Drak just grunted.

"Well," Gil said as he turned back toward the fountain. "All or nothin'." Retaining the cloth, he tossed the three pieces of the Sword into the waiting lava. The fingers of molten rock clutched them.

Boom!

An intense explosion blew the trio across the cavern, through the many cobwebs, and tossed them into the river. Dazed, they pulled themselves to shore and began to recover their sight. They dashed through the webs, smoke, and ash to the lava pool. It bubbled and churned violently, but the fountain was gone and so too were the fragments of the Sword.

"Told you this wasn't wise!" accused Drak.

"Guess you're going for a swim," added Allo.

The fountain suddenly rose once again, sending a shower of sparks in all directions. The trio dodged the falling embers. Gradually, the fountain of lava receded back into the pool, but it left the Sword—the whole Sword—floating in midair. Allo and Drak bowed to their knees. Few living in Trinity had ever seen the Sword whole. The blade was magnificent, made of solid Tork metal with a formidable length and width. It spun slowly about as though wanting the world to see it from all sides. Gil picked up the cloth from where he had dropped it and reached over the lava pool, but he lacked the distance needed to grab the hilt of the Sword. Allo was there and lent Gil a hand. The Elf then grabbed Drak's belt and used him as an anchor.

"No one's laughing about my weight now!" said the proud Dwarf.

Gil again leaned over the pool. With the help of Allo and Drak, he gained precious inches, which allowed him to grab the hilt with the cloth protecting his hand. Drak pulled Allo and Gil quickly back.

The three gazed in amazement at the Sword. Allo put a finger to the blade, and a spark stung his skin.

"May the Gods set my beard on fire!" shouted Drak. "It's whole!"

Gil wrapped it up, and Allo helped him strap it to his back.

"So you were right," said Allo to Gil. "We were sent here for a reason!"

"Sometimes things just work out," answered Gil.

"Now what?" asked Drak.

"We go back," began Gil. "We find the fork in the river and take the left tunnel to the surface." With Gil in the lead, they made their way through the thick cobwebs and back toward the falls to begin their ascent.

"I should get a point as anchor," declared Drak over his shoulder toward Allo. "After all, it was my weight that allowed us to regain the Sword. Do you agree?"

Silence.

"I said, 'Do you agree?'" repeated Drak as he turned. But the Elf was gone!

"Allo?!" Drak screamed as he drew his ax and looked about.

Gil joined him. The huge, shadowy cavern seemed ominous as they looked quickly around its perimeter. The smoke and haze from the earlier explosion still drifted before their eyes, decreasing visibility to a scant few yards. They heard movement far above and looked up. Gil was suddenly hoisted upward toward the cavern roof. He vanished from sight.

"Gil?!" Drak listened for a response. Silence.

"How rude," the Dwarf said. "I don't feel 100 percent, but I might as well join them." Drak put the handle of his ax into his mouth, bit down hard, and jumped upon a thick cobweb. He climbed rapidly upward to the cavern ceiling. There among the thick mesh of webs, he found hundreds of skeletal remains of animals alongside those of humans. Gil and Allo were the only living flesh among them. Their bodies were stuck to the cavern ceiling by a splat of sticky web, and their mouths were filled with goo, preventing them from speaking. Drak swung toward his friends and reached Allo's side. The Elf's eyes were filled with relief, but they bulged as he spied something creeping behind Drak. The Elf desperately tried to communicate with Drak, but he could not move or speak. He motioned with his pointed Elf ears for Drak to look behind himself, but the Dwarf did not heed the warning. Instead, the Dwarf held onto the web with one arm, took the ax from his mouth, and placed it back into his belt. He was defenseless.

"What a nice change!" bellowed Drak upon seeing the Elf's predicament.

Allo continued his frenzied attempt to draw the Dwarf's attention behind him, but to no avail. And so a huge Menka Beast crept closer and closer to its third victim. It had one hundred spiked legs leading to a round, hairy body. Four huge yellow eyes shone in the darkness. Two of its legs began to excrete more web juice in preparation for its attack, but it paused and drew forth its huge red stinger instead. It crept closer.

The Sword began to vibrate with the creature's approach, but Gil could not unbind his arms to reach it, nor did he have a voice to warn the Dwarf. He knew how to kill this beast, but he had been taken by complete surprise. He only hoped that Drak knew how to kill it as well.

"Not very nice of you two to leave me alone like that," Drak continued as he shook a disapproving finger toward a frantic Allo. "Have I ever gone and left you? Have I? No!"

Drak began to pull the goo out of Allo's mouth. Allo burst with frantic joy that he would soon be able to warn his friend, but the Dwarf suddenly stopped. "Wait a minute," said Drak. "I think that I should get a point for finding you so fast. Don't you agree?"

Allo continued his frantic facial gestures to get Drak to turn about, but it did not work. The Menka Beast came closer.

"Don't you agree?" asked Drak again. The creature was now just behind the Dwarf. It raised its red stinger to strike.

Allo quickly nodded yes in the hope that Drak would remove the goo from his mouth fast enough that he might warn the stupid Dwarf.

"Good," said Drak as he reached for more goo. The Dwarf suddenly gave a knowing wink to Gil.

The Menka Beast pounced, shooting its stinger at the Dwarf. Allo knew they were all dead, but Gil smiled, knowing what the Dwarf knew. Drak disappeared before the stinger struck, dropping far below the outstretched weapon. The Menka Beast scurried several yards down its web to look for its prey just as Drak came swinging back up from behind the beast. He landed upon its back and drove his ax deep into its brain. The beast fell dead to the cavern floor. Drak caught a web to stop his own fall and then made his way to Gil and took the goo from his mouth.

"Nicely done!" commended the Guardian.

"Thank you," beamed the Dwarf. "I had lots of practice with them in the eastern Dwarf mines. Nasty things, but they taste good in a hot soup."

As Gil shimmied down a web and to the cavern floor, Drak swung to Allo. The Elf was furious.

"Well?" asked the Dwarf even as the Elf struggled to get free. "I should get one point for finding you and one for saving your sorry life. That puts me ahead by one point."

Allo stared at him.

"Agreed?" asked Drak.

Allo reluctantly nodded.

"Good," said the Dwarf, and he pulled a glob of goo out of the Elf's mouth. Then he raised his ax to cut the web that held Allo. "Oh . . . and I get another point for freeing you."

"No!" screamed Allo. "No more points!"

"So sorry to hear that," said Drak as he slipped down the web and made his way to the cavern floor, leaving Allo affixed to the cavern roof.

Drak joined Gil. The Guardian was looking where the waterfalls had been just minutes before. They were now gone, blocked by an avalanche caused by the explosion.

"Our path back is blocked," said Gil. "The water from the Drownin' Pool must now be accumulatin' on the other side."

"Not good," said Drak.

"Nope . . . not good at all," said Gil.

"Hello!" Allo shouted from above. "Drak . . . let me down. Okay, okay . . . you get another point!"

Gil stared at Drak and shook his head disapprovingly.

"Oops . . . .my fault," said Drak. "I forgot that Allo needs constant attention." The Dwarf grabbed a strand of web and ascended to release Allo.

Gil looked at the sealed path to the west once again and then turned to face the now dry riverbed that led east—deep east. It was the only way out, he reasoned, assuming it was a way out at all. But he had to keep moving. He had to get the Sword to Megani and find the Historian.

CHAPTER 17

DOWN UNDER

Gil, traveling due east, led his companions deeper and deeper into the earth. The large chamber they had left behind gave way to a jagged rock tunnel some fifty yards in diameter through which the river had recently flown. It was now devoid of the water's flow due to the explosion that dammed the river at its source. The air was humid and stiflingly hot. The glowing fungus was sparse, and so they crept forward in eerie shadows as they splashed through puddles that the river had left behind.

"Are you sure we can't go back?" asked Allo, growing more and more uncomfortable in the deep caverns. "Maybe if we try to dislodge the rocks from the avalanche, we can break through and return the way we came."

"We can't," answered Gil. "The landslide closed the entrance and stopped the waterfall. The chamber on the other side of the slide probably filled instantly with water comin' from the Drownin' Pool. If we had tried to dislodge the rocks, the barrier would have broken like a dam, and we would have been crushed as the water forced us down this tunnel. It was too dangerous to even try."

"So we just follow this?" asked Allo as he pointed to the wet channel before them.

"Yep," said Gil. "This river went someplace. We just have to figure out where."

The Elf peered down the long, dark tunnel, but his eyes were not ideally suited for the dark. He could see little. "Where do you think it leads?"

"I have no idea," said Gil. "But the water must have exited somehow. We only have to find out where and how."

"Well then," said Drak. "If I'm going to get lost, I could not think of a better place than this." The Dwarf had fully recovered from the poison, and he was in great cheer for having saved both Gil and Allo from the Menka Beast. The caverns were also well suited to the Dwarf's tastes. "It's not all that different than the summer home my family had in Zak's

Kingdom," he continued. "Not as roomy, but still nice. All we would have to do with this tunnel is add a stone chair here and a stone bed there," Drak gestured around the tunnel, "and it would be very comfortable indeed."

"My family spent our summers in the forests," said Allo. *"Civilized* Races prefer the wide-open places. It gives us a chance to breathe fresh air, commune with nature, and experience all of Anton's blessings."

"Caves are better," proclaimed Drak. "They are solid—strong—with lots of nice hiding places. They make the perfect fortresses and the most durable homes. This tunnel and the caverns would be ideal places to raise a family—or an army. Just look at the magnificent wall structure. That's granite!"

"Forests are better," asserted Allo. "They are versatile, with lots of nice places from which to attack. Forests are alive with plants and animals. The sunshine warms you, the rainfall cools you, and both create life before your eyes."

"No, caves are better," declared Drak.

"Forests are better," repeated Allo.

"You're just afraid of deep, dark places," teased the Dwarf. "All Elves are. It must be the spiders or the centipedes, or maybe it's the Menka Beasts. I understand. The gentle Elf Race could not survive in a place such as this. It would be too great a strain on their overly fragile frames."

"You're just uncomfortable in the fresh air," said Allo, "because it makes your body odor more prominent when compared to the fragrances of the forest. If Dwarves would simply bathe once a month, the stench would be tolerable."

"Sissy Elf," grunted Drak.

"Stinky Dwarf," returned Allo.

"Pointy ears," shot Drak.

"Lard butt," countered Allo.

And so they went for a long while, until the tunnel leveled off from its downward slope. The ceiling of the tunnel began to glisten, and water droplets fell intermittently from the high rock ceiling.

Gil peered at the falling droplets and then looked at Drak. "What do you make of it?"

Allo shrugged. "Don't know," he said, not realizing that Gil had asked the question of Drak.

"He's not talking to you, *Elf boy,"* sneered Drak. "That's because you're not the expert . . . here." Drak caught one of the droplets that fell from the ceiling and put it in his mouth. He tasted it for just a moment, then caught several more and did the same. He rubbed a last droplet between his fingers.

"I know exactly what this is," he proclaimed. "More specifically, I know exactly where we are!"

"Oh, please break the suspense," said Allo sarcastically.

Drak smiled. "We have walked about a full day due east, with a ten-degree declination. We've now leveled off. The water that drops from the ceiling is very high in minerals, especially salt. It is seeping from far above. We are directly beneath the Straits of Devils and are about one hundred yards beneath the ocean's floor!"

"What?!" gasped Allo.

"I suspected as much," offered Gil. "We are already halfway to Devon."

"Very true," Drak added. "And there's more," he said as he stroked his hands over the uneven surface of the wall. "This tunnel was created a long time ago, but it is not natural. Though it was not forged by the river, it wasn't dug out by hand, either. It was blasted out with intense heat. You can tell because the tunnel walls are *melted* smooth. I suspect that a Wizard built this path many ages ago; it may have been an escape between the two lands. But wherever it leads, we may find a Wizard at the end of it!"

"A Wizard?" thought Gil aloud. "In Devon. Perhaps that has been the threat all along. Then we are moving in the right direction!" Gil pushed forward.

Allo grew worried. "But we were supposed to meet Megani at Dire Passage so that we would all make the crossing together. What if she's waiting for us back in Trinity? We will never meet up!"

"Can't help that now," said Gil. "We have no place to go but Devon. We can't go back. When Megani realizes we are not comin' to Dire Passage, I suspect she will go to Devon as well. That's what I would do."

"That's what I would do, too," snapped Drak and then added beneath his breath, "Caves are better."

After a rest and another day's hike, the trio realized that the temperature of the air within the channel was rising higher and higher. Sweat dripped down their faces as they walked through rising mist. The ground became hot, and the companions could see a red glow emanating ahead. After another hundred yards, they entered a huge cavern that had hundreds of firepits dug into the ground. Small puddles of the remaining river water boiled rapidly. It created wisps of vapors that billowed to the high rock ceiling before exiting through the many small tunnels leading upward to pinpoints of light. This was the end of the line. The tunnel and the river that once flowed through it both ended here. There was no apparent way out, except through the tunnel holes in the ceiling.

"Drak?" asked Gil.

The Dwarf studied his surroundings and said, "This is a geyser bed." Gesturing about the cavern, he explained, "The water from the river rushed in here, heated up atop the firepits, boiled, and then periodically shot to the surface through the waterspout tunnels in the ceiling. We are standing in a huge boiler room!" Drak raced along the chamber and peered up through the spouts as far as his sight would allow. "Those spouts go in all directions. They could emerge miles apart on the surface in order to disperse water to various regions. That's where all the water goes."

"What regions?" asked Allo.

Drak shook is head. "Have you been paying any attention whatsoever?"

Gil smiled. "We have reached the shore of Devon," he said to Allo. "Or more accurately, we have reached Devon, down under. The light you see comin' from the small tunnels in the ceilin' lead to the surface. It's just too bad that they are far too high for us to reach."

The Dwarf's keen eyes looked farther into the chamber. "The geyser bed was not naturally made. It may have been created to hide that!" he said, pointing to an outcropping in the solid wall of rock. He walked to the stone.

"What is it?" wondered Gil.

"It was created to look like natural rocks, but rocks don't form like this. It's a step." He touched the solid wall where the step ended then put his ear to it. "And it leads beyond this rock to another tunnel."

"You mean it's a door?" asked Allo.

Drak nodded.

"Impressive," Allo whispered under his breath, quite in awe of Drak's abilities beneath the surface of the earth.

"Thank you," answered Drak, smiling. "And you once said that *my* whispers could wake the dead."

"Perhaps I spoke too soon." Allo returned the smile.

Gil knocked on the rock wall. "How do we get through? I don't see a knob or a hinge."

"I'm afraid we can't," said Drak as he ran his fingers along the faint outline of a door. "It would take Wizardry to open it. And magic is one thing we don't have."

Allo turned abruptly, his senses keenly alert. "Something's coming!"

Drak drew his ax, Allo his bow. Looking for the initial attack, the trio darted toward the center of the chamber and moved back to back to back in a tight circle.

"What is it?" asked Drak.

"I can't tell as yet, but they are coming from the surface," Allo said as he scanned the many tunnel-like holes in the ceiling.

The sounds now reached Gil's ears. "There are hundreds of 'em. On wings." He tilted his head back and forth, trying to catch the faintest sound. "Comin' closer . . . closer. They are talkin' to each other like bats do. I can hear 'em. They are curious why the geysers stopped and are searchin' to find out why. No . . . not searchin'," he continued as he heard their chatter more and more clearly. "They're huntin'." His eyes shot open. "They are after me!"

Hundreds of Devil Rays dropped out of the spouts in the ceiling and swarmed downward, shrieking.

"Ahhhhhhhhhrrrrrrrrrreeeeeeeeeekkkkkkkkkkk!"

Allo grabbed Gil and pulled the Guardian between himself and Drak. The Elf instantly shot three arrows into the swarm and each punctured ten Devil Rays. The beasts flopped upon the ground, but hundreds more descended upon the trio. With the creatures closing the distance between themselves and their victims below, Allo drew his sword and masterfully sliced through the beasts. Ax held high, Drak spun in circles like a top and killed dozens as they strayed into his sharp weapon. A funnel cloud of black death, looking like a giant tornado within the cavern, swirled around the three warriors, the sound of it deafening.

"Ahhhhhhhhhrrrrrrrrrreeeeeeeeeekkkkkkkkkkk!"

"I need just a minute!" yelled Gil above the fury. He squatted upon the ground between his friends and listened intently to the sounds of the beasts.

"A minute more to do what?!" screamed Allo as he battered the beasts. But he never got an answer. A dozen Devil Rays blew past Drak. Though the Dwarf killed many of them, he was thrown backward. His stout body flew over Gil and slammed into Allo from behind, sending both of them rolling to the ground. Hundreds of Devil Rays swooped toward them and began to rip their flesh.

Afraid for his companions, Gil rose to his feet and raised his arms. His sleeve fell, revealing the mark of the Guardian. The beasts instantly left the Elf and Dwarf and darted toward Gil. The black tornado lifted him high off his feet, leaving Allo and Drak stumbling upon the ground but alive. Then a siren sounded, the likes of which was never heard by Man.

"Ahhhrrrrrrrrreeeeeekkkkkkkeeeeerrrrrrrrrsssssrrrrrrrraaaaaakkkkk!

Allo and Drak covered their ears and fell to the floor; Devil Rays began to sputter and fall from flight. The siren did not come from them! It continued with a higher pitch, echoing intensely through the chamber.

"Ahhhrrrrrrrrreeeeeekkkkkkkeeeeerrrrrrrrrsssssrrrrrrrraaaaaakkkkk!

"Grrrrrrrrrr," growled Drak in a futile attempt to keep the wailing out of his brain, but it was impossible. He and Allo rolled back and forth across the floor of the cavern, gritting their teeth. The sound was maddening. Chunks of ceiling began to fall, and firepits sparked and bubbled over.

Then there was silence, and hundreds of Devil Rays dropped from the air, dead. Unharmed but for a few scratches, Gil landed with the instincts of a cat beside his companions. He grabbed his aching throat, which throbbed in pain due to the sound he had created to destroy the beasts. The siren he made would be deadly to the Devil Rays, he suspected, because it was also deadly to bats. And these beasts were very much like bats, he knew. Gil tried to utter a sound but could not; his vocal cords were too strained. He pulled Allo and Drak to their feet.

"What was that?" groaned Drak.

Gil pointed to his throat and then shook his head.

Drak grunted. "I'm not good with games."

"He killed the winged beasts," said Allo, "but it cost him his voice." The Elf turned to Gil. "Is it permanent?"

Gil shrugged. He simply did not know.

"Well," said Drak with as much concern as any Dwarf could muster. "You'll be fine. Allo and I do most of the talking anyway."

Drak abruptly came to a renewed alert. He dropped to his hands and knees and placed his ear to the cavern floor.

"Now what?" asked an exhausted Allo, "Demon dogs with deadly breath? Killer cats with poisoned hairballs?"

"Worse!" Drak said as he jumped to his feet. "It is water—tons of it—coming through the tunnel fast! The dam must have burst. We've got to get out of here!" He darted to the hidden door and began to scrutinize it more closely. The Dwarf threw his weight against the stone wall but to no use.

Gil grabbed Allo's arm and pointed toward the ceiling, with its many tunnel spouts leading to the surface. He made a gesture as though shooting an arrow.

"Got it!" said Allo. "Drak, I need you here!"

The Dwarf sped toward Allo, and the Elf pulled a thin but strong rope from his pack. He tied it to an arrow. "Tell me which spout will surely lead to the surface—one wide enough for all of us."

Drak looked up. "You're crazy! If we get struck in a spout, we'll drown when the water floods the chamber and rises to the ceiling."

Gil shook his head and motioned with a finger, pointing straight upward.

Drak leaned toward Allo. "And what does that mean?"

Allo smiled. "When the level of the water rises to the spouts, the pressure from below will shoot us to the surface."

"Oh!" said Drak. "He wants us on the top of the geyser. More madness. But sure, let's get killed together. We really don't have another choice!"

With Gil and Allo close behind, Drak quickly searched the tunnel spouts along the high ceiling and found one with a strong, glistening, uniform wall. There were no rock outcroppings that might trap them, and it was just wide enough for each of them, if in single file. He could see a hint of light a mile or so up the tunnel, assuring him that it led to the surface. But he heard something that he didn't expect.

Pointing to the spout, he said, "Allo, lend your ears to this."

Allo tilted his ears back and forth. He turned to Gil. "A battle is being fought near the end of this spout. From this distance, I cannot tell much more."

Gil's eyes narrowed with anticipation. If there was a battle upon the surface, he reasoned, it could only mean that Good and Evil had met. If that were true, it was exactly where they should be as well. He pointed to the spout and nodded. Allo shot his arrow. It ascended fifteen feet up the spout and embedded itself into the side wall.

The sound of the approaching deluge grew more intense, and the chamber floor began to rumble. A column of air suddenly blew from the river's tunnel as the water pushed it from behind. The firepits around the trio shot upward with ten-foot flames, growing to match the amount of air they consumed.

Gil stabbed his finger toward the ceiling. Drak and Allo understood instantly. They had to climb the rope and get into the opening of the tunnel spout before the water flooded the chamber, or they would be trapped.

"You first!" yelled Allo to Drak.

Drak flew up the rope, hand over hand. Gil went next, then Allo. They had made it halfway up the rope when a torrent of water roared into the large chamber. Unknown to Gil or Drak, the wave pounded into

Allo, who lost his grip and was thrown about the cavern with the gush of the waves. Drak reached the opening of the spout and looked back. Only then did he see that Allo was no longer on the rope but being carried to the back of the cavern upon a wave. The Elf hit the stone wall hard and slipped under the crushing water.

Instinctively, Drak jumped over Gil and into the torrent. The Guardian looked back and saw that both of his companions were in the drink. The arrow embedded in the tunnel above suddenly bent, dropping Gil back several inches. He wanted to dive toward his friends, but he knew that he had to better secure the line. Gil pulled himself up inside the tunnel spout and toward the arrow. The side of the tunnel was narrow enough for him to use his feet to brace himself on each side of the hole, thus taking all his weight off the line. The arrow was ajar from the wall, and he knew he could not depend upon it to bear the weight of his companions. Gil secured the rope around himself as an anchor for his friends to use. But there was no tension upon it; his friends had yet to find it. The cavern was now swirling with water, and the rope with it. He had an intense urge to jump into the liquid and fish out his friend as he had before, but he could not leave the rope! He watched helplessly as the water rose toward the tunnel rapidly.

Gil suddenly felt tension on the rope! It was light, but discernable. He was sure that something underwater was pulling itself up. Praying that at least one of his friends would make it to the top, he started to pull the rope. The water was just a few yards below the spout now. Gil was still pulling hand over hand when Drak's head broke the surface of the swirling deluge. He took huge, gulping breaths. The Dwarf pulled himself up another few precious inches, and Allo's head broke the surface as well. He was holding tight to Drak's back. The Elf gasped for air. A second later they were out of the water and moving up into the spout. But being out of the water, their full weight was now upon the rope. Gil ached to hold firm. Hand over hand Drak came, and moments later, he and Allo were just beneath Gil in the tunnel. They wedged themselves against the wall to prevent themselves from falling back into the deadly water below.

"Thank you," the weary Allo whispered.

The Dwarf grunted.

The water rose to the opening of the spout. It meant that the chamber below was filled, yet millions more gallons were still pushing into the chamber, and the water's only place to go was up. The water beneath the trio began to bubble. The firepits on the chamber floor were adding to the water's fury. The liquid suddenly shot upward through the spout with massive force, hurling the companions upward toward the light a mile above. They heard both the roar of the water pushing them from behind and the growing sounds of battle from above. Whether they would be alive when they got to the surface was unknown. But of this they were sure: They would be in Devon. And mostly likely, in the thick of battle!

CHAPTER 18

OF WARRIORS AND BATTLE

The Historian dabbed water upon Megani's brow. She was still unconscious, but her lips were constantly moving as she struggled to survive her most fearful dreams. Now and again, her body jerked and she would scream out, but the Historian could not make sense of it. She had been through much, for Megani had been in the Pit of Fears for several days, a long time to face one's fears, he knew. The old Man berated himself for taking her there. He had thought it would save more time than it would take to travel far to the south to circumvent the cliffs, but it had cost them several days anyway. Megani was calm for the moment, so he let her be.

The Historian laid nine flaps of skin near the campfire, each taken from one Guardian. He rearranged them, leaving a blank space where the tenth word, he believed, would be placed.

The Blood of ___ Defeats the Blood of the Wizard.

The Historian gazed upon it for a time and then rearranged the words again and again.

"What are you trying to tell me, Lorelii?" the old Man said, speaking across the centuries to the famed Etha who derived the message in the first place. "What are you trying to tell me?"

Shaking his head, the Historian gathered up the patches of skin and tossed them into the fire. They shriveled in the heat of the red-glowing embers and floated up into the morning sky. He had memorized them by now and was not in need of the messages any longer. He just needed one more—one more word to make it known to him.

Megani began to stir. The Historian bent toward her just as she opened her fearful eyes. He gazed into them. She looked about in a panic, unaware of where she was or how she had gotten there. Her mind then lit with the recollection of a terrorizing, mind-breaking nightmare.

"I died," said Megani in a hoarse voice. "Again and again," she choked and coughed, her mind churning. "It was always the same," she continued as she wrapped her arms tightly across her chest.

The Historian drew closer. "Go on. What fears did you face in the pit?"

"Many, but one . . . one kept coming back . . . ," she trailed off.

The old Man held her hand. "Which one?"

Megani took a deep breath. "The Wizard chained me to a wall in its chamber. I couldn't move. Allo and Drak were dead at my feet. . . . Lyndi was dying. Then he killed me . . . with the Sword of my ancestors!"

Megani clutched her chest where the Sword in her nightmare had pierced her body. Pain exploded with the memory, and instinctively, she opened the top of her robe. Her gaze froze upon the huge scar. Her hands trembling, she stroked it. Dried blood lined the inside of her robe. "It was real!" She began to shake.

The Historian's eyes widened as he caught sight of the scar. "It's the Sword!" he muttered. "I know its mark well."

Megani held herself tight. "It happened then. It really happened . . . again and again . . . a thousand times!"

The Historian held her, moved by her time in the pit and troubled by the depths of her vision. Though he had ventured into the Pit of Fears on several occasions and faced his own demons, he had always been able to put the fear behind him. He was not sure what it meant that Megani could not, and he could not bring himself to share his own recent experience with her. In the nightmare that the pit created for him, the old Man saw himself trapped by the Wizard as well, but he was able to attack the beast, and the act of moving toward the Wizard ended his nightmare. But Megani's dream was not so easily ended.

"You were gone for days," the Historian said.

Megani shook. "It felt like years."

"If you died in your nightmare, then how did you finally break the cycle?" he asked intently. "How did you put the fear behind you?"

"I don't know," began Megani. "It was nothing I did because I could not step forward as you said. I just died. . . . Then a moment later I was entering the chamber again and found myself chained . . . and then I died . . . again and again and . . . ." She took a breath and closed her eyes to calm her nerves.

It was strange, thought the old Man, that Megani's fear did not have a resolution, a chance to break free. It was an omen, indeed, but for good or ill, he could not tell.

"You are being tested," he said.

"Zorca?"

"By whom we do not know. But you are here . . . this moment . . . and we need to keep moving."

Megani looked up, spreading her awareness broadly enough to perceive her environment. The Pit of Fears was now to her west, and she and the Historian were at the edge of what appeared to be vast swamplands. Trees were near her, their crooked, thin branches, stripped of leaves, hung wistfully downward just above their heads. She gazed southeast. Through an opening in the trees, she spied a huge spire some five miles away, rising into a reddish sky. It was the entrance to the Mortal Mines. She was sure of that, though she had never gazed upon it before. A chill came over her. Somewhere in that tower was the chamber of her nightmares. Megani forced her gaze to return to her immediate surroundings. She took a long, slow breath to calm her nerves. But Megani suddenly looked quickly about, realizing that someone was missing—a very important someone.

"Where's Lyndi?!"

"I don't know," said the Historian disappointedly. "I have not seen her since we entered the pit. She either came out before we did and, not finding us, went to the Mortal Mines by herself, or . . . ," he hesitated, "she might be trapped in the Pit of Fears."

Megani grew anxious, rising out of her own melancholy. "We have to go back!" she said frantically. "We have to get her!" Megani's intense desire to save her friend consumed her. She rose sluggishly to her feet and began to stagger back to the pit, drawing her sword—Kendro's sword. "I can't leave her in there!" she cried. "I can't leave her in there!"

Megani could not allow another to die on her behalf. Kendro's death still weighed heavily upon her, as did the deaths of the Elves, Dwarves . . . and her own mother. She was the protector. Her heart burst with concern for the little Wallo . . . the little girl. Though her powers to create were formidable, Lyndi possessed a gentle kindness that kept her forever innocent and forever in danger of those who would seek to harm her. Lyndi was the child who no longer existed within Megani. She could not let Lyndi face her fears alone.

The Historian grabbed Megani's arm and pulled. "You can't find her. She's in a place reserved only for her!"

Megani yanked away from his grip and continued to stagger toward the pit. The Historian grabbed her again and with a jerk, brought her to her knees. Megani collapsed, too weak to rise. He lifted her head and gazed directly into her eyes. He spoke in a low, fatherly tone.

"Megani . . . it's us now. . . . We have to keep moving forward. . . . Our destiny is there." He pointed toward the spire. Megani took a deep, rattling breath. She could not let Lyndi stay in a place as hideous as the pit, and she would gladly sacrifice her life to save her. However, she knew, too, that the Historian was right. They would never find her. The pit was undoubtedly made of Wizardry, she reasoned, and so perhaps the way to save Lyndi was to kill the Wizard itself in order to break the spell. Megani grew calmer as reason welled up within her. Her eyes turned suddenly sharp and deadly. Gone were the panic and sadness that gripped her just minutes before. It was replaced with anger.

"I will kill Zorca with my bare hands," Megani seethed as she rose to her feet. "I'll hunt him down across the land no matter where he hides. I will plunge my father's Sword into his chest and smile as his life drips away. He has already killed me a thousand times. . . . What difference is one more!"

The Historian smiled, "Now you sound more like your grandfather Cyrus than like your father, Jason." The smile grew wider . . . into *pride!*

Megani picked herself up and staggered southeast. The Historian followed. Despite having lost all of her powers along with many friends and family, Megani still marched forward to face the most sinister demon the land had ever known. The Historian quickly wiped a tear away from his eye. If ever there was a human worthy of the name Del, this was she, he thought. Brave beyond compare, more than she realizes. She is not Pita, he knew. She is Megani. The Historian suddenly felt an intense urge to hug her and tell her all that he knew, all of the secrets he was sworn to keep. His heart beating faster, the Historian's frail fingers reached forward to touch Megani, to feel her warmth, to begin to tell her a truth that she had yet to know. But he suddenly withdrew his fingers. It wasn't the time. The air might have ears, and he would have to keep his secret to the end, even if it meant that he might die before having a chance to share it.

The Historian looked back toward the Pit of Fears, hoping to see a blond puff of hair running toward them. But he did not. He, too, felt the loss of this little girl, a little goddess created by Anton to bring beauty into the world. He prayed that he would see her again before the end . . . his end . . . Trinity's end.

The Historian wondered who had created the pit. Was it truly the Wizard as a protection from those who would invade this land from the northwest, or was it someone else, some higher power for some higher purpose? The Historian glanced once more westward, and seeing no signs of Lyndi, he hastened his step, surpassed Megani, and led the way.

The swamps turned quickly to soggy grasslands and then to dusty plains. The trees remained, dotting the landscape with their crooked presence. Now and again they passed huge pools of mud that until recently had been brimming with water. The pools appeared to have fed channels that once sent water toward the Mortal Mines.

"What formed these?" asked Megani, directing the old Man's attention to the mud.

The Historian pointed to a hole in the middle of the mud pool. "That hole is a geyser," he said. "Devon has them throughout the land. The last time I was here, they were all shooting a column of water sky-high every hour or so. The pools were filled with water, and the water ran through channels toward the Mortal Mines, where it continuously filled a huge moat that surrounds the spire. It's very hot there, so the water evaporates fast and needs to be replenished."

"What happened to them?" Megani questioned. "Where did the water go?"

"I'm not sure," answered the Historian. "But it can't be a bad sign. If the moat is empty, it will make it much easier to get across it and into the spire."

"Where does the water for the geyser come from?" asked Megani.

The Historian smiled. "I believe these spouts are fed by the Drowning Pool in Trinity. If so, then something or someone has helped us in our quest." The old Man wondered if the pigeon he had sent to Gil was successful in delivering his message. If the Guardian had plunged into the Drowning Pool as he had instructed, he was sure that he would find the forge in order to recast the Sword. With Gil beneath Trinity, thought the Historian, perhaps he was the one responsible for the geyser's malfunction. But the old Man was not about to share that with Megani. The air might have ears. Never had so much, thought the Historian, depended upon so many to do the right thing at precisely the right time. Maybe the hand of Anton was with them after all.

The Historian selected a secluded path that brought them around the western edge of Devon, keeping the Mortal Mines to the east. They stayed hidden behind trees and low brush as they moved farther south, passing the mines altogether. They climbed up the northern slope of the Misty Mountains, the higher elevation allowing them to peer into the mines themselves.

The air was hot and the moat was nearly dry. The carcasses of huge sea beasts were scattered within it, having died from the lack of water. Surrounding the spire and in front of the moat were thousands of Gorgons wielding their serpent arms. They were dressed in full battle gear with bronze breastplates and helmets. Other serpents slithered separately from the larger beasts, rearing up on occasion to search the horizon. And they had mammoths! All the beasts were on sentry duty. With the moat and sea beasts unable to perform their duty to protect the mines, these creatures were stationed as guards instead. Across the moat, huge tunnels led deep into the Mortal Mines, while above them the spire shot far into the sky. The bridge to the dry moat was drawn.

"They are ready for battle," said Megani. "They must know we are here. Or whatever destroyed their moat has gotten them worried."

The Historian smiled. "So you noticed that too."

"Hard to miss," she said. "Too bad they captured the Dwarves' mammoths; those are more deadly than the Gorgons. I guess our only hope is to wait until the Sword arrives."

"Perhaps," said the Historian. "But we have not heard from Gil, so we should assume that the Sword already is captured by the Wizard."

Megani took a breath. "You are right. Then we go to the very top of the spire."

The Historian glanced at Megani. "Why the top of the spire?"

"That's where the Wizard lives," she said. "That's where the chamber is located. . . . That's where I die."

"Your dream?" asked the Historian.

Megani nodded. "I remember a window at the far end of the room. We were very high up, and I heard the clash of battle from below. The Wizard is there," she ended as she pointed to the very top of the spire where a lone window stood open.

"Perhaps your vision is a trap," warned the Historian. "Perhaps you saw what the Wizard wanted you to see so that you would go to the tower instead of deep into the Mines."

"That's possible," said Megani, "but I know the beast is there, and if you are right and he has the Sword, it will be there, too. And something else . . . there's someone in need there."

"Allo and Drak . . . from your dream."

"No. There's someone else I recall seeing in my vision," Megani said as she closed her eyes and painfully revisited her dream in the Pit of Fears. She saw a whimpering figure in a cage. "It's a woman, I think. She needs my help."

The Historian smiled at Megani. Pride filled his heart.

Megani glanced over and caught the Historian's smile. "Are you ready to tell me all that you know?"

The Historian shook his head sadly. "No . . . not yet . . . not here."

"Then," said Megani, "we have to figure out how to get past the army of Gorgons and across the empty moat in order to reach the spire."

"Perhaps he can help," said the Historian and directed Megani's attention up the slope of the Misty Mountains. She saw a lone figure standing atop it. Megani recognized the Man instantly.

"Sir Joh!" she breathed. "What's he doing here . . . in this place?" Megani's heart leaped at the sight. Squeaky Joh was a boyhood friend of her father and one of the last surviving warriors of the Battle of Meadowtown.

Megani and the Historian climbed up the side of the mountain, staying within deep crevasses to remain hidden from the beasts. They reached Squeaky Joh just below the top of the expanse. He was as old as Megani remembered—as old as the bow and arrows that were draped across his shoulder and the battle-worn sword within its sheath.

"Good day to you, Megani," said Sir Joh as they embraced.

"Why are you here?" asked Megani.

"To help with what little I could," the mayor of Meadowtown said. Then he added sadly, "I never got to tell you how sorry I am for your father's death . . . and I recently heard of your mother's passing as well. I'm deeply sorry for both."

Megani embraced her friend again. He was the last of his kind and the last link to her family. She held back the tears. His presence was special, thought Megani. Squeaky Joh had spent his life defending Meadowtown, the last bastion of humanity on Trinity. But now he was here with them to face whatever evil awaited on this foreign shore.

Sir Joh turned an examining eye toward the Historian. "And you are . . . ?"

"The Historian," said Megani to introduce her new companion.

"Ah, so you're the Historian!" said Sir Joh as he walked slowly to the Man, studying him intently. "We finally meet. Jason told me to send you a message when Trinity was in dire need. I trust that my pigeon reached you?"

"She did," answered the Historian. "The message was valuable indeed."

Megani raised an eyebrow at the Historian. "So you've been sending messages behind my back too."

"Yes," said the Historian. "But I can tell you little else."

Megani paused. "Because you're still concerned that the Wizard Zorca could probe my mind?"

The Historian nodded. "Yes . . . please forgive me. As I said before, I have spent a lifetime training my mind to withstand a mind probe. My defense is more formidable than yours ever was. Let me keep my secrets a while longer."

Megani smiled. "As always . . . it seems."

"So that's what we face," began Sir Joh as his eyebrows cocked upward, his voice steady and sure, "the ancient Wizard Zorca, long thought dead. Well, we will do what we must." Sir Joh continued to carefully examine the Historian. "You are familiar to me," he suddenly declared. "Your voice is familiar to me . . . from somewhere . . . from someone a very long time ago. . . . But the eyes are not right, nor is the . . ."

The Historian drew close and grabbed Sir Joh's arm. "Sweep it from your mind. Don't consider it further; Trinity may depend upon your ignorance. I can shield my mind from the Wizard, but no one else can, so I alone can know who I am!"

Sir Joh considered his words. "Done," he said slowly. "If Jason trusted you, then I will too."

The Historian let Sir Joh go free and then nodded. "Good!"

Sir Joh looked toward the spire. "I assume you want to get into that thing."

"We plan to try," said Megani.

"Then I guess you could use a diversion."

"Any suggestions?" asked the Historian.

"Follow me," said Sir Joh, and he walked to the top of the ridge. As they reached the top and looked south, Megani's jaw dropped. She gazed upon ten thousand men and women dressed in full battle armor, camped along the coast. Alongside them were their children. It appeared that the entire population of Meadowtown, along with the able-bodied remains of Trinity, were now in Devon.

"I thought long and hard about this," began Sir Joh. "We were safe in Meadowtown, but it was only a matter of time before a bigger battle was brought to us. Therefore, I decided to bring the battle here. My forces increased greatly over the past week as families came to the fortress to gain protection from the Gorgons. We trained them all."

Megani hugged her friend. "As you can see, I decided to do the same."

"Gil told me you were headed here," said Sir Joh. "I was not about to have the daughter of my good friend fight alone on this shore. We swept across the southern plains of Trinity, killing any Gorgons we could find. We built ships—the first time we have ever done so—and crossed the calmer, southern part of the straits to land here."

"Then you saw Gil!" Megani beamed. "Was he well?"

"Yes, as were Allo and Drak. They were on their way to recover the Sword, but I have not seen them since. You could have selected none better to find it."

Megani felt reassured by his words.

The Historian shook Sir Joh's hand. "Thank you for bringing your troops!"

"They are at your command," said Sir Joh.

"No," answered the Historian. "They stay at your command."

Sir Joh gazed at the beasts that meandered beside the moat. "Then I suggest a token assault at the center, with a heavy, delayed assault along the sides."

The Historian smiled. "I would have done the same!" He turned to Megani. "Whatever happens, we must stay together all the way to Zorca. In your dream in the Pit of Fears, you did not mention that I was at your side. If we can alter the circumstances—if I can be with you when you encounter the beast—we might be able to alter the outcome. Understood?"

Megani nodded.

The plans were made and orders issued. Megani watched as the force of ten thousand warriors trudged in formation up the southern slope of the Misty Mountains. They left the children behind and upon the shore, protected by archers. Men and women smiled and waved to Megani as they passed. One woman left her formation and approached. She was middle aged, and she wore the accoutrements of war proudly: a breastplate, sword, dagger, and bow and arrows.

"Hello!" she called as she approached Megani. "Remember me?"

Megani looked hard at her face. "Of course I do," she said. "You're Beth, named after my grandmother!" She was the woman that Megani saved from the fist of Mayor Fin back in Olive Branch.

"I took your advice," said Beth, "and left for Meadowtown the very day you told me. Sir Joh saw to it that I was trained."

"Good for you," congratulated Megani.

A voice growled from behind her. "Get back into formation!"

Beth turned and bolted back to her column. Megani found herself facing Mayor Fin.

"Don't disrupt my troops again," spat Fin. "She's part of the Olive

Branch military unit now—*my* unit. I took what little we had left and led the citizens to Meadowtown. Given my leadership skills, Joh put me in charge of all the Olive Branch refugees. Stay away from all of them!"

"Really," shot Megani, "given all of your leadership skills, I'm surprised that you are not dead already!"

Fin grunted, his face becoming red. "Just stay out of my way!" He turned and followed his unit up the mountain.

Sir Joh and the Historian approached.

"I'm not sure that Mayor Fin is the best choice to lead a unit," said Megani.

"I don't like him much either," said Sir Joh, "but his troops do listen to his direction, and as long as he does what I tell him, it will be fine."

More troops smiled and nodded to Megani as they hiked up the mountain. A twinge of guilt and helplessness touched her. "Do they know I have no powers?" she asked Sir Joh. "Do they know I can't defend them?"

"They know. I told them."

Relief washed over her. These people were truly brave, and more importantly, self-reliant. Thank goodness, Megani thought, that Sir Joh had been wise enough to keep Meadowtown strong.

The last of the ten thousand troops positioned themselves just below the crest of the southern side of the mountain. Sir Joh, the Historian, and Megani climbed past the troops to the top of the mountain and looked down upon the Mortal Mines. It was as it had been, with thousands of Gorgons and serpents protecting it.

Megani looked back at their troops. They were divided into three segments, the smallest of which was made up of one thousand troops. It was in the center just behind where she, Sir Joh, and the Historian stood. That segment was flanked by over four thousand troops a half-mile to the east and by over four thousand troops about a half-mile to the west. Each segment had leaders, and within each segment, units were formed of one hundred warriors each that were led by unit leaders.

Megani turned to the Historian. "Is there any chance that the Wizard could manipulate the troops or the leaders by planting false memories within their minds while they are on the battlefield?"

"Good question," said Sir Joh.

"Possibly . . . but not likely," returned the Historian. "Zorca would have to be very close to them to do that, within yards. And the number of sentries he has posted around the Mortal Mines suggests that he's far away, high in the spire as your intuition tells you. As long as the troops don't enter the spire, they will be fine."

"That's good to know," said Sir Joh as he scanned his warriors one last time. "The troops are ready."

"Then let it begin," said the Historian.

With a wave of his hand, the one thousand warriors behind Sir Joh swooped over the ridge and down toward the Mortal Mines. Their swords and breastplates clanged as they dashed forward. A deafening silence erupted around the spire as thousands of beasts turned south and watched the unexpected spectacle, but the silence lasted only moments.

Roar!

Thousands of Gorgons and serpents woke from their stupor and dashed toward the humans. The thousand warriors paused and knelt, each drawing an arrow and letting it fly. Then another. Then another. Then another. The sky darkened as a shower of arrows blocked the light from the sun. Points fell hard upon the beasts. Hundreds of Gorgons and serpents tumbled to their deaths, tripping those behind them. Still more came, trampling the fallen. Serpents sprang from the bodies of dead Gorgons, unleashing two beasts for every one that fell.

As the beasts closed the distance between themselves and the humans, the warriors turned and ran back up the slope. However, the blood-thirsty serpents began to catch up to the retreat, and warriors were grabbed in mid-stride and devoured. Screams arose from the slope as male and female warriors died, unable to overcome the serpents' speed. By the time they were half the distance to the top, hundreds of warriors were dead, and the beasts still came on, pouring out of the mines, over the dry moat, across the plains, and up the slope.

Finally the number of beasts exiting the mines began to dwindle. Sir Joh raised a hand and then pulled it swiftly down to signal the next attack. Thousands of fresh warriors swept over the top of the mountain and down the slope. One massive group was just west of the retreat and the other just east. The beasts were so intent upon capturing the warriors who were still in retreat that they ignored the warriors along their flanks.

The advancing warriors suddenly halted, drew their bows, and sent some nine thousand arrows into the beasts' flanks. They let loose their arrows again and again. Hundreds more of the Gorgons and serpents died, turning the mountainside green with their blood. Stunned, the beasts that remained alive bolted toward the men and women along the new lines.

The ground in front of the moat was now nearly emptied of the beasts.

"Now's our chance," said the Historian to Megani. The two companions already had made their way down the slope and toward the back of the spire, which had become vacant as the beasts raced up the mountainside. They moved quickly across the short plain, down into the nearly dry moat, and up the other side and into the grounds. Megani was surprised at the Historian's renewed strength; there were still reserves of muscle under those robes.

Back on the slope, the serpents burrowed just beneath the surface of the soil and continued their advance in safety. They began to pull warriors into the ground. Men and women dashed to rock outcroppings to escape the serpents' renewed attack, but hundreds did not make it. Those that did sent arrows into the undulating mounds of dirt that hunted them.

Megani turned to witness the sight just as a wave of Devil Rays raced out of the Mortal Mines and descended upon the warriors' positions. Instead of attacking, the beasts ignored the men and women and instead dove through several of the waterspout tunnels and disappeared into the earth.

"What's going on there?!" she asked of the old Man as she pointed at the last of the Devil Rays vanishing into the waterspouts.

"Can't be sure," he said as he found a large doorway that served as the entrance to the spire. They entered.

Five Gorgons standing guard rushed them. Megani pulled her blade and hacked at them, her warrior skills intact as she sliced through each Gorgon and the serpent arms that sought to kill them. Two final serpents sprang from a dead Gorgon and pounced toward her. Though she cut off their heads, the beasts' heavy bodies plowed into Megani, pushing her into the Historian, and both crashed into the spire's wall. Megani found herself buried beneath the beasts' huge corpses. She slowly pulled herself out, but she could not find the Historian beneath the carnage. She yanked at one of the huge serpents, but it wouldn't give. She suddenly spied the Historian's arm beneath the monster's flesh. She reached out but was too far away to grab it.

"Historian? Historian?!" she cried. But he did not move. She glanced about and saw a spiral staircase that led up the tall spire to the chamber at the top. She had the sudden urge to fly up those steps. But she could not. Megani knew she could not leave the Historian; she had to protect him, whatever the costs. She struggled to pull the serpent off of him, but again it would not budge. Then she heard the unexpected.

A woman screamed. "Megani . . . I need you!"

Megani knew that voice, that woman. How it came to be she did not know. Megani's mind raced: She's supposed to be dead. She can't be alive! Was it real . . . or Wizardry?

The voice yelled yet again. "Megani . . . I need you now!"

The screams came from the top of the spire, in the chamber that Megani knew might very well be her doom. She looked at the Historian's arm and tried to reach it again, but she could not. Every ounce of reason told her to stay with him, protect him, and be sure that they reached the Wizard together and thus alter the dream. But the force of the voice was overpowering.

It came again. "Megani . . . I need you," it called. Then in the most cunningly evil way, it added, "Don't make me ashamed that you were not a son!"

Megani turned toward the stairs. The force of the words was too strong, too moving. Sword in hand, she raced up the steps and toward her fate at the top of the tower, calling, "I'm coming, Mother!"

CHAPTER 19

CAPTURED

Men and women warriors continued to fight bravely. Units of one hundred warriors each were gathered upon a multitude of huge rock outcroppings on the slope of the mountain where Gorgons continued their gruesome assault. The rock platforms upon which the warriors fought gave them an initial vantage point because the serpents could not attack from beneath their feet. But the slithery beasts began to leap from beneath the soil and into the air, snaring warriors as the serpents flew over the rocks before diving back into the dirt on the other side of the outcroppings. The technique was taking its toll. Thousands of brave warriors had already died on the slopes that overlooked the Mortal Mines. But they fought bravely, believing that as long as they drew the attention of the beasts, they were giving Megani and the Historian time to find and destroy the Wizard.

The Olive Branch unit, which was now reduced to seventy warriors, fought upon a rock outcropping near the middle of the battle. Fin was safely within the center, protected by the warriors who fought around him. He shouted constant orders, often to position his troops in ways to protect himself. A huge serpent suddenly shot from the dirt, dove through seven warriors, and rocketed straight toward Fin. Panic overtook him. He screamed and ducked while Beth dashed in front of him. The woman warrior wielded her sword, striking the beast hard down the middle of its snout. As the beast's momentum carried it forward, Beth's sword sliced it completely down the center. The two halves of the carcass landed on the other side of the rock platform behind her. Fin staggered to his feet and without thanking Beth, continued shouting orders to his troops.

Sir Joh watched the battle from atop the mountain, sending hand signals to his segment leaders in order to help them maneuver their troops. From his perch, he could tell that the two sides had taken about equal losses. Not the best, he knew, but at least his troops were holding their own.

It was just past midday when the ground suddenly began to rumble. Sir Joh spied a cloud of dust approaching from the Mortal Mines and instantly recognized the sight.

"It was only a matter of time before they used those," he said to himself.

Dozens of Dwarf mammoths, ridden by Gorgons, tramped toward the slope of the mountain and headed toward the many rock outcroppings where the warriors were gathered. Men and women braced themselves for the onslaught. It came. The massive beasts rode up over the rock outcroppings and pounded into the warriors, dozens of whom were trampled and killed instantly. Hundreds more were tossed from the safety of the rocks and onto the ground, where they were instantly devoured by the serpents that lay in wait. The warriors tried to gain the backs of the mammoths in order to unseat the Gorgons, but they failed. The beasts' serpent arms kept them out of reach. Arrows brought many of the Gorgons down, but more remained.

The Olive Branch unit took a beating. Twenty warriors were killed instantly in the first assault as a huge mammoth charged up and over the rocks. Fin hid in a rock crevasse to avoid the beast, but Beth jumped and sliced upward to unseat the Gorgons. Her sword brought it down upon the rocks. The serpent arms shot forth, but they were killed quickly by the fifty or so warriors who remained.

At a signal, all of the mammoths trotted back down the slope so that the Gorgons could regroup. Mammoths that had lost riders were reseated. Sir Joh shouted orders, but there was little that could be done to prevent the onslaught. The warriors upon the rock islands had to stand their ground, and with the addition of the mammoth attack, they were now losing the battle. He knew it would only be moments before the second wave of mammoths came.

Megani raced up the long spiral staircase. It was cold as she spiraled higher and higher. She finally approached a large wooden door at the stair's end. Megani knew this door: It was the same door she opened a thousand times in her recurring nightmare in the Pit of Fears. It was exactly as she remembered it. She hesitated, and looking back down the long staircase, Megani wondered if she was doing the right thing to have left the Historian. After all, this would be the perfect trap!

"Megani?!" called her mother's voice from within the chamber.

Megani grabbed the large metal knob and gave it a twist. *Clank* went the tumblers as the lock opened. She entered the room, her sword drawn. "Keep stepping forward," she told herself.

She entered the same large chamber as in her vision. One window stood near the end of a wall. A faint light squeezed through the dark glass and created more shadow than illumination, the depth of the shadows only enhanced by the flickering light from the torches along the wall. Megani could hear the muffled screams and clash of battle from far below. A podium stood in the middle of the chamber, where a solitary, large chair sat undisturbed. A large cage hung beside the podium. Lying upon the floor of the cage was a woman, whimpering, her body shrouded by her own robe.

Megani ran to the cage, reached within it, grabbed the woman's head by her snow-white hair, and raised it gently aloft to see her face.

"Mother!" she cried upon seeing the worn, dazed look of Bea Del. She could not believe that her mother was alive. Or was she? Was this real or Wizardry?

"Who are you?" choked Bea, not recognizing her own daughter.

"It's me, Megani!" her daughter declared.

"No, I know my daughter . . . and you are not her!"

The mammoths charged up the slopes a second time. Sir Joh knew that this would be the last assault his warriors could take before their ranks broke and individuals ran for their lives. The ground trembled with the approach of the beasts, but beneath that, a new rumble began, one that felt stronger, more widespread, and deeper! Could it be the winged creatures he earlier saw dive into the open waterspout holes at the base of the mountain? wondered Sir Joh. If so, that would be disastrous.

Sssssspppphhhhhhhh!!! came the blast of water as two geysers near the base of the slope blew one hundred feet into the air. From his vantage point, Sir Joh could see similar geysers shoot skyward all across Devon. The battle momentarily stopped as all eyes gazed upon the sight. Amazingly, three figures were blown out of the nearest spout. They were hurled into the air and then landed upon their backs under a shower of water. Sir Joh recognized them instantly. He charged down the mountain to greet them.

"Now what?" Allo asked as he, Drak, and Gil rose sluggishly to their feet after being shot out of the geyser. The three drenched companions shielded their eyes from the water that still showered them from above. They were exhausted, having just defeated the Devil Rays below the surface and survived the deluge that had reignited the geysers.

The trio gazed about to discern their situation. They saw the warriors upon the rocks farther up the slope, bodies of the dead about them. Gorgons were grouped to the north and appeared to be mounting a mammoth attack. The trio could tell that the warriors' positions were weak. Apparently having decided that the newcomers were inconsequential, most of the Gorgons upon the mammoths pulled their attention away from the three figures near the geyser and looked toward their original prey, the thousands of warriors that remained on the slope and upon the rocks. They began a new charge, passing the trio as they made their way up the mountainside. Several of the last Gorgons, however, veered off and rushed toward the trio.

"Well, at least we know where we are," said Drak, " . . . in the middle of the battle!" His eyes turned angry. "And my father's own mammoths are being used against us!"

"How do we stop them?!" shouted Allo as the mammoths charged.

Gil knew the answer instantly, but he could not speak. His voice was still weak from the siren sound he had used to kill the Devil Rays beneath the earth. Gil simply pointed to Drak.

The Dwarf smiled.

"It's me, Mother!" cried Megani as she tried to find a door to the cage, but it was made of one solid piece of metal as though the cage was built around her.

Serpents reached the trio before the mammoths. Allo cut several of them down with his sword while Gil launched directly into the beasts and broke their necks with a kick each. The mammoths drew closer to both the companions and the warriors.

Drak raised his hands to his mouth and called out loudly in a sound eerily similar to that of a Dwarf bugle, "Grunnnnnnntt . . . Gerrrrunt . . . Guuurrrrrranttttttt."

The huge mammoths dropped to the ground and rolled over, crushing the Gorgons that remained on top of them. Dozens of the mammoths continued to roll down the mountainside, tumbling over serpents as they went while avoiding the islands of warriors that still stood upon the rocks. The battle had turned.

"Attack!" commanded Sir Joh upon his descent.

Thousand of warriors left the protection of the rocks and chased the hundreds of remaining Gorgons and serpents, slaying them as they raced down the mountainside behind the mammoths. Minutes passed as the mammoths tumbled over and over again toward the base of the mountain. With the warriors still following right behind them, killing the remains of the Gorgons and serpents, the mammoths finally reached the bottom of the slopes. The mammoths then lumbered slowly to their feet, trotted to Drak, and began to nuzzle the Dwarf.

Allo turned to Gil. "Ya gotta give it to him. The Dwarf is having quite a day."

Having raced down the mountain, Sir Joh dashed toward Gil. "Did you get it?!"

Gil patted the cloth-shrouded Sword upon his back and smiled. "Yes," he whispered. His voice was still hoarse, but at least he still had it.

"Well done!" said Sir Joh. "But haste is needed. Megani and the Historian have entered the tower, hoping to find you there. You must reach them before they find the Wizard. It's the ancient Zorca that they face!"

Gil looked excitedly at the tower. His two reasons for being had meshed together as he had hoped: to deliver the Sword to Megani and his message to the Historian. And now the identity of the evil was confirmed—Zorca—who was thought by all in Trinity to have died long ago!

"Mount up!" Gil said with a painful, cracking voice to Drak and Allo while gesturing to the mammoths.

"Mount up!" the Dwarf and Elf repeated to the first warriors that approached. Dozens of warriors climbed upon the mammoths. Led by Drak, Allo, and Gil, they drove to the moat surrounding the Mortal Mines with several thousand warriors marching behind them. No beasts stood in their path.

"My daughter is bigger than you and has great powers," said Bea angrily as Megani looked on in horror. "Go away!" Bea cried. The Etha shouted again, forcing her voice toward the open chamber door. "Megani . . . I need you! Where are you?"

Megani stood back, not knowing what to do next. Her last memory of her mother was when she had seen her killed by the Beastmaker. Or was she killed? Was that a false memory the Wizard planted, or was this the false memory? Megani's head began to spin. She clasped her hands to her temples to keep her brain from exploding. A voice suddenly drew her full attention.

"Welcome to my home!" it cackled in a wickedly delighted tone.

Megani turned. Her blood ran ice cold, for a mere four feet from her, upon its chair, sat Zorca, exactly as she remembered him from her dream. The long white hair on its head gently mingled with that of its beard as it flowed downward upon its deep-blue robe. Its eyes were a blood red. Its face was pale.

Megani exploded with anger. Drawing her sword, she stabbed Zorca through the heart, but the Wizard only laughed. Stunned by its reaction, Megani withdrew her blade and stabbed the Wizard again and again. Still it laughed. Zorca flicked his hand, and Megani's sword exploded. The force of the blast threw her back against the stone wall. Iron chains instantly clasped around her wrists and ankles. She pulled at the chains, but they held. Megani was helpless. This was exactly where she was in her dream—and from the same vantage point. She was trapped. The dream was becoming reality!

"I can see in your eyes that you have been here before," the Wizard mused as it approached. The beast pulled Megani's robe from her left shoulder and gazed at her scar. "And I see that I kill you here!" It shrilled as it touched her skin. At the touch, searing cold sliced through Megani. The Wizard withdrew its frigid finger.

"But I won't kill you yet," it reflected. "I am having too much fun." The Wizard pinched her cheek. Cold.

"Is that my mother?!" demanded Megani.

Zorca glanced at the cage. "I suppose it is," it said, as though remembering a trivial matter.

"But I saw your Beastmaker kill her!" spat Megani. "I don't believe that is her!"

"How delightful you are," Zorca said cheerfully. "That's why I love playing with you." It strolled to its throne, opened a box on a stand, and pulled out a slab of worm-infested meat. The Wizard tossed it in the cage, where Bea fell upon it and began to feast. Megani's stomach turned.

"She makes a nice pet," Zorca said. "But I'll grow tired of her soon. Besides, she has fulfilled her purpose."

"Which was?"

"To get you here," the Wizard said. "When last we met in Zol, I failed to kill you. But I did manage to plant the memory of your mother's death." Zorca smiled and a note of pride carried its words. "It was so pleasant to make you think she was dead. And better yet, you were so shocked moments ago when you heard her voice that you overruled your better judgment and raced here."

"For all I know," began Megani, "this is the new memory and my mother did die days ago!"

"Could be!" said the Wizard, applauding eagerly with its hands. "You are beginning to understand. That's exactly my fun: No one knows the truth but me. I create it, fashion it, and then plant it. Then I let the new truth take its course."

"Like the Races you butchered!"

"No . . . ," said Zorca as though mildly offended. "They butchered themselves. I simply planted the memory of their princes' murders, and I let fate do the rest. Elves and Dwarves are too bound by stupid, rigid oaths and pledges. They easily forget right and wrong and remember only a duty they invent themselves. They are weak, so weak that I'm surprised they lasted all these years."

"How can you do this?" asked Megani. "You were sent by Anton to rid the land of the Beasts of Becus and protect the Races—not destroy them!"

"Funny *girl,"* Zorca said and smiled broadly, exposing his long, yellow, crooked teeth. "Anton created me and my brethren with great powers. Then he expected us simply to give them up to your ancestors so that you could be the protectors. Anton made a mistake: He left a beast to protect the weak." Zorca then leaned back in his chair and rested one leg across the arm. "And importantly, he really has no true powers here after all. Anton simply guides through the creatures he creates and sends. What a stupid and grossly incompetent thing for a God to do."

"So now you play God!"

"Oh, no!" snapped Zorca. "I don't need to be a God. Let others create. I'm content with manipulating the playthings—like your mother here."

He waved his hand. Bea, who was still eating the worm-infested meat voraciously, suddenly looked about as though aware of her surroundings for the first time. Disgust crossed her face as she spat the raw meat from her mouth. She spied the Wizard, and her eyes widened. She then shot a look at Megani.

"Megani!" she screamed as she rose to her feet within the cage. "Are you okay?!"

Megani melted. With evidence of her daughter's failure all around, Bea's first words were of concern for her daughter.

"I could be better, Mother," she said, forcing a smile.

"I'm bored," yawned the Wizard. With a wave of his hand, Bea dropped to her feet and began to devour the remains of the meat. Blood dripped down her chin. She was lost again.

Megani struggled with her chains, but they would not budge. Blood spurt from her wrists—yet another recollection from the dream.

"Let me see what else we have here," Zorca said.

Megani's mind suddenly flared with pain at an intense intrusion. She could feel the Wizard's thoughts pour into her brain. The beast began to probe her every thought, every experience, every memory. Her whole body was pulled forward by the force, but the chains held. Megani felt a memory of Lyndi being wrenched from her.

"Such a stupid little Wallo," Zorca screeched. "I'll deal with her soon enough—that's if she even survived the Pit of Fears."

A memory of the Historian was yanked upward. "Our Man of mystery," laughed the Wizard. "What can an old Man do?" it mused. "He brought you stories of Guardians and Shaman and ancient wives' tales, but they are nothing but lies for the amusement of old Men!" Zorca released its mind probe, and Megani went limp, hanging from her chains.

"Megani?!" screamed Bea frantically.

Her daughter looked up, but Bea's attention was once again drawn to the door. She ignored her daughter, who hung trapped just ten yards away.

Gil, Allo, and Drak arrived at the moat and jumped down from the mammoths. They watched as the moat continued to fill with water from the renewed geyers, making it impossible to cross by foot. Thousands of warriors massed behind them, with Gorgons and serpents all dead in their wake.

Gil spied the wooden drawbridge embedded in the tower of the spire. "An arrow and rope," he whispered to Allo, his voice still weak.

The Elf tied a rope to an arrow and shot it across the moat and into the drawbridge. He anchored the other end of the rope to a mammoth's leg. The trio prepared to climb the rope across the water.

"We can't follow you there," said Sir Joh. "We need to stay out of the spire in order to safeguard the troops from the mind planter. But we can stay here in case more Gorgons arrive."

"I understand," whispered Gil. "I wish you well."

"And you, too," said Sir Joh. He then gave orders to make camp.

The trio held tight to the rope and pulled themselves hand over hand across the moat. They dropped to the other side of the water, landing just beside the entrance to one of the mines that led deep into Devon. Beyond that was the tall stone spire that jetted up into the dark sky.

"Good," said the Wizard slyly as it moved its eyes slowly to the ceiling of its chamber.

"What's good?" questioned Megani.

Zorca smiled. "Everything is coming along nicely. The Sword is close now . . . very close. I can feel it."

Megani frantically pulled at her chains again. The Sword's arrival meant that Gil must be near, which both elated and frightened her. Was victory also near, or were all the game pieces simply aligning in Zorca's favor?

"We are nothing but puppets to you!" screamed Megani.

"Oh, no . . . not puppets," it said with a smirk. "Think of me more like a loved one who cares deeply for you." Zorca beamed with a sudden idea. "For example, let's play 'Daddy'!"

Megani's heart suddenly burst with joy as she looked into the caring red eyes of her loving father, Zorca! She cherished all the years they had spent together upon Trinity and Devon and recalled how he built Devon in her honor, from her lovely home in the spire to the geysers and pools that cooled and protected them. And he made her pets! She remembered that even as a girl, she played for hours with the friendly and playful Gorgons and serpents. And she was proud of her father, for Zorca the Great had killed many of the Beasts of Becus in order to aid the Races years ago. He even helped Jason Del destroy Pure Evil, using the magic that Zorca gladly gave to him. Then Jason had turned evil and ruled Trinity with an iron fist. If her father, Zorca, had not fled to Devon, he would have been killed. But upon Jason Del's death, his many ungrateful minions had invaded peaceful Devon. Megani hoped her old, loving father would have the strength needed to destroy the vile Races, killing them to the last in payment for their endless treachery!

"I love you, Daddy," Megani said as she returned Zorca's gaze.

Zorca waved his hand.

Megani's mind whirled back to what it had been, and she violently shuttered. Megani couldn't believe that a moment before she had looked upon Zorca with loving eyes. The memories he had momentarily planted within her had been overpowering. She spit repeatedly to purge the last words from her mouth. She now understood how King Alar and King Dal could have been so completely fooled into believing their sons had been murdered. They were duped as easily as she had just been manipulated. How wrong memories can be, she thought.

"Not wrong!" said the Wizard, aware of her every thought. "It's just a matter of perspective!"

The Wizard looked again at the ceiling, its mind sensing that the next phase in its plan was ready. "Good," it said seemingly to itself. "Let them loose!"

Utter blackness enveloped the sky as thousands of Devil Rays poured from the Mortal Mines and attacked the warriors across the moat. Dozens of men and women were instantly carried off into a vortex of wings and devoured in midair. Their bones fell back upon the troops below. Sir Joh began shouting orders. Warriors formed tight circles and began to ward off the blows, but tornadoes of the winged beasts blasted through the defense lines. Warriors killed hundreds, yet hundreds more came.

From across the moat, Gil tried to create the siren sound that he had used to destroy the beasts before, but he could not. His vocal cords were too damaged. Again he tried, and again it would not come. He knew he could do nothing to help the warriors. Allo and Drak tried to reproduce the siren as well, but they could not match the pitch that had emanated from Gil. The last of the Guardians knew he had to get to Megani and the Historian. They were the only ones who could stop the carnage from beyond the moat—but only if the Sword could find its way into Megani's fist.

"This way!" Gil choked to his companions as he dashed around the outer walls of the spire, looking for an entrance to the tower. Allo and Drak raced behind him. Seeing them, three Devil Rays broke from the battle across the moat and darted in their direction. The trio dodged the swooping beasts, but the Devil Rays turned and struck again. The three engaged them, hacking at the winged creatures. The Devil Rays shrieked and fell dead. Hearing their brethren's death call, hundreds of Devil Rays turned toward it. But the companions found a door into the spire, jumped through the doorway, and slammed the door behind them. Silence. They looked about and saw the butchered remains of several Gorgons.

"Megani was here!" exclaimed Allo. "The beasts' deaths were sudden and the blade strokes clean and even."

Gil looked at the spiral staircase. He sniffed the air. "She's there!" he managed to say hoarsely as he pointed to the top of the spire. The trio sidestepped the carcasses of the slain beasts and moved toward the staircase. Gil placed a foot upon the first step.

The Wizard looked up toward the ceiling again. "Good!" he repeated, smiling. "Just as planned . . . and more!" He gazed at Megani. "Things are coming along even better than I had hoped. It won't be long now. Not long at all. I have waited thousands of years for this day. A couple more moments are not long at all."

Megani struggled with her chains as more blood dripped down her wrists and ankles. The puzzle pieces of her dream within the Pit of Fears were coming together. She was headed for destruction. Or was the dream wrong, and was she headed for victory? Destruction or victory? Victory or destruction?

"Why, utter destruction!" answered Zorca with a coy smile. "Haven't you been paying any attention at all, little *girl?*"

CHAPTER 20

A TRIO NO MORE

Gil paused upon the first step of the stone staircase and looked up into the spire. He sniffed the air. As well as the stale smell of ageless dust and more recent Gorgons, he caught Megani's scent from the top of the tower. It was sweet amidst the vile. Gil was sure that she had come this way and had stepped upon this staircase. However, his animal instincts flared as they sensed something else far above him. It was the dark essence of evil. He paused. Allo and Drak took a pace beyond him but then turned back when they saw him hesitate.

"Let's go!" said Drak, eagerly urging Gil onward.

"What are you waiting for?" added Allo.

Gil could see the yearning for vengeance reignite within their eyes. It was a vengeance he thought had subsided. But as Allo and Drak came closer to reaching the creature they held responsible for their fathers' deaths, the desire for blood blossomed once again. It remained unquenched, driven by an oath they took upon their fathers' funeral pyre. Drak and Allo had killed a hundred times since their quest began a week before, but the desire to satisfy the blood oath still burned. Only now did Gil realize that their friendly banter had ceased since they arose from the geyser. It was replaced with stern determination to fulfill a promise made to their departed fathers: to kill all those even remotely responsible for their deaths.

"Well?" asked Allo as he tapped Gil on the shoulder with his bow.

Gil gazed back into the spire, again sensing evil. And more, he sensed that it waited at the top for him . . . and for the Sword. Gil stepped back down off the step. "Not this way."

"What!?" spat Drak.

"We've come so far and the Wizard is close," said Allo. "I can feel it. The three of us can kill it, can avenge my father's death!"

"I can feel it, too," answered Gil as he looked upward once again. "And so can the Wizard. If we get any closer, it'll be able to use our minds against us. It wants us to climb these stairs; it wants us closer. This is a trap. We have to find another way!"

A groan rose from the carnage of serpents near the doorway. Allo readied his bow and Drak his ax, but Gil recognized the sound as human. He raced to a pile of the butchered beasts and pulling one of the massive carcasses up as high as he could, saw an old Man struggling for breath below them. Gil tried to pull him out, but the large Sword upon his back caught on the carcasses and restricted his reach. He pulled the blade, still wrapped in cloth, from his shoulder and tossed it to Allo, who still stood upon the second step next to Drak.

The Elf grabbed it from the air and clutched it close. He smiled with pride that Gil had thrown it to him. An irritated Drak grumbled beneath his breath, "I could have caught it as handily!"

The Elf and Dwarf looked anxiously from Gil and back to the spire again and again, but neither moved to help their friend, for they were too eager to move forward, not back. Gil crawled beneath the serpents to get closer to the Man beneath them. The woodsman pushed his legs and arms up to a kneeling position and then lifted the corpses upon his back upward. Beneath the bodies of the beasts, Gil saw the Man he sought to rescue. He was very old, with a bald crown and yellowing beard. With the pressure of the beasts' weight lifted from his chest, the old Man coughed and drew in many breaths, his chest rising and falling rapidly. The old Man's eyes suddenly flickered open. Though he and Gil had never met in life, they instantly knew each other.

"Historian!" breathed Gil.

"Guardian!" responded the old Man as he touched Gil's exposed tattoo.

Bang!

The door blew open and gale-force winds entered as hundreds of Devil Rays streamed into the tower. They blasted into Allo and Drak before they could react. The black tornado of beasts lifted the Elf and Dwarf off their feet and carried them up into the spire. They were gone in just seconds, the Sword with them, leaving Gil and the Historian hidden beneath the carnage.

Enraged, Gil jerked his body upward and threw the corpses of the serpents across the floor. Only then did he see that his friends were missing. He darted toward the staircase, but another Devil Ray blew into the spire and knocked Gil off his feet. He tumbled and slammed into the stone wall of the spire, falling upon his back. He lost consciousness. The winged beast spied his Guardian's tattoo and began a frenzied attack about his face and neck. A dagger quickly sliced through the beast's chest, killed it, and then pinned it to the stone wall. The Historian, having been freed from the weight of the corpse, rushed to Gil's side. He lifted the young Man's bloodied face to see if he was alive.

Devil Rays flew into Zorca's chamber, creating a whirling black tornado within it. Megani gasped for breath, as the air seemed to have been sucked out of the room. As fast as they had entered, the beasts darted out the window, leaving in their wake two figures spinning upon the stone floor. The Sword of Anton was between them.

"What have we here?" said Zorca with a knowing, wicked voice. "Isn't that convenient?" The Wizard waved its bony fingers and the Sword of Anton leaped into its hand. Zorca sat back upon his throne and gazed at the blade, tilting it back and forth in order to study it from all sides. The light the blade cast bounced around the chamber, intermittently illuminating the shadows. "I have waited a long time to feel this again."

"Given half a chance," seethed Megani, "I will run you through with it and watch your energy pour from you!"

Zorca smiled. "You're cute when you're angry!"

"Allo! . . . Drak!" Megani called.

Still dazed, Allo and Drak jumped unsteadily to their feet. Drak hurled his dagger at the Wizard. Three arrows from Allo followed. The Wizard waved its hand and the weapons exploded.

Zorca smiled, "How amusing."

It turned to Megani. "You really should have told me what a delight your friends are. They will make a fine addition to my collection." He nodded to the cage where Bea sat, still feasting on the remains of the worm-infested meat.

Allo and Drak bolted toward the Wizard. Allo drew his sword, Drak his ax and each jumped headfirst toward the beast. Zorca waved his hand.

Boom!

Light exploded from the Wizard's fist. Megani was momentarily blinded. When she regained her sight, she saw Allo and Drak above the ground, frozen in midflight.

"Why, look at this," said Zorca as he rose from his throne. He walked around the Elf and Dwarf and intently scrutinized them from head to toe. He paid special attention to their weapons. "If I am not mistaken by what I read in your mind, Megani," began Zorca as he inspected Drak's ax closely, "I believe this ax was owned by Drak's father." It then inspected Allo's sword. "And this sword was owned by Allo's father. How interesting . . ."

Devil Rays continued to pour from the mines one by one to attack the warriors. The men and women killed hundreds, but the beasts took a similar toll. From a starting force of ten thousand, only about half of the warriors remained. Blood poured from everything and upon everyone. The Olive Branch unit was down to their last twenty warriors, so they merged with other units in order to create a greater force with which to defend themselves against the winged beasts. Fin continued to shout orders while ducking behind his warriors. A black tornado descended upon them and pulled the ten warriors surrounding him into the air and to their deaths. Only Beth remained nearby. Seeing the two exposed, a line of Devil Rays darted toward them. Fin pulled Beth in front of himself as the beasts closed in on them. She struggled to free her sword hand, but she could not pull her arms from Fin's grip.

A figure suddenly tackled Beth from the side, breaking Fin's grip. She tumbled with her savior toward a line of warriors who protected them from the threat above. Fully exposed, Fin was pounded by the Devil Rays, which quickly carried him off into the sky. His bones fell upon the battlefield just moments later. Her savior pulled Beth up from the ground. It was Sir Joh.

"Thank you!" she screamed above the fury.

Sir Joh glanced back at Fin's bones. "You both got what you deserved!"

Joh looked toward the Mortal Mines. If only the Devil Rays would stop rushing from the caves below, he thought, they might be able to outlast the winged beasts. If only . . .

A small, eager boy with bright brown eyes and blond hair played within a dark, damp tunnel. His hands were filthy with dirt as he grabbed and shaped the mud in a puddle before him. First he shaped the mud to resemble a bear and then a big whale. He spied a stick nearby.

"Oh, goodie!" he squealed as he grabbed the stick and jabbed it into the whale's blow hole, pretending it was a water fountain. It was a nice diversion, for the little boy had been sick thanks to a very bad Elf, he remembered, who had shot him with three arrows. But he was now on the mend.

The boy suddenly looked up, having momentarily forgotten his task in the amusement of the mud. He grabbed a bat that hung from the ceiling of his small tunnel home. He gazed at it intently, right down to the smallest of particles that makes a bat. Finding what he needed, the boy touched the bat every so slightly. A hideous mutation began.

Poof!

The bat turned into a huge Devil Ray and darted out of the tunnel to join its brothers. It only knew that it was to attack, to kill the humans on the surface. It was driven to do so; it was instinct. But at a much lower level, it was genetic; it was its task in life.

"Hurrah!" cheered the little boy as he grabbed another bat, then another, then another as they each were transformed into a creature of death and flew to their destiny. Just as he was about to grab another bat from the low ceiling, a different bat darted into the tunnel and perched itself upon the boy, hanging downward from his chin.

"Hey there," said the lad as he grabbed the furry winged creature. "I guess it's your turn." He gazed into its skin, down through the building blocks of life, and was about to transform it, but he stopped. "Wait a minute!" he said as he gazed at the minute elements that comprised this creature. "I know you!"

Poof!

The bat transformed into its proper self—its original self—a little blond-haired girl. She slapped the boy hard across his face!

"You've been a very bad Wallo, Togi!"

"Oh, Lyndi! Why did you hit me so hard?"

Megani swallowed hard. The individual visions of her torment in the Pit of Fears were becoming reality. She should never have left the Historian, she now knew. She could very well die because of it, and all of Trinity would be in endless peril at the hands of a beast that delighted in people's agony.

Zorca continued to gaze upon Allo and Drak as they hung in the air. The demon smiled now and again as it considered its next step. The Elf's and Dwarf's eyes wiggled desperately back and forth, signaling the frightful attentiveness of their minds.

"They are truly flawed creatures," Zorca considered. "I can't imagine why Anton made them in the first place. Elves and Dwarves have no place here. They are too dedicated to nothingness, to odd oaths and silly honor." He turned to Megani as though seeking reassurance. "After all, their Races killed themselves."

"Nonsense!" she shot.

The Wizard was taken aback. "You don't still think I killed them, do you?"

"You altered their memories!" raged Megani. "You made each king believe that the other killed his son. That's the blackest of deeds."

Zorca smiled. "Ah, so you think the truth is always best. You think it would be best that these pitiful Races know things as they really are. You believe that truth will lend itself to eternal, blissful peace."

"Yes!"

"Then let's try a dose of truth and see where it gets us." Zorca waved his hand.

Allo and Drak fell to the floor. Each still carried a weapon: Allo, his father's sword and Drak, his father's ax. Zorca waved his hand again. Both princes staggered a moment. They then looked at each other, their faces growing angry, their bodies rigid. They began circling each other, a prelude to battle. Allo's eyes grew intense, matching Drak's own.

"What did you do?!" screamed Megani to Zorca as she watched her friends.

"Why, I gave you want you wanted . . . the truth!"

Megani pulled against her chains. "What truth?!"

"The truth you held in your mind and kept from these fine boys: that each king killed the other king. And how fortunate it is," mused the demon, "that each son just happens to have the weapon that did the dark deed."

"I thought you were my friend, but your father killed mine!" roared Drak.

"Mine should have killed you too!" yelled Allo.

Drak lunged at Allo, repeatedly slicing with his ax as the Elf backed up to prevent being disemboweled.

"Allo! Drak!" Megani screamed. "Stop this. It's the Wizard. It's making you battle; it's controlling you!" Her words could not penetrate the minds of her friends. Each was too intent on righting a wrong, on fulfilling a blood oath.

Allo leaped over Drak and landed ten feet behind him, giving the Elf ample space to better use his sword. He began to direct short thrusts toward the Dwarf. Drak backed up.

"You see," said the Wizard as it yawned, seemingly indifferent to the battle as it slumped in its chair. "They have the truth—all the truth— and yet they cannot reason with it."

Drak pivoted around a thrust. Allo stabbed forward again, but Drak rolled beneath the sword as he had in the western forest. He came up slamming his ax into Allo's chest but not before Allo stabbed him with his jewel-handled knife. The two combatants fell to the floor with a heavy thud. They gazed at each other, their faces just inches apart and their life blood flowing from them.

"You see!" boasted Zorca. "Their fathers died for a lie. The sons are dying for a truth. No difference."

Grieving, Megani could not take her eyes off her friends, nor could she save them from their fate. Helpless. She noted a strange smile come to Drak's quivering, dry lips. Allo returned it. It was as if, in the throes of a menacing death, they found a common place.

In unison, over breathless lips, they whispered, "Tied!"

Their bodies went limp. They were dead.

"Oh dear," said the Wizard. "Perhaps I forgot to remind them that this all started when I planted the memories of their deaths in their fathers' minds." It mused sweetly, "Do you think that would have made a difference?"

The Historian examined Gil's wounds. The young Man was bloodied and unconscious, with pieces of raw flesh hanging from his face and neck. One eye had been plucked from its socket, and several fingers were sheared off, but he was alive—barely—his breathing shallow but steady. The Historian slid his pack under Gil's head to give what little comfort he could. He then retrieved his knife and found the tattoo on Gil's arm. He hated to be so callus, but he had no choice. Megani was gone. The Sword was gone. Both, he suspected, were in the hands of the Wizard, and he had yet to decipher the entire message, a message that traveled for over a thousand years in order to reach him this day. He cut into Gil's flesh.

Togi held his sore nose. "You didn't have to hit me!"

Lyndi smacked him again, this time on the top of his head. "What do you think you are doing? We don't see each other in a couple of thousand years, and then I hear that you are calling yourself the big, bad Beastmaker. What's that about? And I even had to go through the Pit of Fears to get here. I faced the Beasts of Becus all over again. I had to face the loneliness again. Then I had to face fears I didn't even know I had. Turns out I'm afraid of getting fat, and there I was, eating pie after pie after pie. I was huge. It was just terrorizing!"

"Oh, shut up!" cried Togi, pouting. "It's always about Lyndi. Well, there are more things in this world than you! I was lonely too after our brothers and sisters died. The Wizard understood. . . . He knew what it was like."

"But you had me! We had each other!"

"You were always telling me what to do," Togi argued. "'Don't make this creature,' or 'Don't create that.' It was always don't, don't, don't. The Wizard lets me make lots of different things. And he doesn't talk on and on like you do!"

"But he's bad," said Lyndi, shaking her brother's shoulders.

"Awwww!" Togi yelled as he pulled away from Lyndi. "My chest is hurt. A bad Elf shot me with arrows a couple of days ago. Just like Zorca said: Elves are bad; Dwarves are bad; Men are bad."

"Don't be silly," said Lyndi. "They are all good, all created by Anton."

"So was Zorca!" countered Togi. "He was created by Anton, too, you know."

"But he became bad!" argued Lyndi. "Can't you see? The things you are creating, like these Devil Rays, kill people."

Togi smiled with pride. "Neat, huh! I also made Gorgons out of people who came to Devon, and I turned snakes into their arms. That took me a hundred years or so to figure out, but I did it!"

Lyndi stamped her feet. "Just because you *can* create things doesn't mean you *should* create things. That's why all of us Wallos used to vote about what we could and could not create. We had to figure out how the world should work. Every time you make one change, it can affect so many other things."

Togi looked bored. "There you go again telling me what to do." He turned angry, his voice growing low. "You better leave now, Lyndi. I have work I need to do." He reached for another bat upon the low ceiling. Lyndi grabbed his hand and yanked it back down.

"I'm not going to let you be bad anymore, Togi!"

"Just try to stop me!" growled the Wizard's apprentice.

"I will if I have to."

"Then go ahead!"

"You go first."

"No, you go first."

Togi transformed into a cobra and lunged at Lyndi.

The little girl suddenly became a mongoose and somersaulted above the snake, landing upon its back. The beast became a ferocious crocodile and snapped at the mongoose. Catching the small animal in its jaws, the crocodile began to chew. The smaller beast squealed in pain. The crocodile then swallowed it whole.

Poof!

Togi grabbed another bat from the ceiling, examined it closely, and transformed it into a Devil Ray. The creature zoomed toward the battle. Togi was proud of his work, and he knew that Zorca would be proud of it too. After all, the Races had treated both of them very badly for many years. This was a way to repay them for all of the hardship they had endured. He felt a twinge of guilt about killing Lyndi, though. They did have fun many years ago. But then his little Wallo heart hardened.

"Maybe I'm a little sorry, Lyndi," said Togi as he licked his lips. "But I'm only sorry a little bit. After all, I warned you fair and square!"

The silence was unbearable. The Wizard sat upon his throne, admiring the Sword. Allo and Drak were dead at Megani's feet. Her mother was in a heap at the bottom of her cage, exhausted from consuming her meal. The room was nearly aligned to the nightmare Megani encountered in the Pit of Fears.

"You can't rush these things," said the Wizard abruptly, still knowing her every thought. "They have to be carefully considered . . . carefully planned. Just like the day I created this magnificent Sword."

Megani roused herself from her own stupor. "The day my descendents put you to sleep," she sneered.

"Yes . . . of sorts," began the Wizard. "The Sword was created to house the power of the last remaining Wizards. I plunged it into my two brothers and drew the entire life source from each. They died because of it, as intended. Then it was my turn. But a fraction of my powers was to be left intact so that I could awaken before your father's battle with Pure Evil. My task was to instruct him on the proper use of the magic he possessed—my magic—which I did." The Wizard smiled as he recalled someone else from his past. He gazed at Megani. "You remind me so much of Pita Del."

Megani stiffened. This was not the comparison she desired. Pita ran from a beast after the Wizard was put to sleep. She died for her cowardice and almost got her father killed too. "I know the story!" Megani shot. "I'm not Pita. . . . I entered your chamber, didn't I? I didn't run. I came to attack!"

Zorca looked deep into the Sword's luster while recalling the past. "Yes, exactly as Pita did!"

Megani gasped. "But the histories throughout the ages said that she ran from a beast spawned from the Wizard's demise."

Zorca laughed. "I love me. I placed that memory in all those who were present because I did not want them to know the truth."

"Of what?"

"That there was no beast spawned from the Wizard's demise. The beast was me! I moved against Angeloti Del and his daughter, Pita. I refused to have them take my powers as I had my brother Wizards. I wanted the power for myself, so I attacked Angeloti and nearly killed him, but Pita gained the Sword and plunged it within me. Even as the power left my body, I began to strangle her, but she refused to let the Sword go . . . refused to run. Then, just as I was about to die, she pulled the Sword out so that I would go into a long slumber instead, as was the plan, so that I could train your father, Jason, ages later. Though I was weakening, I continued to squeeze, and Pita died in my hands. She could have killed me instead, but she knew that I was needed later. She was such a dedicated girl, really. And as I faded to sleep, I knew that I needed to plant a different memory—a different history—in the minds of all those who were still present. I did not want history to know that I attacked them because I did not want to be killed while I slumbered. Too, I needed an explanation as to why Pita was dead and her father wounded. So I contrived the memory of a monster to explain the events. I'm truly an artist!"

Megani cast her eyes downward. "And all these years . . . for all history . . . Pita was known as the Del who shamed the family. It kept generations of women from fulfilling their destinies within the Royal House of Del."

"That was particularly pleasant," said the Wizard, quite proud. "After all, I couldn't have the world think that a silly little girl could defeat a beast, me or otherwise! So you see, when I said you were like Pita, you should take it as a compliment. I should know since I'm the one who killed the wretched little thing!"

Togi reached above his head and grabbed another bat. He focused, attempting to find just the right elements to transform it into a Devil Ray, but he could not concentrate. His head spinning, the little Wallo blinked his eyes and they burned. He let the bat go free.

He sneezed! It was an odd feeling, for he had never sneezed in his life. He wiped mucus away from his nostrils and examined it carefully. "What's this?!" he said as he rubbed the sticky fluid between his fingers. Sweat beaded thickly upon his brow. He felt suddenly dizzy. Togi wiped the sweat away and examined it too. He swayed back and forth.

Togi tried to swallow, but pain seared his throat as he clutched it. Togi then breathed deep, but he could not satisfy his lungs. Sweat now poured freely down his face. The tunnel seemed to revolve about him. He fell to his side and began to cough, blood spurting up and spraying the tunnel walls. He took another breath then another and went still. His heart stopped beating. Dead. Mucus dripped from his noise and hit the tunnel floor.

Poof!

A little blond Wallo appeared from the fluid. Lyndi shook her head sadly as she patted Togi's head. "I had to stop you, Togi. I had to do it." She gave him a kiss on his forehead and then began to skip out of the tunnel. She turned back suddenly. "Oh . . . and I think I'll call that a virus."

A moment later, she turned into a bat and darted out of the tunnel.

Thousands of warriors continued to battle the Devil Rays and take heavy losses. Hundreds already had been bitten to death on the battlefield or carried off and devoured. But a decided turn suddenly came in the warriors' favor, Sir Joh noted. The winged beasts stopped pouring out of the tunnels. Maybe, he thought, just maybe that might turn the tide.

Megani pulled at her chains. "I will finish what Pita could not do in her age: see you dead by the Sword!"

"Mighty words for someone so close to the end herself," said the Wizard. "Besides, it doesn't quite work the way you think it does." The Wizard immediately turned the Sword of Anton around and plunged it into his body. Megani's eyes grew wide. Nothing happened.

Zorca laughed as he pulled it out. "You see, there are still truths left untold."

At that moment, a bat flew into the window and landed near Megani. It instantly transformed into a little Wallo.

"Beastmaker!" exclaimed Zorca angrily as he gazed upon Togi. "You are supposed to be making lovely Devil Rays. I suggest you get back to that!"

"Well . . . okay," said the Wallo. He winked at Megani and then strolled past the Wizard and toward the open window. Without warning, the Wallo transformed into a giant tiger and leaped toward Zorca. But it did not get any farther.

Boom!

Lightning exploded from Zorca's fists. The tiger flew back and slammed into the rock wall beside Megani. Just as the creature transformed into Lyndi, chain restraints clamped onto her legs. The little Wallo was unconscious and bleeding profusely from a gash on the back of her head.

The Wizard smirked. "Wallos are truly stupid things. Oh, well. Events are coming along quite nicely. Just about everything is in place!"

The Historian cut Gil deeply and removed the flap of skin with the final message. He raised it up to the scant light of the spire. The skin was deeply scratched by the Devil Ray's attack, making the word hard to read. The Historian turned the message around and around in an attempt to discern it. His eyes suddenly shot open. He *knew* the tenth word. His mind spun as he tried to place the ten words in various orders within his mind, building different sentences with the words of the message. His mind sparked.

"I've got it!" he proclaimed as he dashed onto the stairway and sped up the spiral staircase as fast as his ancient limbs would take him.

"Some visions are more real than others!" Zorca laughed. "Some are real enough to kill you. Then there are those visions that *are* real!"

Megani froze. Those were the very words Zorca used in the Pit of Fears before she was killed.

The Wizard took one step closer and into the torchlight. He lifted his clenched fist high, and a brilliant light flashed. It was the Sword!

"Thank you for the gift!" it cackled. "It's precisely what I needed your friends and you to do: deliver the Sword." The beast looked lovingly upon the blade. "Imagine that in the entire world, this is the only thing that could have stopped me . . . and you did not even know how to use it." It laughed and the chamber echoed with its shrill voice.

"All your friends are dead or dying," it heckled. "You are so much like Pita. You have no idea!"

Zorca suddenly threw the blade, hurling it toward Megani's heart. Fear exploded within her, and she struggled to get free, but she could not. The blade looked like an icicle against the dark cavern. She tried to step forward—to take just one step—but she could not! This was the dream and the moment of her death. She did exactly what she was not supposed to do, and so she played right into the Wizard's hands. In a moment, she knew, she would be dead.

CHAPTER 21

FATES

The Sword spun as it came. The scar Megani received in the Pit of Fears throbbed as though waiting to be sliced open anew. She pulled one last time at her chains, but they held as blood from her wrists and ankles continued to pour. Allo and Drak were dead at her feet, and her mother was collapsed and disoriented in a cage. Lyndi hung beside her, dying. A moment later, Megani would be dead too.

Megani stared intently upon the blade as it rocketed toward her. In her final moment, she refused to give into the fear. She refused to shrink from her fate. Though she was at the moment of failure, she would die with bravery. Rather than pull herself back against the wall as though to shrink from the blade, Megani arched her body forward to receive it. She would die like Pita, with courage, yet in all likelihood, she would have the same undeserving reputation long afterward, the reputation of another woman from the Royal House who had failed.

Defiant, Megani was ready. The blade was just feet away, and she stared angrily upon it as though daring it to strike. But a blur obscured her view just as the blade pierced her chest!

"Ahhhhhhhhhhhhhh!" moaned Megani as the Sword sliced through her body and pounded deep into the wall behind her. But its trajectory was off! It had cut through her left shoulder and not her heart. In front of Megani was the Historian, pinned through his left shoulder with the same Sword, his back pressed hard against her. Where did he come from? Megani wondered, startled to be ready for death one moment and saved the next. Clearly, the old Man had jumped between Megani and the blade, an action that shifted the Sword's path just enough to save her. Was there now reason for hope? But how could there be? They were both helplessly pinned to the wall.

"What fun is this?!" said the bemused Wizard. "I sliced two silly humans with one stroke. It's truly a magnificent day for me . . . far better

231

than I had hoped. I will remember this blessed day for a thousand years!"

The Historian turned his head painfully back and looked deep into Megani's eyes. The old Man suddenly smiled. Megani noted not a trace of fear or defeat upon his face, only confidence and courage. He winked and then whispered to her in a deep, calm voice, *"We'll face this together."*

Though her shoulder throbbed with pain, Megani's full attention was drawn to the old Man's words. They were familiar . . . very familiar. Where had she heard them? When had she heard them? She knew they had been spoken in just the past few days. Megani suddenly remembered and gasped: She had heard those words in the Plains of Temptation. They were spoken by the Man who saved her from the comfortable cottage that had been her prison!

The Historian grabbed the handle of the Sword with his right hand and with a mighty yank, pulled it from the wall. Megani winced in pain as the blade was withdrawn from her body. Blood flowed down her left shoulder and onto her chest. Unpinned from the wall, the Historian took a staggering step forward, the blade set comfortably in his hand though his left shoulder spewed blood as well.

Zorca stepped back a foot, then another. For the first time, Megani saw fear in the creature's blood-red eyes.

"It can't be!" hissed the Wizard. "The Sword should have burned your hand. Only members of the Royal House of . . ."

"It is what it is!" said the Historian, cutting off the demon's words. The old Man took another step forward.

Recovered from his initial shock, Zorca bore down, concentrating with utter determination, and Megani knew exactly his intent. The beast was using his mind probe to throw a full assault upon the Historian's defenses. The old Man was forced back a step as the probe hit. He battled to keep the Wizard out of his mind—out of his thoughts—as he had practiced during his many years in seclusion. The Wizard's face winced as it pounded its mind into the Historian's. Megani waited for the outcome. Was the Historian's ability to deflect Zorca's probe great enough? The answer came soon.

The Historian smiled. "You have no force here," he said and took another brave step forward, gritting his teeth as his mind continued to ward off the Wizard's attempts to gain access. "It took many years," he said, "but Lyndi was able to shield thought after thought after thought within my mind!"

Of course, thought Megani. Lyndi also must have altered the old

Man's eyes to be brown instead of green and his hair yellowing instead of red, the telltale signs of a . . .

"Who are you?!" shrieked the Wizard, releasing his mind probe, exhausted of its power. "All the remaining Dels are dead!"

The Historian glanced upon the Sword and watched as the blood of Megani and his own mixed upon the steel. A light suddenly exploded upon the metal as the Sword shone more brightly than most had ever before witnessed. The blood of two brought it to life. The Historian took another step forward, slowly chanting the message from across the ages: "The Blood of *Two* Defeats the Blood of the Wizard."

Zorca nervously stepped back again. The beast glanced about the room as though looking for an escape route. It was now off the podium and behind its chair. "Who are you?!" it repeated again.

Megani smiled, knowing the answer that would come. The Wizard was so intent upon the old Man that it didn't bother to search her mind for the answer that was suddenly there. This was truly beyond belief, she thought, yet it was so. It all made sense to her now, though how it came to be was still a mystery. The beast did not have to wait long for the answer it sought.

The Historian took another step forward and began to swing the Sword masterfully before him. "I am a descendant of Angeloti. I am the great-great-grandson of Matthew Del the Tempest Slayer. I am the husband of Beth. I am the father of Jason. But of most importance, I am the proud grandfather of Megani!" He paused, leveling the Sword at the Wizard. "I am Cyrus Del!"

The Wizard's eyes flashed.

The warrior hooked the Sword into the nape of his own robe and used it to throw the garment aside. Beneath it was the well-worn buckskin of an aging warrior, the same that Megani saw him wear in the Enchanted Forest when the mist rolled in around them. This was the true Man beneath the Historian's garb. Blood continued to flow from Cyrus's left shoulder, but the warrior gave it no notice.

"This is the Sword that once helped destroy Pure Evil," said Cyrus Del as he waved the blade in front of the Wizard. "It will do for you as well."

"You're dead!" screeched the Wizard. "I had your ashes brought back to me . . . uncovered from your grave at the Fallen's Memorial. The Beastmaker confirmed that it contained the remains of your very flesh right down to every detail."

Cyrus touched the Sword to the stump on his left shoulder. "It was worth the cost of my left arm to fool you," he began. "Jason and I planned this many years ago. Having helped me fake my death in the north, he brought the ashes of my left arm back to be buried. We knew that after the fall of Pure Evil, you might reappear once you thought that only one Del remained. So I waited in seclusion, aided by Lyndi, should the time come when you moved against us."

The warrior glanced at the little Wallo who was chained and dying upon the wall. His eyes darted to Megani and then back to Zorca. Cyrus grew angrier. "When my son died, you wasted no time in moving against Trinity, believing that only Megani survived. You thought that as the only remaining Del, she would not have been able to bring the Sword fully to life by mixing fresh blood . . . *the blood of two!*"

Megani watched and listened intently. Her heart swelled with love for her grandfather, for he was a link to her family, her father, her past. This was Cyrus Del, who had led the Battle of Meadowtown and wielded this very Sword during his own son's battle with Pure Evil. Megani struggled with her chains but still could not gain freedom. She was afraid that her grandfather, though in possession of the Sword, was still not a match for Zorca. Cyrus was old and weak despite his physical appearance.

Her grandfather's words came back to her: *"We'll face this together."* Megani suddenly realized that he needed her—her strength, her abilities. Cyrus glanced quickly at Megani, then at Lyndi, then back again to the Wizard. She saw it in his eyes now. He was too old and too weak to kill the Wizard by himself. Cyrus knew that. He was simply stalling, waiting for her to break free of the iron chains that shackled her to the wall!

"Lyndi," Megani whispered to her friend. "Lyndi, I need you!"

The Wallo's eyes began to quake as though her mind heard Megani's plea. The little girl's fingers twitched ever so slightly.

Still concentrating solely upon Cyrus, Zorca took another step back. "But how did you discover the power of the Sword?"

"Before she died many, many years ago," said Cyrus, taking a step forward, "the Etha Lorelii had a vision, one that revealed the real events on the day the Sword was forged. She must have recalled that Angeloti and Pita had to mingle their blood upon the blade in order to bring it fully to life so that it could be used to pull the power from the Wizards! That was a history that you eliminated from the minds of those present that day because you did not want us to know the real secret. Knowing the truth, Lorelii sent a message across the years to be delivered now—this day—to me!" Cyrus smiled as he tilted the Sword back and forth, allowing the red blood to drip all about its blade. "So now we have come full circle, and the blood of two Dels once again ignites the Sword!"

Cyrus lunged at the Wizard.

Boom!

Light exploded and the chamber rumbled. Zorca blasted Cyrus with an intense, constant stream of energy, but the warrior shielded the blows with his mighty blade. Zorca pivoted the power to the right and then left, but Cyrus swung the Sword well and protected himself as he took another step closer. Megani noted that the blade was as much a part of him as was his remaining good arm. Rocks began to fall from the ceiling. Megani watched intently. It was so similar to the dreamlike battle she witnessed between Cyrus and her father in the Plains of Temptation, when her grandfather saved her from the prison of her isolated cottage. Megani suddenly realized that in doing so, Cyrus Del was able to practice his swordsmanship as well. That, perhaps, was his own temptation: to save Megani from evil. He was now fulfilling the dream in real life!

Boom . . . Boom . . . Boom . . . .Boom!

Zorca relinquished the constant stream of power and began shooting fireballs from his fist. They pounded into Cyrus's Sword, pushing him back. One of the balls suddenly shot low and caught Cyrus by the feet, kicking his legs from underneath him. The old warrior crashed upon the rock floor.

"Lyndi!" screamed Megani. "I need you. . . . Lyndi!" The little Wallo's eyes fluttered wearily open as blood leaked from the corners of her eyelids. Lyndi was badly hurt, and she herself knew it. In all her years, the Wallo had never been this close to death. She glanced around the chamber and immediately discerned her friends' predicament—and her own. Lyndi also knew that she had only the power left to save herself or perhaps . . .

The Historian pivoted and rose to his knees, shielding himself from a renewed attack.

Boom . . . Boom . . . Boom . . . Boom . . . Boom . . . Boom . . . Boom!

Hundreds of small fireballs burst from Zorca's fists. Still upon his knees, Cyrus swung his Sword in all directions and batted many of the missiles away, but there were far too many of them. They began to pelt Cyrus, burning his flesh in dozens of places. With each hit, Cyrus wavered, which allowed more fireballs to find their mark.

Boom!

Seeing Cyrus falter, the Wizard sent a massive ball of energy directly at the old Man. The Sword flew from his hand and was hurled behind him. The force blasted Cyrus Del off his knees and sent him spinning across the floor. He tried to rise, tried to fight, but he fell back, completely unprotected.

Boom!

A final blast of power exploded upon Cyrus Del. His body tumbled across the chamber. He was dead!

Zorca smiled. "The end for you!" it sneered at Cyrus, but the Wizard's eyes suddenly widened in terror as the Sword continued to whip through the air behind Cyrus.

Slap! It landed snugly in the outstretched hand of Megani!

Megani still had the chains clasped about her wrists and ankles, but they were no longer embedded in the rock wall. The face of the wall, in fact, was no longer rock at all but a soft mud, thanks to the final and loving act of a gentle Wallo. Touching the rock with her final life force, Lyndi had turned it soft in order to free Megani from her chains. The effort had cost the Wallo her life.

Megani looked upon the blade. It felt far lighter than she had imagined, and it fit her hand perfectly, as though forged solely for her. She turned her attention to Zorca. Her bright-green eyes burned with hatred as she stared at the Wizard through locks of her long red hair. Her robe was drenched by the blood that still dripped from her left shoulder. It was the same color as her anger.

"You will do no more damage here!" Megani seethed through clenched teeth. "I will finish what Pita started!" Megani leaped across the chamber.

Boom! came the sound of Wizardry as light exploded once again from Zorca's fist. Megani was more agile than Cyrus. She bounced over the energy and landed behind the Wizard. The beast turned quickly to face her.

Boom . . . Boom . . . Boom . . . Boom . . . Boom . . . Boom . . . Boom!

It sent hundreds of fireballs toward her, attacking from all directions, the same tactic that worked so well with her grandfather. Megani swung the Sword quickly and efficiently, knocking all the missiles from the air before they struck. The Wizard then bore down on her mind, trying to plant a false memory, some thought that would save it. But the beast could not; it was too weak from battle to concentrate.

Megani moved closer and closer to the Wizard, all the while spinning about as she defended herself from the continuous stream of fireballs. She was the last remaining Del to carry the blood of the

Royal House. Her concentration was steadfast as she moved closer to her enemy.

Thousands of warriors in the yard began to gain the upper hand against the Devil Rays, killing hundreds as they circled above them. Sir Joh and Beth fought side by side. The victory was within reach.

Megani took another step toward the beast. The chamber was alive with hundreds of fireballs flying toward her from all directions. The Wizard was intent upon killing her. Smoke and sparks filled the chamber as even more balls of energy flew from Zorca's fist, yet Megani was magnificent as she dodged, whirled, spun, and pivoted her way toward the demon, smashing fireballs as she advanced. But Megani felt herself weakening, the strength flowing out of her body with each ounce of blood she lost. Megani knew she probably would have only one opportunity to thrust the Sword into the Wizard in order to pull the power from the beast. She was very close now, just feet away. She suddenly realized that all the years she spent at her father's side were invaluable. This was the moment for which he had trained her so thoroughly for all those many years.

Zorca abruptly cut off his attack and directed his energy toward the cage, encircling it with the bright-white light of his power. Megani paused when she saw her mother look up, bewildered by the light.

"Another step and I'll kill her. . . . Drop the Sword!" demanded Zorca. The light fell upon Bea and began to choke her. The Etha gasped for breath.

Megani's eyes peaked from beneath her long red hair, glancing shrewdly back and forth from Zorca to her mother.

Her mother spoke fearfully, straining and choking to squeeze the words out. "Listen to him, dear. . . . Put down the Sword. . . . *Back away.*"

Megani's eyes flashed at those words. She again glanced back and forth from the Wizard to her mother. Megani then began to lower the Sword ever so slowly. A small smile reached the Wizard's dry lips.

"That's right, dear," choked Bea as she spoke gently, cautiously. "That's right. . . . Back away."

The Wizard's smile grew wider. But it was short lived. Megani lunged forward and with her right hand, plunged the Sword of Anton deep into Zorca's exposed chest. Her left arm held the beast tight within a deadly embrace.

"Ahhhhhhhhhhh!" Zorca screamed as its power began to get sucked out of its being and into the Sword. The beast's entire body began to stretch toward the blade, but Zorca struggled to keep itself from sliding into it. The Wizard was still strong.

Megani whispered in its ear, "My real mother would never have told me to *back away*. She would die before she told me to run!"

The cage instantly vanished and with it, the image of Bea. Megani had realized just a moment before what the Wizard knew: Bea was already dead, killed by the Beastmaker days before in Zol. Her heart breaking, Megani felt as though she had lost her mother twice, once for real and now again in falsehood. But she could not let that interfere with her current effort. Zorca must die, and she would need every bit of concentration and strength to do it.

The two were smothered in white power that whirled hot about them. Zorca grabbed Megani's throat and began to squeeze just as he had with Pita. Megani could not catch her breath. She felt her lungs ache and her mind began to dim for want of oxygen.

"This is all too familiar!" Zorca said as it struggled to laugh.

With a mighty jerk, Megani threw her painful left arm upward and broke the arm that held her throat. She grabbed the Wizard's throat instead. "Pita kept you alive so that you would one day help my father learn the use of magic. I don't have that restriction!"

Megani squeezed. Zorca's red eyes bulged from their sockets while she continued to grip its throat with her left hand while twisting the Sword with her right. Megani thought of her parents and all that they had suffered to ensure that she was prepared for this moment. She understood more than ever now why they trained her so. Losing her youth seemed to be a small price to pay. Their only intent was to keep her alive.

As the white power continued to envelop them, sending sparks throughout the chamber, Megani whispered again to the Wizard. "I may have inherited my strength and skills from the blood of my father," she twisted the Sword, "but I inherited my determination from my mother. I . . . don't . . . lose!"

Megani recognized that her mother's stern behavior, even her ridicule, had only one goal—one objective—to make her strong enough to kill this beast. Her mother did not really need or want a son; her mother needed a child strong enough to kill a Wizard. And that's exactly what Bea had borne. By reminding Megani that she was not born a son, her mother made her strive for greatness. Cruel, perhaps, but effective!

Zorca continued to struggle. He pounded Megani with a massive fireball, which exploded upon both of them. Her grip held. Zorca's image stretched more and more as it slipped into the Sword. Still he struggled against it as he tried to pull his figure away from the blade.

"Imagine . . . ," Megani whispered devilishly as sparks continued to ignite about them, "that the greatest of Wizards was destroyed . . . by a *girl!*"

Boom!

Megani was hurled back. She crashed against the wall just as the last of Zorca's powers—and his entire being—were pulled into the Sword with devastating force. He vanished within the blade. Megani lost consciousness, and her world went black.

CHAPTER 22

SPIRIT LAKE

Springtime brought an abundance of flowers and fresh green grass to the meadow that surrounded Spirit Lake. The water was the lightest of blues this time of year, and the lake bed was visible many feet below the calm surface. Tall trees circled the meadow, their bright-green leaves swaying to a gentle breeze from the east. A deer reached to eat leaves from a low-hanging branch. Birds chirped as they flew from treetop to treetop, and a large family of white rabbits sipped water from the lake while bees danced from flower to flower. The midday sun illuminated it all as it shone brightly upon a heavenly blue, cloudless sky.

Megani sat in the meadow, wondering. It had been a month since she buried her grandfather Cyrus as well as with those of her mother, Bea, whose remains she found in Zol, where the Beastmaker had killed her. She had carefully placed their ashes at the Fallen's Memorial, a fitting place for the brave who had given their lives for the protection of Trinity. She had carried the ashen remains of Drak and Allo to the Valley of Despair so that they would have a resting place where their fathers had died. She placed Lyndi in the tunnels below Trinity, a place where the Wallos created much of the world thousands of years ago. It was a fitting place for one so gentle, creative, and true.

So many good people had died, Megani thought again and again. Her mind could not erase the images of her loved ones' deaths. The visions created an indelible imprint upon her mind. Her mother died in her cottage. Allo, Drak, Lyndi, and her grandfather Cyrus died in the Wizard's spire. Kings Dal and Alar died in the Valley of Despair. Thousands of others throughout the land had had their own final moments, not knowing for what purpose they had been slain. Megani struggled with the senseless nature of it. She could not comprehend it, and her heart ached with the loss of so many loved ones in such a short period of time.

And so Megani Del waited at Spirit Lake, a place where the souls of those who had gone before sometimes returned to speak to those who remained behind. This was the place, too, where her father met the end of his days. She would wait an eternity if necessary. Megani wanted answers.

"How much longer do you intend to wait?" asked Gil as he approached. The young Man walked with a cane, and scars lined his neck and face, the remnants of a Devil Ray's sharp talons. A patch covered the hole where his left eye once had been. But he had lived, which was a great blessing. What had begun as a sweet, gentle affection between the two had become a permanent bond. Their relationship had grown tenfold, forged by a shared, hideous experience. They had not parted since Megani found Gil near death at the base of the spire. She nursed him for a week until, little by little, he regained his strength. He had stayed close to her ever since, helping bring her loved ones to their final resting places.

Megani smiled sadly as Gil knelt beside her.

"Come on," prodded Gil, returning Megani's smile. "How much longer do ya intend to wait?"

"I'll stay here until I get satisfaction," she said.

"But satisfaction from what?" asked Gil. "Ya did what ya had to do, and ya did it well. That is a noble goal for any of us. What more satisfaction do ya need? What other answers do ya expect?"

Megani shrugged. "I don't know, but something tells me to stay here in this spot until it comes." She had a deep, nagging feeling that the circle of her life had not yet been closed. There was so much that needed attention in Trinity since the rise of the Wizard, and she did not know where to direct her efforts. Megani wanted that direction. But more than that, she felt the urge to wait at Spirit Lake. Something from beyond this world was coming. She could feel it. Until the sensation passed, she would wait.

Gil sat beside her. His smile grew. "Then I'll continue to stay as well . . . until ya get the satisfaction ya deserve." He glanced over the meadow. "I could not have picked a better place to spend eternity anyway!"

Megani put a tender hand upon his. Gil's sincerity and faithfulness were unblemished by the battles that disfigured his flesh.

"Besides," said Gil as he turned and began to pull lunch from his pack, "I'd kinda like to see what a ghost looks like. I suspect it would be all wrinkly and old and miserable."

Megani had never told Gil that she waited for a spirit, but she realized her intent was obvious. Still, she could not be sure it would be a spirit at all. Her skin suddenly tingling, Megani only knew that its arrival was imminent. Megani rubbed her arm and noted a small spark, as though the air were preparing for the approach of someone or something. She glanced quickly about herself, but the meadow was undisturbed. The wildlife still moved to and fro, taking advantage of the lake and abundant grasses and flowers.

"Water?" Gil asked as he turned to Megani, holding a canteen in one hand and a wooden cup in another. "I just scooped it up from the lake all by myself." He smiled once again. "I had to battle some bunnies to get it, but it was well worth it. Those varmints can be nasty, particularly when they all attack at once. It was a very scary experience; I barely escaped with my life!" He winked.

Megani nodded. "Yes, please. I would love some water, particularly since you bravely went through such effort to get it." She took the wooden cup and held it out as Gil began to pour. "Bunnies can be nasty indeed," she continued with a smile, "especially when they are as ferocious and frightening as you say."

Silence suddenly engulfed the meadow. The water from the canteen stopped in midair on its path into the cup. Gil became completely static. Birds that had been swooping toward the lake were frozen in midflight, as were the bees that flew between the flowers. The breeze was nil and the trees stood completely still.

Megani released her cup and it stayed similarly suspended. Her heart pounding, she slowly scanned the meadow and found everything just as motionless. The tingling sensation grew until it shook her entire body. When it passed, she rose slowly, knowing that she was within the moment . . . a moment similar to what her father must have experienced before his death. If ever she were to be contacted by the great beyond, this was it. Her heart continued to pound.

After a few anxious moments, Megani spied a figure walking slowly through the trees on the eastern side of the lake. Passing around the frozen bees and swooping birds, Megani stepped forward to meet the visitor. As Megani came closer, she could see that the figure was dressed in buckskin and wore the accoutrements of battle, a sword, an ax, and a jeweled knife. But it was not a male warrior; it was a female warrior! Megani recognized the womanly figure's long, beautiful red hair and sharp green eyes, the physical characteristics of the Royal House of Del. She was an ancestor, a spirit from the past. But who?

wondered Megani. The apparition appeared to be no more than fifteen years old at best. The two came within feet of each other and stopped, each gazing into the other's eyes. The apparition smiled warmly. Megani then saw the bruise upon the spirit's neck. Inspecting it intensely, she realized that the shape of the bruised skin fit perfectly with the slender, crooked fingers of a Wizard.

"Pita!" Megani exclaimed. Megani lowered herself to one knee, holding back the tears. Of all the spirits she imagined would come, Megani had never thought it would be one of the most ancient. It was Pita Del, the ancestor who was brave in life but falsely disgraced in death. Pita, the ancestor who died trying to contain Zorca, giving her life so that the Royal House and all of Trinity could survive. It was her memory that motivated Megani to be her best. "I honor you," said Megani. "And I owe you my life."

"Let's have none of that," said the spirit, smiling as she placed a hand under Megani's chin and urged her upward until they were once again eye to eye. "It is I who owe you. Without your bravery, the world would still be in grave danger. Without your persistence, my name would still be remembered among the cowardly. Thank you, Megani."

Pita embraced her, and Megani was surprised that the spirit had substance and warmth.

"Let's sit," said Pita, motioning toward a fallen tree trunk. They settled in. "You have questions," said Pita. "Ask them."

Megani wiped a tear from her eye as she struggled to contain her emotions. "I'm incomplete . . . unsatisfied," she stammered, "and I don't know why. Do I have another quest . . . another task?"

"None," said Pita as she reached to tenderly hold Megani's hand. "You have given much, and nothing more will be asked of you. Anton was very pleased with your effort. You honored him magnificently. Your task is done."

Megani frowned. "But I feel otherwise."

Pita smiled. "That's natural, as you have dedicated your life to Trinity. It's hard to have such vast responsibility one moment and have it removed the next. The only obligation you have left is to yourself."

"But the people still need me," Megani said. Her heart ached for all those who remained in Trinity, their lives disrupted and even destroyed by Zorca's evil designs. However, she had no powers left that might aid them as the people began to rebuild the land and their livelihoods. "I only wish I had powers to help them."

Pita shook her head. "Don't you see? Your powers needed to be taken out of Trinity. They were too dangerous. Just as the once-gentle Wallo, Togi, turned evil, so too could a future descendent of the Royal House. Anton wanted all the powers gone from the land, that of Wallo, Wizard, and the Royal House. It was the only way that Man could have a future absent of the powers that make one far greater than the rest."

"This was all preordained?" Megani asked. "You mean the Lord Anton knew this would all come to pass exactly as it did?"

"No," said Pita. "Not in that sense. For a long time Anton knew that there was an imbalance of powers in this world that had to be reconciled. As the imbalances became dangerous, such as the Wizard's betrayal, Anton put a series of events in place that would help to counter the Wizard's powers and wipe them from the land. But the outcome was uncertain until you made it certain. He put his trust in you as well as your relatives and friends. Anton felt assured that your strengths would sustain you. And they did."

Megani saddened. "But the Dwarves and Elves are gone forever."

"Upon Trinity they are gone, but there are many places in other worlds where they flourish even now. All that there is, is far greater than you can ever imagine. The downfall of goodness in one place brings an uprising of the same in another. Balance is maintained on the whole, even though this world might appear imbalanced to you."

"And Mankind?" asked Megani.

"Man has proven to be the most balanced of the Races in this world. That's why they have survived many trials and are apt to survive many more, but they still have a very long road to travel before the Race is truly secured. There is both darkness and light on their horizon, and no one can tell which will reign supreme."

"Is this just a test?" asked Megani.

"In some ways it is. The history of this world is still being written. It's still under development, still evolving. And importantly, you have knocked Mankind out of its complacency."

"How so?"

Pita laughed. "You are so close you can't see it. Ten thousand warriors—male and female both—risked their lives to venture to Devon. In ages past, few would have dared the trip because they were too content in Trinity. Their peril and their desire to save you made them face their fears . . . much like you faced yours in the Pit of Fears."

Megani's mind sparked with knowledge. "Anton created the Pit of Fears . . . and the Plains of Temptation . . . and the Enchanted Forest! Didn't he?"

"Yes!" declared Pita. "They were early gifts he gave to all those upon this world, but few ever cared to face their greatest fears, their greatest temptations, or their inner selves. Had they done so, they would have, like you, left ages ago to reach other lands. Instead they avoided these gifts and stayed where they were born." Pita smiled. "Now, because of you, many who ventured to Devon have decided to stay there and explore more. Many in the northern country are beginning to move deeper into the forests to discover their mysteries. And none, fortunately, will rely upon you to help them. They have their self-reliance restored, and they will take fate into their own hands."

"How much is there to explore?" asked Megani.

"This world is over a thousand times bigger than what the Races ever knew. They just needed someone with the courage to show them. You brought the battle to Devon, facing your innermost fears to do so, and many followed your lead. This world will never be the same again . . . so isolated . . . so afraid. You should be proud."

Tears came to Megani's eyes.

"And more," said Pita. "You restored an equal partnership among men and women, a partnership that was destroyed ages ago by the devious Wizard who invented a lie to promote his own evil plans. We all thank you for that. But I thank you most of all." Pita rose to her feet. Megani joined her and they embraced once more.

"My time here is coming to a close," said Pita Del.

"What of my friends and family who have passed?" Megani asked urgently, afraid that the apparition would disappear before she discovered what little she could about her loved ones. "Are they well?"

Pita squeezed Megani's hands. "They are smiling upon you."

Megani took a deep breath. Her heart calmed. It felt good to know that somewhere, somehow, she was still connected to those she loved.

"Then what of me?" Megani asked lastly. "You say that my task is complete. What do I do now?"

"It all depends upon whose advice you care to take," Pita said, smiling as the two began to stroll toward Gil. "And this is why I am truly here."

"Advice?" Megani asked. "Whose advice?"

Pita put a comforting arm around Megani as they walked, giving her a gentle squeeze. "Your father asked me to tell you to follow your heart. Your mother hopes that you care for the youth inside of you, the one she regrets she took from you too soon. Your grandfather Cyrus suggests that you explore the world. Allo and Drak want you to find a friend with whom to share it."

They reached Gil. Pita motioned for Megani to return to the spot where she was sitting before the world stood still. Megani did so, her tears continuing to flow. Her heart was gladdened to discover that those she loved were truly safe in a world beyond this one . . . and watching . . . and giving her loving advice. Megani grabbed her cup once more.

"Oh," continued Pita with a laugh. "Lyndi suggested that you marry Gil and have a thousand babies, the first of whom she wants you to name after her!"

The water poured once more. Pita was gone. The birds swooped above the lake as the sights and sounds of life exploded within Megani's ears.

"Why are ya cryin'?" asked Gil, startled at the sudden rush of tears.

"Because I have never been happier," Megani said. After a pause, she whispered, "I'm ready to go now."

Gil shot her a startled smile. "That's wonderful. Tell me where, and I'll see to it." Then he added with a blush, "That's . . . if you'll let me."

Megani reached over and kissed his cheek. "I'll go anywhere, as long as it's with you."

EPILOGUE:
THE SWORD REMAINS

A History from the Book of Endur,
Submitted during the Watch of Megani

It was a great privilege that I was entrusted with the keeping of the ancient Book of Endur, and I was honored to add my histories alongside those of the great Ethas of Trinity. With this, I offer my final submission to the Book. Further text, if any, I leave for my descendents to add.

In the past fifty years since Zorca was destroyed, Mankind has flourished abundantly. Explorers have discovered new lands and seas filled with a rich assortment of life. Small villages have been established in far-away places. Some of these villages have become large townships, and some of the large townships have even become immense citadels. It was amazing to behold.

Mankind has proven to be as inventive as the Wallos. What it lacks in God-given creative ability, it makes up for with persistence and ingenuity. Mankind has proven to be as diligent as the Elves and Dwarves. What it lacks in loyalty, it makes up for with intense determination.

Despite such positive qualities, Mankind's desire for power and riches is troublesome. I now fully understand why Anton pulled the abilities of the Wallos, Wizards, and Dels out of this world, for our strengths were far too tempting and thus dangerous. Unfortunately, Mankind does not heed that warning. This Race wishes to re-create such powers through other means. Various forms of governments have been created throughout the known world, many of which place power not in the hands of the people but in the hands of kings. A king's frivolous, selfish desires often destroy the ability to satisfy the needs of many. Even a just king becomes corrupt as empires grow. Dangerous forms of warfare have also been developed, not just for defense, but for aggression. Mankind has found ways to extract natural minerals from the earth,

247

refine them, and use them as means of destruction the likes of which rival the Wizard's own. Disputes over land and resources have turned to war.

Pita's prophesy has come to fruition: Mankind does travel through darkness and light. Though I have tried to use my powers of persuasion to prevent conflicts and turn Mankind away from darkness, my counsel has proven to be of little use. I am regarded as an anachronism, out of place with the world as it now exists.

I am curious why, in Anton's infinite wisdom to extract my powers from this world, he saw fit to leave the Sword behind. I cannot imagine that it was an oversight; he must have left it for a purpose. But I also know that it was not meant for me to wield again. It must be destined for another's fist. So before I leave this world, I have found a hiding place for the Sword from those who might seek to use it for evil purposes. It's within this riddle that its location can be found:

> I have made the Sword invisible, yet in plain sight; in the company of multitudes, yet alone; in the township of Fastf, but within the grasp of the world.

That is all I can say regarding the Sword's whereabouts for any of my descendents who might need it to correct humanity's course.

This is the last the world shall hear of me. I leave with my husband, Gil, and our three children to travel deeper into the frontier to taste even more of the abundant goodness that Anton bestowed upon the land. I leave the trials of Mankind for another to resolve.

Faithfully, *Megani*

107